Everybody love

"An outrageously good time. Fast, fun, and fiery hot. Everybody's going to be talking about *A Willing Spirit!*"
— Suzanne Forster, bestselling author of *Blush*

"Deb Stover's *A Willing Spirit* is one of the quirkiest, sexiest, funniest time-travels I've ever read. Full of riotous turns and twists, it showcases a new author at her best."
—Anne Stuart, bestselling author of *The Prince of Swords*

"Sassy, snappy, sexy . . . *A Willing Spirit* is a most unusual and highly entertaining time-travel with a twist. Deb Stover is the genre's newest star!"
—Kathe Robin, *Romantic Times*

"Deb Stover weaves magic!"
—*Pen and Mouse*

"You are an exceptionally talented writer. Your combination of laugh-out-loud humor with dark subjects, lightning timing, and heartwarming hope makes for an extraordinary read."
—Khrys Williams, Barnes & Noble Booksellers

"This is totally original. . . . Creativity, thy name is Deb Stover!"
—*Heartland Critiques*

Open the pages of A WILLING SPIRIT,
and find out what you've been missing!

**If you liked this book, be sure to look for others
in the _Denise Little Presents_ line:**

A WILLING SPIRIT

Deb Stover

Pinnacle Books
Kensington Publishing Corp.

PINNACLE BOOKS are published by

Kensington Publishing Corp.
850 Third Avenue
New York, NY 10022

Pinnacle and the P logo Reg. U.S. Pat. & TM Off.

First Printing: October, 1996
10 9 8 7 6 5 4 3 2 1

Printed in the United States of America

This book is for Dave, my rarely embarrassed husband who never met a stranger.

As always, my eternal respect and gratitude to the Wyrd Sisters: Laura, Pam, Karen, Paula, and Von.

And special thanks to Denise Little, a.k.a. "Dream Editor."

One

Divorced—every time Winnie Sinclair thought about that horrible word it was a painful intrusion.

Her stomach roiled in protest, a reminder that she'd promised herself a day of relaxation. True, this would be a working vacation, but anything was better than spending the weekend at home. Alone.

Besides, redecorating a houseboat would be a unique experience to add to her resume. This was a first. When her boss asked her to take the job, she'd jumped at the opportunity. The owner, whoever he was, wouldn't be on board all weekend. She could work, plan and measure at her leisure. Winnie knew that the odds of receiving another opportunity to spend a weekend on a private houseboat were remote, at best.

She wouldn't be sailing, but she'd be able to go up on deck and be surrounded by soothing blue-green water. It would be heaven. Sighing, she leaned back in the deck chair. This was just what she'd needed—a day away from the turmoil of the city to bask in the sun. A gentle breeze teased her skin and toyed with the curling tendrils of her hair.

But even the serenity of the lake couldn't prevent the memories of her marriage and its demise from intruding on her thoughts. Eight years ago she'd been so sure . . .

But now it was over.

Staring at the distant horizon, Winnie considered the destruction of her marriage. Well, the reason for it really wasn't too hard to figure out. The root cause was a blond bimbo whose talent for mayhem and whose ability to hone in on a vulnerable target rivaled a patriot missile's. Everything had started downhill the day that woman went to work for Dirk's construction firm.

Winnie's anger returned. Just when she thought she had it all under control, that she'd put everything into perspective and knew what to do with the rest of her life, she got plain old-fashioned pissed again. No doubt Dirk's blond bimbo would provide him an entire houseful of little peroxide replicas of herself.

"That son-of-a-bitch," she bit out, startling some gulls into flight.

She'd never been capable of hiding her emotions. Her father'd often told her she wore her heart on her sleeve. Well, that was one habit Winnie was determined to halt. She needed nothing less than a suit of armor to shield her true feelings from the world.

And when she thought about the blood-sucking divorce lawyer Dirk had hired . . .

The barracuda-lawyer had been smooth, managing to look like a *GQ* cover model, invading her dreams and fantasies, then coming in for the kill when she'd least expected it. Not that he'd given her a second thought, beyond minimizing her property settlements, of course. She'd just . . . fantasized about him. It made her sick to her stomach every time she remembered being attracted to such a monster.

God.

Struggling to her feet, Winnie stretched and decided to get back to work. She was, after all, being paid to decorate the luxurious houseboat, not to lounge around on it for the weekend. She was expected to do something besides soak up sunshine for her salary.

She lifted the hatch and stepped down into the living quarters of the *Sooner Sunset*. The main cabin had potential, but its share of problems, too. She sighed, turning in a full circle to examine the neglected decor. The vessel was far from new. She suspected it was older than she was, which would make it old enough to run for president . . . and then some.

A smile tugged at the corners of her mouth as she went to peer out the porthole toward the open water. What a view—but wishing the houseboat belonged to her wouldn't make it so.

She retrieved her pad and pencil from the bar and jotted down a few notes. She envisioned lots of soft beige with splashes of blue. Her boss had mentioned that the owner was a bachelor, so she assumed certain concessions would have to be made with regard to color and tone. She hoped he wasn't one of those types who'd opt for red velvet and mirrors. Ugh.

After finishing her measurements in the cabin, Winnie peered out the porthole again. The sun was setting, leaving the water a glistening, golden expanse, stretching out before her. Green hills and lush forests lined the shores of Lake Oologah. It was a beautiful spot, off the beaten path.

She took a deep breath and closed her eyes for a moment. She'd sleep well tonight.

She stripped off her clam-digger pants and T-shirt, and donned a pair of baby-doll pajamas, wishing she'd packed something warmer. She was unaccustomed to the lake, and it had never occurred to her that a chilly fog would creep across the water at night. The temperature was dropping; thunder rumbled in the distance. Thunderstorms in June were as commonplace in Oklahoma as ticks and mosquitoes.

Winnie glanced around the room, shivering. The bar drew her attention. With a shrug, she walked over and poured herself a brandy. As she sipped the warming liquor, she giggled and decided to fill the snifter again. Why not? She didn't have to drive and was completely alone. A little self-indulgence might do her some good. She settled down with her favorite author's newest book . . . and another snifter of brandy.

The bathroom—the head—was a small space which defied any decorating ideas she'd toyed with. Clutching her brandy snifter, Winnie wedged her way into the claustrophobia-inducing room. Thankful for the tiny porthole and the meager amount of light it provided, she was left with no choice but to close the door. It was physically impossible to utilize the facilities with it open.

At least she had running water to wash her face, even if there weren't any lights. That was something. What little light the setting sun had provided was nearly gone.

She lifted her glass to her lips and took another long swallow. Then another. As a rule, Winnie almost never drank, and brandy was as foreign to her as Romulan ale.

A slight shifting of the houseboat distracted her as she held her glass to keep it from spilling. It would be a shame to waste such good brandy.

The rocking sensation came again. Was the boat moving? As if in answer to her unspoken question, Winnie was thrown against the back wall. Brandy sloshed over the rim of her glass and across the back of her hand.

Giggling, she licked the droplets from her skin and brought the glass to her lips again. With a shrug, she tilted her head back and emptied the goblet. That was one way to keep it from spilling.

The boat lurched again and brandy dribbled down her chin. "Damn." Confused, Winnie tried to open the door, but the knob came off in her hand. "What the hell's going on?"

Trying not to panic, she stared hazily at the doorknob and reminded herself to add a new one to her list. Then the vessel gave a lurch and started rocking slowly to and fro. It was getting dark fast. And it felt like the boat was moving.

Panic threatened her from all sides, but she swallowed hard and forcibly quelled it. "Calm down, Winnie. You're all right." It was probably just her imagination or the wind. Wasn't it?

Or the brandy.

But the moving sensation grew stronger, and she knew it was much more than her imagination *or* the brandy. This boat was heading out into the center of the lake . . . with her aboard.

But who was the designated driver?

The pitching and rocking became more intense and Winnie's stomach suddenly rebelled. She dropped her empty glass, gripped her abdomen, and moaned, then glanced in the mirror. There was still enough light to permit her a glimpse of her sickly face.

"Oh, my. What an awful shade of green." She took a deep breath and covered her mouth with her hand.

Winnie Sinclair, professional landlubber, was seasick.

Paul Weathers raked his fingers through his hair and thanked his lucky stars. He'd been spared from a tedious weekend behind a pile of depositions—an absolute miracle.

He was where he'd much rather be. Always. Someday, when he could retire from his busy Tulsa law practice, he was going to move onto the *Sooner Sunset* full time. The thought of sleeping every night on board his houseboat, waking each morning to the sounds of the waves sloshing alongside and birds calling out a greeting to the world was his idea of living.

Someday.

The boat needed work. There was no denying it. A little at a time he was having her restored to her original beauty—the way she'd looked when his father'd first bought her.

She was seaworthy, though the old engine had its share of idiosyncracies. The new one wouldn't be in for weeks. But who cared? He chuckled, gazing out at the moonlight reflecting off the still water.

A gentle but steady breeze lifted his hair away from his face as Paul steered the vessel toward the lake's center. With the generator out, the only running lights he had were reflectors, totally dependent on other sources of light to be effective. But he wasn't planning to venture out too far before dropping anchor for the night. Just enough to escape the artificial lights and sounds of civilization.

He took a deep breath and closed his eyes for a moment. This was the life. Perfect. No court dates, custody battles, or divorce settlements.

The wind shifted directions suddenly, and Paul opened his eyes open in alarm. Holding his breath as he slid across the deck, he jammed his rubber-soled deck shoes into the teak floorboards, got his balance, then glanced up at the darkening sky.

Ominous, threatening clouds boiled and rumbled above, blotting out the moon and stars that had been so prominent only moments ago. It looked like he'd have to wait for that perfection. It was a little late to say "oops," he thought. "Looks like I'm in for it."

The weather forecast hadn't included a single word about a storm when he'd rushed out to the lake at the end of his workday. Clear skies were what he'd been promised. But spring weather in Oklahoma wasn't exactly known for consistency . . . or clemency.

Paul didn't fret to much over his dilemma just then. It was a sudden squall—the weather could calm down just as quickly. But the least the National Weather Service could do with the tax-payers' dollars was give an accurate forecast.

The wind took on an unholy howl that sent shivers down his spine. Rain pelted his bare arms and face as he turned to head back toward the shore. He was in the middle of the lake, with no working radio, a motor held together with chewing gum and a prayer, and no navigational equipment, except an old compass which was pretty well useless, since he didn't know exactly where he was. Everything was being refurbished, repaired, or replaced. The *Sooner Sunset* was practically stripped of anything resembling modern technology.

After locking the helm, he gripped the railing and looked toward shore, but the rain had obliterated his view of land. The way the wind was picking up, he knew navigation would be impossible and foolish. Cursing against the gale, Paul managed to stagger back to the helm just as the lake grew angry enough to really worry him. The boat was lifted high and driven low by the angry lake, reminding him of a roller coaster. He'd practically grown up on the water, but couldn't recall having ever seen a storm brew quite this fast before.

The hatch. At the very least, he needed his slicker. The dock was still some distance away. Of course, he was assuming he'd make it that far. Paul hesitated. Maybe he should just let the storm blow over, rather than try to sail blindly out of the tempest. But he was running out of options pretty fast.

The wind and rain intensified. He'd better just drop anchor and go below deck to ride it out. With any luck, the squall would blow over before it did any real damage. He pulled at the anchor, tossed it overboard and waited until it caught.

Soaked and shivering, he stepped down into the cabin. With trembling fingers, he retrieved a box of matches from a drawer under the bar. It took him a few moments to light the gimballed lantern as the cabin pitched around in the storm.

One day soon, he promised himself, he'd have the generator replaced. Right now, though, it was rather pleasant. Except for the damned weather. He peered through the starboard porthole and groaned. Lightning flashed all around and the wind was ominous.

Paul peeled off his wet clothing and slipped on his University of Tulsa sweat suit. He didn't keep much aboard, just a few changes of clothing for emergencies. It didn't matter what he wore right now. There was no one here for him to worry about trying to impress. And he had more important things to worry about.

He poured himself a brandy at the bar. Holding the snifter beneath his nose, he inhaled the heady aroma with satisfaction. This would warm his bones.

He took a long, slow sip of the fiery liquor, igniting a smooth burn as it passed down his throat, immediately spreading warmth throughout his body. He was tired. Damned tired. Life as a divorce attorney wasn't all it was cracked up to be. Not at all what he'd had in mind when he graduated from the University of Tulsa.

He took another sip of brandy, then walked over to the narrow door that led to the head. But when he reached for the doorknob, all he found was a circular hole where it should have been.

"That figures," he muttered, reaching inside the door to press the workings with his index finger until the door popped open. "One more thing to—"

"Stay away from me," a frantic feminine voice called from inside the head.

"What the hell . . ." Paul opened the door wider, permitting the lantern's golden light to flood the small space. A woman—a scantily clad one—was cowering in the head. "Who are you and what the hell are you doing stowed away on my boat?"

"Your . . . boat?" The woman wrapped her arms around her middle. "I . . . I'm the interior decorator." She hiccuped, shrugged, then gave a nervous little laugh. "I was told no one would be on board this weekend."

Paul groaned as his memory returned in a rush. "Oh, God. That's right, I forgot about it. I'm sorry."

It was nearly impossible to see her clearly in the dim light. Plus, he was blocking a good portion of it. But he could see his unexpected guest well enough to know she was worth a little eyestrain, and then some. Red curly hair framed her small face and grazed her shoulders. She was fairly tall and slender, and there was something vaguely familiar about her . . .

"I was planning to stay overnight and finish taking measurements in the morning, when there's more light. My boss said you're a friend of hers, so she was sure it would be all right."

Paul nodded and held his palm out in front of him in self-denial. "Yeah, I told her that'd be fine. Would've been anyway." He laughed again and shook his head. "I just forgot. I managed to get away at the last minute and never paused to consider this. It's my fault—really." He extended his hand. "By the way, I'm Paul Weathers."

"Paul Weathers?" The woman repeated his name as if he'd said he was Attila the Hun. "Of Klein and Weathers?"

Oh, nuts. Was that where he knew her from? Had he handled her divorce? "I'm . . . at a slight disadvantage here. You know me, but I can't place you."

"Oh, *really?*" She stared drunkenly at his still extended hand. "I can't believe this. It's just *perfect.* If my life was a damned soap opera, it couldn't get any worse than this."

She's plastered. Lifting his eyebrows, Paul was properly impressed with her display of temper . . . and level of inebriation. "Would you care to explain that bit of philosophy to me?" He waved his hand over his scalp. "I'm afraid it went right over my head."

She stomped her foot. "I'd rather be on a boat with Conan the Barbarian," she whispered fiercely, then pushed past him.

"What? C'mon, I'm not *that* bad." He turned to follow her into the cabin, chuckling at her obvious vehemence. Maybe if he could get a better look at her face . . . "You don't even—"

His voice froze in his throat as she bent over an overnight bag that was sitting on the bunk in the corner. His gaze riveted to the sight before him. Good Lord, the woman obviously didn't realize what a spectacle she offered for his torment and entertainment.

The golden lantern illuminated her very shapely bottom as she continued to rummage through her bag. Long, slender legs peeped out from beneath a pink nightgown that left the very sexy dimples on her buttocks exposed to his enthusiastic perusal.

"Damn fine," he muttered, tilting his head to one side as she straightened to glare at him.

"Excuse me?" She lifted an auburn brow and sneered. "What did you say?"

Paul shifted his weight to his other foot, feeling a growing discomfort in certain regions of his anatomy. What an eye-opener. Here he was on his private houseboat, adrift in a storm, with a gorgeous woman wearing a sexy nightie. His luck was definitely on the upswing.

"I was just admiring your, uh . . ." He grinned, lifting his gaze to her lovely face. The lantern clearly illuminated her features now. He frowned as recognition hit him full force. *Oh, shit.* "You're . . . Dirk Sinclair's—"

"Wronged ex-wife," she finished. "That's right, Mr. Divorce Attorney, also known as Barracuda Lawyer, Inc."

"Ooookay." Paul sucked in his breath. Maybe his luck wasn't on the upswing. This was torture, instead. He was being punished for excelling at his chosen—rather, inherited—profession. All right. Well, he could deal with this. "Winifred, or Winnie, isn't it?"

She put one hand on her hip and turned to face him. The light displayed her full length. He sucked in his breath as his gaze traveled down her silken throat to the exposed vee at the top of her nightgown. Full breasts rounded out the front of her gown, their peaks distinctly outlined beneath the thin fabric.

Definitely torture.

"Winnie Sinclair." She nodded and started to push past him again. "If you'll excuse me, I'm going to dress and get off this tub."

"Whoa, not so fast." He touched her shoulder, but she

flinched away from him. "We're stuck in a storm . . . in the *middle* of the lake, Winnie." The boat gave a mighty lurch and she swayed, nearly losing her balance. *She was* really *drunk.*

"*Ms.* Sinclair," she insisted, righting herself with admirable dignity.

But her stare could freeze active volcanoes, which was precisely how his libido was reacting to her close proximity. The woman exuded sensuality, from her sultry green eyes, exotic red hair, small upturned nose, full lips . . . and that body. Lord, if this was punishment, someone sure as hell had chosen the most effective weapon.

"Y'know, you look different than I remember from court." He sighed, then smiled. "Ms. Sinclair."

"Oh, I'm sure you were paying *real* close attention." She lifted her chin a notch. "You just didn't bother to recognize the fact that Dirk Sinclair actually had a human being for a wife. Not that he's one, of course."

With a sigh, Paul nodded. "I'm ashamed to admit you're correct, of course."

She seemed surprised. "You are?"

Her nipples became even more prominent as he watched her. Torture—pure torture. It was a miracle he didn't pass out on the spot, the way his blood flow redirected itself. And when her tongue passed over those lips, leaving a glowing sheen behind, well . . .

"Yeah, I am." He wanted to touch her so badly he ached. This was one appealing woman. He couldn't imagine why Dirk Sinclair'd wanted a divorce. The grounds had been simple incompatibility, though he'd suspected through the entire proceedings there was more to it.

She shook her head and pursed her lips. "So, how far out are we?"

Those lips were full and sexy. "Out?" His gaze drifted downward again to those breasts. He couldn't recall having

ever been so tempted by a woman's breasts before. Hers
were . . . outstanding. Magnetic.

"Out in the lake, Mr. Weathers?" She tilted her head and
stared at his face. "Earth to Mr. Weathers."

"Oh, the lake. Yes." He cleared his throat and took a deep
breath. If God took him right here and now, it would be sweet
relief. Remaining stranded here with this half-dressed
woman, without being able to touch her would kill him for
sure. "I'm not certain."

"Oh, that's just dandy." She laughed in open derision.
"What kind of sailor are you?"

"One without any equipment, I'm afraid." He chuckled
at her stunned expression. "Not much of a motor, no generator, no radio. Hey, this isn't a very big lake."

"Oh, boy." Winnie shook her head. "So you're telling me
I'm stuck here . . . with *you?*"

He sighed. "Care for another brandy, Ms. Sinclair?" He
walked over to the bar and lifted the decanter. "I'm afraid
it's going to be a very . . . long night."

Winnie swallowed with difficulty. Brandy—yes. She
wanted *lots* of brandy. The whole damned bottle. She remembered Paul Weathers vividly from her divorce hearing.
Despite the circumstances, she'd noticed his heart-stopping
appearance even then. But he looked even better now, on
this boat, wearing a sweat suit with University of Tulsa
printed across its front.

But she'd bet a million—if she had it—that few college
sweatshirts had ever been filled out so . . . nicely. Lifting
her gaze, she noticed the cleft in his chin was as striking
now as it had been in the courtroom, when he'd been wearing
a three-piece suit.

She had to be the only woman alive who could manage
to become stranded with her ex-husband's divorce attorney.
Talk about irony. Another thought made her stomach lurch.
"Oh, God," she groaned.

"Pardon?"

"Dirk'll love this one."

Paul's full lips turned up at the corners and he dragged his fingers through his dark hair. His blue eyes glittered in the reflected light. Then he shook his head and started to chuckle.

Winnie stared open-mouthed at him. "What the hell's so funny?" she demanded, taking a step closer as he poured a brandy and handed it to her.

He gave a casual shrug. "Well, you'll have to admit, this is . . . unusual."

Winnie gave a noncommittal grunt and took a tentative sip of the brandy. The warm liquid burned its way down to her stomach. She could really get used to this stuff. "Mmm." At least her initial seasickness seemed to have passed. Apparently, shock and brandy were instant cures. "Strong stuff. But I like it."

"Brandy usually is strong. I like it, too." Paul took a sip from his glass, but his eyes continued to twinkle at her over the rim.

The expression smoldering in his eyes sent indisputable messages ricocheting throughout Winnie's body. Good Lord, this was one handsome man. Just her luck—stranded with a Tom Selleck look-alike, who turned out to be Dirk's divorce lawyer. *Not fair, not fair, not fair.*

She was suddenly aware of his gaze on certain parts of her anatomy. Then she remembered her scanty nightie. *Uh-oh.* He probably thought she was advertising. It hardly seemed likely she could possess a commodity he might be interested in, though. Winnie took another sip of brandy as her gaze darted beyond him to the head. She should put her clothes back on.

"Cold tonight." She turned and pulled a small blanket off the bunk and draped it over her shoulders. Her face flooded with heat when she realized from his gaze he knew exactly why she'd picked up the blanket.

Instinctively—maddeningly—her gaze was drawn back to

his. Riveted, really. The warm caress in his eyes was mes-
merizing. This was classic. She . . . *wanted* her ex-husband's
divorce attorney.

The howling wind increased suddenly, making the houseboat lurch and bob in the angry lake. Winnie's pulse thudded
at the base of her throat. She stared warily at her impromptu
host.

Paul walked over to the porthole and looked outside, then
turned to face her. He glanced down at the floor and sighed,
obviously avoiding her gaze.

"It's bad, isn't it?" she asked in a small voice, gasping
when he lifted his gaze to meet hers. Deep furrows marred
his handsome brow. "Oh, God."

"If you have any influence in that direction, it couldn't
hurt."

"Oh, God," Winnie repeated, groaning as she lifted the
brandy snifter to her lips. She tipped her head back and
gulped the fiery liquid in one smooth motion. Her eyes watered and stung as she held out her glass. "I think you'd
better refill this. I'm not much of a sailor."

Paul lifted a speculative brow as he crossed the room and
refilled both their glasses. She took hers with trembling fingers and lifted it to her lips. His gaze followed the movement,
making her feel warm and languid. She took a slow sip of
the amber liquid, savoring the warmth that followed, insig-
nificant when compared to the sparks of yearning beginning
to flare in her belly.

"You're very beautiful, you know," he said in a silken
whisper as his gaze dipped lower.

He was a hungry wolf on the prowl. No doubt about it.
Her pulse escalated. Winnie could feel his gaze on her. It
was almost as if he touched her—caressed her with those
beautiful blue eyes. He was Superman, with superhuman vision that could see right through the blanket, still clutched
in one hand, while she held her brandy in the other.

Damn. She gulped another mouthful of brandy, feeling its

impact clear to her toes. It wouldn't take much of the potent liquor to make her fall right into this man's arms. Though she'd never engaged in a one night stand before in her entire life, it *had* been a while since she'd felt a man's touch.

"Oh, Lord," she murmured, draining her glass again and not offering a protest when he refilled it.

The houseboat continued to pitch and rock as the wind howled overhead. "I really thought the storm would've blown over by now," she said nervously, biting her lower lip. If only he'd stop staring at her like that, then maybe she could get a grip on her libido. She felt like a teenager.

"So did I."

"So did you, what?" Flustered, she half-turned away and sipped from her glass. Winnie felt warm and cozy all over. A dangerous combination of tipsy and aroused. Actually, despite the raging storm inside and out, she felt rather marvelous.

A giggle bubbled up from her chest when she glanced at him. He tilted his head to the side and smiled in a slow, sexy way that made her laughter dissolve into a gasp. His blue eyes darkened to cobalt.

"We're both consenting adults, Winnie," he said in a low tone. "I can think of a very pleasant way to . . . pass the evening."

Winnie nearly gagged on the lump in her throat. "Oh, Lord."

"I think you said that already."

"Did I?"

"Uh-huh." He reached toward her then, ran his fingers along her bare arm, sending shivers of anticipation skittering along her spine. "Very pleasant . . ."

Winnie didn't respond—verbally. She wasn't sure she *could* speak even if she tried. Blatantly wanton thoughts raced through her mind. She hadn't been with a man since her divorce. Her woman's body wanted it—wanted Paul Weathers.

In her overnight bag, she knew there were several packaged condoms left over from the last trip she and Dirk had made together before their break-up. *Could* she? *Should* she? No, of course she shouldn't.

But *could* she?

Such . . . decadent thoughts.

Such marvelous possibilities.

She cast Paul a surreptitious glance as he continued caressing her upper arm with his fingertips, tracing the curve of her shoulder, then traveling up the side of her neck. Her pulse leapt and raced as he grazed her lips with his thumb.

Was it the brandy? Her head swam, the wind howled, the houseboat pitched to and fro. Flashes of lightning illuminated the room, clearly defining the expression in his eyes.

Her gaze met his. What was wrong with a night of pure carnal indulgence? Men did it all the time. All her life she'd been a pretty good girl—a lady. Other than one serious relationship in college, Dirk was the only man she'd been intimate with. But now . . .

Now she was a grown woman. Alone. She had needs, just like everyone else. But she hadn't acted on them.

Yet . . .

How sophisticated could she become for this one night? No one need ever know. Her gaze locked with his. Could he read her thoughts? Did he know she wanted him to kiss her, touch her, make love to her?

The boat tipped suddenly, knocking the brandy from her grasp and flinging her into Paul's waiting arms, his warm embrace. His firm body prevented her fall to the floor, but she knew it would be the catalyst for her descent into indecency.

As the houseboat righted itself, Winnie made no effort to free herself from the protective circle of his embrace. Her gaze riveted to his as he tightened his arms around her.

With a growl, he covered her mouth with his.

He molded her close to his rock-hard body with strong

hands as she returned his kiss. Vulnerable to the thrilling tumult his touch generated within her, Winnie slid her arms around his neck and clutched him to her. He lowered her to the floor, their lips never breaking contact as he eased himself down beside her.

This was like something straight out of a romantic movie—or a black comedy. Things like this never happened to Winnie Sinclair. Was this real? The heady sensations swirling around in her head while the tempest roared outside were foreign, exotic and wonderful.

Their tongues entwined and met, parried and withdrew, emulating a far more intimate activity. Winnie pressed herself against him, savored the delicious waves of pleasure his touch created within her.

He lifted his lips from hers and gazed into her eyes. Winnie thought she could drown in their blue depths. The lantern light flickered overhead, casting a golden illumination over them.

"I want you," he whispered, his scintillating gaze never leaving hers.

"I know."

"I don't have—"

"I do." A secret woman's smile tugged at the corners of her mouth as his eyes widened, then became even darker. "In my bag."

He stood, pulling her up beside him as they traversed the short distance to the bunk. She reached into a side pocket of her overnight bag and withdrew a small square packet. Hesitating for just a moment, she searched her mind for the voice of her conscience. Wasn't it past time for the real Winnie Sinclair to step forward and halt these scandalous proceedings? She sighed, then pressed the packet into his palm.

"How many of these do you have, Winnie?" His voice was low and hoarse, filtering inside her to do a titillating dance.

She moistened her lips with the tip of her tongue. *Oh, Lord.* "Several."

Without hesitation, he reached for the hem of her nightie, lifting it until the cool night air caressed her breasts and belly, then he dropped it to the floor. Winnie didn't cringe beneath his scrutiny, surprising herself with such brazen behavior.

"You're beautiful," he murmured, running his fingers along both sides of her rib cage, teasing the tender undersides of her breasts. "Beautiful."

Winnie trembled and tugged on his sweatshirt. "No fair," she teased. "Your turn."

He peeled off his sweatshirt and dropped it to the floor beside her gown. When he growled and pulled her hard against his bare chest, Winnie gasped at the intimate contact, the scorching heat of his flesh against hers. The brandy seemed to become more powerful as her libido fueled its potency within her veins.

Her nipples hardened and ached for his touch. The hairs on his chest teased and tantalized the sensitive peaks until she felt like screaming in frustration. Then he lifted her slightly against him, blatantly brandishing his uncompromising arousal.

"Oh, Lord." She gasped in anticipation as he lowered her to the bunk, pushing aside her overnight bag in the process. With a crash, it fell unheeded to the floor.

Winnie moaned when his mouth again covered hers, stealing her breath in a kiss so hungry it made her blood boil. There was nothing hesitant or restrained in the way he kissed her now. There was a primal need throbbing between them that would rule all until sated.

He dragged his mouth from hers, reached for her lace-trimmed panties and stripped them from her. Then he released the drawstring at his waist and pushed his sweatpants down as well, kicking them away to reveal his magnificent male body. She cast a furtive glance downward. His erection

was large and hard . . . and ready. Her heart did a little somersault of anticipation.

He nuzzled the sensitive lobe of her ear, teased the side
of her neck with his tongue, then cupped her breast in his
hand. She felt herself swell and fill his palm as he brushed
her nipple with his thumb, then displaced it with his warm,
hungry lips.

She arched against him, pressing her flesh more fully into
his mouth as he continued his delicious torture. Cradling her
breasts in his palms, he shared himself equally between them
as she writhed and moaned, entwining her fingers in his hair
to hold him to her.

Winnie glanced down, saw his mouth welded against her
breast. Her gasp of pleasure strangled in her throat. The air
was thick and heavy, crackling with energy, rivaling even the
storm outside.

Reality slipped away. Winnie was insatiable, raking her
fingernails across his shoulders and down his back. He slid
his hand down her pelvis, found her heated female flesh and
manipulated her sensitive core.

She moaned as he kissed his way down her abdomen. She
felt empty and hungry inside, desperate for something—for
him. His fingers parted and filled her, giving promise of
more to come.

"Oh, God," he muttered against her abdomen, then his
mouth dipped lower, covering that sensitive nub with his lips
while his fingers moved within her.

Winnie gasped as he shifted between her thighs and she
draped her legs over his shoulders. His wonderful, talented
mouth continued to give her such mounting pleasure, she
felt death was imminent. It had never been like this before—
she'd never felt like this before.

Millions of tingling fingers of pleasure culminated at her
core as he tasted and teased her. She felt all her strength
converge around his probing fingers and possessive mouth.
Her blood heated and pooled as she reached a pinnacle of

completion. She wrapped her fingers in his hair to hold his head against her greedy woman's flesh, as wave after wave of ecstasy poured through her. She was filled with liquid heat, suffused with a satisfaction unlike anything she'd ever experienced, or even anticipated before.

A loud clap of thunder, followed by a blinding flash of lightning, punctuated her climax. Winnie burst into billions of tiny pieces, becoming the stars in the sky floating slowly back to earth, one by one.

He eased himself up her body, caught her before she'd landed in reality, kissed her nipples until she moaned with renewed longing. She still hungered for more. Much more.

She reached between their bodies, found the velvet tip of his sex and traced the ridge encircling it with her fingertip. He flinched and tensed at her side. A perverse sense of power swept through her as she wrapped her fingers around the smooth, hot shaft.

Paul growled as her explorations grew bolder. He retrieved the square packet she'd given him earlier and tore it open with his teeth. This woman was driving him insane. He couldn't wait much longer to bury himself inside her.

She took the contents of the packet from his hand as he lifted himself from her just enough to enable her to maneuver her hands between their bodies. He gasped, then groaned as she rolled the condom down the length of his throbbing erection. He felt like a bomb about to explode. She made the entire process of practicing safe sex quite pleasurable indeed. He couldn't wait to discover how wonderful the main event would be.

Pressing himself against her, he felt the folds of her womanhood open to receive him. Paul held his breath for a moment to bring himself under control. He was so aroused it was downright dangerous. This fiery redhead was a lethal weapon. There was no doubt about it.

She opened like a blossom to the sun, unfurling her petals to take him inside her. "Oh, God," he muttered as he slowly penetrated, wondering if he'd be able to last long enough to bring them both the pleasure they so desperately sought. Winnie Sinclair was one hell of a woman.

She was hot and tight, enclosing him within her velvet sheath. Paul froze with his body buried deep within hers. Millions of tiny rivulets of pulsing pleasure seemed to surround and contain him. She fit him like a glove, drew him in and held him fast.

As he moved within her she matched his rhythm, angled her hips to more fully meet his powerful thrusts. A staircase spiraling toward pure hedonism drew him upward. Paul's movements became more desperate as he neared his completion.

She tensed beneath him, bucked and cried out in feral delight. He felt her fingernails rake his shoulders as her legs tightened around his waist, drawing him even deeper inside. This was pure, uninhibited sex. It was wild, crazy, hungry, all-encompassing.

It was the best he'd ever had. *She* was the best he'd ever had.

He became an erupting volcano as he burst within her. Tensing and straining, he gasped as she pulsed around his shaft, drawing every ounce of energy he could muster from deep in his core. Everything he had converged in this single glorious moment, taking him over an edge, into a pit of rapture unlike anything he'd ever known.

Panting, he slumped against her, kissed her damp brow, felt her tense, then relax beneath and around him.

Thunder rumbled and the houseboat tipped again, tossing them onto the floor. She giggled and his chuckle soon joined in. This woman was absolutely delightful. And he'd thought he wanted to be alone this weekend. He couldn't have been more mistaken. This was infinitely better.

"Winnie," he whispered, lowering his lips to toy with the corner of her mouth. "How many of those little packets did you say you had with you?" He lifted his gaze to watch her slow, sexy smile.

"Several."

He gasped at the provocative expression in her green eyes. "I have a feeling we're going to need every . . . last . . . one of them."

Her catlike eyes glazed over with passion as she moistened her lips with the tip of her tongue. "I'm counting on it," she purred.

"Oh, God."

Two

Winnie awoke with a start, confused and clutching the blanket to her bare breasts. *My God, I'm naked.* She never slept in the buff. And where the hell was she?

And more importantly, whose warm body was pressed intimately against her backside?

Oh, Lord.

Memories tore at her, filling her with remorse. She winced and bit her lower lip in self-chastisement. How could she have been so . . . impetuous?

So *stupid?*

Had she really done it? Slept with her ex-husband's divorce attorney?

Oh, yeah. I did it and I . . . liked it.

A soft groan grew in her throat. This was lower than low. She shook her head in disbelief.

Tacky, Winnie. Really tacky.

It was difficult to accept such uncharacteristic behavior from herself. But the memory of the glorious hours she'd spent in this man's arms would not be denied. She'd done it.

She glanced over her shoulder at the sleeping man. The cleft in his chin was softer in slumber. His dark lashes rested against his tanned cheeks so softly it made her heart do a little flutter in her breast. He was gorgeous.

Would she do it again under similar circumstances?

Yep.

The memory of Paul's potent kisses waged a bold assault

on her rising regret. She took a shuddering breath, acutely
aware of his breath tickling the hairs on the back of her neck.
He was sound asleep, obviously unaffected by the tossing
and pitching of the boat.

Winnie placed her hand over her stomach and winced as
the rocking continued. Last night, she'd overcome seasickness once, but she'd been distracted.

Wonderfully distracted.

Her throat was dry. The brandy she'd consumed had left
a foul taste in her mouth . . . and in her conscience.

"Damn," she whispered, trying to free herself from Paul's
clinging grasp. In slumber, his weight seemed far more significant than it had last night.

Winning her freedom, she stood beside the bunk where
they'd made love into the wee hours of the morning and
stared down at him. He was still extraordinary, even asleep
with dark beard stubble marring his complexion. Heat
flooded her face when she noticed the empty square packets
scattered all over the floor. *One, two, three, four . . . five?*

Oh, Lord.

A wave of nausea accompanied more vigorous rocking
of the boat. She needed an antacid and a drink of water—
desperately. Holding her hand to her forehead, Winnie decided a couple of aspirin might not be a bad idea either as
she walked into the head.

She stared at the face in the mirror. Her hair was a mess,
plastered to one side of her head. *No danger of anyone wanting to seduce me now.* She filled a glass with water and took
the medication, then brushed her teeth to rid herself of the
foul taste in her mouth.

Her clam-digger pants, T-shirt, and sports bra were still
hanging on the back of the door. Remembering the missing
doorknob, she only partially closed the door and pulled on
her clothing. Cursing herself, she involuntarily recalled all
the ways and places Paul had touched her last night. It was
maddening. Infuriating.

Stimulating.

"Damn." A wave of heat flashed through Winnie, making her consider seeking more of his magical touch. *No!* She wouldn't succumb to such weakness again. Surely she had more self-restraint than this. *Somewhere.* Lurking in her subconscious . . .

Barefoot but dressed, she tiptoed into the cabin, pausing again to gaze at the still-slumbering man. And what a man! Her face flamed with embarrassment and something more, as she stood staring at him. No man had ever taken her to . . . such heights of rapture before.

Heights of rapture? C'mon, get a grip, Winnie.

She'd learned many new things last night. Things she wasn't apt to forget, nor was she likely to experience them again. Paul Weathers was more than her lifetime quota of flings. Besides, it was doubtful anyone else could measure up after such beautiful lovemaking.

Beautiful lovemaking? Don't be a fool, Winnie. It was plain, old-fashioned sex. Well, maybe not so plain or old-fashioned.

With a sigh, she turned her back on the desirable hunk and opened the hatch to crawl up on deck. A dull gray dawn heralded a new day. Surely the storm wouldn't last much longer. The wind and rain seemed to have diminished somewhat, so she ventured up on deck to investigate. For some inane reason, she needed to know how far they were from shore—not that swimming was uppermost on her list of possible escape plans.

A life vest hanging from a hook caught her attention. It couldn't hurt, especially since the water was still so choppy. *Better safe than sorry.* Groaning, Winnie tried to combat a mental image of herself starring in an ad campaign promoting the practice of water safety *and* safe sex. "I can't believe this."

After shrugging into the bright orange garment, she secured the front and grabbed the railing to pull herself completely onto the deck.

Squinting, Winnie tried in vain to see the shore. Paul had mentioned he'd dropped anchor. But how far out had he sailed before doing so? There was no sign of land, and Lake Oologah wasn't a huge body of water by any means.

The wind began to howl again, making the boat pitch and rock violently. She lost her balance and groped blindly for the railing just as the vessel took a precarious dip into the lake, then popped back up with such force it sent her flying.

Over the railing and into the cold water.

"Help!" she cried, spitting out the fishy water as it filled her mouth and nose. Thank God she'd donned the life vest. "Help!"

But there was no sign of Paul, who was undoubtedly still sound asleep. After all, wasn't that what all men did following great sex? *Great—just great!*

Was this her fate—to drown after falling into the arms of her ex-husband's divorce attorney? *God!* Dirk would get another laugh out of that. He'd probably think she'd committed suicide from a broken heart.

Then another far more disturbing thought assailed her. Winnie hadn't found the time to change the beneficiary on her life insurance yet. If she drowned today in the midst of this unexpected tempest, Dirk Sinclair—adulterer—would become a very wealthy man.

That'll be the day.

The boat vanished from sight as she was swept away in the swirling, churning current. The life vest offered some, albeit slight, solace as the water tossed her to and fro like a fishing bobber. She was far too small to prevail against the fierce storm and angry reservoir.

A whirling sensation began near her feet, tugging mercilessly at her toes. Winnie kicked and waved her arms in the turbulent water, struggling against the terrifying sensation.

Suddenly, she was drawn into the whirlpool and began to

spin counterclockwise, slowly at first, then faster until she felt herself become one with the lake. It was almost as if she'd left her body back on board the boat. Her mind was whirling and she closed her eyes against the unknown, praying for a cessation to the horror.

Drowning was supposed to be a peaceful way to die, but this was far from tranquil. Yet she must be dying. What other explanation could there be? If this was death, it was sure as hell taking its sweet time about ending her misery. Winnie's struggle continued against the cold water for what seemed like hours as it tried again and again to suck her under.

But fight she would before Dirk Sinclair would see a dime of her life insurance.

The spinning gradually slowed and she was freed from the whirlpool's destructive grasp. With her eyes still tightly shut, she gripped the life vest with all the strength remaining in her battered body, then gasped when her foot struck something. She was so tired she could scarcely keep her eyes open, let alone her death grip on the front of her life vest. Just when she thought she'd imagined the solidness, her foot struck it again.

C'mon, Winnie. Open your eyes.

Dragging her gaze upward, Winnie nearly wept with joy. The beach was just ahead, less than twenty yards away. A burst of determination inspired her to paddle and kick as the storm vanished as suddenly as it had appeared. It seemed she'd weathered yet another tumult in her less than memorable life.

Land felt glorious. Winnie staggered onto the beach, gasping for precious air as she fell to her knees on the wet sand. Down on all fours, she considered pinching herself to ensure she was alive, but realized that had she been dead, the horrendous pain in her head wouldn't be troubling her any longer.

Dirk would never know how close he'd come to inheriti a cool half million. A tired smile tugged at the co her mouth as evil but victorious thoughts flashed through her mind. Unless she told him, of course.

And she would.

As she flopped onto her back, shedding the life vest in the process, Winnie closed her eyes. She was so tired. The sun felt warm against her face; a gull called out to the world as it sailed past. Was it morning or evening?

Her eyes grew heavy and her mind even foggier than before. She couldn't even see her hand in front of her face, let alone find her way back to the dock.

She must sleep. . . .

Winnie struggled into a sitting position, blinking several times to clear her vision as she rubbed her aching head.

She was lucky to be alive. Very lucky.

A shudder swept through her as she considered how close she'd come to losing her miserable life in the storm. But the world wouldn't have been any worse off with one less interior decorator around. And as she'd been reminded by her ex-husband on more than one occasion, hers was a less-than-impressive profession. He'd certainly never complained about her paycheck, though.

What had become of the houseboat? Probably still anchored in the lake with the womanizing Paul Weathers snoring away in the cabin. *Creep!* The memory of her ordeal made Winnie shiver. A headache was a trivial consequence of such a near-disaster.

Groaning as she tried to stand and failed, Winnie took several deep breaths and heaved herself to her feet. She swayed slightly, but for the most part she wasn't in bad shape . . . considering.

"There she is!"

"ale voice carried across the beach, making Winnie with relief. Someone *was* searching for her. Her only other person who'd known where she was going for the weekend. With no family to speak of, she'd assumed no one would care enough to wonder where she was. At least, not so soon.

The theme song from *Gilligan's Island* flitted through her mind as she swayed and shook her head, trying unsuccessfully to bring her wooziness under control. She staggered a bit, wondering if the owner of the voice would think she'd been drinking. The truth be told, she felt as if she'd consumed no less than a fifth of Jack Daniels—not to mention the brandy.

Falling to her knees, she laid her face in her hands, wishing the spinning would cease. It was making her very nauseous. If she kept her eyes tightly shut, it didn't seem quite so bad, though the light-headedness continued unabated.

"Ah, hell. You ain't her." A low groan punctuated the man's strange remark. "But what do I care? Your hair's the right color, so you're gonna be her. What the hell difference does it make? You got a good job waitin' for you at Hopsador's ranch."

What nonsense was he blabbering? Baring her face, Winnie tried to bring the dizziness under control in order to properly greet her rescuer. She opened one eye, then immediately closed it. She must be hallucinating.

Grimacing, she opened her other eye. From her kneeling vantage point, she was face to knee with a pair of filthy jeans, patched with three different colors of fabric. Looking down, she noticed a pair of very old boots with a hole in one toe. What kind of welcome party was this? She was all in favor of live and let live, but at the moment, she wasn't exactly in a politically correct frame of mind.

She opened both eyes, confirming her suspicions, and moaned slightly in bewilderment. Rescued, but by *what?* Surely this wasn't a responsible, dependable sort—not dressed in such tattered clothing.

Of course, it must be a costume. But why? This guy looked like he'd just stepped off the set of an old Western. Or maybe he was from one of the nearby tourist attractions. It was nowhere near Halloween, so what other explanation could there be?

The way her luck had been running lately, he was probably an ax murderer. *And the way my head still hurts, I can only hope . . .*

"Git up."

Definitely a male voice, with a decidedly Western twang. How appropriate. She managed a grunt and a nod, finally summoning the strength to drag her gaze upward until it encompassed the top half of the strange man.

A multicolored shirt, with a broad assortment of patches and crudely mended tears, topped the dirty jeans. A leather strap crisscrossed his chest and carried enough ammunition to blow away half the population of Tulsa. And guns—two of them in a leather holster slung low on his hips. Surely no one would carry loaded weapons around in public like this.

What the hell had she gotten herself into now? Winnie felt giddy. This unusual and astonishing character did absolutely nothing to assist her return to reality.

The man reached down and grabbed Winnie's arm, dragging her unceremoniously to her feet. Wincing from his brutal grip, she mentally shook herself and managed to thank him for his assistance. She chose to ignore his ominous-looking guns—it seemed her wisest move at the moment. Besides, they couldn't be real. Could they?

After all, simply because he *looked* like someone who'd recently escaped from the penitentiary was no reason to be rude. But the way he continued to gape at her was anything but polite. He was staring at her in open disapproval.

"What in tarnation is you wearin'?" he finally asked, scratching his head. He shook his head and clicked his tongue. "Hopsador ain't expectin' a woman who wears britches. I can tell you that for sure."

Winnie grimaced at the man's loud and ridiculous observation. "What the hell do you propose I wear to go boating?"

she asked in a slurred voice which barely resembled her own, swaying against him in the process. *Jeez, he probably does think I'm drunk. But I'm not . . . anymore.*

"Boating? Is that what you call it?" Chuckling, he rolled his jaundiced eyes. "I reckon you ain't no worse'n we expected." His sneer was quite profound as he turned and pulled her along with him. "I can't figger what in hell the old fart expected, anyway."

"Huh?" The man's breath was horrible—bad enough that Sadaam Hussein would probably try to use it as a weapon in chemical warfare, if given the chance. None of this made any sense at all, and at the moment Winnie couldn't have cared less about anyone else's problems. When he didn't bother to explain, she shaded her eyes and looked into the distance, thinking she might spot the boat, now that the storm had passed.

Winnie blinked several times to clear her vision. As she swung her gaze left and right, she realized with a start they weren't at the lake at all. Somehow, she'd managed to end up in a river, rather than the lake. But that wasn't possible. She couldn't have been swept over the dam. She definitely would've remembered that!

The wind had been fierce, but certainly not *that* powerful. And the possibility of her drifting *upstream* into the Verdigris was even more ludicrous. Then how could she be here, walking along the riverbank with no lake in sight?

Weird.

Besides, June was typically one of the most popular times for lounging at the lake—uh, river. It seemed odd that, besides Stinky here, there was but one lone figure as far as she could see in either direction. They were heading toward him.

"Where the hell's the damned lake?" Her stomach lurched in protest and her head throbbed. "The lake . . ."

She could actually feel her "rescuer's" continued perusal. He probably *really* thought she was nuts, now. But his interest seemed far more intense than even this insane situation called for. Of course, the way she staggered along, periodically gripping his forearm for support, probably gave him all sorts of ideas. "What are you gawking at?"

"I was just wonderin'." The man looked away and chuckled again. "Can't figger out why you'd wanna . . ."

"What?"

"Well, dress that way—it just don't make no sense."

Another voice barged in on their meaningful conversation.

"That ain't her. Who the hell's *this?*" The second man she'd noticed earlier had an accent and crude attire similar to her rescuer. His expression reminded her of Oscar the Grouch from *Sesame Street. Oscar and Stinky—rescuers from hell.* He joined them as they neared a primitive collection of buildings along the waterfront.

"Hush up and use your brain. This has to be the right woman. We ain't got no choice. Got it?" Stinky spit on the ground near Winnie's bare feet, inducing her to curl her toes under for protection. "Only one here, *and* her hair's the right color. Besides . . . Hopsador ain't never seen her."

"And she's sure as hell been in the water." Oscar guffawed as his gaze raked the length of her. "Looks like a drowned rat. Scrawny thing. But as long as we deliver a woman with red hair, I reckon that's all that matters. But what in tarnation happened to the other one?"

Deliver a woman with red hair? Other one? This certainly didn't sound encouraging. Winnie lifted her chin a notch and sneered at the second man, noting that his costume was even more outlandish than the first. "You guys on your way to a costume party or something?" She was beginning to feel a bit more stable, but infinitely more confused. Where the hell was the damned lake . . . and the boat?

And Paul.

Ignoring her question, the peculiar men conversed quietly for several moments, leaving Winnie to her own devices. Testing her sea legs, she soon discovered herself capable of remaining in a vertical position without assistance. At least that was something.

Along with her vertigo went the nausea. Other than exhausted, hungry, thirsty and dirty, she felt relatively normal, all things considered.

"I dunno how Hopsador's gonna feel about them britches." Oscar the Grouch shook his head in open disapproval. "I reckon the othern's trunk's probably at the ranch by now, though."

Trunk? Winnie stared at the twin nut-cases with a frown. "You guys obviously have me confused with someone else," she said quietly. "Were there others lost in the storm?" What about Paul? Was he still safely napping on board the boat?

Both men looked at her as if she'd grown another head. Stinky seemed incapable of doing anything more difficult than spitting, while Oscar glowered at her in an arrogant manner that offended every feminist bone in her body.

"Storm?" Oscar the imperious folded his arms across his bullet-laden chest. "There weren't no storm, woman." He chuckled and shook his head. "It's like this . . . the minute we let it slip that old Rufus is half-Cherokee, you *jumped,* yellin' somethin' about savin' your scalp."

"The *hell* I did!" Outrage swelled within her, making her blood pressure escalate. This was ludicrous. Scalp? Winnie was furious. She didn't know what kind of game these strange men were playing, but she wasn't about to assume any role in it. "I was caught in a freak storm and swept off the deck of the *Sooner Sunset.* It's a miracle I'm alive at all. And I've *never* seen you two goons before in my life!"

"*Sooner Sunset?*" The man's crude laughter pervaded the quiet riverbank. "I ain't ever heard that ferry called the *Sooner Sunset* before. Have you, Lemuel?"

Winnie took a deep breath and shook her head. *Lemuel, Stinky—what's the difference?* "Look, I'm pooped. Bobbing around in a . . . a lake can do that to a person." She laughed derisively. Where *was* the lake? "All I really want is a ride back to the dock where I parked my car yesterday. Then I'm going to drive straight home—if I can find my keys—for a hot bath and something to eat. If you can't give me a ride, do you suppose you could at least manage to point me to a phone so I can call someone to pick me up?"

"Phone? Y'mean a telyphone?" Stinky laughed as if her requests were ludicrous, rather than quite ordinary. "I reckon you won't find one of them newfangled talkin' things anywhere around here."

Newfangled talking things? Where the hell have these guys been? "Damn. Why are you doing this?" Winnie kicked at the rocky riverbank that *should* have been a sandy beach. She was quite certain no one but her could manage to attract two less helpful rescuers. She had a gift for such strokes of luck. Last night had certainly been vivid proof of that. "Thanks, guys, but I'm outta here. I appreciate your . . . help, though. But I've had enough of this little game."

When she turned to walk away from the pair of miscreants, her forearm was captured in a steely grip. "You're gonna be governess to Rufus Hopsador's daughter. Got it?" Oscar said in a warning tone. "I don't much care who you really are, or where you come from. So don't try nothin'."

Oh, Lord. What had she gotten herself into? These men had obviously mistaken her for someone else. And they certainly didn't show any indication of releasing her in the near future. Playing along seemed her only alternative at the moment. "Governess?" *God, these creeps think I'm Mary Poppins. If only I had my magic umbrella.*

The men didn't talk as they dragged her along until they came upon three horses tied in the trees. Winnie remained silent as her confusion escalated.

She tried to plant her bare feet in the slippery mud when they pulled her close to one of the waiting beasts—*way* too close. "Hey, I don't like horses."

"Well, ain't that just too bad." The first man laughed and

spit again. "You mean they don't got no horses back in Boston?"

"Boston?" Winnie shook her head. "I've never been to Boston in my entire life."

"Uh, you ain't been to Boston?" The second man's face reddened and he looked at the ground while his cohort laughed uproariously. "How the hell we gonna pull this off, Lemuel? She don't know nothin' she's supposed to know. Hell, we don't even know her name."

Winnie barely managed to suppress a shudder as realization swept through her. She was their prisoner. What the hell was wrong with her? Seeing the men's guns and ammunition should've triggered a mental alarm. But *no!* She was still so spaced out from her encounter with the storm, the brandy, and Paul Weathers she couldn't think straight. God! These men were *dangerous.*

She opened her mouth to argue, but thought better of it. Something warned her such efforts would be wasted. Who were they? What did they want with her? Was she being punished for one night of decadence? One lousy—well, not so lousy—night?

"Git on up there." Stinky held the reins and pointed at the saddle.

Winnie looked at the tall horse. It was big—really big. A lump of cold fear formed in her throat. "I . . . I don't know how."

"Tarnation, how the hell you gonna get by out here without knowin' how to ride a horse?" The man slapped his thigh and shook his head. "Lemuel, throw her up in that saddle. We gotta git back to the ranch. Hopsador's gonna have our hide for this."

"Nice horsey," Winnie murmured, reaching out to touch the animal's neck. She took a deep breath. The horse's hair was soft and smooth, soothing her somewhat. Until the beast looked at her from the corner of its eye. "He . . . he doesn't like me."

"He's a she and I don't give a damn if she don't like you."
Stinky-Lemuel grabbed Winnie's arm and pulled. "Git on
the horse. *Now!*"

Winnie sighed and put her right foot in the stirrup. She
gripped the saddle horn with both hands, but realized that
couldn't possibly be right. She looked down at her foot in
total confusion, mingled with growing trepidation.

The truth struck her full force . . . and she didn't like it
one bit.

She was being kidnapped.

"Chrissakes, woman!" Oscar, whose real name Winnie
was still blissfully ignorant of, placed his hand on her backside and pushed. "Put your *left* foot in the stirrup and swing
the other'n over the horse. Unless you plan on ridin' back-
wards. Sorry, but we ain't got no sidesaddle for your high-
ness."

*Yeah, a sidesaddle would make all the difference in the
world. Jeez!* Gritting her teeth, Winnie took a deep breath
and did as the man had instructed. It was a miracle, but she
found herself sitting—facing forward—in the saddle. "Okay.
I'm up here." She gripped the saddle horn so tightly her
knuckles turned white.

"What's your name?" Oscar demanded as he climbed on
his horse. When she didn't answer, he shook his head and
chuckled. "Have it your way. Hopsador's expectin' a woman
named Kathleen MacGregor. So, that'll be your name."

Winnie chewed the inside of her cheek. Her head was
throbbing again. She was tired and hungry. This MacGregor
woman was expected to do something for someone named
Hopsador. *Oh yeah, be Mary Poppins for his little girl.*

She tried to ignore acid churning in the pit of her stomach.
God, she was in big trouble. Governess or hostage? These
guys knew very well she wasn't the right woman. Could they
be planning to hold her for ransom, instead? If so, they'd
have a long wait ahead of them. Her personal fortune only
kicked in after she died. She had no family to speak of, and

she sure as hell didn't know anyone with the kind of money kidnappers would be interested in.

Except maybe Paul Weathers.

Silently chastising herself, Winnie took a deep breath. She had to get control of her thoughts and emotions. If she told them her real name, then they'd realize they couldn't possibly extract ransom from someone for a hostage named MacGregor. Right. That'd work—she hoped.

"My name is Winifred Sinclair," she said very clearly. "Most people call me Winnie, but *you* may call me Ms. Sinclair."

The men, both mounted now, laughed as if she'd said something hilarious. Winnie straightened in the saddle, relaxing her grip on the saddle horn somewhat in the process. "I don't see anything amusing about this at all."

"Nope, I don't reckon you would." Stinky grinned at her. It was a friendly smile, one that made her wonder whether or not she might be able to trust him. Perhaps he could help her escape from Oscar.

"So, Hopsador's gonna think somebody made a mistake back in Boston," Oscar said, grabbing the reins to Winnie's horse. "The MacGregor woman didn't come. They sent this'un instead. Got it, Lemuel?"

Stinky seemed hesitant. He rubbed his chin for a moment, then nodded. "Yep. Reckon we don't got no other choice."

Winnie sighed, abandoning hopes of any assistance from him. *Damn.* What were these men planning to do with her? More importantly, what was this Hopsador character planning to do with her? She found it hard to believe all they expected was a governess. How ridiculous! There were agencies that handled things like that. People didn't have to go out and kidnap domestic help. There was something far more sinister about this situation. She recalled their earlier words.

As long as we deliver a redheaded woman.

That didn't sound like an appropriate prerequisite for a governess by any means. Winnie suppressed a shudder as they started to move. The horse plodded along steadily, but the side-to-side motion was foreign to her. It was all she could do to keep her balance in the saddle. She didn't dare release her death grip on the saddle horn.

They were heading away from the lake—rather what should've been the lake—traveling uphill. Trees closed in around them, but before they were completely swallowed in the dense forest, Winnie forced herself to look back over her shoulder. From her high vantage point, she had a view of the entire Verdigris Valley.

There was no sign of a lake. None at all.

It was impossible. Yet undeniable.

If there was no lake, then where was the boat? Where was her car? She blinked as a sinking feeling washed over her. This was, without a doubt, the strangest experience she'd ever had. She felt like Dorothy in *The Wizard of Oz*. Casting a surreptitious glance at her alleged rescuers, Winnie almost laughed. This sure as hell wasn't Munchkin Land and she wasn't sitting astride the infamous horse of a different color. This one was plain brown.

Paul's face flashed through her mind. He was smiling at her, making that wretchedly handsome cleft in his chin appear even deeper.

Damn that man. This is all his fault.

Turning to face forward again, Winnie blinked back her stinging tears. She was in trouble, but the last thing she needed was to burst into tears. That wouldn't do her a bit of good. She drew a shuddering breath, then released it very slowly.

If the lake isn't where it's supposed to be, then. . . .
Where the hell am I?

Three

Paul rubbed his eyes and moaned as the houseboat tipped precariously low in the water. "What the hell . . ." The roller-coaster ride dumped him off the couch, reminding him with a start how he and Winnie Sinclair had rolled onto the floor in a similar manner the night before. Together. Connected.

Intimately.

The boat's pitching made old-fashioned fear crowd his libido for supremacy. Just when he thought the vessel was going to capsize, it righted itself. Releasing a breath he hadn't even realized he'd been holding, Paul scrambled for his sweat pants and a life vest.

Once the vest was secure, he looked around the cabin. There was one life vest missing, which had positive and negative connotations. It meant she may have gone on deck, but it also meant she had some protection if the disaster struck. Not yet ready to assume she'd gone out in the storm, Paul glanced in the head. No sign of Winnie.

That woman had to be the surprise of his life. How could he have known she'd be such a fiery lover? Lord. He'd never had such an experience before, not even in his most erotic adolescent dreams.

But where was she now?

If she wasn't in the cabin or the head, then she had to be . . . on deck. He took a deep breath, forcing himself to accept the truth. There was nowhere left to search.

The way the boat was rocking and pitching, she wouldn't

last five minutes up there. His heart pounded frantically as he threw open the hatch and gripped the railing to heave himself onto the precarious surface. *Barefoot—brilliant move, Einstein.* Without his rubber-soled deck shoes, he didn't stand a chance of maintaining his footing on the slippery surface.

Paul held onto the railing with both hands as he strained to see through the driving rain. His eyes stung and his skin felt as if it was being peeled from his flesh by the vicious wind. Still, there was no sign of Winnie.

"Damn." He eased himself closer to the railing, peering over the side and into the choppy water. She'd gone overboard—there was no point in denying it any longer. His gut twisted into a vicious knot.

That was the only place she *could* be—in the water.

"Oh, God, Winnie," he whispered, easing his way along the deck so he could check the other side. He had to make sure. Didn't he owe her that much?

The thought made him cringe. That was one of the most chauvinistic thoughts that had ever crossed his mind. Modern women didn't feel men "owed" them anything—he hoped.

Had he driven her to this? Could she have been so desperate to get away from him that she'd been willing to endanger herself this way?

Then he recalled her feral abandonment, the delicious way she'd responded to his touch . . . No, she hadn't been anxious to get away from him at all. They hadn't been able to get close enough to each other—then.

Winnie Sinclair was one hell of a woman—one he planned on getting to know much better. As soon as he figured out where the hell she'd gone.

A flash of lightning momentarily blinded him. The houseboat pitched again, viciously tearing Paul away from the railing. He groped through the furor for something, anything, to grab onto.

Cold terror seized him as the boat left the lake's choppy

surface, then plummeted back into the water. Before Paul had the opportunity to consider his limited options, a huge wave reached over the railing and ensnared him. It seemed almost human—clutching him in a watery fist to pull him off the *Sooner Sunset*.

I'm in for it, now.

The boat quickly vanished from sight as the swirling, churning current swept him away. Thank God for the life vest, he thought, coughing and sputtering as he bobbed around in the vicious water.

Something tugged at his feet, seeming intent on sucking him into the murky depths below. He began to spin counterclockwise with the mighty current. Paul imagined himself something like a lone ice cube in a cocktail, being mercilessly spun by an avenging swizzle stick.

Just when he thought he was a goner for sure, the spinning slowed. Clutching the front of his life vest, Paul took great gulps of air, not daring to open his eyes, knowing his stomach would heave if his surroundings continued to spin.

The watery grave would have to wait for some other sucker. He wasn't ready to die, yet. There was still too much of life left to enjoy.

Like Winnie Sinclair.

Dragging his eyes open, he saw land and paddled toward it. Surely, if he could survive such an experience, Winnie could have, too. She was young and strong—didn't he know it?—more than capable of making it to shore.

Paul staggered onto solid ground, falling to his knees as he gasped for air. He clutched his middle, leaning on one palm for support. The *Sooner Sunset* was nowhere in sight. He sighed, silently praying the boat hadn't been destroyed.

The vessel was a legacy from his father. He couldn't lose it—it was all he had left of his family.

Shaking his head, he rolled onto his hip and sat, hugging his knees to support his trembling upper body. He rested his forehead against his crossed arms for a few minutes, then lifted his gaze to peer out at the water. Maybe he'd catch a glimpse of the boat.

Or Winnie.

As his stomach lurched again, he shaded his eyes to scan the horizon. There was no sign of Winnie or his boat. But something else was wrong. Different.

Something . . . incredible.

He blinked several times at the unexpected sight before him. It was a river. *A river?* Where was Lake Oologah? More importantly, where was *he?*

Paul lurched to his bare feet and took a few shaky steps toward the bank, shedding his life vest in the process. This was nuts. He knew he'd been in the lake. Hell, the boat was too big for the river. This was more than just a little weird.

And where was Winnie? Was she back at the lake—wherever *that* was. Had she survived the storm? Raking his fingers through his hair, he took a deep breath. The authorities needed to be notified so they could start searching for Winnie.

Or for her body.

"No, not that." He shuddered, then shook his head as if to confirm the denial. Why the hell was he so concerned for a woman he barely knew? "Damn." He knew the reason. "Because she was on my boat—*my* responsibility."

He raked his fingers through his hair. "God, I don't believe this. How the hell did I get myself into *this* mess?" he muttered, glancing up at the cloudless sky. The crystal blue mocked him, almost as if the storm had never occurred. He took another deep breath and felt more stable.

A movement downstream drew his attention. Could it be Winnie? Instinct took command, prompting him to migrate quickly toward the figure crouched on the riverbank. About twenty yards from the person, he paused behind a clump of trees, realizing the shadowy figure was male—definitely not Winnie.

The man half-turned, peering out across the water as he

straightened to his full height. *What the hell . . . ?* It was like looking in a mirror. Paul held his breath and his heart banged in his chest. How could that be? Was he a relative—a distant cousin, perhaps?

I guess everyone in the world really does have a twin.

Paul suppressed the urge to rush over to the stranger. Instinct told him to remain hidden for the time being, until he figured out exactly what was going on. Maybe he was unconscious and dreaming all this. What a relief it would be to waken and learn that was true. He closed his eyes for a moment, then reopened them.

This was no dream.

Swallowing the lump in his throat, Paul watched his double stoop down to pick up a rock. He was a big man, every inch as tall as Paul. The man's hair was considerably longer than Paul's, but the color was identical.

This man's profile was a precise copy—albeit a bit more tanned and rugged—of his own.

Paul's gaze traveled downward. The man looked as if he'd just stepped off the set of a John Wayne Western. His costume screamed cowboy from the top of his dark hat to the toes of scarred leather boots. Was someone shooting a movie in the area? Paul couldn't recall reading anything about a film crew on location. That sort of news usually got around, especially in Oklahoma.

A strange sound—some kind of animal—distracted him from his puzzling thoughts. Instinct maintained control, insisting he keep his back against the tree until he'd identified the source of the soft whinny. It was a horse.

Of course, what was a cowboy without a horse?

There was another soft nicker, almost as if in answer to the first. Two horses—two cowboys?

The figure near the water's edge immediately tensed, commanding Paul's attention. He noticed the silver star flashing on the man's broad chest. Then he saw something else—something far more significant.

A gun.

Two guns, to be exact, hanging in a holster worn low on the man's hips.

He has to be an actor. Who the hell else—

Another body suddenly seemed to fly through the air and collide with the cowboy. They tumbled into the river, rolling over and over in the shallow water. A fist connected with a jaw, filling the air with the sickening sound of flesh striking flesh. The men punched and swung at each other, repeatedly falling into the water, then leaping back to their feet.

Stuntmen?

Paul tried to convince himself this was fake—that the men were actors. However, a nagging voice in the back of his mind refused to accept such a simple explanation. This was too real.

The attacker's red hair fell across his face, partially concealing his features. Blood trickled from the corners of his cut mouth. Real blood? It looked real enough.

Paul started to take a tentative step from behind the tree, then hesitated. If this was a movie crew, they'd be furious after staging such a realistic scene only to have a bystander screw it up.

And if this wasn't acting? If it was real?

Another thought struck him. If these were stuntmen, where was the movie crew? Lights? Camera? Action? They only had one out of three here.

Confused, Paul shook his head, then turned his attention back to the struggling, grunting men. Their hats had fallen off when they first tumbled into the river. Water streamed off their bodies and clothing, mixing with the blood from split lips and noses.

Real blood?

Paul's heart slammed against his ribs when sunlight glinted off something silver. The flash came again, then he realized with another surge of adrenalin that the object in the attacker's hand was a knife.

The other man—his duplicate—froze, staring at his adversary's face. Paul wondered how his twin kept his gaze from straying to the menacing blade clutched in his opponent's fist. Paul couldn't tear his gaze from that face—so like the one in his bathroom mirror each morning.

A muscle twitched in the dark-haired man's jaw—his eyes narrowed to mere slits. Every muscle in his body was blatantly tensed in readiness. Paul felt his own muscles tense in anticipation.

"I didn't wanna have to kill you, but you wouldn't let me alone. All I wanted was a chance to go straight. You shoulda stayed away and left me alone, Weathers," the redheaded man taunted.

Weathers?

Paul's blood turned cold. What the hell was going on here? Had he stumbled into some alternate universe or something? Was this man his alter ego? Freud would've loved this.

Paul Weathers hated it—a hell of a lot.

"You'll swing," the dark-haired man said, never shifting his gaze from the threatening blade.

"Maybe someday I will." The armed man chuckled. "But you ain't gonna live to see it and it'll be your own damned fault for not leavin' me be."

Paul moved from behind the tree again as the men resumed their battle. He had to intervene. This had gone too far already. As he took a few steps toward the river, a horrifying sound reached his ears.

He knew without really knowing that the dull thud was the sound of steel piercing flesh and muscle, deflecting off human bone. A low grunt followed as the lawman crumpled and fell.

Paul resisted the impulse to rush forward. He was unarmed and he wouldn't help this stranger—relative?—by getting himself stabbed, too. The best he could do was wait for the attacker to leave, then try to help . . . if it wasn't already too late.

The redheaded man hovered above the other figure, knife still clutched between bloodied fingers. His chest rose and fell with his rapid breathing. As the man grabbed his victim by the collar and dragged him toward the bank, Paul shifted back into hiding.

Paul's nerves were tuned to an almost painful awareness, despite his long night and near-drowning. Gut instincts tugged him in opposite directions. One moment he wanted to rush forward to offer assistance—the next he wanted to hide. His fight-or-flight instinct was alive and well, and making him a nervous wreck. He should know better than to risk being seen by an armed man—a killer. This entire situation was the most impossibly bizarre experience he'd ever known.

Paul's gut instincts demanded he accept the truth. This was real.

My God—have I witnessed a murder?

Maybe the man wasn't dead. Paul peered around the tree as the assassin stooped and dug through his victim's pockets. The murderer removed what appeared to be a couple of coins and stuffed them into his own pocket.

Had the man been murdered for loose change? Paul swallowed hard as the killer kicked the body on the ground, then chuckled. With one swift movement, the assailant spit on his victim, then turned and walked away.

Paul strained to see the attacker's face, but all the reddish-brown hair prevented a clear view. There was no way he'd be able to identify the man's face, but the hair color was very distinctive. He wouldn't forget it—ever.

The murderer disappeared into a clump of trees. A few moments later, the sound of hoofbeats signaled the all clear.

Paul rushed over to the injured man and dropped to his knees, feeling the victim's carotid artery for a pulse. There was none. "Damn."

He tore open the man's bloodied shirt to expose the deep wound. There was a copious amount of blood. No one could've survived this. Either Paul could help the guy breathe until help came, knowing it was probably a lost cause, or he could just walk away. No, he couldn't do that. He had to at least try. Paul pulled a dirty bandanna away from the man's neck and pressed it against the wound, then held it firmly in place with his knee.

Trying to remember the CPR training he'd never used, Paul rolled the victim's head until sightless eyes were staring straight up at the sky. "Oh, shit." The face looked even more like his own than he'd originally realized. "Oh, *shit.*"

Panic threatened. Paul squelched the cold terror which jeopardized his resolve. He had to at least try . . .

Counting and alternating chest compressions with artificial respiration, he worked on the man for what seemed like forever. Finally, spent and panting, Paul flopped down onto the bank beside the body.

The man was dead. There was no way to revive him—whoever he was.

"What a crappy day." Paul stood on legs that felt totally inadequate and staggered to the river to rinse the blood from his hands, then splashed his face with cool water. He'd never even considered possible exposure to HIV. God, that was stupid in this day and age.

When Paul forced himself to turn around and look at the dead body again, a chill gripped him, eliciting a shudder from deep in his gut. He felt as if he was being watched.

He just wasn't accustomed to being around dead bodies, that was all. "You're losing it, Paul." He shook off the eerie sensation and combed his fingers through his hair. This was nuts. Where were the cops when you really needed them? No paramedics? Nothing. He didn't even know where the hell he was. Not on Lake Oologah—that was for certain.

"Shit."

He looked directly into the vacant eyes, noting they weren't exactly the same shade of blue as his. This man's were more gray than blue, but the resemblance continued to unnerve him.

The eerie sensation returned, stronger this time. The hairs on the back of his neck stood on end as Paul turned slowly to look up the bank. He was being watched. His gut told him this wasn't a simple case of paranoia.

There was a figure standing on the bank. "Oh, my God." A white glow surrounded the almost translucent image. Paul swallowed hard and his pulse reached the critical level in record time.

This was like being trapped in an episode of *Picket Fences,* only worse. The figure on the bank—there was no mistake— was another replica of Paul and the dead man. This was becoming more and more like the damned house of mirrors at a carnival.

Then realization hit home—hard. "Oh, God." The newest participant in this comedy of errors had to be . . . a ghost.

He couldn't recall having ever been so frightened of anything or anyone before. That was . . . until the image started down the hill toward him. Then Paul discovered what real terror felt like. The . . . thing was literally floating. Paul's stomach tightened—his chest constricted. He frantically looked from side to side. There was nowhere to hide. Would the spirit hold Paul responsible for his death?

This is crazy—I don't believe in ghosts.

At least, he hadn't until now. Paul took a few steps backward, splashing into the river, then promptly fell on his butt. The ghost hovered over him, staring down at Paul with an expression of obvious disbelief.

"Who the hell are you?" the image demanded, lowering himself to the ground right in front of Paul. His voice was loud, with a built-in echo. "You look just like me, except you're a sissy."

Paul scooted back in the water, not bothering to stand. Hell, why bother? He'd just as well save himself the trouble of falling down again. "Yeah," Paul finally whispered, his gaze riveted to the . . . thing. "I noticed." *Beetlejuice? Ghostbusters?*

The figure grew—his glowing gray eyes widened. "I asked you a question." His voice grew louder, echoing around and into Paul until he felt his bones vibrate.

Paul nodded. "Yeah, I heard." He took a deep breath and got to his feet, wondering how the specter would feel about what Paul was about to tell him. There was only one way to find out. "Paul Weathers."

"Weathers?" The spirit backed away. "I don't have any brothers still livin'. Just a son over in Fort Smith, Arkansas, still wet behind the ears." He scratched his head.

Paul's gaze traveled down to the spot where the knife had torn through the man's shirt earlier. The bloody stain and ragged tear were identical to the shirt adorning the dead body. But the guns—*thank God*—weren't strapped around the ghost's hips.

Here he stood, carrying on a conversation with a damned ghost. What was next? Men in white coats coming to take him away, no doubt.

"Tell me how it is you got my last name and look just like me." The image folded his arms across his bloodied chest.

Paul shook his head and laughed. It was a crazy sound. What the hell—he must *be* crazy, so why fight it? Sane people didn't have hallucinations like the ones he'd experienced today.

His laughter died in his throat. These events couldn't be hallucinations. That explanation was far too simple for this situation.

"Well, I'm waitin'," the ghost reminded Paul in an exasperated tone.

The lake was gone, Winnie had vanished, and he had a dead body next to him. Paul glanced around again, dragging his fingers through his hair. When he looked up at the ghost, he was stunned to discover the spirit's hand running through his hair in much the same manner.

A mirrored image.

"Damn, this is queer," the ghost said. He took another step back and looked down at his lifeless body. "Guess I ain't gonna get back up this time." There were a few seconds of strained silence while the being obviously struggled with the realization that he was dead—*really* dead.

Paul shook his head. For some reason, he felt sorry for this entity. The ghost—the man—was dead. Something, a thought that wouldn't quite form, nagged at Paul.

"That son of a bitch got me this time." The image sighed and shook his head in obvious disgust. "I almost had him, too."

"Had him?" Paul took a step forward. If he was going to accept this, he'd just as well go all the way with it. "What happened?"

The ghost looked up, then back down at his body. "I was so close. Damn close. I been tryin' to catch up with that no-account son of a bitch for ten years."

Paul furrowed his brow as nagging memories continued to haunt him. There was something he should remember, yet he couldn't quite grasp it. It was hovering on the fringes of his mind, teasing yet refusing to make itself clear enough to do him any good at the moment.

"Was he someone you knew?" Paul suspected somehow that the ghost didn't mean to harm him. He had no idea why or how he felt that way, since none of this made any sense at all. He just knew.

"His name's Buck Landen. He murdered a woman." The ghost's voice was quieter now.

Paul frowned and chewed his lower lip. "He killed you, too. I saw." What the hell did all this mean? *That you're losing your mind, Sherlock.*

"You saw it all?" The spirit's glowing gaze narrowed and he loomed nearer, threatening.

Paul shrank back. God, all he wanted was a ride back to his car so he could call someone to help him search for Winnie. He sighed in exhaustion. "Look, I never laid eyes on that scum before in my life," he explained. "But I'll make damn sure the police get a description of him. I'll testify. Don't worry about that."

The spirit nodded in obvious satisfaction. "That's good." He rubbed his jaw and tilted his head to one side as if contemplating Paul again for the first time. "It beats the hell outta me how we can look so much alike. I sure don't remember no cousins."

"Neither do I. Our eyes aren't exactly the same color, though." Paul returned the being's stare. "What the hell *are* you? A . . . a ghost?"

"Hell if I know." The spirit chuckled. "I ain't had any experiences like this before. But I reckon this is somethin' that only happens to a body once. I've had my share of close calls, though. Bein' a United States Marshal's dangerous work."

"United States Marshal?" Paul chuckled and shook his head. "Like Rooster Cogburn, eh?"

The ghost wasn't laughing.

"What's so funny about bein' a marshal?" he demanded, towering over Paul, then shrinking again. "And what's a Rooster Cogburn? One of them fancy fightin' cocks?"

Paul shrugged. "Sorry, my mistake." Surely everyone had heard of John Wayne's Oscar-winning role. Where'd this guy been hiding? "So . . . you have a son?" *Make small talk, Paul. Why not?*

The ghost's expression softened. "Yeah. His name's George. He'll be three his next birthday." He stared toward the east. "He's been livin' with my sister-in-law over in Fort Smith since my wife died."

George—like my great-grandfather? "I see." But he really didn't see. Paul shook his head. He knew the man—ghost—must be realizing that he'd never see his child again. Suddenly, Paul became angry with this entire situation. "Why the hell do things like this have to happen? I don't understand any of it. None of it. Crime, war, homelessness. Why? I wanna know *why.*"

The ghost smiled. It was a cynical, knowing kind of grin that made Paul feel, for just a moment, as if they were kindred spirits. *Spirits, hell.*

"So, you'll testify against Landen?" he asked, rubbing his jaw with a thumb and forefinger. "Judge Parker'll string him up for sure this time. We gotta catch him first, though. Take him in."

"Whoa, what do you mean *we?*" Paul held a hand out in protest, then noticed an odd twinkle in the spirit's eyes. "What are you thinking about, Marshal? I'm already an officer of the court."

"Oh?" The ghost tilted his head to one side and arched a brow. "What kinda officer of the court? Out here in the Territory wearin' practically nothin'? Not even a pair of boots." He shook his head and clicked his tongue.

Paul lifted his chin a notch and took a deep breath. "I'm an attorney." When the marshal's brows lowered, Paul took a deep breath and rushed on. "A lawyer."

"I ain't never had any use for lawyers, but I do need an officer of the court." The spirit moved upward and traveled in an imposing circle around Paul. "At least, one in a sound body."

A sound body? "What . . . what are you doing?" Paul turned with the ghost. He had no intention of turning his back on the being. He still didn't believe the marshal meant him any harm, but Paul was certain the spirit was up to something. The problem was, he didn't know what.

"Checkin'."

"Checking what?" Paul narrowed his gaze and glowered at the wraith.

"To see how much you really look like me."

This was getting uncomfortable. Damned uncomfortable. Though he had no way of knowing what the ghost was up to, Paul was growing very uneasy. "Why?"

"I was wonderin' . . ."

"Wondering *what?*"

"Oh, don't worry about it." The spirit settled near his body again. "You'll need my guns . . . *and* my badge."

Paul chuckled nervously and shook his head. "If there are two things in this world I definitely don't need, it's a gun and a badge."

"Maybe you don't . . . but *I* do."

What the hell was this thing up to? His heart lurched into his throat when he met the being's gaze again. The specter looked at him in an almost . . . hungry way. Possessive. Good God, what was he thinking?

Then the spirit moved toward him. A mischievous smile played about his lips as he kept coming, showing no indication of moving aside.

Paul tried to sidestep his approach, hoping to avoid coming into contact with the ghost, but the marshal altered his course until he ran right into Paul.

Into him in the very literal sense of the word.

Paul screamed. A terrible pain seared through his chest, flooded his head, made every nerve in his body leap to attention. He clutched his head as the spirit melded into his body, became one with him.

The pain subsided as Paul straightened and released a long sigh. He still felt like himself, yet he knew someone else was . . . borrowing his body. They were both here. He and Sam Weathers. *Sam Weathers. George.* Those names were familiar in a distant sort of way.

There was a sensation of coldness in the pit of his stomach, or maybe more in the region of his heart. He placed his hand over his chest as the sensation passed and he felt warm inside again.

Paul's memory suddenly was flooded with images from Sam's past. They mingled with his own to create a catalog of thoughts and experiences unlike anything he could've ever imagined. This was bizarre, to say the least.

Then he remembered what should've been obvious the moment he'd heard Sam's name. Sam and George Weathers were Paul's . . . great-great-grandfather and great-grandfather. *Oh, my God.* His own great-great-grandfather.

Sam was battling for control. It was terrifying. This was a force over which Paul had no power—no knowledge. He couldn't see it, couldn't escape from it. Was this how people with multiple personalities felt? God, how bizarre.

A different brain took command of his body, made it move in a direction and do something Paul didn't want to do. He tried to halt his steps which moved him into the trees to a tall black horse. *Nice horsey.* The beast turned dark eyes toward Paul, then he bent his head and resumed munching on the short spring grasses.

Paul reached into the saddlebags as if he knew exactly what he was doing, and why. This was so strange, following his body's lead rather than having his body follow his mind's commands. How long would Sam Weathers put him through the paces? Hadn't the joke gone on long enough?

Clutching a pair of jeans and a chambray shirt in his fist, Paul pulled off his sweatpants and donned the marshal's clothing. Then he turned toward the dead body, wanting desperately to halt his steps, but he couldn't.

Sam Weathers was powerful and stubborn as hell.

Sam Weathers was a damned parasite.

The melody "Tubular Bells" flitted through his mind as he did his great-great-grandfather's bidding.

Continuing to wonder how and why he was doing it, Paul stooped beside the corpse. He bit his lower lip as he released the ornate belt buckle. *Why am I doing this? I don't want the damned thing.* Sweat beaded his brow. He had to fight and regain control.

Within a few moments, Paul had the dead man's holster buckled around his hips—complete with guns. The silver badge was pinned to his chest and the worn leather boots encased his feet. He looked down at himself in total confusion. He was lost—bewildered.

Was this his punishment for seducing Winnie Sinclair? Was she safe? If he could find her, maybe she'd get him back to Tulsa—help him find his way out of this mess. This nightmare.

Help him find the best psychologist money could buy.

Or maybe a priest would be more appropriate, under the circumstances.

Who's Winnie?

Paul gasped. "What—who—don't do that." Sam Weathers was talking to Paul from inside his own brain. "Will you get out of me?"

Nope, not until we take Buck Landen back to Fort Smith to hang.

"Hang?" Paul scratched his head. "I don't think they still hang people in Arkansas."

The hell they don't.

"This is nuts." Paul tried to unfasten the belt buckle, but Sam wouldn't permit his fingers to perform the task.

Calm down there, or I'll have to take over completely. I'm just borrowin' your body for a while. I reckon you was right about us bein' family, so's it seemed like the right thing to do. Sam chuckled. *I don't see how you could be my great-great-grandson, though. Now, that's a hoot.*

"I'm not laughing. And this isn't the right thing to do at all—not to my way of thinking." Paul shook his head as if he could rattle the spirit right out of his body. "God, I'm talking to myself."

Nope, you're talkin' to me. I figgered on lettin' you keep part of yourself, but I think I can take over all the way if you make me. You gonna cooperate?

"Do I have a choice?"

Good. I think you're startin' to understand. Now, we gotta get rid of my body.

"What?" Paul glanced down at the corpse and gulped. "Why?"

So nobody'll know I'm dead, fool. What good's it gonna do you to be me, if everybody knows I'm dead?

"Good question." Paul dragged his fingers through his hair, then down his face. "How the hell'd my great-great-grandfather's ghost get here—now?" He looked up at the sky and sighed. "All right. Let's get this over with, then we can go into town and call the cops. Let the law take care of this. That's what our taxes are for."

Huh? I'm the law out here in Indian Territory. We are now, I reckon—you'n me.

"Indian Territory?"

Yeah, where in hell'd you think you was?

Paul gazed up at the sky. It was getting late and he had no idea what had happened to Winnie. Despite his best efforts, his memory unleashed a string of erotic images that made his gut twist and his groin tighten.

I'll be. This Winnie must be one helluva woman, the voice in his head insisted. *I can't wait till we meet up with her.*

Paul frowned. "Will you stop reading my thoughts?"

Sam laughed. *They're pretty entertainin' thoughts. Not bad at all. I was right. We must be related. Keep 'em comin'.*

Paul felt defiled—violated. "This is really sick." He closed his eyes for a moment. "Do you have a car parked around here somewhere?"

Car?

"We need transportation."

Yeah, remember my horse is tied in the trees there.

Paul shook his head. "I don't know how to ride a damned horse. What's more important, I don't *want* to know how to ride a horse." He slapped his thigh in frustration. "How the hell are we—am I—supposed to get to town?"

On Lucifer, but we ain't goin' to town. There was an exasperated sigh from inside Paul's mind. *You ain't givin' me no choice. I'm takin' charge—at least for a while.*

"No, wait. I—"

Paul grabbed his head as another pain shot through it. When he straightened, letting his hands fall to his sides, a smug grin tugged at the corners of his mouth. With an alien swagger in his gait, he walked into the trees and calmly released the horse.

Leading the animal, he returned to the body on the riverbank and rolled it over and over until it landed in the water with a splash. Then he waded into the river and shoved the corpse with his foot until it was in water deep enough to allow it to be swept away by the swift current.

With the ease of a man accustomed to horses, he swung himself into the saddle, glancing back once at the vanishing body floating downriver.

"It weren't much good to me no more anyway."

Four

Winnie had no idea the human backside could experience such incredible pain. The perpetual motion of the horse jarred her bones until she was sure she'd never move under her own power again. When the parade leaders finally stopped, she forced her gaze straight ahead.

The landscape varied from rolling hills to open pasture, where a magnificent house graced the top of a slight hill. It was built of native stone and appeared relatively new, though the style and construction resembled architecture from the last century. As she glanced around, Winnie was struck by the obvious prosperity of the place. Various outbuildings, well-kept grounds, and numerous fattening cattle indicated a successful business. Civilization at last.

Not exactly your typical kidnapper's hideout.

A wooden sign at the front of the house swung in the persistent breeze on squeaky hinges. *Lazy H* had been burned into the wood. With any luck, very soon she'd be able to find a phone and call for help.

Lemuel reached up and literally dragged her from the smelly horse. "Ouch." Her bottom and the saddle seemed to have fused together during the ride. Superglue remover might have made the separation a bit less traumatic, but she wouldn't have guaranteed it for any amount of money.

"Well, it's about time," a booming voice called from the front of the house.

Staggering, Winnie stood on her feeble legs. Sharp stones

bruised the bottoms of her bare feet. God, she wished she was still on the boat.

Even with Paul. *Especially* with Paul.

"We run into a little trouble, Mr. Hopsador," Oscar the Grouch said as he approached the house, leaving Winnie behind with Stinky.

She lifted her gaze to stare at the huge man on the front porch. He was dark, obviously Native American, with a rotund abdomen hanging over a huge belt buckle. His dark eyes were gentle, belying his size and clear-cut physical strength.

"What kinda trouble, Cal?"

Cal—that figures. Winnie squinted, swaying as she watched the exchange between the pair. Stinky Lemuel reached out to steady her, then led her very slowly toward the other two men.

"C'mon, Winnie," he urged, not unkindly.

"Ms. Sinclair," she hissed from between clenched teeth, stepping gingerly on the rocky drive until they paused in front of the big man.

"Mr. Hopsador," Stinky called up to the larger man. "The woman . . . fell off the ferry and we had to drag her outta the river."

"Liar." Summoning her dwindling strength, Winnie met Rufus Hopsador's gaze straight on. "I was swept overboard in a storm. But not from a ferry, that's for su—"

"Storm?" Interrupting, Hopsador scratched his head and furrowed his brow. "What storm?"

"Was one of them fast-movin' ones," Cal quickly explained, casting Winnie a look that could kill. "Sorta come outta nowhere and disappeared just as fast."

That's certainly no lie. Feeling rather smug with the scent of victory in the air, Winnie lifted her chin a notch. Her abductors would soon regret their actions. "I have no idea why these men have brought me here, sir." She laughed nervously. God, she was so tired. "All I asked for was a ride to my car."

"Car?" Hopsador frowned again. "Miss MacGregor—"

"Sinclair," she interrupted with a smile. "Winnie Sinclair, sir." Now that the truth was out, he was sure to end this nonsense. He certainly didn't seem like a kidnapper. Maybe she'd been mistaken about that. At least, she sure hoped so.

"They sent a different woman for some reason," Cal continued with his fabrication, fidgeting with the hat in his hands. "Don't rightly know why, sir."

Hopsador sighed and shook his head. Then he turned his dark gaze on Winnie. "Are you sure you're qualified to be a governess, Miss Sinclair? If you'll forgive me, your clothing is kinda . . ."

Winnie rolled her eyes. The man wasn't being rude—he was simply misinformed. "Of course, I *can,* but—"

"Daddy."

A flurry of blue fabric and frothy lace interrupted Winnie's explanation, as she stared in shock at the strange creature who bounded out the door and grabbed Hopsador's elbow. Why was a teenager dressed like *that?* Winnie blinked several times; the girl's costume remained unchanged. No designer jeans here. The lovely young lady was dressed like Scarlett O'Hara.

Winnie couldn't believe this. What was this wilderness outpost? And the people were all characters from a history book, or maybe a novel. This all seemed a bit too dramatic for actual history.

"I don't understand any of this," she whispered, ignoring the conversation between the man and his daughter on the porch. Something unbelievable had happened. The hairs on the back of her neck stood on end as she glanced at the gathering, then around them at the obviously prosperous ranch.

There were no power lines, though they could've been underground. She held her breath. There were no vehicles

of any kind. Everyone was dressed as if they'd just
off a western movie set. A ranch this size should ve had
tractors and trucks, satellite dishes, computer networks and
modems, telephone systems, everything modern technology
had to offer.

Yet there was nothing—at least not from her vantage point.

"What the hell's going on here?" Winnie was frightened.
Suddenly, she felt absolutely desperate for something—any-
thing or anyone—familiar and comfortable. Even Paul
Weathers would be better than this.

In fact, his warm embrace would be remarkably welcome
about now.

Trying to suppress the nagging sense of foreboding that
gripped her, Winnie shivered involuntarily. She was plain
old-fashioned terrified. But it was no longer the men she
feared—it was this entire bizarre situation.

"Miss Sinclair." Hopsador stepped off the porch, disen-
gaging his daughter's grasp. "Are you ill?"

Winnie nodded, unable to speak. She was frightened, out-
numbered and confused.

"We'll show you your room so you can rest now." Mr.
Hopsador gripped her elbow and led her into the house and
down a dark hall. "Amanda, send June to Miss Sinclair's
room, please."

"Oh, Daddy. I don't want a stupid old governess anyway,"
the girl whined in a shrill voice that sliced right through
Winnie. "Just send her back to Boston. I heard what Cal
said. If she jumped off the ferry, she don't wanna be here
anyhow."

"Amanda, do as you're told."

The girl stomped her foot, whirled around and walked
away as Rufus half-led, half-dragged Winnie down the hall.
She tried to inspect her surroundings, but suddenly felt vulnerable—an emotion unfamiliar to her. She was alone in a
strange house with a strange man.

One hell of a big man.

She swallowed hard as he opened a door and led her through. Bright sunlight filled the spacious room, forcing Winnie to blink as she glanced around. The focal point of the room was a huge four-poster bed.

A bed. *What had Stinky and Oscar said? Deliver a red-headed woman . . .*

What did Rufus Hopsador plan to do with her?

Winnie glanced at the big man. His expression was solemn, filled with concern. There was no indication he intended to harm her in any way. She heaved a sigh of relief and continued her perusal of the interesting room.

Mint-condition antiques were artfully arranged. Her trained decorator's eye thought at first the furnishings were replicas, but they seemed genuine.

"I hope you'll be comfortable here, Miss Sinclair," the man said, leading her to a chair near a cold hearth. "We had the room redone in honor of your arrival. June will be here soon to help you with anything you need."

He was being so polite and hospitable—innocuous. Winnie relaxed somewhat and sank gratefully into the chair. But when her backside made contact with the wooden surface, she winced in silent agony.

Damn you, Paul Weathers. This was all his fault. If he'd just stayed away from the damned boat last night, none of this would be happening.

After a few moments, a petite Native American woman shuffled into the room. She didn't speak a word as she moved around the room, then paused before Hopsador, maintaining her silence as she stared at the big man.

This woman's clothing also looked as if it had come straight from a history book. She wore a long skirt which brushed the floor as she walked. Her salt-and-pepper hair was parted down the center, in neat braids on each side of her head. Leather moccasins graced her small feet and distinctive embroidery trimmed her blouse.

"June, Miss Sinclair is very tired from traveling," Hopsa-

dor explained. "I think a warm bath and a nap'll pe
right up, though."

And a phone, a cab, a copy of Mel Gibson's latest film,
an entire carton of strawberry frozen yogurt, and at least
twelve hours of sleep.

The woman nodded, then Hopsador returned his attention
to Winnie. "June doesn't speak, Miss Sinclair, but she hears
and understands everything just fine. Anything you need or
want, just ask. I'll leave you to rest now."

Winnie nodded. "Thank you, Mr. Hopsador." It seemed
strange to thank the man when she'd been brought here
against her will, but it seemed even more inappropriate not
to.

He smiled. She'd been right about his eyes. They were
gentle. In fact, the man exuded kindness and sensitivity.
There was nothing the least bit menacing about him, despite
his enormous size. She felt certain she had nothing to fear
from him. Too bad she couldn't feel such confidence about
the rest of her strange circumstances.

"Your trunk arrived this morning, so I'm sure you'll find
everything you need."

There's that trunk nonsense again. Winnie smiled weakly
and nodded. There was no point in arguing with the man.
He thought she'd been sent here to serve as governess to his
daughter. Besides, until she figured out what was going on,
she had no idea what to say to him. Soon, she'd go in search
of a telephone. She'd call her boss or maybe the police . . .

"Here at the Lazy H, we got the only indoor facilities in
this part of the Territory. Windmill's out back." He puffed
up with obvious pride. "There's a tank in here that heats
water, too. We lit it for you this mornin'."

Lit it for me? Winnie frowned, but managed a slight nod.
"Thank you," she murmured, trying unsuccessfully to smile.
"It's all very . . . nice."

"You're welcome." An odd expression crossed the man's
face when his gaze met hers. Then, with a sigh, he turned

toward the door. "I hope you're feeling up to having dinner with the family this evenin'. Take care, Miss Sinclair."

After the door closed behind Hopsador, Winnie pushed herself up from the chair, and off her sore bottom. June was moving around the room, laying strange garments out on the bed. Winnie's gaze traveled to the open trunk beneath the tall window. Considering how everyone else in this nut house was dressed, she had little doubt the trunk was filled with prim Victorian clothing.

What the devil's going on?

June opened another door and Winnie soon heard running water. In anticipation of soaking her aching body, she shuffled toward the open door, but when she went into the room, she blinked in incredulity.

"Wow." Antique porcelain fixtures greeted her eager gaze as Winnie entered the museum-bathroom. This was incredible. Her boss—a certified antique nut—would've had a fit.

Steaming water flowed at a trickle into a huge tub. Winnie couldn't wait to sink into the warm water. She peeked at June, who was busily unpacking the strange trunk which everyone seemed hell-bent on insisting belonged to Winnie. Right now she didn't care. Nothing mattered except getting into warm water and clean clothes. Anyone's clothes.

She walked over to the bed and picked up a slip of some sort and a pair of what she supposed Scarlett O'Hara would've called pantalettes. Winnie picked up another item which defied comfort of any sort. *A corset?* She pinched the boning which had been carefully sewn into the hideous-looking garment, imagining what being laced into it would feel like. Suppressing a shudder, she dropped the contraption back onto the bed.

June stared at her as if she thought Winnie'd lost her mind and Winnie still wasn't convinced she hadn't. Sighing, she gave the woman a sheepish grin and a shrug. "When in Rome," she said with a smile, then carried the unusual but clean garments into the bathroom.

She had no idea what was going on, but as soon as she was bathed and dressed, she was damned well going to find out. First things first. Nothing was more important than that tub full of warm water. It was obvious to her now that Hopsador and his men meant her no harm. She was just a victim of an absurd misunderstanding. Calm logic would prevail in the end, she was certain.

And in the meantime, it made perfect sense to take advantage of the hospitality extended to her. Lord knew she'd been through enough hell for one day. For a lifetime, actually.

After stripping off her soiled clothing, Winnie stepped into the huge cast iron bathtub. With a moan, she sat down gingerly, wondering if her bottom looked anything like it felt— black and blue.

"Some relaxing weekend this has turned into," she grumbled, leaning back to permit the warm water to cover her aching body, wishing it was deep enough to come up to her neck. Well, at least Rufus Hopsador—who thought he was her employer, of all things—was a decent host.

Her tense muscles released and she closed her eyes. "Oh, God, this feels good."

Winnie wiggled her toes and lifted one leg, then the other, savoring the feel of warm water sloshing across her skin. When she opened her eyes, she couldn't help noticing a single droplet clinging to the side of one rosy nipple.

In her mind, she saw Paul Weathers's tanned face against her breast, drawing her sensitive nipple into his wonderful mouth. "Oh, God." Moaning, she closed her eyes again, but despite her best efforts to the contrary, her thoughts exploded with memories of his sizzling touch.

A pang of longing shot through her, made her insides coil into a tight spring. She dunked her head under water, struggling against her deluded memories as she blew bubbles from her mouth, then leaned back and shook her head. She certainly didn't need to deal with this now—not with everything else.

"Paul Weathers, leave me alone," she whispered furiously, opening her eyes and pushing herself up to a sitting position. She had to face facts. Trying to force the memory of her indiscretion into submission wouldn't make it any less real.

I slept with Paul Weathers.

There. She'd admitted it—faced it. Now, all she had to do was get over it.

But for some infuriating reason, Winnie couldn't erase the images from her mind. He'd branded her, left his signature upon her soul. *Signature on my soul? Cut the theatrics, Winnie.* Deliberately or not, Paul had made an impression on her that was determined to remain, whether or not they ever laid eyes on one another again.

And if Winnie had anything to say about it, never would be too soon. The mere thought of being in his arms again made her libido do a Texas two-step. She could just imagine her reaction if she had to actually face the man after practically throwing herself into his arms. Such a possibility was degrading beyond belief. No, she couldn't face Paul Weathers again—not after last night. It would be too humiliating.

Winnie's stomach rumbled hungrily. Her hangover had passed and she was more than ready for food. Like it or not, it was time for this heavenly bath to end. She had no idea what time it was, but the entire day must be nearly gone.

A day which shall live in infamy . . .

Glancing around for a bottle of shampoo, Winnie finally decided the most important thing was to get the lake water and dirt out of her hair. The bar of soap June had left for her would have to do. After lathering her long curls twice with the harsh soap, she rinsed them and searched for the drain. There wasn't one. How strange.

Her muscles were much more limber when she stepped from the tub than when she'd climbed in. After drying herself with an inadequate linen towel, Winnie held the bizarre undergarments up in front of her. This was becoming more outlandish by the minute.

Grimacing, she put on the soft cotton pantalettes, then pulled the slip over her head. Her bra was too filthy to put against her skin and the trunk hadn't contained anything even remotely similar. Well, it wasn't as if she really *needed* one, after all.

She hated leaving her dirty bath water in the tub, but there was no alternative. She'd have to wait for June to return to show her what to do with it. It was growing late by the time Winnie decided on the simplest of the old-fashioned dresses she found laying across the bed.

This was nuts.

Just as she pulled the odd garment over her head, a knock at the door preceded June's entrance. The silent woman closed the door behind her, then hurried into the bathroom without even glancing in Winnie's direction.

Winnie quickly buttoned the fitted bodice of the gray dress, which left no room for doubt about the proportions of Kathleen MacGregor's bust. Twiggy had to have more curves than the mysterious missing governess. The fabric stretched tight across her breasts, gaping open between some of the buttons. Thank goodness for the slip, camisole, or whatever it was. She sat on the edge of the bed to slip on a pair of high-topped black shoes.

Granny boots.

Giggling, she struggled with the strange shoes. Button-hooks? She bit her lower lip and discovered an odd-looking instrument which she assumed was for the shoes. It took several minutes, but she finally succeeded in closing the ridiculous footwear. The boots were stiff and narrow, pinching her feet and squeezing her toes. She wouldn't be able to wear them for very long without losing all the circulation in her toes. Great—just great.

The dress was a bit shorter than it probably should've been, barely covering the tops of the boots. Winnie sighed in resignation. This was infinitely better than running around half-naked and barefoot. She looked down at her feet and flinched. At least it was better than half-naked.

A strange sound drew her attention, and Winnie popped her head around the corner into the bathroom and saw June bailing her bath water and pouring it out the open window.

"I'll do that," Winnie insisted, rushing over and grasping the handle of the bucket as June turned to dip into the murky water again. The thought of someone else cleaning up after her disturbed Winnie. She wasn't accustomed to such luxury. She'd always seen to her own needs, scrubbed her own toilets, and done all her own dirty work. Why should she change now?

June stared at her long and hard, then grinned, displaying gaping holes where several teeth were missing. With a nod, she permitted Winnie to take the bucket.

Winnie stared after the unusual woman, then bent down to remove the remainder of her bath water. From the corner of her eye, Winnie saw June stooping beside the huge copper-bottomed tank at the head of the tub. She opened a small door at the tank's base, then leaned closer and blew out the steady blue flame inside.

Recalling her host's explanation about hot water earlier, Winnie merely shrugged and rolled her eyes. What a strange place. She'd be gone from here soon, though. What did she care if these peculiar people chose to live under such primitive conditions?

June turned and smiled again as Winnie moved toward the window with the last bucket of water. The woman's obvious approval was heartening, though Winnie didn't know why it should matter to her. She was leaving. Soon.

Going home.

To her tiny Riverparks apartment, her nineteen-inch color television set, seventeen-year-old stereo, and the 1968 Volkswagen she'd bought used during her first year of college.

Alone.

She almost laughed out loud at her foolishness. Why was

she thinking about all the negative things in her life? She should be eager to return to Tulsa, to resume her . . .

To resume her . . .

Damn. Winnie groaned quietly and chewed her lower lip in frustration. She didn't need this right now. What she *did* need was a way out of this loony bin and back to her car. Remembering where her purse and car keys were, she closed her eyes in reluctant acceptance.

The boat . . . and Paul.

There was no way around it. She'd have to return to the boat to collect her belongings. Maybe Paul would be gone by the time she returned.

Or maybe not. Which would she really prefer?

Winnie's stomach lurched in hunger and protest. Her heart hammered within her breast, echoing and mocking her conflicting sentiment.

"Oh, Lord," she whispered, knowing the truth and hating herself for it.

Paul was losing.

He continued to fight his crazy guest, but to no avail. Sam Weathers was determined to control Paul's body—make him do things Paul wouldn't have considered doing in a million years.

His butt—and other parts of his anatomy—were killing him. The person who'd invented a saddle should be shot—or worse. Why wasn't there a pocket or indentation to allow for male anatomy? The wisdom in the use of sidesaddles was becoming increasingly apparent with each jarring step of Lucifer, the stallion from hell. What Paul couldn't understand was why men never used sidesaddles. The anatomical implications—benefits—were obvious.

Painfully obvious.

He could struggle and fight, but Sam obviously wasn't going to relinquish control. Paul resigned himself to being . . . possessed for the time being. He was Sam's very reluctant host—or prisoner. Continued struggle was obviously futile.

There had to be some means of escape—of ridding himself of his unwanted alter-ego. Sam commanded Paul, who'd never ridden a horse in his entire life, to urge Lucifer over a bone-jarring rut. Paul didn't even have enough control to grit his teeth, or wince . . . or cuss.

Conjuring up every expletive he could summon, Paul flooded his mind with his displeasure. But much to his dismay, Sam Weathers merely laughed and shook Paul's head.

This is nuts.

"Nuts?" Sam repeated.

Paul's suspicions had been confirmed. It was possible to communicate with his ancestor telepathically. *What the hell is going on?* Paul demanded from the prison within his own body. *Get out of me.*

Sam clicked his tongue and shook his head again. Paul's tongue. Paul's head.

"I done told you, I ain't leaving without takin' Landen to hang."

Paul sighed. *Sam, how did you get here?* A nagging suspicion took root and grew. Was it possible? What was he thinking? How could it be any *less* possible than what he was experiencing right now?

"What do you mean, how'd I get here?" Sam shrugged and guided Lucifer up a muddy slope, then onto a flat open area. "I rode my horse." The lawman laughed out loud.

Paul was grateful for the gift of sight. Even if he couldn't roll his eyes in disbelief, at least he was being permitted to see where this lunatic was taking his body. *I mean here . . . in this time.*

Sam stopped laughing and pulled on the reins until Lucifer came to a halt. "What nonsense are you spoutin' now?"

Was it nonsense? He had to ask—there was no other

choice. It was way past time for him to learn the truth. *How— what year is it?*

"Year?" Sam laughed even louder. "You musta been on a drunk before I run across you. Can't figure out why else you'd be out here in the Territory without your boots."

Paul's suspicions grew—exploded, actually. *God, is it possible?*

Sam chuckled again and nudged Lucifer with his knees. The horse proceeded across the meadow at a slow trot. "I ain't never been called God before."

I wasn't talking to you, dammit.

"I'm the only one here." Sam fell silent, guiding Lucifer onto a crude, dirt road. "Quit your stalling. What is it you really wanna know?"

Paul would kill to be able to rake his fingers through his hair—a habit he'd picked up from his father. As he thought about doing it, Sam did it. *Can I control my body through thought? Is it possible?*

"Could be, I reckon."

What?

"You might be able to control your body if you think hard enough." Sam took a deep breath and paused on the crest of a sloping hill. "But I wouldn't recommend it."

Why's that? Of course, Sam didn't want Paul to regain control, but that was just too bad. Paul was damned well going to take command of his own body again at the first opportunity. Maybe he could control his thoughts enough to keep Sam from figuring out everything he was thinking. He needed some privacy.

"Well, I'm goin' after Landen." The lawman pulled his hat low over his eyes. "Be dangerous business, and *I* know how to handle it. I don't think you do."

Paul's thoughts froze. He had to know the truth. This was getting more ridiculous by the moment. *What . . . year is it, Sam? Really.*

Sam didn't laugh this time. "You gotta be the craziest . . ."

He shook his head and gazed into the distance at some fluffy white clouds. "It's 1896."

1896?

"That's what I said."

Paul's brain was fried. That's all there was to it. This couldn't be happening. Logic just wouldn't permit something this ludicrous to happen. *Where am I—over the rainbow?*

"I ain't never heard of that before. Must be a new way of sayin' heaven." Sam laughed quietly, continuing to guide Lucifer along the dirt road. "This is a nice place, but I don't reckon it's close to heaven."

Heaven? Am I dead?

Sam clenched his teeth and held his breath for a few moments, then released it in a loud whoosh. "Nope. You ain't dead . . . but *I* am."

I've traveled backward in time. . . .

"What the hell are you talkin' about?" Sam whistled low. "You really are crazy. I reckon you're lucky I come along when I did."

Lucky? You call this lucky? Paul didn't know whether to laugh or cry. This was insane.

But true.

"At least *I* ain't crazy." Sam clicked his tongue and urged Lucifer into a faster, bone-wrenching trot. "We're almost there, now."

Paul needed to maintain some semblance of awareness. This was *his* body. He needed to at least try to protect it. It was the only body he had, even if he was being forced to share it. If something happened to him in this strange place and time, it wasn't as if *he* could just take over the next body that happened to come along. Or could he?

This had to be more than simply coincidence. How had he traveled back in time to the exact location and moment of his great-great-grandfather's murder? Was it possible that sailing his houseboat near the murder scene had been enough of a catalyst to create this . . . *supernatural* phenomenon?

And what about Winnie? Was she . . .

"So, you think you've traveled back in time?" Sam wasn't laughing now. "Do you know how stupid that sounds?"

Not any more stupid than it sounds from this side.

"Yeah." Sam turned the horse up a long lane and through a wooden gate. "We're here, now. This was the last place Landen worked at anythin' honest. If you know what's good for this body of yours, you'll stop fightin' me. It's sure as hell clear I can take better care of it than you can."

Paul thought over his ancestor's suggestion. If Sam truly intended to take them into some dangerous situation, then perhaps Paul would be better off to permit his great-great-grandfather to maintain control for a while longer. At least until he figured out how to get out of this mess. *Don't do anything dangerous. This is my body.*

"That it is." Sam chuckled. "Well, here comes Amanda."

Amanda?

"Yeah, Amanda Hopsador. She's been sweet on me for years." Sam clicked his tongue. "She's a pretty young filly, but I'm near as old as her Pa."

Is it really 1896?

"Yeah, really," Sam answered disgustedly. "Now, will you stop chatterin' away inside my head and let me think?"

It's my head—I think. Paul allowed himself to turn his attention back to the scene before him. He had no idea what had happened. What force could have transported him back through time?

And why? It couldn't be a mere coincidence that he'd appeared in this exact time and place. There had to be more to it than that.

Sam slowed the horse, then stopped it before the long front porch. As he swung a leg over the saddle and dropped to the ground, Paul mentally grunted and groaned, earning him his ancestor's brutal thoughts in return.

Forcing his attention to the woman standing in front of

the house, Paul almost laughed. She was nothing but a girl, a very pretty one, but still a girl. A child.

Amanda whatever-her-name-was sure wasn't Winnie Sinclair. Paul's thoughts were filled with images of Winnie bared before him on his boat. Those breasts . . .

Oh, Lord.

Much to his dismay, Paul was aware of his great-great-grandfather's thoughts following a similar pattern. Paul's body, under Sam's command, responded to the images Paul was broadcasting. Maybe he could have private thoughts, but obviously when it came to mental pictures, he was an open book. He tensed and hardened with a fierce, primal hunger.

"Marshal Weathers," the girl greeted in a seductive tone that belied her age, as Sam took a step toward her. "It's been a long time since you come for a visit."

"Yeah," Sam returned, swallowing hard as he removed his hat and clasped it in front of him, below his belt. He exhaled slowly, then raked his fingers through his hair.

Paul was excruciatingly aware of the longing he shared with his ancestor. It was disconcerting, to say the least. Paul's thoughts of Winnie had turned Sam on.

Damn.

"That's for sure."

"Excuse me, Marshal?" The girl took a step nearer and touched Sam's chest. "I ain't sure I heard you right."

Paul was worried. Would Sam use Paul's body to satisfy that hunger? Talk about unprotected sex.

Paul didn't want to engage in group sex, and that's precisely what it would be. Two women and one man . . . maybe. Two men inside the same body, making love to one woman? No way. *Down, old man.*

"I ain't that old, but I'm too old for this'n," Sam whispered, then grinned at the girl. "Miss Amanda. Is your Pa home? I need to see to him about somethin'."

Amanda's bright smile dimmed and her hand fell to her side. "Yeah, come on in."

"Thanks."

The ranch seemed well maintained, but the lack of modern utilities was further confirmation of his bizarre situation. As Sam stepped into the cool, dim house, Paul allowed his thoughts to follow his ancestor's gaze.

"Come on in and have a seat, Marshal," the girl invited, flashing him a brilliant smile. "I'll fetch Pa."

"Thanks."

Paul contemplated the sad condition of his butt as Sam flopped down into a leather chair near the cold hearth. Last night, Winnie'd told Paul he had great buns. He couldn't help wondering what she'd think of them now.

Jerking his thoughts back to the present, Paul admired the magnificent room. Even in his confused, bedraggled, suppressed condition, he couldn't help noticing the beamed ceiling, the masculine leather and wood furnishings.

As he felt himself finally begin to relax, a voice bolted right through Paul. Sam turned his head toward the sound, then shot to his feet, dropping his precious cowboy hat in the process.

The woman moved slowly across the room, her expression reflecting the same incredulity surging through Paul's mind. As she paused before him, Paul struggled again for control. He had to talk to her. *She's here with me. Good God, Sam, let me out. Let me out.*

"Howdy," Sam said in a low voice, while he silently battled with Paul.

A name went from Paul's thoughts to Sam's, then obtained fruition.

"Winnie."

Five

It can't be.

Winnie's mouth went dry—her heart struck a staccato rhythm. She placed her hand over it as she stared at the incredible sight before her eyes. A low buzz began in her ears until it filled her head, then slowly dissipated. She drew a long, slow breath and forcibly quelled her trembling. She could handle this.

"Winnie," he whispered.

Involuntarily, she bit down hard on her knuckle. She wasn't prepared to face Paul so soon. The memory of the way she'd behaved last night bombarded her and brought a flash of heat to her face.

Oh, Lord.

"Paul?" She forced herself to look directly into his eyes. His beautiful blue—

"Gray?" she asked aloud, squinting as she stared into his eyes—his very gray eyes. "Your eyes . . ."

Paul tilted his head to one side, then grinned in a devilishly crooked manner that nearly knocked her senseless. "Yeah, my eyes is gray," he answered. "And yours is the color of clover."

The color of clover? What an odd choice of words for the Paul Weathers she knew. Then . . . she didn't really *know* him—his mind—did she? But his eyes—she'd been so certain . . .

Contacts. Of course, he was wearing contacts. Or had he

been wearing blue contacts last night? She looked again—he was still smiling. Despite her embarrassment and confusion, Winnie couldn't help herself. She returned his smile with a tentative one of her own.

"How'd you find me?" She moistened her dry lips, then looked down at his feet in embarrassment. He was wearing cowboy boots. *Cowboy boots?* Paul Weathers, Mr. *GQ*, in cowboy boots?

Stunned, Winnie permitted her gaze to travel slowly up his long, lean legs, now encased in a dirty pair of jeans. Paul certainly hadn't seemed like the type of man who'd allow himself to get this dirty.

Winnie's gaze swept over the trim hips, where a wide buckle flashed just above his . . .

Oh, Lord.

The memory of how intimately she knew his body after one absolutely magnificent night rampaged through her like an Oklahoma thunderstorm. A burst of strong, healthy lust flew to her toes, then settled mercilessly in her middle.

Then something very unexpected drew her attention away from his extraordinary male body. Something unbelievable . . . so *un*-Paul.

Guns—two of them. Paul Weathers, yuppie metropolitan attorney, was wearing guns.

"Paul?" Frowning, she glanced up at his face. There was a strange twinkle in the silvery depths of his eyes. "Why . . . why are you wearing . . . *those?*"

He glanced down to where she was pointing and shrugged. "First of all, my name ain't Paul." He grinned when she looked up with a gasp. "And second . . . I don't never go nowhere without my pistols."

Never go nowhere? Not Paul? What the hell was going on? Winnie shook her head and chewed the inside of her cheek. "Of course you're Paul." Yet even as the words left her lips, she realized the man spoke the truth.

Somehow, some way, he *wasn't* Paul.

At least not the Paul she'd known last night. This rugged man wasn't the man who'd held her in his arms, who'd touched her ever so gently, then taken her over the edge of decency to discover a part of herself she hadn't even known existed.

A very exciting part.

Winnie swallowed the lump in her throat. Was he . . . ill? Mentally ill? Did Paul Weathers suffer from some sort of personality disorder?

Her gaze locked with his. The devilish gleam in his eyes remained consistent.

"You all right, pretty lady?" he asked in a slow drawl.

"If you aren't Paul, then how'd you know my name?" she challenged, lifting her chin a notch and praying for strength. Hunger and exhaustion were seriously impeding her ability to think straight. She'd had more than her fair share of shocks for one day . . . and night. It was far past time for her to go home. "Well?"

The man's face actually reddened. Color suffused his cheeks as he averted her gaze and glanced down at his boots again. "I . . . don't know your name."

"I heard you say it." Winnie took a deep breath, then closed her eyes for a moment as she released it. "If you don't know me, then that means you can't remember . . ." *Could it be true?*

Was her secret safe? She took a deep steadying breath. How could she consider saving her self-respect at the expense of someone's sanity? But it wasn't *her* fault he was confused. If he couldn't remember who he was, or who she was, then that meant . . .

She was the only living soul who knew the truth about last night.

Guilt quickly overshadowed relief. She'd been a consenting adult—very consenting. Besides, it was obvious Paul needed help. She had to get him back to the lake and drive him into town.

The trick would be convincing him to accompany her at all. Clearing her throat, she met his gaze again. There was something disconcerting about those eyes. She was positive he had at least a vague, unconscious memory of her—he had to. He'd very plainly whispered her name when she first entered the room. The twinkle in his gray eyes was almost a silent "I've got a secret" taunt.

"Sam, it's good to see you," a booming voice intruded on her preoccupation.

Sam? Winnie turned quickly to stare in incredulity at Rufus Hopsador as he entered the room. The big rancher walked directly to Paul as if they were old friends and extended his hand.

"Good to see you again, Rufus," Paul returned, grinning at their host as his eyes twinkled at Winnie. "Been too damned long."

What the hell is going on? Winnie's mind reeled. She took a step backward and almost fell over the braided rug in the center of the huge room. How could this man know Paul as . . . someone else?

Unless . . . this *really* wasn't Paul.

"I see you've met Miss Sinclair." Hopsador reached back to offer Winnie a steadying hand. "She had a little accident down at the ferry crossing. Are you feelin' better now, Miss Sinclair?"

"We was just gettin' acquainted." Paul—er, Sam grinned at Winnie. "Wasn't we?"

Rufus turned to cast a questioning glance in her direction when she didn't answer his inquiry. Winnie wished the floor would open up and swallow her. *She* was going insane—not Paul. None of this was happening. It couldn't be.

Could it?

"Miss Sinclair?"

Winnie jerked at the sound of her own name, then forced her gaze to meet her host's. "What?"

"Are you all right?" His expression was filled with concern. "Maybe you should lie down for a spell."

"No." Winnie battled instinct, which was one hundred percent in favor of a one-way trip to Tulsa. Adrenaline pumped through her veins and clouded her judgment, demanding immediate action. She couldn't think. She *mustn't* think until she was far away from this crazy place and these demented people.

Somehow, despite her desperation, she suspected that running away from the Lazy H wouldn't free her from this nightmare.

Something bizarre—terrifying—had happened.

And the really horrible part of all this was that it had happened to *her*.

Rufus tightened his grip on her arm. "Sit down, Miss Sinclair," he urged, guiding her to a rocking chair in the corner. "You don't look too pert."

As she lowered herself into the chair, Winnie's gaze was drawn back to Paul or whoever he was. Concern etched his handsome features. His brow furrowed and his gray eyes grew solemn as he watched her.

He knows me. He knows me. I know he does.

"You must be starved by now," Hopsador concluded, straightening and turning toward his other guest. "Sam, would you mind stayin' here with Miss Sinclair while I see how long supper's gonna be?"

"You go ahead. My business can wait a spell."

Winnie trembled when she realized she was alone again with . . . with . . .

His expression changed as she studied his face. He knelt beside her chair and gazed long and hard, directly into her eyes. "I ain't Paul," he repeated, blinking once as if trying to hide something from her probing gaze.

"No, you're not Paul." She sighed and covered her face with her hands before looking openly at him again. There was a new emotion in his gray eyes—one she clearly recognized. It was the same naked desire she'd seen in Paul's last night. This man—whoever he was—wanted her.

"Unbelievable," she whispered, shaking her head. "Men are all the same. They think with their . . ." Heat engulfed her face.

"With their what?"

He was grinning. It was a wicked, mischievous, drop-dead gorgeous grin. *Damn.* She didn't need this right now. What she needed was to figure out what the hell was going on, and more importantly, how to get herself out of it.

"If you aren't Paul," she said, drawing a deep, steadying breath. "Then who the hell are you?"

A strange glint of colored light flickered in his eyes. What color? Blue? No, it couldn't be. Wishful thinking, no doubt. Winnie blinked and leaned forward, staring intently into his eyes, but the glimmer was gone. She must've been mistaken. "I asked you a question."

He grinned again. "Marshal Sam Weathers, at your—"

"Weathers?" Winnie lurched to her feet, but a wave of dizziness made her sink back to the chair just as quickly. "Sam . . . Weathers?"

He nodded and his expression softened. "That's right. Sam Weathers, United States Marshal, assigned to Indian Territory outta Fort Smith."

Indian Territory? Winnie fell back in the chair, her head hitting with a soft thud. "Indian Territory?" she echoed. *Here comes the infamous ripple effect. Insanity begets more insanity.*

"I dunno what it is with folks these days, not even knowin' where they are." With a sigh, Sam straightened and shook his head. "Yep, this is Indian Territory. Where'd you think you was?"

This man's voice was similar to Paul's, but his accent and vocabulary were very different. And he wore guns. Winnie stared at his chest, stunned to see a silver star winking back at her. How had she managed to miss that? He'd said he was a marshal.

"Oklahoma, I guess."

"Oklahoma Territory's farther west." Sam clicked his tongue. *"This* is Indian Territory."

Winnie nodded. Arguing with him wasn't doing her a bit of good. Besides, if he wasn't Paul, she needed to find out who he was and where *she* was. "So, you're Sam Weathers—a United States Marshal. And we're in . . . Indian Territory." *Take a deep breath, Winnie.*

"That sums it up real good, I'd say." The tall lanky lawman grinned again, then knelt in front of her. "What's your given name?"

Winnie blinked. "I heard you say it," she insisted, but his gaze was unwavering. Maybe she'd imagined it. But deep in her gut she knew that wasn't so. Somehow, this man had known her name, yet now he insisted he didn't. Was he lying or confused?

Or insane?

Laughter bubbled up from her chest. If anyone was confused, it was her. Confused as hell.

"What's so funny?"

When she met his gaze again, Winnie found laughter in the silver depths. But he wasn't mocking her now. The glint of humor was warm and genuine.

Her nervous giggle died a sudden death. "This . . . situation is almost funny, I suppose." Winnie sighed and shook her head. *But I'm not laughing anymore.* "All right, now let me try to understand. This is Indian Territory. You're not Paul Weathers—you're *Sam* Weathers, a United States Marshal." *I said that already.* She trembled slightly, then rushed on. "And this is . . . is . . ."

He reached out and covered her hand with his. Warmth radiated from him. When she glanced down at his hand, Winnie gasped. His palms and fingers were covered with angry blisters. "Your hands."

He jerked them back and looked down at his palms. "Damned tenderfoot."

"Tenderfoot?" Winnie frowned. He was calling himself names now. What next?

"Well, it seems you two are sure getting friendly," a shrill voice intruded. Amanda Hopsador swept into the room wearing a gown of burgundy silk. The neckline was daringly low, accentuating her firm, full breasts, reminding Winnie of her own inadequacies in that area. Though Paul hadn't seemed to mind . . .

"Miss Amanda." Sam straightened, then turned to face her. "Yep, we was just talkin'."

"Miss Sinclair is hired help, Marshal." Amanda blinked rapidly and folded her arms across her middle, providing far more uplift than any underwire bra Winnie'd ever seen. Amanda tilted her head to one side and glared at Winnie. "She's supposed to be my governess. At least until I convince Pa I don't need one, that is."

Yeah, and I'm at least twice your age. Winnie couldn't suppress the cynical smile that tugged at her lips. This girl didn't need a governess. She needed a juvenile detention center matron. Mischief and cunning oozed from her every pore.

"What are you grinnin' at?" Amanda's scowl grew even more pronounced, if that was possible. "I didn't want you to come here, you know. It was Pa's idea."

"Yep, it sure was." Rufus Hopsador ambled into the room with a broad smile on his ruddy face. "One of my better ideas, I think. Your ma wanted you to learn the kinda things Miss Sinclair's come to teach you. And by golly, you're gonna let her do her job."

Amanda rolled her eyes. "Nowadays, girls don't have to learn all that lady stuff Ma was always talkin' about."

"Nowadays." Rufus exchanged glances with Sam and chuckled in paternal indulgence. "You'd think it was the twentieth century already, the way she carries on."

Twentieth century? "But . . ." Winnie bit her lower lip to silence her protest. She didn't want to be rude to her host, who'd treated her very well since her unwilling arrival at his ranch. Surely, he'd just made a slip of the tongue. He must have meant the *twenty-first* century.

"Well, it almost is." Amanda thrust out her lower lip in open defiance. She tilted her chin slightly and stared at her father through veiled lashes. "Only four years."

Four years? Four years away from the twentieth century? No. It was four years until the twenty-first century. Winnie drew a deep breath and stole a glance at Marshal Weathers. Sam—Paul—whoever he was. The man's jaw twitched and his lips were set in a grim line. Tension poured from him.

Why?

Bizarre, terrifying thoughts surged through Winnie's mind as the room began to spin. Thank God she was sitting down or she would've fallen for sure. Her blood pounded through her head as a list of incredible possibilities rolled by like a runaway computer macro.

Was it possible?

Blinking to clear her vision, Winnie lifted her gaze to stare at her odd companions. They were all dressed as if they belonged in the nineteenth century. This was crazy. No matter how hard she tried, Winnie couldn't remember having seen anything even remotely contemporary since washing ashore from what *should* have been a lake.

But it was preposterous. The mere notion of—

"No." Winnie gripped her head and pressed inward, trying to forcibly obliterate the insane thoughts from her mind. Time travel? Quantum physics? "No, it can't be."

"Miss Sinclair?" Sam Weathers knelt before her again. "You all right?"

Winnie was vaguely aware of others in the room talking in hushed tones, though she couldn't focus on one voice clearly enough to discern exactly what was being said.

There was movement around her, then a pair of strong

arms lifted her from the chair. A spicy fragrance teased her
senses. For a moment—a delicious, impossible instant—she
was sure it was Paul who held her so protectively. The expensive cologne he'd worn last night surrounded her, soothed
her frazzled nerves.

Cradled in his arms with his hard chest supporting her
head, Winnie rested against him. Strength flowed from him
into and through her, offering solace in the midst of chaos
and hopelessness.

Darkness and the man who held her were all that existed.
They were moving, floating really, then she felt herself being
lowered downward and enveloped in softness. A moan rumbled up from her chest, then a whimper of protest as he
moved away.

Don't leave me, Paul.

Paul was grateful for the warm bath and soft bed. Though
he couldn't control his body's movements at the moment, he
certainly felt every ache and pain. Sam Weathers was bru-
talizing Paul's body.

"She's a looker all right," Sam said with a shake of his
head as he stared up at the patterns of light and dark on the
ceiling over the bed.

She's hurting, Paul tried again to reason with his ancestor.
There had to be a way to help her understand this insanity.
Not that he understood it, of course. *Winnie doesn't under-
stand what's going on and neither do I.*

Sam sighed, then folded his hands behind his head.
"Y'know, I been doing some thinkin' on this. I think I might
have it figured out."

And? Paul had been trying very hard *not* to read his great-
great-grandfather's thoughts. It was confusing enough to
share his body with another person, but sharing his mind
was just too much.

"I reckon you really are my great-great-grandson, like you said."

Paul released a mental sigh. *Yeah, that seems to be the general consensus.* Here he was, sprawled out in bed carrying on a conversation with someone who'd been dead for a century. Well, really just a day.

"That's just it, Paul," Sam said in a quiet tone. "I don't rightly know how this happened, but I reckon you really did come back in time."

Great, just great. Paul had been trying to avoid that nagging thought since they reached the ranch, but here it was out in the open. It was time to face reality. If this *was* reality. There was still the possibility he'd lost his mind and was hallucinating this entire situation. Though after seeing Winnie's horrified expression, that hardly seemed possible. Surely, she must suspect the same thing. *This is really nuts.*

"It's weird. That's for sure." Sam took a deep breath and scratched his head. "I reckon the good Lord sent you here to me."

Ah, hell. Don't start getting religious on me. I don't see anything good or righteous in any of this. Paul wished he had his body back so he could hit something. Anything.

"Heck, I ain't never been a real religious man either, Paul, but dyin' kinda makes a body look at things." He chuckled and shook his head. "This is really somethin', though. My own kin's come back to help me take my killer to justice."

Stunned into silence, Paul digested this bit of philosophy. Was it true? Had a divine power—God—sent him back in time for such a grandiose purpose? But what about Winnie? Had she been caught in the crossfire, so to speak—in the wrong place at the wrong time? Was he really supposed to believe that God had bad aim when it came to miracles?

No, of course not. Winnie was just a victim of circumstances. There was no reason for her to be here. No reason at all.

"Well, we don't know that for sure."

Sam's words startled Paul. *You're reading my mind again, old man.*

"I might be your great-great-grandfather, but I ain't—wasn't—any older than you are." There was a moment of strained silence, mental and actual. "Guess I never woulda been."

No, I guess not. For some insane reason, Paul felt guilty. Here he'd been bemoaning his own situation and Sam Weathers was dead. Dead. But why did Paul have to be the lucky descendant—the chosen one—to travel back in time to see justice done? *Damn. I could make a fortune selling this idea to Spielberg or Copola when I get . . . back. Sam, just how the hell are we supposed to get back?*

Sam was silent for a few moments. Paul felt—shared—his ancestor's torment.

"I dunno," Sam said finally, then rolled onto his side to stare out the open window. A gentle breeze wafted through, carrying with it the scents of springtime. "What was you doin' when it . . . happened?"

A mad rush of images flooded Paul's mind as he recalled the night he and Winnie'd spent together aboard the *Sooner Sunset.* He clearly saw her in his mind's eye, standing in the doorway of the head, half-drunk and looking absolutely delectable in that skimpy pink nightie.

A rush of blood to his loins made Paul realize he still had some involuntary control over his bodily functions. Then another thought destroyed the memories of Winnie in his arms. Sam was reading his thoughts again. Was Paul's body reacting to Sam's horny, depraved thoughts? Or was it the other way around?

Hey. These are my memories and I'm not in the mood to share. Paul was furious yet powerless. It was disconcerting and frustrating, to say the least. He was a prisoner inside his own body. *My memories . . .*

"Yeah, and they're fine ones at that." Sam chuckled, then

closed his eyes, blocking Paul's view of the fluttering curtain. "So you and Winnie . . ."

What? On top of losing control of his body and being forced to do whatever Sam wanted him to, the lack of privacy was really irritating. He couldn't even think about making love to a beautiful woman without sharing the experience with this parasite. *Just leave Winnie alone. I'll figure out some way to get her—us—out of this mess.*

"I reckon you're entitled to keep some things to yourself." Sam pulled the blanket up over his shoulders. "So you was on a boat?"

My houseboat—the one my father left me when he died. Paul mentally shook himself, still wishing he could hit something or someone. *Winnie was with me and there was a violent storm. She—we—were washed overboard.*

"Together?"

Paul recalled the panic he'd felt upon discovering Winnie missing . . . this morning? It seemed like an eternity ago, though it had been less than a day. *No, separately.*

"But from the same boat on the same day?"

Yeah. So?

"I'm just tryin' to figure this out." Sam yawned and curled up into the fetal position on his side. "Your body's too soft, boy."

Boy? I thought you said you weren't any older than me. Paul almost laughed. The entire situation, if it had been happening to someone else, would be hilarious. Absolutely deranged. Maybe, instead of Spielberg, he should sell the story to Monty Python. It was just bizarre enough. *Winnie was just unlucky. She should've stayed away from me, I guess.* Trying to get away from him had driven her out into the storm in the first place. Hadn't it?

"Paul?"

What?

"Assumin' you really was sent back to help me catch Landen . . ."

Paul had an uneasy feeling he knew where this conversation was leading, and he didn't like it—not one bit. *Yeah?*

"It stands to reason you won't be able to go back before the job's done."

I know. I already thought of that. Paul mentally winced, but it wasn't the least bit satisfying. He wanted his body back to wince anytime he pleased. He'd give almost anything to be able to hit, kick, cuss, spit—to vent the fury and futility that gripped him. If he could have, he'd have held his breath, too. *Looks like I'm stuck for a while.*

"So, you'll help me catch Landen?" Sam punched his pillow and pulled it up into a ball beneath his head. "Then we'll see about how to get you'n Winnie back where you belong. And me . . . wherever it is I belong."

Again Paul was struck with the fact that Sam Weathers was dead. He'd been murdered and wanted to see justice done. Was it Paul's duty—his destiny—to do everything within his power to see that happen?

Do I have any choice?

"Sure don't seem like you do. That's a fact."

Who would be in control of his body once Sam went to sleep? Would the first one awake have command? Could he stay awake all night and find out? There had to be a way out of this mess. A way to talk to Winnie.

Paul's thoughts were far from sleepy, though his body ached. He wanted to roll over, to sleep in a position he was accustomed to. *Hey, I sleep on my stomach. You're borrowing my body, so the least you can do is sleep the way I'm most comfortable. Roll over.*

"Damn sissy," Sam grumbled, then threw the pillow onto the floor and flopped over face down on the bed. "Happy, now?"

Paul wasn't happy, but he was satisfied. For now. *Thanks, I appreciate it.*

"Hearin' a voice in my head is gettin' mighty irritating."

Objection—my head.

Six

Winnie rolled onto her back and stretched as she opened her eyes. She blinked several times, then eased herself into a sitting position to survey her dark surroundings. She was sure of only two things—it was the middle of the night and this was *not* her room.

"Oh, my God." She brought her hand to her mouth and chewed on her fingertip, waging a futile campaign to forget yesterday's disturbing developments. Of course, refusing to remember wouldn't change the facts.

She was trapped in some sort of nightmare. Was it all in her mind or was this *really* happening? Drawing a deep breath, she slipped from beneath the patchwork quilt and stood beside the bed for several moments. Her heart thundered wildly as her gaze darted around the moonlit room.

"What the hell is happening to me?" She staggered to the window and stared out at the night. The moon was almost full, lending additional, though unnecessary, ambience to her spooky circumstances.

"I wanna go home, dammit." She dug her fingers into her hair and pulled until tears stung her eyes. "This can't be real. Why is this happening?"

Paul's handsome face flashed through her mind. Was this *punishment?* Was she paying penance for her night of decadence?

Her heart lurched, then hammered wildly in her chest. Logic screamed, insisting that the very idea of punishment for her sins was ludicrous. She wasn't even dead; damnation shouldn't begin while she was still breathing. Should it?

Am I still alive?

Winnie probed the side of her neck for her pulse, which thundered along to the cadence of *The 1812 Overture—with* cannon. She wasn't dead and the Lazy H definitely wasn't hell. It also wasn't home.

Her car, purse, keys, suitcase were all back at the . . . lake. Lake Oologah. Winnie's mind reeled as she rubbed her face with both palms, then walked over to the door to feel the wall for a light switch.

"Of course there isn't one," she muttered to the empty room. "What could I have been thinking?" She shook her head in bewilderment.

Stepping into a pool of silver moonlight beside the bed, Winnie looked down at her wrinkled dress. She'd slept in her clothes—or rather, Kathleen MacGregor's clothes.

Tears stung her eyes, but she blinked them into submission. "I'm not going to cry," she vowed, sitting on the edge of the bed with her chin in both hands. *Be calm, Winnie. Look at the evidence.*

She lifted her head and groaned in disgust. "Jeez, I sound like a lawyer." Like Paul Weathers? Rubbing her temples, Winnie mulled over the entire sequence of events, beginning with her arrival on the houseboat.

Everything had been going splendidly until Paul Weathers showed up and decided to take a twilight cruise. In a storm, no less. And more importantly, with *her* on board.

Now, here she was stranded . . . somewhere. *Say it, Winnie.* She drew a shuddering breath and went cold—downright icy as she forced herself to face reality.

Not somewhere—some*when.*

"Oh, God." Moaning, she covered her face with her hands and rocked her head from side to side in a rhythmic pattern. If only she could erase the last two days . . .

She needed answers. No one in their right mind could sit

here and consider the possibility that they'd traveled back in time without irrefutable proof. But then, maybe she wasn't still in her right mind. There was the very real possibility that she'd gone totally insane and none of this was really happening.

She gripped the bedpost and pressed her cheek against the cool wood. The smell and texture of solid oak anchored her in reality.

No. This was happening—whatever *this* was.

Answers. She'd damned well have answers. *Now.* Standing, Winnie walked slowly toward the door and pulled it open. She hesitated, then poked her head out the door and looked left, then right.

A movement in the hallway seized her attention. Easing back into her room, she peered around the corner as the man fumbled with the doorknob, then entered the room next to hers.

Her breath caught in her throat as recognition seeped in. It wasn't Paul—it was his clone, Sam Weathers. Did *he* have answers? Did he know why she was here and what had happened to Paul? Was he really Paul wearing contacts and playing an insidious game with her sanity?

But why?

Dirk? Could her ex-husband be up to something? Had he paid Paul Weathers to do this to her? No, it wasn't possible. Dirk had everything he wanted. He had everything, *period.* The house, car, savings account . . .

Winnie gnashed her teeth and continued to stare down the hall until the faint click of the closing door jarred her out of her stupor. Enough was enough, and she'd passed her quota of believability back on that damned boat.

Filled with determination, Winnie squared her shoulders and tiptoed down the hall. Pausing before the closed door she'd seen Sam Weathers go through only a few seconds earlier, she held her breath and searched for the deflated courage that, only a moment ago, had spurred her into undertaking this quest for truth.

She lifted her hand to knock, then reconsidered. Sam Weathers wasn't going to have the opportunity to send her away without answers. Gripping the crystal doorknob, Winnie recalled the less ornate one that had come off in her hand on the boat. A sense of déjà vu rippled through her, but she shook it off, renewing her resolve.

Taking a deep breath and lifting her chin, Winnie turned the knob, entered the room and closed the door behind her in one smooth motion. A warm hand clamped over her mouth from behind and jerked her against a tall hard body.

A very male—very *naked*—body.

It took only a split second for her to regret her impetuous decision. A lamp, turned low on the nightstand, provided pale golden light for her frightened gaze. As she frantically searched for some means of escape, she caught a glimpse of herself in the mirror across the room. Standing directly behind her, with his hand fastened over her mouth and her body pulled intimately against his, was Paul Weathers.

"You oughta know better than to sneak into a man's room at night," he whispered against her hair. "He might be gettin' ideas."

Sam Weathers—not Paul.

Winnie's knees went weak as terror was instantly replaced by an insidious warmth emanating from deep within her. The memory of Paul's lovemaking wreaked havoc on her common sense. This man felt so familiar—so intimate—it was disarming. A part of her ached for Paul's embrace just now. Such comfort was just what she needed.

And exactly what had landed her in this mess in the first place.

Filled with purpose, she struggled against his iron grip, but he tightened his hold in response.

"Stop fightin' me and promise not to scream, then I'll let

you go." His breath was hot against the side of her neck as he whispered in her ear.

Winnie nodded, aware of his hand following her slight movement. Ever so slowly, he relaxed the pressure on her mouth and eased his hand away. His other hand was still locked around her waist, holding her effortlessly against his solid frame.

He was so much like Paul. How could two men be so much alike? Before she'd fainted, Winnie'd heard her name on his lips and seen desire in the marshal's eyes. And damn her soul to hell, she couldn't prevent her body's immediate reaction to this man's close proximity.

As if reading her thoughts, her captor's body hardened and pressed familiarly against her backside.

Winnie's face flashed with a sudden heat born from a combination of frustration, humiliation and desire, all rolled into one deadly package. She really was crazy, feeling desire for a man she didn't even know. Closing her eyes, she silently reminded herself that this wasn't the first time.

As he loosened his hold on her waist and brought both his hands to her shoulders, Winnie instinctively turned to face him, dazed by his intimate position. Acutely aware of his hardness boldly pressing against her lower abdomen, Winnie forgot for a moment why she was here . . . and who he was.

And wasn't.

She didn't dare look anywhere except straight into his eyes. The urge to glance down between them, thinking she might somehow convince herself this man really *wasn't* Paul, threatened to overwhelm her at any moment.

"What are you doin' here?"

His voice was like raw silk, rough in places and smooth in others, pouring over her as the gnawing ache in her loins intensified. Her breaths became short and rapid as he eased his hands down her upper arms and paused.

"I asked you a question," he reminded her, his thumbs tracing tiny circles on the soft insides of her elbows.

Winnie swayed and her knees buckled. He swept her into his arms in one smooth motion; then carried her the few short steps to the bed—*his* bed. As he bent over to lay her down, she was overcome with the need to feel his lips on hers. Perhaps then she could convince herself once and for all that he was *not* Paul.

She reached behind his head and clasped her hands together at the back of his neck. He made no move to straighten, seeming to accept her semi-embrace without question. "You're playin' a dangerous game, Winnie."

Moistening her dry lips with the tip of her tongue, she marveled at how the lamplight flickered across the planes and angles of his rugged features. "Kiss me," she invited, tilting her head to a more convenient angle.

"Holy shit, woman," he whispered, lowering his lips a fraction of an inch closer to hers. "He ain't gonna like this."

Winnie didn't have the vaguest idea who or what he was talking about, nor did she care. All she could think about was feeling his lips on hers. Was he Paul? Would kissing him prove or disprove his claims? Put her doubts to rest once and for all so she could concentrate on the rest of her dilemma?

Paul struggled against his own libido and his great-great-grandfather as Sam bent closer to Winnie. Raging hormones clouded Paul's judgment, inadvertently empowering Sam to take Winnie in his arms. As his lips made contact with hers, Paul's concerns about sharing this moment with his ancestor wavered, then vanished into a black hole as he remembered her softness, her passion on board the houseboat.

Forgetting Sam, he became himself, deepening the kiss as he explored and savored her. Winnie whimpered in his arms, arched upward against his chest, pressing her firm breasts against his chest. He brought his hand over to cup one soft round globe, brushed its taut peak through the fabric of her dress, and felt his body nearly explode with the need to possess her again.

With Winnie, he could forget all the horrors, and relive the pleasures of the past thirty-six hours. Reaching for the buttons at the front of her dress, he paused as a voice only he could hear infiltrated his thoughts.

"Down, boy," the voice warned. "I ain't gonna be able to hold myself back if you don't stop urgin' me on."

Paul mentally jerked himself away from Winnie, and Sam physically followed. Backing away, Paul looked down at the woman on Sam's bed. *Sam's bed.* Paul had almost allowed himself to get carried away enough to take a companion along for the fun. He was all for sexual experimentation, but this was ridiculous—not his thing by any stretch of the imagination. Paul Weathers preferred having his women all to himself—especially Winnie.

Dammit. Ménage à trois? No.

Winnie's lips were swollen from his kiss. Her face appeared flushed in the lamp's inadequate light. A cascade of auburn hair formed a frame around her small, perfect face.

He saw her gaze sweep over him, then waver. "You're not Paul," she whispered, then sat up in the bed. "I'm sorry—I shouldn't have come."

As she swung her legs over the edge of the bed and stood, Paul couldn't help noticing her gaze drop to his very eager—downright impudent—erection. His body had a memory, too, it seemed. Sam chuckled, reminding Paul again that he and Winnie were not alone.

She gasped and jerked her gaze away from his body, looking beyond him toward the closed door. "I was hoping . . ."

"Hopin' I was Paul," Sam said slowly. "But I ain't. I think I told you that already."

Damn, damn, damn. Paul saw her pain. Felt it. He might be able to offer her some assurance if only he could speak for himself. He was being held prisoner inside his own body. *Sam, tell her I'm here.*

Sam remained silent. After a frantic moment, Paul realized how insane that would've sounded. Poor Winnie had enough trouble without hearing that the man she'd made love with was possessed by his great-great-grandfather's spirit. What a mess.

Winnie nodded and turned toward the door. She was like a sleepwalker as she reached for the knob, glancing back over her shoulder once to stare at his face. "What the hell happened?"

She must've gotten caught in the crossfire when he was swept back in time. She'd been in the wrong place at the wrong time. But if she hadn't been there, they wouldn't have had their night together.

"I kissed you, like you asked me to," Sam answered, ignoring Paul's thoughts. "What was you thinkin', comin' in a man's room in the middle of the night? Heck, I ain't even dressed. Dropped my britches to climb in bed just before you walked through the door." Sam tilted his head to one side. "But I reckon you know that by now."

With a gasp, Winnie opened the door and fled as Paul urged Sam to follow. His great-great-grandfather moved as far as the open door, peered into the hallway, then closed the door and returned to the bed.

Dammit, Sam, she's scared—I need to talk to her. Paul was totally helpless. Even though he barely knew Winnie Sinclair, he owed her something. Hell, he owed her some sort of explanation, after someone explained it all to him. Maybe he could help her accept the situation.

Until what?

Damn.

"Damn what?" Sam mumbled as he turned down the lamp, then flopped into bed, tugging the quilt up to his chin.

Damn you for dragging me into this mess.

"I ain't the one who brung you back in time," Sam stated very calmly, then yawned and closed his eyes. "Musta been somebody a whole lot more powerful than you or me."

God? Paul tried to digest this bit of philosophy. Was it possible? He would've laughed if he had control of his own vocal chords. Yet how could he doubt the possibility of *anything*, considering his ridiculous situation?

He wasn't ready to accept or admit that his little adventure was an act of God.

He wasn't exactly denying it either.

Winnie seriously considered walking right out the front door and never looking back. She'd just walk back to her purse, her car, her life.

But she didn't.

A niggling voice told her such an attempt would be futile. Even if she managed to find the exact location where she'd left the houseboat, she knew it wouldn't be there.

And she knew *why*, but still wasn't ready to accept it. Not completely, anyway.

She leaned heavily against the closed door of her room and sighed. The sun was creeping up, casting long shadows across the floor at her feet.

Of course, she realized that walking back to Lake Oologah wouldn't do her a bit of good, because there was no Lake Oologah. She swallowed the lump in her throat and took a deep breath, forcibly quelling the voice—the very demanding voice—trying to make her admit something she didn't care to even consider.

"No, I won't think about it." She pressed her hands over her ears, then walked to the tall oak wardrobe where she'd seen June hang some dresses the day before. "I'm going to find out what the hell's going on and figure out how to get home."

She froze. Her eyes smarted again. One lonely tear managed to escape, despite her best efforts to the contrary. Leaning her forehead against the edge of the wardrobe's open door, Winnie released her insistent tears.

There was no use lying to herself any longer. This was no nightmare—no hallucination. The missing lake should've made her immediately wary. And Stinky and Oscar the Grouch should've really clinched her suspicions. Maybe subconsciously she'd perceived the truth and had been in a state of denial for the past twenty-four hours.

Time—somehow I've traveled back in time.

Was this punishment for her sins?

She almost laughed through her tears. "Yeah, right." Winnie drew a shaky breath and squared her shoulders, then wiped her eyes with the backs of her hands. *One night of pure decadence nets me the vacation of a lifetime.* She trembled as the memory of her visit to Sam's room assailed her. Talk about stupid—walking right into a strange man's room. She'd had to make certain he wasn't Paul. The resemblance—all over—was uncanny. Except for those silver eyes.

"I'm just lucky, I guess." Winnie mentally shook herself and sorted through the dresses in the wardrobe. They were all similar to the wrinkled gray one she still wore. It didn't really matter. All she wanted was something clean and un-wrinkled. With a sigh, she selected a simple blue dress—calico or something equally archaic, she supposed—and laid it over her forearm.

Her stomach grumbled angrily. "Wonder what they have to eat in this place. I'm starving," she murmured, remembering she hadn't eaten since night before last. Before Paul Weathers had come into her life.

Winnie turned toward the bed, pausing to withdraw clean underwear from the open trunk near the window.

Movement from outside caught her attention, distracting her from her growling belly. She pulled the lace curtain aside and stared at the man strolling toward the barn.

"It's Paul—no, stop it, Winnie. You know it isn't Paul." She bit the inside of her cheek in total confusion tinged with a modicum of reluctant acceptance. "It's his ancestor. He has to be. Looks too much like—" Winnie's heart swelled and pressed into her throat as she struggled against the on-slaught of emotions which tore at her. Even if the handsome lawman had been Paul, why should she care? She only knew Paul Weathers as her ex-husband's divorce attorney . . . and as her once upon a future lover.

My one—no, five—time lover.

Besides . . . this was all *his* fault.

And what difference did it really make? With a groan, Winnie recalled her silent wish never to come face to face with Paul again. A cynical laugh bubbled up from her chest and she shook her head. She felt like the kid in *Home Alone* when he woke up the morning after wishing his family would disappear and discovered his request had been granted.

Who could have known that in order to avoid seeing Paul again after their wild night together, Winnie would have to move to another century?

"I still don't believe this."

Deciding it might be better to make her wishes a bit more specific in the future, Winnie watched Sam until he disappeared into the barn, then she turned back toward the bed. Regardless of what was going on, Winnie had to see to her basic needs, like food and shelter. Hopsador expected her to play governess to Amanda-the-Hun. That was her only alternative at the moment.

Until what?

Winnie's breath caught in her throat as she considered her predicament. *Would* she be able to find a means of returning to her own time? The thought of never returning terrified her. How would she get by in the nineteenth century?

Chuckling derisively, she shook her head. "The same way you were getting by in the twentieth century, dummy." She took a fortifying breath and closed her eyes for a brief moment. She was a liberated woman, capable of taking care of herself in any situation. Right? Wasn't she?

"Damn straight."

With a sniffle, Winnie squared her shoulders and removed

her wrinkled clothing. Turning in a full circle, she recalled the "indoor facilities," as Hopsador had called them.

The toilet consisted of what would one day be called a commode. A chair, with a lid and a removable . . . receptacle. How civilized. Then again, it beat trotting to an outhouse every time the urge hit.

Outhouse? I really don't believe this.

Forcing herself to concentrate on the mundane task of preparing herself for the day ahead, Winnie washed her face and straightened her hair with the missing woman's brush and comb. After slipping on the blue dress, she paused to stare at her image in the mirror above the dressing table. A near-stranger stared back at her. Without makeup she looked years younger. Her pale lashes and brows did nothing to give her any semblance of sophistication. Faint freckles seemed to mock countless years of painstakingly concealing them with foundation and powder.

"I look like a kid." Winnie made a face in the mirror, then glanced down at the hairbrush's carved handle. A feeling of melancholy washed through her. Who was Kathleen Mac-Gregor? What had happened to *her?*

Were people in the twentieth century wondering the same thing about Winnie Sinclair?

She looked again at the face in the mirror, watching her pupils dilate in astonishment as another possibility dawned on her. Had she and Kathleen traded places in time? Winnie brought her hand to her mouth with a horrified gasp. Imagining how difficult life in 1996 would be for a woman from the nineteenth century made her own plight seem somewhat less dramatic. Almost.

The entire situation defied explanation. She had no way of knowing what had happened to Kathleen MacGregor—no more than she could figure out how and why she'd traveled back in time.

A quiet knock startled Winnie from her musings. Drawing a deep breath, she turned and went to the door, but she couldn't quite bring herself to open it yet. She paused for just a moment to gather her wits before turning the knob.

A devastating grin greeted her when she swung the door open. Sam. Winnie's heart accelerated as she fidgeted with the folds in her skirt, hoping to hide her trembling. Her mouth was dry and she was so hungry she felt sick. Her messed-up brain needed fuel and this Paul look-alike cowboy-lawman wasn't doing a thing for her ability to think straight.

"Rufus thought maybe you'd be ready to try'n eat somethin," he said in that low drawl, so like Paul's, yet different at the same time. "I do think you seemed a mite more perky . . . earlier."

His eyes bored into her as Winnie met his gaze. Silver lights with the faintest hint of another color flashed near his pupils when he grinned again. "Eat?" she echoed, ignoring the burning sensation in her throat. Shaking herself, she took a shuddering breath. "Yes, I think that would make me feel much better. Thank you . . . Marshal."

He nodded and offered her his arm. *Chivalry is alive and well, and living in the nineteenth century,* she thought sarcastically, laying her hand in the crook of his elbow. Physical contact with this man was unnerving, especially after her stupid predawn visit to his room. He was so much like Paul that his mere presence released a barrage of memories Winnie knew she should try to forget.

Permanently.

She couldn't help herself. His clean, soapy fragrance mingled with leather and horse, creating a masculine aura that turned her insides to Jello. She'd never been partial to macho men before, but Sam's family resemblance could influence her opinion—dangerously so.

She glanced at his profile and an irritating warmth spread through her body. When he turned to look directly at her, his gray eyes startled Winnie into a shocking realization.

It wasn't Sam who created the longing ache deep inside

her—it was her memory of Paul. Her subconscious wanted to believe this was Paul. Winnie tried to smile at her escort as they made their way down the hall toward the back of the large house, but she couldn't. A perplexing sense of despondency imprisoned her.

And enraged her sensibilities.

She was pining away after the barracuda lawyer. She meant nothing to him, nor did she harbor any romantic fantasies about him. Sex, yes—romance, no. All they'd shared was sex. Pure, simple—actually rather creative—sex. Not love, or anything bearing any resemblance to that singular emotion. There'd been no whispered promises or any other such nonsense.

Get over it, Winnie.

Besides, Paul was one hell of a long way from where and when she was at the moment. Even so, when she cast another surreptitious glance at Sam, she had to remind herself again he wasn't Paul.

He isn't Paul . . . and I'm glad.

The last thing in the world she needed right now was to deal with her peculiar feelings toward a man she'd spent one night with. One night. It wasn't as if he was her ex-husband.

As they entered the dining room, Sam grinned at her again. "Reckon you must be half-starved, since you missed supper last night," he said in a low voice, then paused to pull out a chair for her to slide into. "Rufus and Amanda went to call on a neighbor. They already had breakfast."

Had they gone to town? Winnie turned her head so quickly she felt dizzy. "A town?" she asked in a small squeaky voice which bore little resemblance to her own. "Did they go to . . . town?" *Tulsa?*

Sam chuckled and took a seat across the long narrow table from her. "No, just down the road a piece."

As he unfolded a linen napkin and tucked it into his open collar, Winnie was again reminded of the differences between the marshal and Paul. They had the same last name.

That, combined with the uncanny resemblance, meant Sam had to be Paul's ancestor—no question. It was a given. She closed her eyes for a moment, then opened them to see June as she walked in and silently placed platters laden with ham, eggs, potatoes and biscuits on the table.

June poured steaming coffee into a china cup. Its scent wafted up to Winnie's eager nostrils, making her forget what she'd been discussing with Sam before the food interrupted. Nothing was more important to her at this moment than filling her empty stomach and fueling her brain. *Especially* fueling her brain.

Winnie ate in total silence, ignoring the man across the table from her. Her fat intake be damned. She consumed a huge slice of salty ham, a mound of fried potatoes—prepared in lard, no doubt—and two eggs over-easy, then crumbled two biscuits onto her plate and ladled gravy over them. *Triglycerides, yum.*

As she lifted a final forkful of the fat-laden yet heavenly concoction, her gaze met her breakfast companion's. Embarrassment flooded her face with heat, but she placed the utensil in her mouth and ate the food anyway before laying her fork aside, in spite of Sam's knowing grin.

"June's a good cook," Sam said quietly. There wasn't a hint of mockery in his tone.

Winnie nodded in agreement. She was stuffed. Contentment made her smile when she should have snapped at him for staring, but she felt so much better—stronger—it was impossible for her to feel angry at the moment. Drawing a deep breath, Winnie brought her napkin to her lips, then set it aside.

"Feelin' better, now?" Sam asked with a crooked grin. He lifted his cup to his lips but continued to stare at her over the rim.

"Much, thank you." Winnie lowered her gaze for a moment. "I don't remember ever being so hungry before. Makes me appreciate and understand what Mother Teresa's been trying to do in India."

"Pardon?" Sam tilted his head to one side, setting his cup aside and leaning forward.

Winnie's face flooded with heat again. "I'm sorry." She swallowed hard and reached for her coffee cup. The warm liquid invigorated her—made her feel almost human again. A human in one hell of a pickle.

At least now she could think. Her brain was functioning again. Sighing, she lifted her gaze to Sam's again. *He's not Paul,* she reminded herself for at least the hundredth time. "I'd like to apologize for . . . for coming into your room earlier. It was a . . . mistake." Her voice fell to a ragged whisper. "A terrible mistake—all of it."

"All of it?" he repeated in a voice that resembled Paul's more than ever.

Winnie stared in astonishment at his flickering gaze. He had the strangest eyes she'd ever seen. They seemed to change color at times, darkening and lightening from silver to—

No. She pressed her hand over her eyes for a moment, then sighed as she removed it. She was really imagining things, now. For just a moment—a wonderful moment—she'd imagined his eyes had turned blue. Her imagination—nothing more. It was impossible.

Any more impossible than time travel?

Winnie felt cold as she met the marshal's gaze again. His eyes were as gray as they could be now. No evidence of the blue light she'd seen—rather, imagined. None at all. *Not blue. Gray. Get it straight this time.* Breathing a sigh of relief, she managed a shaky smile.

"As I was saying," she continued, "I really shouldn't have . . . come into your room like that." Men had never intimidated her in her own time, so why should they now? They shouldn't. The increased blood supply to her face felt like liquid fire.

Sam rubbed his chin slowly with his thumb as he studied her, grinning mischievously the entire time. "Y'mean, you shouldn't have asked me to kiss you?"

"Well, I never."

Winnie turned quickly to the sound of the irate feminine voice.

"Just wait until Daddy hears about this," Amanda Hopsador continued. The girl gave Winnie a look of pure hot rage that could thaw the Arctic Circle. No problem.

Winnie's stomach lurched. She wondered for a few moments whether or not her breakfast was going to beat a hasty retreat. Amanda Hopsador's adolescent outrage was just what Winnie didn't need right now. Drawing a deep breath, she pushed away from the table, then stood. She dropped her napkin beside her empty plate, then slowly approached the antagonistic young woman.

"Amanda," Winnie began in what she hoped was an exasperated tone, because that was precisely how she felt at the moment—at herself and Amanda. "Your behavior is completely unbecoming. Didn't your father say he wanted you to learn to act like a lady?"

"Well . . ." Amanda's gaze darted from Sam to Winnie, then down at the floor. "So?" She looked up again and lifted her chin defiantly. "I heard what he said about you. *You're* no lady."

Winnie mentally counted to ten, then slowly smiled. "My dear, what I know about being a lady will amaze you." *And me.* "I'm feeling much better today, so we'll begin right away." *Lord, I hope I can pull this off.* "And the first lesson you're going to learn today is not to eavesdrop on other people's conversations."

"But—"

"Let's go." Winnie gripped Amanda's elbow and steered her from the dining room, nearly colliding with a chuckling Rufus Hopsador.

"Papa." Amanda wailed as Winnie avoided the girl's father's gaze and continued down the hall with her charge.

"I think we'll begin with voice, Amanda," Winnie continued. "You sound like Phyllis Diller on one of her good days."

"Papa!"

Seven

All right, Winnie. Now what? You have to teach Amanda-the-Hun how to be a lady. Images of Eliza Doolittle and Professor Higgins popped into Winnie's mind. It was worth a try. She sure didn't know what else to do.

"Repeat after me, Amanda." Winnie struggled to suppress a grin . . . and to resist the urge to sing. "The Rain in Spain."

"I don't wanna." Amanda turned her back on Winnie and folded her arms across her middle. "This is the silliest thing I've ever heard."

That makes two of us. Winnie sighed in exasperation and sat down on the edge of Amanda's bed. How could she continue to argue the point when she was in total agreement with the girl? Remembering her "place" and behaving like a lady were nothing less than criminal acts for a woman, as far as Winnie was concerned.

If she never found her way back to the twentieth century, Winnie decided she'd search out Susan B. Anthony and become a suffragette. She scratched her head, trying in vain to ignore Amanda's continued complaints about learning to "talk proper."

Winnie brightened as she remembered something from her high school history class. "Hey. Don't women in Wyoming have the vote?"

"Where's Wyoming? Besides, who cares?" Amanda stomped her foot and whirled around to stare in open hostility. "Why, in heaven's name would a woman want to vote? Is that part of being a lady, too?"

Winnie lifted her brows and suppressed the grin which threatened to betray her at any moment. "Why . . . yes. Yes, it is, Amanda. A very important part, as a matter of fact." She cleared her throat and turned her brightest smile on the girl. "Someday, women will be able to run for office—maybe even be president."

Amanda's mouth formed a perfect circle, then she shook her head and pursed her lips. "Well, *I* don't wanna do it, so why do I gotta learn to talk all over again? Besides, what makes you so sure?"

Because I've seen the future, you dimwit. Winnie rubbed her temples and silently counted to ten. If someone were to multiply all the times during her two days at the Lazy H that she'd counted to ten, she felt certain it would total at least a million. Amanda Hopsador was the most infuriating teenager Winnie'd ever encountered—not that she'd been around very many. Amanda's easy acceptance of the subordinate female role in society fueled Winnie's ire most. Even the girl's crude comments about Winnie and Sam's two-day-old conversation at the breakfast table were tolerable compared to Amanda's lack of interest in women's rights.

Winnie drew a deep breath and reminded herself of the year. Times *would* change. Inwardly she cringed, wondering if she could bear living in such a place and time. Fear and insecurity threatened her demeanor, but she quickly squelched them. Such self-indulgence was a luxury she couldn't afford at the moment. She must remain cognizant of anything and everything . . . and wait for some sort of clue which might help her return to her own time.

Where she belonged.

"I heard Marshal Weathers say you *asked* him to kiss you," Amanda whined for at least the hundredth time. The girl's tone betrayed an undeniable degree of jealousy.

"I told you I don't care to discuss it with you, Amanda,"

Winnie said slowly, then chewed the inside of her cheek, hoping to prevent her hot retort. "Marshal Weathers and I are adults—*you* are not."

Glancing up at the girl, Winnie saw pure hatred in her dark eyes. *Uh-oh.* She'd done it, now. Amanda was mad enough to commit murder and it didn't take a genius to determine the identity of her next victim.

"I bet I'm more woman than you, anyway." Amanda flipped her long dark hair over one shoulder and sashayed toward Winnie. "I know what men . . . like." Her last word was blended with as seductive an expression as Winnie'd ever seen. Marilyn Monroe could've taken lessons from the volatile Miss Hopsador. Amanda oozed sensuality from every pore.

Trying to ignore the taunt, Winnie couldn't prevent the telltale heat from creeping to her cheeks. Paul Weathers hadn't found her lacking in sexual ability. Had he? Uncertainty brought a flash of reassuring memories. The memory of Paul's touch, his kisses, the decadent manner in which she'd responded, all combined to restore her self-confidence and assault her composure.

"I'll bet you haven't even *done* it."

Ha. Wanna bet? Winnie took a deep breath and met Amanda's glower. Surely, this young girl hadn't been with a man. She was just bragging. That was all. "And I'm equally sure you haven't either," Winnie lied, hoping her own guilty conscience didn't betray her. If she was going to act as Amanda's governess—as if she really had a choice—then she was damned well going to do a good job of it.

The silence lengthened. Winnie cast the girl a furtive glance, concerned by the expression on Amanda's face. Worry blended with obstinance were all too common traits for a twentieth-century teenager. Apparently, some things never changed.

Had Amanda been intimate with a man already? Winnie took a deep breath and released it, then decided it would be best to change the subject. She couldn't undo what the girl had already done, but if she could instill some self-respect and values in Amanda for the future, she'd consider herself successful.

Successful? Was this the reason she'd been dragged from her world to this primitive place and time? Winnie almost laughed aloud, but explaining it to her reluctant pupil would've spoiled the moment. Winnie felt like Alice when she was ten feet tall. Now if only she had a mushroom to nibble on, that would make it all better again.

Suppressing her smile, Winnie decided to call it a day. There was only so much of this lady business she could handle in one day, and she'd passed full and moved on to gut-buster shortly after lunch—er, dinner. *Breakfast, dinner and supper, Winnie. There is no lunch in 1896.*

"And no pizza either."

"Pizza?" Amanda sat down beside Winnie on the edge of the bed. "What's that?"

"A . . . a pie. A meat and cheese pie." Winnie's face flooded with heat, but she knew, given the opportunity, she might have killed for a pizza with thick crust, Canadian bacon, pineapple, green peppers, onions, freshly grated garlic, and artichoke hearts. Her stomach rumbled in anticipation.

"Oh."

The girl plucked at her skirt and stared down at her lap for several moments. It was obvious she had something on her mind. *Good.* As long as Amanda was preoccupied with other matters, perhaps she wouldn't realize how inept her governess really was. Winnie could only hope Rufus wouldn't notice and throw her out of the house. Then where would she go? What would she do? She had to learn as much as possible about current events before trying to strike out on her own. History hadn't been her best subject in school. Unfortunately.

"Pa says we might go to the dance Saturday."

"Dance?" Winnie's interest immediately piqued. This

could be interesting—a real opportunity to check out the life and times of Indian Territory. A good history book would've sufficed, but under the circumstances, firsthand would have to do. "What dance?"

Amanda sighed dramatically, a habit Winnie'd already learned to associate with the girl's manipulative techniques. "The Morrisons is having a barn raising on Saturday, and there'll be dancing after the work's done." She grimaced and rolled her eyes. "I hate barn raisings, but come dark they can be lots of fun." The girl's face turned red and she lowered her gaze for a moment.

Winnie made a mental note of Amanda's reaction to "after dark." Maybe the girl would bear watching. The thought of Amanda throwing herself away at seventeen, while under Winnie's influence—a subjective term if she'd ever known one—didn't set well with her at all, even if she wasn't supposed to be here. In order to watch the girl, Winnie'd have to attend the dance. Would she be invited? She was, after all, hired help.

Yeah, from QTEA, Inc.: The Quantum Theory Employment Agency.

"Pa says I can't go unless you do," Amanda said in a calculating tone, glancing at Winnie through veiled lashes. "He said maybe you can learn me how to be a lady in public, too. Will you go?"

"Teach, Amanda—not learn," Winnie said absentmindedly. For just a moment, Amanda's expression softened to something at least marginally human. The girl was actually very beautiful. Winnie stared at her as very unexpected memories of another face flashed through her mind. She remembered a portrait of a beautiful young woman—a Native American woman.

Winnie's stomach contracted as she remembered where she'd seen the woman's face. Her grandmother'd had a portrait hanging in the entryway of her house out in Claremore.

She smiled in remembrance, then saw the portrait again

in her mind's eye. A lump formed in her throat. The half
Cherokee woman in the painting had been Winnie's great-
grandmother. People were always stunned to learn of Winnie's Native American ancestry, which wasn't difficult to
understand, considering her red hair and green eyes.

*A couple of generations of Irish blood can do that to a
family.* Winnie smiled and took a deep breath. When she
looked up at Amanda, she was reminded of the portrait of
her great-grandmother, whose name Winnie couldn't recall.
She tried, but the name was buried in childhood memories.
Undoubtedly, her great-grandmother's first name would
come to her sooner or later, but Winnie definitely had no idea
what the woman's maiden name might have been. For all
she knew, the Hopsadors could be . . . relatives.

Winnie swallowed hard, but the lump remained. Her heart
thudded in her chest as she pondered this possibility. No,
impossible. Ridiculous.

"So, will you go?" Amanda was openly agitated by Winnie's delayed response to her question. "I ain't got forever,
y'know."

"Oh, of course." Winnie stood and smoothed her skirt,
shaking the uneasy feeling that there was something more
she should remember. She had no reason to suspect any direct relationship to the Hopsadors, though it was possible,
since they were from the same tribe. Distantly related, of
course. Very distant.

". . . and like I said, the dancin' will start after the sun
goes down." Amanda sighed. "The men'll lay out a wood
floor and sprinkle it with sawdust. Then folks'll bring out
their fiddles and such. You'll see—it'll be fun."

At this moment, the girl seemed almost pleasant. Winnie
smiled and nodded. "I'm sure we'll have a nice time,
Amanda." A thought forced itself to the forefront of her mind.
She couldn't help remembering the way Amanda had looked
at Sam Weathers, not that it really mattered to Winnie, of
course. "Uh, Amanda?"

"Yeah?" Amanda looked up from her seat on the bed.

"Um, do you have any boyfriends?"

"Boyfriends?" Amanda giggled. "I never heard that before. You mean boys who are friends? Or do you mean suitors?"

Winnie's face warmed and she chewed her lower lip, searching her mind for that mystical wisdom of mothers and grandmothers. "Either or both." She met Amanda's gaze steadily as the girl stood and faced her. The expression smoldering in the girl's dark eyes was mysterious—secretive. What was she hiding?

"I've had some . . . *men* come to call." Amanda looked down and lifted her green muslin skirt with the toe of her shoe. "And Marshal Weathers is sweet on me, too. Why else would he keep comin' back like he does? He pretends like he's just coming to see Pa, but I know better. He may have left yesterday, but I know he'll be back. You'll see."

Winnie detested the surge of jealousy that threatened her ability to reason. When she'd learned of Sam's departure yesterday, the sinking feeling in the pit of her stomach had made her feel sick. Sam Weathers wasn't Paul, and even if he was, it shouldn't make any difference to Winnie. Amanda was welcome to him, except that he was way too old for her, and Winnie was sort of responsible for the girl right now.

"Marshal Weathers is old enough to be your father, Amanda," she said steadily, recognizing the competitive gleam in the girl's eyes.

"You just want him for yourself."

Not Sam—just his body. Sort of.

Paul didn't know how much more he could take. Whistling off key, Sam guided Lucifer around a muddy place in the road. Since leaving the Lazy H the previous morning, they'd been rained on, hailed on, and fallen in the mud twice while leading Sam's horse through slippery clay.

Paul was dirty—dirtier than he'd been his entire life. Even during childhood, when boys wore more dirt on their bodies than anything else, he'd been cleaner than this. *Sam, I need a hot shower, er bath.*

"It ain't Saturday, yet," Sam said as if Paul's request was the most ridiculous idea he'd ever heard. "Are all men in the twentieth century like you?"

Paul knew when he was being insulted. *If you mean, do they like to be clean, I'd have to say yes. Most of them, anyway.* He had an itch low on his back where Sam's belt dug into his flesh. This was like wearing an invisible straitjacket. *Hey, scratch my back for me.*

"Yeah, I feel it. Hold your horses." Sam reached behind him and scratched the irritating spot until Paul felt the relief clear to his toes. "Better?"

Yeah, thanks. They'd crossed the border into Kansas early this morning. A trip that would've taken a couple of hours by car, had taken them all of one day and the better part of the next morning on horseback. Where was a Holiday Inn when you really needed one? Paul would give anything for a hot shower and a good night's sleep in a soft bed.

"We oughta reach Coffeyville before noon," Sam said, scratching the offensive place on Paul's back again. "I reckon we could use a bath. Before I forget again, I gotta tell you I owe Rufus for loaning me some money after that bastard robbed me. You see to it Rufus gets repaid."

Paul would've cringed, but settled for a mental shudder instead. Robbing Sam was the least savage act Buck Landen had committed. Reminded of his great-great-grandfather's fate, Paul was painfully aware of the full implication of Sam's request. The bottom line was that Sam wouldn't be around to fulfill that obligation himself. Unfortunately, Paul had no income—not for at least a century, anyway.

"I'm gonna send a wire to Fort Smith while we're in town and get next month's pay. Funny thought—a dead man drawin' pay." Sam brought the horse to a stop and looked down into a valley, heavily treed with a river running through it. "Yonder's Coffeyville. It's one of the prettiest little towns I ever had the chance to visit."

Paul looked down at the town through different eyes. Though the cornea and optic nerve were the same, the thoughts and feelings behind his physiological perception were far more alert—receptive. Sam, or his spirit, were helping Paul learn to appreciate some things he'd taken for granted all his adult life.

Making money as a divorce attorney had been the most consistent thing in Paul's life since graduating from law school. He hadn't allowed himself to see the other side of life—the people whose lives were devastated by the divorce proceedings from which he reaped a tidy profit. Especially the children.

He recalled Winnie's reaction that night, when she'd first realized his identity. She'd looked at him with pure loathing in those gorgeous green eyes. Was such animosity justified, simply because he'd represented Dirk in their divorce?

Maybe.

A flood of new perceptions bombarded him. The scent of rain-kissed grass, the sun glittering on the droplets which clung precariously to the tips of oak leaves. A scissor-tailed flycatcher flew overhead, then perched on a branch to sing its beautiful melody.

God, I'm getting downright sensitive. Next thing you know, I'll be watching Donahue.

"Who's Donahue?"

Startled back to the present—the past—the current present—Paul broadcast a silent chuckle. *He's a celebrity from my time. Some people call him a feminist.*

Sam tensed. "Y'mean one of those fellows who . . . don't like women?"

No—not that. Wouldn't Sam be amazed by how much things would really change over the next hundred years? More than technology, the people were so different. Morals were looser, that was for sure. *Donahue believes in women's rights. He has a television talk show—*

"A tele-what?" Sam gave Lucifer his head, allowing the horse to pace himself as they made their way down a slippery slope. "Never heard of that before."

Paul searched his mind for some way of explaining modern technology to his ancestor. *Well, it's a . . . little box and you watch people in it.*

"Y'mean they shrink folks down to fit inside a little box?" Sam brought the horse to a stop again. "You're pullin' my leg for sure now."

Paul sent Sam an exasperated groan. *No, like photographs. I'm sure you must know what photographs are. I know they've been invented. I've even seen some from the Civil War.*

"Sure, I know what they are. What do you think I am?" Sam reached into one of his saddlebags and withdrew a small oval frame. "This here's my wife and boy." He was silent a moment. "George."

Paul looked at the woman and child in the photograph. Recognizing the squeezing sensation in his throat as Sam's reaction to his loss, Paul's eyes stung with unshed tears. He wasn't sure if they were his own or Sam's. Both, probably. *George. My great-grandfather.*

Sam nodded. "He'll be all right with my sister." The lawman took a deep breath and stared at the photograph for several minutes longer. "Paul, can I ask you a favor? Another one, I mean?"

Somehow, Paul sensed what his ancestor was about to ask. *Yeah?*

"When you go back to your own time and all—"
If I can find my way back.

"You will. I feel sure of it." Sam took another deep breath and held it for a few minutes. "You take this photograph with you. My sister's got others and I want you to have it."

A priceless gift from the past—a memento of his adventure through history. *Thanks. I'd like that.* There were a few moments of mental silence between them, for which Paul was eternally grateful. He needed to get his act together before their combined emotions made him—them—start bawling.

"Good." Sam slipped the photograph back into the leather pouch at his side, then prodded Lucifer toward town again. "I reckon we could get us a bath, seein's how you ain't used to good old-fashioned dirt."

Old-fashioned—that's for sure.

Sam chuckled, and Paul couldn't help wondering again whose emotions had triggered the reaction. *A bath would be great, Sam. Thanks.*

"And a drink." Sam smacked his lips. "A shot of bourbon would hit the spot about now."

Bourbon'll do, but it's a little early for me. Paul remembered the brandy he and Winnie had shared, including the aftereffects.

"There you go again, fillin' my head with pictures of that redhead."

I wish you wouldn't do that. Paul hated sharing his memories, especially of Winnie, but he hadn't determined a way to prevent Sam from seeing the mental images precipitated by Paul's thoughts. Yet.

"I can't help it," Sam said, shaking his head in disgust. "And I can't help getting hard as a year-old corn dodger every time you fill my head with them pictures either."

Sam sure as hell wasn't alone in that. Were Paul's memories of making love to Winnie accurate? Or had the trauma of these past few days slanted them? Was it possible she hadn't been as warm, as giving, as sexy, or as spectacular as he remembered?

Then again, maybe she had.

"I think you oughta do right by her."

Paul's thoughts immediately skidded to a halt. *Uh, excuse*

me? Surely, Sam didn't mean what Paul thought he might. *What do you mean by "do right by her?"*

"I dunno what it's like in your time, but these days a man's honor-bound to marry a gal if he tarnishes her reputation."

Tarnishes her reputation? His ancestor actually thought Paul should marry Winnie Sinclair simply because he'd spent the night with her. Of course, it had been the most sexually satisfying night of his life, but that hardly seemed justification for marriage. It wasn't as if she'd been a naive, virginal young girl. *I don't think I tarnished her reputation in either century.*

"Huh. From what I've seen—a whole helluva lot more'n I wanted to—you done a pretty thorough job of soilin'."

Soiling? Anger and resentment clouded his thoughts. Maybe he shouldn't react this way to Sam's archaic morals, but it wasn't as if he'd been the only consenting adult on board his houseboat that night. *What kind of man do you think I am? We both wanted it, Sam.*

Sam gulped. "I ain't sayin' she didn't *want* to . . . be with you like that, but she probably thought you was gonna marry her." He sighed. "Women do."

Not modern women, Sam. Besides, Winnie's been married before.

"She's a widow, then." Sam squinted as he pulled on the reins and brought Lucifer to a stop before a wooden structure. He hopped down and tied the reins to the hitching rail. "All the more reason to do right by her."

She's divorced. Paul regretted the words the moment they left his gray matter. He should've kept his thoughts to himself. The worst part of it was, he had a great deal of respect for Winnie Sinclair, yet here he was putting her down to make himself look better in his ancestor's eyes. Tacky. Really tacky. *But her ex-husband's a real jerk. I represented him, so I oughta—*

"I don't reckon I wanna hear any more of this." Sam drew a deep breath and walked into the livery stable. Gritting his

teeth, he turned toward a short, heavyset man with a beard.
Under his breath, he added, "Now hush up so folks won't
think I'm talkin' to myself."

Paul was furious—with himself as much as Sam. The true
insult to Winnie had been made less than two minutes ago,
not the night of their midnight rendezvous. Of course, Sam
couldn't understand that. Things were different now than they
would be in 1996.

Sam handed the proprietor a handful of coins, then the
short man led Lucifer away. Thank God. A hot bath and some
time away from that smelly horse were just what Paul needed.
There was something else concerning him more at the moment, however.

I'm sorry, Sam.

"Good." Sam looked across the street. "Ah, bourbon."

Wait a minute. You said we were going to take a bath. Paul
couldn't believe he was talking about a group bath, but he
certainly didn't have anything he should, or could, hide from
Sam.

"They got baths upstairs." Sam grinned and rubbed his
hands together as he made his way across the dusty street.
"Soft beds, warm baths, smooth bourbon and hot women—
what more could a man want?"

Women? Paul's imagination went crazy, fueled by Sam's
thoughts. *Hey, wait a minute. This is my body and I don't
want to catch anything.*

Sam hesitated for a few moments. "You been fillin' my
head with pictures—real clear pictures—of you'n Winnie."
He shook his head then stepped onto the boardwalk in front
of the saloon. "The women here get paid for pleasurin' a
man. There ain't nothin' wrong with it."

It's my body, Sam, Paul was helpless. There was nothing
he could physically do to prevent Sam from using him this
way. *I don't want you to do this with my body.*

Sam gritted his teeth, then pushed the swinging doors open
and stepped inside. The floor was covered with sawdust.

Brass spittoons were in every corner. The dark stains on the sawdust surrounding the receptacles made the origin of the substance obvious. *Gross.*

"I've had about all of you I'm gonna take."

There's a simple solution to that problem. Paul sensed he was pushing his ancestor farther than common sense told him he dared, but he didn't want to have sex with a nineteenth-century prostitute. Or maybe saloon girl was the correct term. All Paul knew was that he couldn't let this happen.

Obviously choosing to ignore Paul's suggestion, Sam stepped up to the bar and pushed his hat back on his head. The bartender paused in front of him and nodded.

"Gimme a bourbon and a beer."

"Comin' right up, Marshal." The bartender poured the requested refreshment, then placed them on the polished surface in front of Sam. "Ain't seen you in a while."

Sam took a long sip of beer, then shot the bourbon down his throat in one smooth swallow. He followed the entire gut-burning procedure with yet another sip of beer.

Damn. Slow down, will you? Paul felt liquor-induced warmth spread through him like butter in his veins. Even his stiff muscles relaxed as the alcohol worked its magic. *On second thought, a little more wouldn't hurt.*

Sam grinned, then turned his attention back to the bartender. "Yeah, it's been a while, Fred." He sighed and took another sip of beer. "Gimme another shot."

As the bartender poured the amber liquid, Paul tried to read Sam's thoughts, but they were carefully masked. What the devil was the old man up to?

"Seen Buck Landen lately?" Sam asked in feigned indifference, then gulped the bourbon and sipped the beer.

The bartender stared long and hard at Sam, then frowned. "You look different, Marshal."

Paul was aware of heat flooding Sam's face and knew his ancestor was blushing. Did he look different? Then he recalled the color of those sightless eyes staring up at the sky

on the banks of the Verdigris. Gray—Sam had gray eyes.
What color were Paul's eyes right now? He hadn't seen himself in a mirror since Sam entered his body. The fool never
even used a mirror to shave. For all Paul knew, he might be
walking around with another man's eyes.

Dead eyes.

"Yeah, just different," the bartender said, refilling Sam's
shot glass. "And no, I ain't seen that bastard, Landen since
last year when he was through here." Fred shook his head
and sighed. "And that's just fine with me and everyone else
in this town."

Sam looked beyond the bartender at the huge, ornate mirror hanging behind the bar. Paul's gaze followed his ancestor's. *Gray. My eyes are gray.* No, they weren't Paul's eyes.
They were Sam's gray eyes staring back from Paul's face.
Sam's dead eyes.

Paul stared long and hard, realizing by Sam's fluctuating
expression that the lawman knew exactly what was happening. For the first time since Sam's spirit had entered Paul's
body, Paul was seeing his own face.

His face, but not his eyes.

What'd you do with my blue eyes, Sam?

Sam shook his head very slightly, then returned his attention to the bartender. Placing his empty glass on the bar, he
held out his hand to indicate he didn't want another refill.
"Louise workin'?"

"I am for you, Sam Weathers," a sultry voice said from
directly behind them.

Oh, no.

Sam turned around with a devilish air that made Paul want
to scream. The old fart was going to use Paul's body after
all. Sam was going to have sex with a prostitute, against
Paul's will. This was sick.

Don't do this, Sam.

"Shut up and enjoy it, Paul," Sam whispered so low, no
one else could have heard him. "Louise, you're lookin'

mighty fine. I swear you look younger every time I come to Coffeyville."

Paul followed his great-great-grandfather's gaze, down the length of the buxom beauty and back up again. She was beautiful, in a round sort of way. *She's fat. I don't like fat women.*

Sam sighed in frustration and closed his eyes for a minute. "She ain't fat."

"Fat?" Louise echoed. "Who're you callin' fat, Sam Weathers?"

Sam smiled at the woman again, but she'd already turned around and was heading back up the stairs. "I wasn't talkin' to you, Louise, honey."

The voluptuous brunette paused on the stairs and glanced back over her shoulder. "Well, I sure as hell hope whoever you was talkin' to can keep you warm, Sam. And take care of . . . other things, too, 'cuz I sure as hell ain't." Her gaze dropped suggestively, then she turned around and flounced back up the stairs.

"Oh, you've gone and done it, now." Sam turned back around to face the bar, but stopped short when he saw the bartender's shocked expression.

"You all right, Marshal?"

"No, Fred. I ain't all right. I ain't been all right for a coon's age." Sam walked over to the bar and drained his beer mug. "We want us a bath."

"Us?" Fred's lips twitched suggestively and he cleared his throat. "Sure. A bath for . . . two?"

"One." Sam closed his eyes and drew a deep breath, resting both hands on the bar for a few moments. "Just one, Fred." He opened his eyes and smiled tightly. "We—" He bit his lower lip and closed his eyes for a minute. "I want fresh water, too."

"Hell, Sam. Leftovers is half price. Y'know that, don't you?"

Fresh, Sam. There's no way I'm going to let you put my

body into someone else's secondhand bath water. No telling what they might have left behind.

Sam closed his eyes again, then reopened them and bared his teeth. Even though Paul couldn't see Sam's expression clearly in the cloudy mirror, he knew it wouldn't even come close to resembling a real smile.

"Fresh. Fresh water, Fred." Sam barely moved his lips when he spoke, gnashing his teeth at the same time. "And a room for the night."

"For one?" Fred was grinning openly now.

Sam leaned on the bar and narrowed his eyes. "Yep, just one."

Ah, victory is sweet.

A menacing whisper filled Paul's mind. "And dangerous as hell."

Eight

Mesmerized, Winnie watched the dancers as if they were part of a bizarre dream. Unfortunately, she knew all too well that this was no dream. It was a nightmare gone bad.

She leaned against the side of the newly constructed barn, listening to the whining strains of Mr. Elston's fiddle as he tried—without success—to play his unique rendition of a song Winnie couldn't begin to name. As he hit a particularly hair-raising note, a title popped into her mind: "The Goose Pimple Waltz?"

Another man pulled a harmonica from his pocket and stepped onto the makeshift stage—an elevated platform, specifically arranged for the musicians. His subtler tones were a welcome accompaniment. Winnie sighed as the fiddler's music gradually became less offensive. Either that, or she was losing her hearing along with her mind.

The dancers were dressed like ordinary people—by nineteenth-century standards—though most of them were obviously at least part Native American. Winnie sighed in disappointment. She hadn't realized until this moment that she'd been hoping to see tribal members in native dress. This was Indian Territory, after all. She should've known better. Now, if she'd only been twenty or thirty years earlier . . .

"Bite your tongue, Winnie," she whispered to herself, remembering her wish to never have to face Paul Weathers again. A dream come true? She knew better than to tempt fate a second time.

"Nice evenin'."

Winnie turned with a start toward the all too familiar voice. "Pa—Sam—I mean, Marshal Weathers." *Get a grip. He's just a man.*

A man who looked exactly like someone she'd once known *very* well. No wonder her tongue felt tied in knots each time she tried to speak with him.

"Sam'll do fine." He placed his hand on the wall beside her and leaned against it. His casual air was charming and masculine.

And very disarming.

"I . . . thought you left." She took a deep breath, thankful the darkness hid her fiery face. As her lungs filled with fresh evening air, she girded her resolve and forged ahead. The pioneer women didn't have anything on Winnie Sinclair. "Didn't you?" Jeez, she sounded so foolish and . . . dumb blonde. That was it—she was expressing herself like the subject of one of the dumb blonde jokes that had swept through the country in the last couple of years—rather, a hundred years in the future. Maybe she could start a new trend of dumb redhead jokes. Somehow, she didn't think the present mainstream of society would embrace such a fad.

"I did for a spell, but I come back. I owe somebody . . . somethin'." He sighed, then removed his hat and raked his fingers through his hair. "I was anxious to get—uh, did you miss me?"

"Miss you?" Winnie narrowed her gaze as she eyed the man through the semidarkness. Lanterns had been strewn from ropes surrounding the dance area, but the light they provided was minimal. Still, she knew all too well what Sam looked like—*who* he looked like. She didn't have to see him clearly to form a picture of his handsome face in her mind. All she had to do was correct his eye color. Her memory was becoming more aggravating with each passing day.

"Well, did you?"

She saw a flash of white teeth in the dark and knew he

was smiling. The man was coming on to her. There was no point in denying it. Was Paul's ancestor a John Wayne style pick-up artist? Must run in the family. *Great—what next?*

"Miss you?" she repeated, feeling really stupid and hating it. Winnie sighed and half-turned to fully face him. He loomed over her in the darkness, even though she was above average height for a woman. Sam had everything his descendant did except the blue eyes . . .

Everything? Winnie's cheeks flamed as she found herself wondering if Sam resembled his descendant in other more intimate ways. Graphic memories flooded her mind. The vivid memory of Paul's potent kisses, his exquisite touch and the urgent way he'd possessed her, filled Winnie's senses, created a fierce, wicked hunger she cursed herself for even acknowledging.

Lord, give me strength—but hurry.

"You look mighty pretty this evenin', Winnie," he said quietly, his tone warm and gentle. "Would you like to dance? I don't dance too bad. I can probably manage to keep from stompin' on your pretty toes."

Winnie bristled. How did he know what her toes looked like? *You're losing it, Winnie.* She almost laughed aloud at her foolishness. He didn't know, of course. Sam was just making conversation, which she was misinterpreting. Paranoia was making her think and say witless things.

She drew a deep shaky breath. It was considerably past time for Winnie Sinclair to reaffirm jurisdiction of her life— as much as possible. She might not be able to expedite her return to the twentieth century, but she could certainly assume a more aggressive role in what transpired in the here and now.

She flashed Sam Weathers her most brilliant smile, realizing he'd seen it when he gasped quietly. "Yes, Sam," she said with far more conviction than she felt. "I'd love to dance. Just remember, I'm not . . . not from around here, so I might not be familiar with the dances you know. I'll try not to step on your feet, too."

He chuckled, then pushed away from the barn, bending his elbow and offering it to her. Winnie hesitated only a moment, then slipped her arm through his. Her stomach lurched and her heart took off like the Orient Express. Swallowing hard, she tried to come to terms with the sensations of déjà vu which swept through her.

Despite her best efforts, Paul's face flashed through her mind. His infuriatingly wicked and highly effective grin, the same one he'd wielded against her defenses that night on the houseboat, made her feel warm and tingly in one not-so-innocent flash of introspection.

And this man could be Paul's twin. It wasn't fair—not one damned bit.

Winnie bit her lower lip as Sam led her slowly toward the sawdust-covered dance floor. Her feet felt like lead and regret filled her mind and heart. She should have remained in the shadows, hiding from the crowd. Hiding from her own doubts and insecurities.

He isn't Paul.

Memories made her heart flutter and her libido take off like the Concord making its New York to Paris run when she was around Sam. This was dangerous, she realized with a jolt. Long-term abstinence and too much brandy had been the only necessary catalysts to make her fall into Paul's waiting, eager, and very talented arms. Could she be as easily swayed into Sam's bed?

Oh, Lord.

Winnie cast a surreptitious glance at Sam's inspiring profile as they passed directly beneath a glowing lantern at the edge of the dance floor. Her heart swelled into her throat. God, he must be Paul. How could it be possible for two men—albeit, a hundred years apart—to look so much alike? This just wasn't fair. Not at all.

"You all right?"

Winnie gasped at the sound of his voice. She'd forgotten for a moment where she was. "Yes. I'm fine."

They stepped onto the platform and he slipped his arm around her waist and caught her right hand with his left. The fiddle and harmonica worked together to create some sort of waltz. Winnie wasn't familiar with the melody, but at least the three-four beat was helpful. It could have been much worse. Maybe.

Sam flashed her a devastating grin and tightened his arm around her waist. "I always was partial to a good old-fashioned waltz." His expression softened. "And redheaded gals."

Oh, boy. Winnie nodded, not trusting herself to speak as he held her close. Her gaze darted around the gathering, noting that the other couples on the dance floor didn't stand nearly as close together when they waltzed. Sam's actions put her in an awkward situation. She should remember her position as governess. Her presence at this party was strictly to oversee and guide Amanda Hopsador's behavior, as soon as she found the girl.

Winnie Sinclair—worried about appearances? Her mother wouldn't have believed this.

Winnie was accustomed to dancing this close in *her* time, but now was very different. If she did something scandalous in public, she might jeopardize her position with the Hopsadors. That would never do. At least, not until she'd determined her best course of action. Should she make the best of her situation in the nineteenth century, or try to figure out how she'd arrived here and how she might possibly return?

Reality struck as Sam guided her through the simple steps of the familiar dance. She really had no choice. The answer was so painfully simple she wanted to drop to her knees and cry right here in front of God and everybody.

She was stranded here. Forever?

Stunned to her very core by this reality check, Winnie

lifted her chin and gazed into Sam's eyes—his very *gray* eyes. She'd have given anything at this moment to find blue eyes staring back from that familiar face. But they remained a silvery, twinkling gray. She was unable to suppress the sigh which came from her very soul. Winnie wasn't only a time traveler, she was lost in time—stuck here in this place, this new present. A prisoner in time.

An exclusive San Quentin for time travelers? No . . . San Quantum.

It wasn't a simple matter of making the best of a bad situation. She had to do better than that. Winnie Sinclair must make a new life for herself.

Though the realization that she'd traveled through time had struck her days ago, the true magnitude of her predicament was new and raw. As she continued to stare at Sam's handsome face, she saw his jaw twitch slightly, then he furrowed his brow in open concern. It was almost as if he'd read her mind, shared her anxiety, her bewilderment. Her hopelessness.

"It'll be all right, Winnie," he said reassuringly, rubbing her back with the flat of his palm as the music came to a stop.

Winnie stared at him. Was her shock that obvious? How did he know she was worried about something? Her heart thudded mockingly in her chest. For some reason, she felt certain this man knew things about her that logic demanded he couldn't. She was suddenly as sure of this fact as of her own name. Yet how could he?

"Sam, you . . ."

What was she supposed to say? Dare she ask if he knew she was a time traveler? Chuckling in disbelief, she shook her head and glanced around the dance floor again. Anything to distract her mind from this comedy of errors. It was imperative that she anchor herself in something simple and tangible, to preserve her sanity against this madness.

Then she saw Amanda on the arm of a tall young man who appeared very near the girl's own age. Good. Reminded of her duty, the reason she'd attended this function in the first place, Winnie met Amanda's gaze. The open hatred so clearly depicted on Amanda's lovely face unnerved Winnie.

It didn't take a rocket scientist to figure out why Amanda was looking at her governess as if she could commit murder without a moment's remorse.

"Uh-oh." Winnie sighed and bit her lower lip in consternation as Sam led her back toward the barn.

"What?" Sam asked, tilting his head at a cocky angle as he turned to face her. "Uh-oh, what? And what was you gonna say before?"

Winnie frowned for a moment, trying to remember what she'd been about to say before she caught sight of Amanda. It had been something important. She searched her mind, then suddenly remembered and jerked her chin upward to stare at Sam in amazement. Her knees went weak and she felt hot all over. "You know about me," she said accusingly, waiting for his answer. "What—who I am?"

Sam turned slightly away and she saw his lips moving in the inadequate light. He was talking to himself—thinking out loud? "Sam." She touched his arm. "I must know. Do you know who I am—where I'm from?"

Clearing his throat, he turned to fully face her, his expression grim. "Nope." The word was so short and precise, it couldn't be mistaken for any other.

"Sam." Winnie was certain he was lying to her. What she couldn't understand was *why*. First of all, how could he possibly know she was from the future? And why would he bother to hide that knowledge from her? With each passing moment of strained silence, Winnie became more convinced that he really knew. It was utterly insane, yet she couldn't shake the suspicion. "You *do* know something—I can tell."

"Winnie." He rubbed his hand over his face as he released his breath in a ragged sigh, then met her gaze. "Don't ask me no more questions. I ain't sure how to answer them and I don't wanna upset you."

"Upset me?" Winnie shook her head as unshed tears stung

her eyes. "I'm not some stupid Victorian lady who needs a big strong *man* to protect her from the cold, cruel world, you jerk. I'm a liberated woman, who knows how to take care of herself." A tear trickled down her face, mocking her bravado. Grateful for the darkness, she rushed on. "I had a man—a husband—once. Take care of me? Ha. Not on your life. I was the one who—who took care of him *and* myself." She bit back the sob that tore at her throat. "I want—*need*—the truth, Sam. What do you know . . . and *how* do you know it?"

Paul knew as he watched Winnie Sinclair stand up to his great-great-grandfather, that she was the finest woman he'd ever known. *Sam, what are we going to do?* He felt totally helpless as his ancestor tried to talk to Paul's fellow time traveler. Poor Winnie hadn't asked for any of this.

Of course, neither had he.

She was a victim of circumstances—very bizarre circumstances. Maybe if he hadn't sailed the *Sooner Sunset* into the middle of the lake, none of this would have happened. If they'd remained in the dock, with the boat securely moored . . .

He never would've experienced the most memorable night of his life.

Here she stood, bathed in lantern light, touching his arm and not even aware of his presence. She thought the man standing before her was Sam Weathers, and in a way he was. Paul could see her, smell her clean soapy fragrance, feel the gentle touch of her hand on his arm, see the pleading look in those gorgeous green eyes . . .

Yet he was powerless.

Sam. Paul couldn't think of anything to ask his great-great-grandfather to say to Winnie. All he knew was that he wanted to comfort her. He ached to touch her and to hold her in his arms again.

He focused his gaze on her lips, remembered the sweetness, the softness of her kiss. His memories became images, filled his mind and triggered a physical response.

A shared one.

Oh, no. I did it again.

"You sure as hell did," Sam whispered, hiding his mouth behind his hand.

Remembering how he'd interrupted Sam's intentions in Coffeyville, Paul tried without success to suppress a terrible thought. Would Sam seek revenge? Would he try to seduce Winnie Sinclair to get even with Paul?

Winnie stepped closer, continuing to wait for an answer. Paul wanted desperately to tell her to run away from Sam, but he couldn't. She reached up to place her palm on his chest and stared into his eyes.

Whose eyes did she see?

Sam, let me talk to her. There was no answer. Paul tried to read Sam's thoughts, but they were vague and jumbled. All he knew was, from a physical standpoint, he felt like a twelve-year-old with his first hard-on. *Oh, Lord.*

"What do you know about me?" Winnie asked in that sultry voice of hers. She leaned closer. "Tell me."

Paul sensed and shared Sam's physical reaction to her close proximity. No, it was *his* physical reaction. Sometimes Paul had to remind himself that this was his body. He was beginning to feel like a passenger, rather than a host. *Don't you even think it, Sam.*

Sam didn't respond to Paul, but he inclined his head toward Winnie. "What is it you want me to tell you, Winnie?" the lawman asked in his slow drawl. "Tell you that you're the prettiest gal here tonight? Well, you are."

You son of a bitch.

"Tell you I've wanted to kiss you since the minute I first seen you at the Lazy H?" Sam leaned closer to her.

Damn you, Sam Weathers. Paul hated his ancestor at this moment. The man had taken everything from Paul, leaving him with nothing—not even his own body. Now it looked like Sam wanted Paul's lover, too. It wasn't as if Paul had

any claim on Winnie. One night didn't grant him any special
privileges. *You owe me . . . Grandpa.*

Sam straightened, withdrawing from the tempting proximity of Winnie's lips. "Woman, you best keep your distance,"
he said quietly. "I'm rough around the edges sometimes, but
my ma raised a gentleman." He drew a shuddering breath. "I
got my limits, though."

Thanks. Paul's mind filled with relief. Winnie was safe
from Sam—for a while. If only Paul could find a way to
speak to her directly, instead of through his unwelcome and
often uncooperative passenger. Though, at this point, Sam
seemed more like a chauffeur than a passenger. He was definitely behind the wheel.

Winnie nodded and stepped back slowly. "Then answer
my question." She pulled her lips into a thin line and tilted
her head at a cocky angle. "If you're really a gentleman,
then tell me how and what you know about me. I can tell
you're hiding something."

He isn't the only one.

Sam sighed and shook his head. "Winnie, I don't know
nothin' about where you come from or who you are. Does
that answer your question?"

Paul saw tears glistening in her eyes. Lantern light glittered on a lone tear trickling down her lovely face. He ached
to reach out and brush it away, if only he could. He was
useless. Winnie needed help, but he couldn't give it to her.
If only he could find a means of letting her know she wasn't
alone. Maybe knowing she had company in this nightmare
would offer her some reassurance. Maybe.

Guilt manifested in Paul's mind, then bloomed into something almost tangible. He felt his gut twist and churn, despite
Sam's control over Paul's physical being. The lawman laid a
hand across his abdomen. It seemed only fair that Paul should
be able to effect some discomfort in his own body, particularly
since his anxiety was causing it. After all, if Paul's thoughts
could trigger Sam's libido, why not a little heartburn?

Poetic justice.

"Must be them beans."

Winnie touched his arm again, concern etched across her features. "Are you all right, Sam?" She frowned. "You look sort of . . . green."

Sam clenched his teeth and delivered a string of silent curses that would've made Cheech and Chong blush.

Paul couldn't resist rubbing it in a little. *Satisfaction. It feels good. Damn good.*

"Speak for yourself," Sam whispered.

"Excuse me?" Winnie leaned toward Sam. "Did you say something? Are you all right?"

"Yeah." Sam straightened and drew another deep breath. "I'm all right now."

"Maybe you'd better sit down for a while."

"Yeah. I reckon so."

Just keep your hands, and the rest of your—my—body off Winnie.

"See. There they are." Amanda pointed at the couple as they moved toward a bench near the dance floor. "My new *governess* and Marshal Weathers. See? He *is* here, just like I told you."

Buck Landen leaned against the top rail of the rough fence as he contemplated this interesting development. How the hell could Sam Weathers be up walking around? Corpses didn't walk, talk or dance. "Shit."

"I'll thank you to watch your language around a lady," Amanda said, batting her inky lashes.

"Lady, my ass."

Her gasp of outrage was almost believable. Buck smiled inwardly, then turned his attention back to the impossible sight of Sam Weathers—alive and well.

How could it be? Rage welled up within him, clouded his judgment for a few moments, then settled low in his gut to guide his thoughts. Weathers was alive. As impossible as it seemed, the lawman had obviously survived Buck's well-aimed blade. He took a step backward, away from the dance floor and out of the lantern light. It would never do for the marshal to see him just now.

Dammit, Weathers. I didn't wanna kill you in the first place—now you're gonna make me do it again.

"Well?"

Amanda's whining penetrated his thoughts and rattled his bones. God, that girl was infuriating. He raked her with his gaze. She was also a hot-blooded woman when the need arose, which it often did. Sighing, he decided that more than made up for the other. It wasn't every day a man was granted the opportunity to bed a girl half his age. She was young and supple, plump in all the right places.

"Well, what?"

"Didn't you hear a word I said?" She sighed dramatically and put her hand on her hip. "Why're you hiding back there in the dark, Buck Lan—"

"Shh." He grabbed her wrist and pulled her toward him, easing his way back into the shadow of an old shed. When she parted her lips to speak again, he covered her mouth with a smoldering kiss. He lifted his face to gaze down at her, hoping he'd distracted her for a moment so he could think. "Mmm, you taste good, woman."

Amanda giggled. "Ah, Buck. You're so naughty and nasty. Daddy'd whip us both if he heard you talk like that." She tilted her head to the side. "Will you help me get rid of that woman?"

Surprised by her request, he straightened and moved slightly away, but kept his arms around her shoulders. "Get rid of her?" He studied her for a long moment, wondering if she knew exactly what she was asking. Moonlight revealed the fury blazing in her dark eyes and gave him his answer. She knew, all right. Chuckling, he shook his head. "Amanda, sometimes I think you're worse than me."

Amanda laid her cheek against his shoulder. "I'll . . . *do* it again with you." She pulled away and looked up at him. "If you'll do this for me."

Hell, he knew she'd lay with him even if he refused to help her get rid of the woman. She was always willing, even before he'd been fired from his job at the Lazy H. Now, every time he showed up at the ranch, she was there, ready to give him what he needed. He glanced at her. There was something about Amanda that made him feel almost guilty for taking advantage of her innocence. If he could get rid of Weathers once and for all, then he might be able to finally settle down . . .

She pressed her full breasts against his chest. Raw, physical need vanquished his brief flash of guilt. He didn't have time for that—not right now. Buck was a wanted man in Kansas, Missouri, Arkansas, and Oklahoma Territory. Not so long ago, Indian Territory'd been his only safe place to hide. Until Sam Weathers. Getting rid of that pesky lawman would simplify things considerably.

Almost had.

"Damn lawman."

"Hmm?" Amanda looked up. "What'd you say, Buck?"

"Nothin' important." He reached up to test the weight of her breast. "You want rid of that governess lady awful bad, Amanda. Why?"

Amanda tensed in his embrace. "I . . . I just do."

" 'Cuz she got too close to somethin' you want."

Amanda looked toward the dance floor, then back up at Buck. "Yes," she hissed, her black eyes glittering angrily in the moonlight. "You ain't ever gonna make an honest woman out of me, so why not Sam Weathers? I gotta look out for myself. Besides, Pa likes him."

Jealousy built deep inside Buck, twisting his gut into a knot, but he'd be damned if he'd allow it to overshadow his sense of reason. What did it really matter if Amanda wanted to hitch herself up with an old man? That didn't mean she couldn't continue to pleasure him from time to time. And like she'd said, he wasn't about to get married. At least, not as long as he was a wanted man.

He grinned. Besides, Sam Weathers wasn't going to live long enough to walk down the aisle with anyone. He looked toward the bench where the lawman sat laughing with the redheaded governess. Maybe Amanda was right about them. If Weathers really was sweet on the woman, Buck may have just found a soft spot in Sam's tough hide.

Getting rid of Sam Weathers would solve more than one problem. It'd help Buck keep Amanda for himself and get the law off his trail.

Filled with determination, he dragged in a deep breath. That nagging voice in the back of his mind wouldn't let him rest until the running was over. He knew that now. Buck Landen didn't desire to be a wanted man for the rest of his life. If he could get rid of Weathers, he'd be able to assume a new identity here in the Territory—with Amanda.

"Yeah, Amanda," he promised, continuing to stare at the couple. "I'll get rid of her."

"All right, but don't hurt her," she warned. "Just . . . take her away somewhere and scare her real good."

He looked down at her, noticed the soft trembling of her lower lip. Why did this young girl make him go all soft inside? Any other woman would have had him heading in the opposite direction by now, but he kept coming back for more with this one. It wasn't his way, but it was the way he wanted it. For now.

He sighed, then shrugged. "Not until you gimme what you promised," he said suggestively, turning toward the dark woods beyond the barn. He tugged on her hand. "C'mon."

Amanda giggled, then permitted Buck to lead her away from the festivities and into the forest. "We'd better hurry, or Pa'll have *her* lookin' for me."

Buck chuckled. "You ain't gonna have nothing to worry about from her much longer." *Sam'll be the one lookin' . . . but it'll be for her, not you.*

Nine

Sam shifted his weight in the saddle, then guided Lucifer up a hill toward the ranch. "You're gonna do right by that girl."

Paul couldn't believe this. Here he was, stranded in the past with a maniac in control, being informed that *he* was the villain of the piece. *Stay out of it, Sam. It's none of your business.*

"The hell I will. I reckon as your great-great-grandpa, I got some rights. Even if I am dead. I spent some time with her this evenin', but you know that. She's a nice woman, who deserves to be treated fair."

How could Paul argue with that bit of wisdom? Winnie was a nice woman and she did deserve fair treatment . . . and then some. Had Paul really mistreated her, though? Guilt crowded its way into his thoughts, ignoring the fact that there was no room. *Damn.*

"Rufus said we could bunk at the ranch again for the night."

A curious blending of melancholy, guilt and excitement flooded Paul's mind. *Winnie's there.*

"Forget it."

Damn, damn, damn. Will you stop reading my mind? Over and over again, Paul had to remind himself that he had no physical privacy and very little mental. *You're so concerned that I do right by Winnie—whatever the hell that means—yet every time I even think about her, you jump down my throat.*

Sam laughed and shook his head. "I reckon I really did jump down your throat, in a way. Didn't I?"

You got in here somehow. If only Paul could figure out how to reverse the situation, not that it would really do him any good. Like it or not, Paul knew he wouldn't abandon Sam in his quest, even if the opportunity presented itself. More and more, Paul realized this was his destiny. Sam's murderer *should* be taken to justice. What possible reason could there be for fate to have swept Paul back in time, if not to remedy that historical error?

No matter what it took, Buck Landen would go to jail. And much as Paul hated to admit it, if the law of the land demanded Buck be hanged, then so be it. So much for his opposition to capital punishment.

So, when do we find Landen and take him to jail? It was past time to get this mission underway and over with. *I'd like to finish this trip to the dark side as soon as possible.*

"Dark side? It ain't so dark tonight." Sam looked up at the nearly full moon. "Not with that big moon hangin' over us. Look. You can even see the man in the moon tonight. Besides, what's your hurry?"

What's the hurry? Now that's a stupid question, if I ever heard one. And if you think the man in the moon's impressive, remind me to tell you about men walking on the moon sometime. Paul would give almost anything for the simple ability to punch something, preferably his great-great-grandfather.

Sam chuckled and shook his head. "Men walkin' on the moon. Boy, I dunno what you're jawin' about now." He sighed. "You didn't answer me. What's your hurry?"

I have an eight o'clock tee-time on Friday.

God, I just want to get back to my own life—my own world. My own time. Can't you understand that? If you'd been brought forward to my time, wouldn't you want to find a way to get back here?

"I reckon. For George, I'd do about anything." Sam sighed, then shrugged. "What about Winnie?"

What about her? Paul suppressed the disturbing thoughts popping into his mind. He didn't want Sam to know his true feelings on this issue. As the days went by, Paul was becoming more and more efficient at keeping his thoughts to himself. At least, with a little luck, that might grant him *some* intellectual confidentiality. Besides, his musings about Winnie Sinclair were confusing enough when he was the only one reacting to them.

"Now, are you gonna do right by her?"

Paul tried to think of something really disgusting to bombard his great-great-grandfather with, but all he could think of was Winnie. It was his fault she was here in this mess. She'd been in the wrong place at the wrong time . . . and with the wrong man. She didn't deserve any of this. What if he did manage to return to his own time without her? Was it possible? Maybe Sam was right. He did owe Winnie something. Identifying it was the problem. *Will you please define, exactly, what you mean by "do right?"*

"Oh, I reckon you oughta know what I mean easy enough. Besides, I remember tellin' you once before, when we was goin' up to Coffeyville." Sam guided his horse through the gate at the Lazy H, then stopped to dismount. As he dropped to the ground, he released his breath in a slow whoosh. "What the hell do you think I mean?"

Judging from your Victorian morals, I suppose you mean . . . marriage, but—

"You suppose right." Sam shook his head, then led Lucifer toward the dark barn.

The ranch was quiet and serene, bathed in moonlight. Stars were sprinkled across the sky like diamonds across a bed of black velvet. An awesome silence held the night in its grip. Each star seemed to promise adventure. Paul was beginning to understand the power of the land that had attracted so many emigrants westward during the nineteenth century. It was chilling, humbling and intriguing. *Beautiful night.*

"Yep, but I ain't gonna let you change the subject. You

slept with her, now marry her. 'Course, it should've been the other way around."

Paul was more than a little uncomfortable with this line of conversation, and he wasn't ready to ask himself why. For some reason, he wasn't prepared to hear or accept the potential answer. *This is none of your business.*

"The hell it ain't." Sam opened the gate and led Lucifer into the paddock, where he loosened the cinch, slid the heavy saddle off and slung it over the fence rail. "I reckon it's on account of me she's here. The least I can do is see to it my offspring does right by her."

I'm not your offspring, dammit. My great-grandfather— George—is your offspring.

"Yep, that's true." Sam shook his head. "It's kinda comforting, knowing my son'll really grow up an' be a pa someday."

Yeah. Sam really knew how to play that line to the hilt. Problem was, it worked. Paul tried to keep his perturbing thoughts to himself while Sam whistled low and rubbed Lucifer down with the rough saddle blanket. After measuring a ration of something that looked like lumpy Cheerios for the animal, Sam turned toward the house. He stood staring in that direction for several minutes.

"Tell me somethin', Paul."

What now?

"Why *don't* you wanna marry up with Winnie?" He rubbed his jaw, shifted his weight. "She's sure pretty enough. Smart, too."

Yeah, she's gorgeous and the best—er, never mind. I never planned to marry anyone. I'm a confirmed bachelor. I like it that way. How could Paul make his great-great-grandfather comprehend the world Paul and Winnie had left behind? Marriages were no more resilient than a paper license . . . or divorce decree. *Why didn't you want to marry fat Louise up in Coffeyville?*

"She ain't fat." Sam clenched his teeth. "Besides, Louise

is a whole lot different than Winnie. I think even you can see that." He removed his hat and raked his fingers through his perspiration-drenched hair. "Louise chose to be what she is. She even told me she likes workin' in the saloon. So, if you're tryin' to tell me Winnie Sinclair's a harlot, I ain't gonna believe you."

Harlot? Oh, you mean a prostitute. No, of course not. Guilt, guilt and more guilt surged within Paul. Why the hell was Sam doing this to him? It was bad enough the man had commandeered his body. Now Sam wanted the rest of Paul's life—what was left of it, anyway. *It's nothing against Winnie personally, I just don't want to get married. Besides . . . she wouldn't want me, anyway.*

"Now I don't believe *that* either." Sam shook his head again and clicked his tongue. "A lady like Winnie don't just up and . . . give herself to a man if she ain't at least thinkin' about marriage. And there ain't nothin' you can say to make me believe she would."

Not only was Sam able to read Paul's thoughts, he was beginning to predict them. Real inconvenient. *That's now, Sam. In my time, women are liberated. They do what they want, sleep with—*

"Hold on a minute. I don't wanna hear this." Sam pressed his hands over his ears. "Ah, hell. That ain't gonna work, is it?"

Welcome to the club. It was Paul's turn to chuckle. If only he could actually laugh, feel tears of hysterics sting his eyes and get a really good catch in his side. His unsatisfying mental mirth abruptly ceased. This was the pits.

"So, you gonna do right by—"

Will you just shut up about that for now? Paul needed time to think—in private. *Besides, it isn't exactly like I can walk up the aisle under my own power.*

"I dunno. There might be a way." Sam pursed his lips together. "For now, though, I reckon we can put it to rest for the night." He walked slowly toward the house. "Rufus said we could take my usual room. Said he'd tell June to leave the door open for us."

Us? Really?

"You know what I mean." Sam continued to grumble beneath his breath as he made his way onto the porch.

Why'd we really come back here, Sam? I thought you were looking for Landen.

"I am."

Suspicion filled Paul's mind. There was more going on here than his ancestor was saying. *Sam?*

Sam paused and sighed, turning to look out across the pasture. "I got a pretty good reason to suspect that Landen shows up here on a regular basis."

Here? I heard Rufus say he hadn't seen him in a year. The possibility of a cold-blooded murderer lurking anywhere near the Lazy H terrified Paul. *Ah, hell.* He knew the real reason for his anxiety. Forget the ranch, he was worried about Winnie.

"Oh, I don't reckon Rufus *knows* Landen comes around." Sam chuckled and released the kerchief at his throat. After wiping the perspiration from his face, he stuffed the soiled article into his shirt pocket. "Landen comes around to see Amanda, not Rufus."

She's just a kid.

"Yep." Sam sighed again. "But she's been in one helluva big hurry to grow up ever since her ma died."

I see. Paul contemplated this information for a few minutes. *So, you think Buck Landen and Amanda Hopsador are having an affair.*

"That's the way I figger it." Sam chewed on his lower lip, then leaned against the porch railing. "I think it's been goin' on for quite a spell, too."

That's sick. What is she—about seventeen?

"I reckon." Sam shrugged. "There's lots of women married with a houseful of babies by that age in these parts. I'd say most of them."

Again, Paul grappled with his emerging awareness of the drastic differences between the nineteenth and twentieth centuries. At this moment, he was doubly glad he wasn't a father, especially one with a daughter. A seventeen-year-old girl having an affair with an outlaw? *That sucks.*

Sam chuckled. "Well, if that means it's a bad thing, it sure as hell does."

It does. Paul wondered what all this really meant—how it affected his situation. *And Winnie's.*

"So, you gonna do right by Winnie?"

Back to that again? Dammit, I told you marriage isn't in the cards for me. Will you leave it alone? Paul was furious and helpless, a combination worthy of masochistic distinction, for sure. *Winnie doesn't want to marry me anyway. Why don't you just accept it? I don't think she'd be happy to see me again—ever.*

Sam was quiet for several moments, for which Paul was grateful. A barrage of unanswered questions exploded in his mind, threatened his resolve against a lifelong commitment to any woman.

"I know you still want her the way a man wants a woman on a cold winter's night, and lots of other nights, too." Sam blew out his breath very slowly. His voice was low and hoarse. "By God, you've made that clear as rain."

What man wouldn't want her? Except for her ex-husband, Dirk Sinclair, the idiot. *She's gorgeous.*

Sam nodded. "I still think you should do the right thing and propose."

God, give me strength. Sam, she doesn't . . . want . . . to marry . . . me. Did you understand that this time? I tried to explain this to you the other day, but you wouldn't listen. By God, you're going to listen now. Paul mentally counted to ten. *I was Winnie's husband's divorce lawyer. Do you know what that means?*

Sam stiffened and pulled away from the railing. "You were what?"

Oh, great. I've really screwed up this time.

"You're what kinda lawyer?"

Paul wasn't frightened of telling his great-great-grandfather what he'd done for a living. He was ashamed. Being a divorce attorney hadn't been his chosen profession. When his father'd died, Paul had inherited a partnership in the old man's law firm. Paul had promised himself it would only be temporary, until he made enough money to open his own law office somewhere, practicing criminal or constitutional law. Something noble.

He wanted respect in the legal community—something readily available to almost any type of attorney except those specializing in divorces or frivolous malpractice suits. Then again, maybe chasing ambulances would've been a more worthy endeavor.

The financial reward from marital destruction was too easy. The steady stream of clients, most with simple uncontested cases, had provided Paul with a comfortable income. Months turned into years and his grandiose plans faded into the background as his bitterness toward matrimony in general festered.

How could a single man watch relationships dissolve for years the way he had without feeling a great deal of reluctance toward taking the plunge himself? Marriage was a farce, one he had no intention of experiencing.

No way.

"I asked you what kinda lawyer you said you was," Sam said in a carefully controlled voice.

A divorce lawyer.

"Divorce." Sam shook his head. "That's a terrible business. I've heard of it, but never know'd anyone who'd done it before. Shameful, just shameful."

Paul didn't bother to respond. The life he'd left behind—rather, ahead—now appeared in a different light. From his present position, a hundred years in the past, he saw it as more distinct and unsatisfying than it had been when he was right in the middle of it.

It wasn't that he'd assisted people through divorces which made him feel like a failure. He'd provided people in a very precarious situation with a service; whether divorce was right or wrong was irrelevant. No, he was disgusted with *himself,* not so much for guiding people through divorces, because most of them had really needed and deserved any help he could offer, but for allowing his own dreams to be pushed aside, unfulfilled. Not pursuing his dreams was nothing less than criminal.

Shameful. Yeah, that's the word.

Winnie placed her hand across her stomach and frowned. For the third morning in a row, she'd awakened with a queasy sensation she'd rather not define. It couldn't be. They'd been careful.

Five times.

"Oh, God." Groaning, she pressed her hand to her forehead and swung her legs to the floor. She drew a deep, fortifying breath and held it for a few seconds, then slowly released it. Feeling a little more stable, she pushed to her feet. Her head felt light and the room went black for a fleeting moment.

"No," she whispered, gripping a bedpost. "Oh, no. Not that—anything but that."

Yet she had to consider the possibility. "I don't believe this." She waited until her vision cleared, then walked slowly into the bathroom to splash her face with cool water. Feeling considerably more human, she dressed for the day, then stood staring at the mirror in the corner of her room.

She took a step closer to study her reflection. "I don't look any different. Except for these stupid clothes." She glanced down at the beige calico dress, the tiny brown flowers seeming to mock her melancholy with their simplistic cheeriness.

As her gaze traveled upward, taking in her slim waist, Winnie gasped when she noticed how tight the fabric was stretched across her breasts. "Uh-oh," she murmured, laying her hand over her swollen breast. She closed her eyes in disbelief. Reluctantly, she reopened them. Her breasts looked heavy and were tender to the touch.

"Gee, Winnie," she said with a grimace to the image in the mirror. "If you'd paid closer attention in sex education class, maybe you wouldn't be in this mess. At least you might remember the symptoms."

There was one symptom she should've been aware of right away. Winnie's eyes grew round and her face paled noticeably, prompting her to turn away from the mirror and stagger to the bed. She slumped down to the edge of the feather bed and searched her mind.

Be logical, Winnie. Think. Numbers were logical—weren't they? *One, two, three, four* . . . "Oh, Lord. That can't be right." Her last period had been a couple of weeks before . . . that night. Shaken, she recounted the weeks since her quantum leap—*as if I did it deliberately*—using her fingers for accuracy this time. There was no point in arguing with herself. Six weeks had passed since her last cycle. Six weeks.

"I'm pregnant."

How could that be? She searched her mind, recalled the morning after her decadent night of abandonment. In her mind, she again counted the empty packets on the cabin floor. There'd been five of them, so how could she be pregnant? It wasn't possible. Five condoms for five . . . times. Surely she'd have known and remembered if one of them had broken.

Wouldn't she?

"Oh, Lord."

Winnie ran her hand over her face and moaned. Another image flaunted itself in her mind, bringing a flash of heat to her face. "Five times. Right? *Only*—jeez—five?"

As she considered the enormity of her situation, Winnie forced herself to remember each time in as much detail as she possibly could. She remembered the first time the most graphically, that sweet urgency with which Paul had made her his . . . at least for a night. Yes, they'd very definitely used protection.

She brought her hand to her lips—it trembled as she recalled him tearing open the packet and allowing her to roll it slowly down his very impressive erection. Her insides coiled into a tight spring, aching to burst free in sexual abandonment.

Again.

"No, Winnie. That's the last thing you need." She drew a deep breath, then forced herself to make a mental mark for one episode. "That's one."

She closed her eyes for a moment. The room was very warm. She tugged at her collar, loosened the top button and mopped moisture from her neck. *Think, Winnie.* The storm had sent them rolling onto the floor, where they'd proceeded to engage in some additional rolling on their own. Paul had reached into her upended overnight bag and grabbed an entire handful of packaged condoms, opening one and putting it on himself that time. As she recalled, he'd been in a big hurry. Still, they'd taken the time to protect themselves.

She had a vague recollection of Paul pouring them each another brandy. *Just what I didn't need.* They'd been on the bunk, both sipping their drinks, when the storm had caused the boat to rock, knocking Paul's glass from his hand. A slow smile of remembrance tugged at the corners of her mouth as she warmed all over. The brandy had spilled across her breasts and abdomen. Paul had insisted they not waste a single drop. . . .

My, were we that creative? Again, she recalled helping him put on a condom. "All right. That's three."

She stood and walked over to the window. The ledge beside the window reminded her of something else that had happened that night. "Surely not." A throaty chuckle bubbled up from her chest. She recalled something amazing about a barstool, with Paul on his feet.

Had they really done it that way, too?

Oh, yes—we did.

Winnie opened the window and leaned out to look at the bright and mocking new morning. "Did we use protection?" she whispered, chewing her fingernail in contemplation. A very detailed image of her barely putting it on before he'd filled her with himself provided her answer. Relieved, she sighed. Yes, they had. "That's four."

The fifth one was easy. Her face grew warm as she remembered Paul telling her she had magnificent breasts. He'd actually said magnificent. Involuntarily, her hand fell to her breast where she felt her nipple harden into a bud of anticipation.

"Oh, Lord."

Just the thought of that night—of that man—aroused her beyond any sense of reason. She wasn't even drunk now, so she couldn't place the blame on the brandy. Only on herself . . . and nature.

That fifth time—the sex people only dreamed of—had been the best. Winnie felt warm and funny inside, like gelatin that hadn't completely set. Her insides liquified in expectancy and she cursed herself for wanting him again. Foolishly wanting him.

Well, it didn't matter what she wanted. Paul Weathers was a considerable distance from her. She struggled with a surge of disappointment, then drew a deep breath and closed her eyes. *Think, Winnie.*

She'd sat astride him while he laid on the floor, propped against the edge of the bunk. He'd been buried deep—*really* deep—inside her as she permitted herself to completely let go, to take him in a way she'd never imagined a woman could. The sense of control had been—

But did we use protection?

Yes, she remembered, as relief flooded her. *That's five.* She was safe. Unless the condom had leaked . . . That was unlikely, though. She was simply being paranoid. After all, time travel probably messed a woman's cycle up royally. Her gynecologist would've had a field day with this one.

A movement out by the barn drew Winnie's gaze. Sam. He was staring at her as he leaned against the corral fence. From this distance, his resemblance to Paul took Winnie's breath away. It was incredible. Tears stung her eyes and she wondered briefly why she was reacting so powerfully to her imagination. Sam wasn't Paul, and even if he had been, it shouldn't matter to her. Not one bit.

Yet it did.

"Why?" she asked herself, chewing her lower lip in consternation as she watched him lift his hand to wave. Hesitantly, she waved back. As nice as Sam was, at this moment Winnie would have given anything for the power to magically transform him into his descendant—her one-night lover.

Watching Sam brought another memory to her mind in a flood of realization that struck her like a tornado, twisting her emotions and fears into a unique blend of awe and terror.

Winnie forced herself to turn away from the handsome lawman. She rushed to the mirror and stared in dawning realization, half expecting to see a reenactment of the truth in the silver. "Oh, my God."

She clutched her collar and loosened yet another button, pulling it away from her constricting throat as she struggled to breathe. The memory returned, stronger this time, insisting she face it. "Oh, my God."

Again, she closed her eyes, which only served to sharpen the images in her mind. Winnie was in Paul's arms. He was carrying her into the head, where he turned on the crude shower and bathed her with lukewarm water. He'd tasted and teased her until she'd been ready to scream from the sheer want of him. Her face heated as she graphically recalled imparting equal treatment to his magnificent body.

Then he'd taken her—filled her with all of him right there in that tiny shower stall. Completely unprotected—drunk and dauntless.

Winnie swallowed hard and forced her eyes open. Heat flooded her face as she recalled the ecstasy of being with Paul again and again.

One time too many.

Ten

"Marshal."

Dragging his gaze from the window where Paul had seen Winnie only a moment before, Sam turned to face Amanda. "Mornin'."

She moved closer than she should have, provoking Sam to step back. Unfortunately, he was right against the corral fence, unable to retreat any farther from the steadily advancing female.

She's on the prowl, isn't she? Paul mentally squirmed while his great-great-grandfather struggled with the natural male reaction to the nearness of an attractive member of the opposite sex.

Sam leaned away as Amanda stepped nearer, actually brushing her full breasts against his chest. Even Paul felt the physical reaction to the girl's seduction. It couldn't be called anything else. Despite her youth, she was coming on to Sam with everything she had.

And she had plenty.

Damn. Tell her to go home and play with dolls or something. Paul took comfort in the knowledge that Sam didn't want Amanda. Even though he couldn't prevent a natural physical response, Paul felt confident that this time Sam could resist the urge to appease it without assistance from Paul.

"I'm glad you come back for me, Marshal Weathers. Sam," she added in a sultry whisper, then stepped even closer, pressing herself against him even closer. Black lashes veiled her dark eyes as she leaned into him. "Real glad."

"I think you best go on back to the house, Amanda." Sam's voice was gruff and strained, precisely echoing Paul's feelings. "Your pa wouldn't like this."

Her pa isn't the only one.

Amanda bristled, but made no effort to move away. "But he likes you, Sam." She moistened her lips slowly, sensuously. "And I *really* like you."

"No, Amanda. This ain't right." Sam shook his head with deliberate slowness. "I'm near as old as your Pa. Besides, Rufus happens to be a friend of mine. He trusts me and I reckon I'd like to keep it that way. I know what you think you're after, but I ain't so sure you *really* know what you're doin'."

"Oh, I know." Amanda rubbed herself back and forth across his chest, then brought her hand forward in the folds of her skirt to press it against his erection. "See? You do want me."

Oh, damn. This is sick. Paul could just imagine himself being tried for having sex with a minor. What had his fraternity brothers called girls like Amanda? *Jail bait. San Quentin quail.*

"San Quentin what?"

"What'd you say?" Amanda asked, pursing her lips into a sensual pout. "I know you want me, Sam. This proves it, don't it? You can't hide that from me or anybody else." Her lusty laughter surrounded them.

Sam nodded. "Ain't many men who wouldn't want it when it's flaunted in front of them. Just 'cuz it's being offered, don't mean I'm gonna take it, though. Now go on up to the house before somebody sees you carryin' on like this."

Bingo. As Amanda straightened and stepped back, Paul felt a sigh of relief, even if he couldn't actually manage the real thing.

Amanda jerked her hand back with the obvious intention

of slapping him, but Sam grabbed her wrist, intercepting the action. "That's enough. Go on back to the house now." Sam's voice was carefully controlled.

"You're gonna be sorry," she taunted. "B—uh, I'm gonna take care of her."

Sam tensed. Paul was aware of every nerve ending in his body coming to life as his ancestor sprang to alertness. "What'd you say?" Sam's voice held a virulent edge.

Amanda flipped her dark hair over one shoulder and her black eyes flashed. The air between them snapped with anger. "I know you want me, Sam," she insisted again. When Sam failed to respond, she narrowed her lips to a thin line. "Fine. You'll learn. After *she's* gone, you'll see that I'm all the woman you need."

Amanda turned and stomped toward the house. Paul watched with Sam until the girl was near the front steps, at which point she turned to stare. Then she brought her hand to her lips and blew him a kiss.

She's not going to give up that easy. You know that.

The moment Amanda was inside, Sam took three long strides and bent down to retrieve a crumpled piece of paper from the ground. Clutching it in his hand, Sam moved to the side of the barn, where they couldn't be seen from the house.

What's that?

"I reckon you read as good as me. Probably better." Sam unfolded the paper and held it in front of him. "Ah, hell." He sighed, but every muscle tensed. "Damn. That's what I was afraid of." He started to stuff the crumpled paper into his pocket.

Wait. I didn't get a chance to read it.

Emitting a sound of disgust and impatience, Sam retrieved the note and held it in front of his eyes again. "There, now read it and you'll see what it is I been worried about."

Buck—take her tomorrow night.

"See?"

Buck? It must be Landen. What does it mean, Sam? Fear

clouded Paul's sense of reason until realization dawned. *Oh, my God. Winnie.*

"That's how I got it figgered." Sam sighed and shook his head. "Amanda's jealous, and somehow she's found a way to contact Landen." He balled one hand into a fist and punched his other palm. "She musta been plannin' to leave this note for him."

Paul tried to follow his ancestor's meaning. Why was Sam so worried when the note was right here? *Well, now he won't get it.*

"I reckon she'll just write another. Either way, she's gonna get hold of Landen. That's clear."

And convince him to . . . take Winnie away?

Sam nodded, then shoved the paper into his pocket. "I reckon we could wait and ambush him after he—"

No. Paul knew beyond all suspicion that he couldn't allow Sam to endanger Winnie. She meant something to him— something much more important than a one-night stand. *Sam, I care about her.*

"Well, it's about time you figgered that out." Sam chuckled and nodded, then rubbed the back of his neck. "Now you gonna do right by her?"

Paul had walked right into Sam's trap. A sudden suspicion struck him. *Is the note real, or did you make this all up to trick me?* For some reason, Paul didn't mind being trapped this time. He hadn't spent enough time with Winnie to know what it was about her—exactly—that drove him crazy with wanting her, but he knew enough to realize it was a whole hell of a lot more than just sex. Even more than great sex.

"Nope, it's real." Sam chewed his lower lip thoughtfully. "Tell you what, Paul."

Uh-oh.

"You promise to do right by Winnie and I'll see to it Landen don't get his hands on her tonight."

Blackmail, Sam?

"Yep." Sam nodded emphatically, folding his arms across

his chest as he looked up at the sky. "Whatever it takes. I've spent enough time with that gal to know she'll be a good ma for my great-great-great-grandchildren."

Paul couldn't argue with that. Funny thing was, he didn't want to. Was he losing his mind? Marry Winnie? Here and now? He knew what had to be done. More importantly, it was what he wanted. Of course, deep in his gut, he knew Sam would never let Landen harm Winnie, even if Paul refused to do his bidding.

If Winnie'll have me, you've got yourself a deal, Sam.

Pacing the floor in her room, Winnie clutched the crumpled paper in her hand and shook her head. She was so bewildered. Each time she came face to face with Sam, that nagging doubt plagued her anew. And now *this*.

Logic insisted he couldn't be Paul and she'd always prided herself on being a sensible person—except for one very memorable night. Then why was she persistently plagued with dreams of her brief liaison with Paul? Wonderful, erotic dreams that left her quaking with longing when she awakened, tangled in sweat-soaked sheets.

Alone.

Suppressing a shudder of primitive longing, Winnie drew a deep breath and unfolded the note. She blinked twice, checking to see if the words had changed from the last time she'd read them. They hadn't.

Winnie, If you want answers, I got them. Meet me out behind the barn at midnight. Sam.

She ran her fingers beneath the curls on the back of her neck and lifted them to permit the evening air to reach her damp flesh. It was hot, even for early July. God, how she missed air conditioning, refrigerators full of cold beverages, and freezers with ice-makers.

"You're avoiding the issue, Winnie," she said aloud in a mocking tone. *Ooookay—so do I go?*

She sat on the edge of the bed and stared at her open window, where the lace curtains fluttered in the breeze. Why couldn't she get Paul out of her mind? This note wasn't from Paul, no matter how much his ancestor might look like him. It was from Sam Weathers, a nineteenth-century lawman. Was this Sam's way of luring her out so he could . . .

Oh, Lord.

Was she destined to be tormented by a member of the Weathers family, regardless of the century? *That's ridiculous.* But even as she tried to force the thought aside, it insistently took root and flourished. "Just what I needed—a man for all centuries." Of course, her near certainty that she was carrying Paul's child didn't do a thing for her ability to reason.

How could she explain all this away as simple coincidence? "Well, you see . . . I spent the night with my ex-husband's divorce attorney, woke up the next morning and traveled back in time, found out I was pregnant, then had an affair with his ancestor. Just to make sure?"

Would Paul end up being his own great-grandfather? "Oh, yuck. Will that make me his . . . great-grandmother?" Groaning, Winnie rolled her eyes and looked up at the ceiling, then flopped back on the bed with her legs dangling off the edge. "God, this is really crazy."

She held the note up in front of her face while she remained flat on her back. Yet again she was reminded of Paul's searing touch, his fiery kisses, the urgent way he'd made love to her . . . a hundred years in the future.

The note only said Sam had answers. Problem was, how'd he know she had any questions? Her first impression, that he was simply trying to get her alone to seduce her, seemed more plausible every time she thought about it.

No matter how much she fantasized, yearned or needed, the man who'd written this note wasn't Paul. And it was Paul she wanted—not Sam. That damned attorney was still messing up her life from another century.

This gives entirely new meaning to the long distance phone company's slogan to "reach out and touch someone."

Instinctively, Winnie laid her hand protectively across her lower abdomen. Was Paul's baby growing inside her? She swallowed hard, then drew a deep breath.

If she was stuck here, then didn't it make sense for her to start thinking of a future for herself? For the baby? *Future—cute, Winnie.* Maybe even marriage and a father for her child?

Sam Weathers?

Her baby's real ancestor, with the same last name.

Winnie's heart raced even as her mind screamed "No," and she sat up straight in bed to stare at the small clock on the mantel. Dare she meet him? It was almost time.

She looked at the note again. He had answers. Lord knew she needed them. Drawing a deep breath, she squeezed her eyes shut for a moment, then opened them as she stood.

Right or wrong, she didn't want Sam, or any other man for that matter. She wanted Paul Weathers, a man she'd known intimately for one night. The most memorable, and unfortunate, night of her life. Was she doomed to pine away after a man who didn't care a thing about her, other than as a convenient bed partner on a stormy night? And more importantly, a man who hadn't even been born yet?

She almost laughed when she realized—should her pregnancy prove true—that Paul's offspring would be born before his or her father. The expected laughter didn't materialize, however, as Winnie struggled with a surge of conflicting emotions. How could she feel such a powerful bond with a man who'd represented her ex-husband in court? Paul Weathers had seen to it that the only thing Winnie'd walked away from her marriage with was herself and her car. Thanks to Paul's expertise, the house and business had remained with Dirk.

Nevertheless, Winnie had to resolve this issue once and for all. She smoothed her skirt and shoved the folded note into her pocket. It was past time she faced Sam Weathers about this. Those long looks he'd been broadcasting spelled "I want you" in a big way. She'd have to explain to him that she couldn't . . . do that. What she couldn't figure out was *why*. It wasn't as if she was married or engaged to anyone in any century. And she certainly found Sam attractive.

Yeah, and just look at how much trouble your last fling got you into, she silently chastised, then moved toward the door.

She'd just go out to the barn and tell Sam he was mistaken, that she didn't want him at all.

Though he could certainly pass as a substitute for the man I really do want. No, no, no.

There was always the very remote possibility that he really did have answers to her questions. The thought gave her pause. Could he know she was from the future? If so, he might be able to help her return.

No, he couldn't possibly know. She furrowed her brow in growing confusion. *Then how does he know I'm looking for answers?*

"Well, there's only one way to find out."

Lifting her chin and squaring her shoulders, Winnie quietly opened the door and stepped into the dark hallway. She took quick, silent steps down the hall and slipped out the back door.

It was cooler outside. She drew a deep breath, savoring the heady scents of honeysuckle and summer. The air was heavy with moisture, thick with pollen from the fertile countryside. Oklahoma summer nights were gorgeous in any century, she decided, then deliberately compelled her thoughts back to her current situation.

"Let's get this over with," she whispered into the night, turning toward the silhouette of the large barn, a short distance down the hill behind the house.

She hesitated at the front of the barn, then glanced nervously back toward the house. Her palms turned clammy and she wiped them against her skirt, regretting yet another im-

petuous decision. Should she turn around and go back? This
was a mistake. An alarm went off in her mind just as the
flesh on the back of her neck crawled, warning her she wasn't
alone.

Too late to turn back. She had to face Sam. And more
importantly, she had to face herself. It was time she put her
desire for Paul in the past—er, future—where it belonged.
She had to get on with her life, apparently in this time. *This
time* . . .

Squaring her shoulders, she half-turned to face the dark
figure leaning against the side of the barn, only a few yards
away. Moonlight bathed him in silver as he pushed away
from the building and swaggered toward her.

Definitely not Paul.

This cowboy-lawman was a far cry from the sophisticated
lawyer she'd spent the night with, yet every bit as sexy. She
took a deep breath and prepared herself to face him. It was
way past time she put this childish infatuation to rest.

"You came," he whispered, pausing less than an arm's
length away. "I didn't think you would."

Like Paul's, his voice crawled right inside her and did a
sexy little dance—just what she *didn't* need. "I—we need
to talk." Commanding herself not to tremble, she reached
into her pocket and retrieved the note, holding it out to him
in her open palm. "About this."

He nodded and took a step nearer. "What about it?"

Winnie moistened her dry lips as she struggled against an
onslaught of indefinable emotions. Why'd he have to be so
tall, so handsome, so sexy . . . so much like Paul? *Why?*
"What sort of answers do you have? If this is just a ploy
to . . ." She bit the inside of her cheek, then rushed ahead.
"I can't. I don't . . ."

He reached out and touched her shoulder, his fingers just
barely grazing her through the thin cotton fabric. "Can't
what?"

Winnie's knees trembled as she stared up at him. She felt

so feminine, so vulnerable . . . so damned foolish. "This," she blurted out, taking a nearly frantic step back. "I can't . . . *be* with you."

Sam sighed, long and deep. "Well, I didn't ask you to." He shrugged almost imperceptibly in the darkness. "You gotta come with me anyway if you want your answers."

Had she been mistaken about his intentions? Or did he mean to take her against her will? Winnie frowned and took another step back. "What do you mean, I have to come with you? Where?" She had a very bad feeling about this, which became even more pronounced when he took two steps toward her for each one she took in retreat, until she felt his breath on her cheek. The scent of leather and horse mingled with something else—something appealing and vaguely familiar.

Realization clobbered her. He smelled like *Paul*. No, that was impossible. There was absolutely no possibility that Paul's expensive cologne could have been invented yet. She was imagining things. Stimulating, dangerous things.

"I need to go back to the house," she whispered, suddenly fearing her own ability to maintain control. Had she spent her entire life being good, only to succumb to the charms of a man in the Weathers family *again?* No, she wouldn't let this happen. Look what it had cost her the first time.

Besides, this *wasn't* Paul. And, God help her, it was Paul she wanted. Only Paul.

Oh, Lord. A devastating sadness crept over her, enveloped her and squeezed her heart. Was she in love with Paul? Really in love with a man she'd spent one night with? No, she couldn't be. Could she?

Her throat convulsed as he took another step nearer. "Winnie," he whispered in a voice so like Paul's it made her ache. "Come with me. You really gotta."

Tears pricked her eyes and she looked up at him, silently pleading for his answer. Could he turn his Paul imitation on and off at will? Sam couldn't even know about Paul, except for the few times she'd accidentally mentioned his name, let alone pretend to be him. Imagination was a powerful and dangerous thing. "You're not Paul."

"Nope." He sighed and shook his head. "I ain't Paul. You know that, though. Don't you?"

She nodded slowly, flinching when he reached out and took her hand in his large, rough one. The calluses on the pads of his fingers sent shivers down her spine. "You're not Paul, and I'm losing what's left of my mind."

"No, you ain't." He sighed again, then mumbled something under his breath. "Listen, you gotta trust me. Come with me and . . ."

There was a moment of strained silence while Winnie tried to determine what he'd been about to say. Was he ready to tell her the truth? There was no doubt in her mind that he knew something more. She'd suspected it the night of the barn dance, but now she was certain. "You'll what?"

"I'll tell you everything," he promised, giving her hand a reassuring squeeze. "Listen, you're in danger here, Winnie. You gotta come with me."

She stared at his face in the moonlight for several moments. The silvery light made him a collection of colorless planes and angles. If only she could see his gray eyes, then she might convince her crazy imagination once and for all that he wasn't Paul. Some primitive instinct from deep inside her made Winnie's decision for her. She had to accompany Sam and learn what it was he wished to tell her. Did he know she was a time traveler? If so, could he tell her the secret that might help her return to her own time? Going with Sam Weathers was a risk she had to take.

"Okay, I'll come with you." His sharp intake of breath revealed his surprise at her decision. She drew a deep breath and lifted her chin. "Where are we going?"

"Just away, for starters." He pulled her toward the back of the barn. "I'll tell you why after it's safe."

"Safe?" Winnie didn't have the vaguest idea why he

thought she wasn't safe. Rufus Hopsador had treated her well since her arrival at the Lazy H. There was no reason to think she was in danger. "I am safe."

"You gotta trust me, Winnie. Remember, I'm a United States Marshal, sworn to uphold the law." He paused at the back of the barn and released her hand. "Just git on my horse now."

Winnie looked at the huge beast. Even in the darkness, she could tell this wasn't the same gentle, tolerant horse she'd ridden that lamentable day mere weeks ago. This one was as dark as the night and the whites of its eyes glowed when it turned its head to snort at her.

"No way." She took a step back, never taking her eyes off the beast. "I'm not getting on that thing."

Sam chuckled and pulled her hand. "Yeah, you are. Lucifer ain't as mean as he looks." He pointed to the saddle. "Now, please." He sighed and shook his head. "This is one stubborn woman."

He had a horse named Lucifer and now he was talking to himself. Maybe she should reconsider her decision. "I've changed my mind. I'm—"

"No, you ain't." Sam grabbed her around the waist and swung her into the saddle in one smooth motion. "Paul said for me to git you outta here, so that's what I'm gonna do."

Paul? Winnie felt as if the wind had been knocked right out of her. She couldn't draw a breath for several seconds. Was Paul here, too, in this time? With her?

"Paul's . . . here?" she asked, looking down at Sam from her equine perch. "Don't lie to me, Sam."

He stared up at her in total silence for several agonizing seconds, then pushed his hat back farther on his head and sighed. "All I can say for sure right now is you'll be seein' him real soon."

See him soon, her mind echoed. She was speechless as Sam put his foot in the stirrup and swung his long leg over the back of the horse. He was taking her to Paul, then maybe they could get out of this mess.

Together.

Sam settled his long, muscular frame behind her in the saddle, jarring Winnie from her reverie. She was suddenly and acutely aware of her backside and his groin in intimate contact as he guided the horse away from the Lazy H.

Except her mind was on another man and another night. In another time.

Paul couldn't imagine how he was going to manage this one. It'd been hell, convincing Sam to go along with his idea, and he wasn't about to give up now. After discovering Amanda's plans to have Winnie taken away by that murderer, he had to do something. Even Sam had agreed with that reasoning. It was about time they agreed on something besides when Paul's bladder was full.

Of course, there'd been a price to pay for Sam's cooperation. Now Paul was expected to "do right by Winnie." For all he knew, Sam could be taking Winnie to the nearest preacher. This was one hell of a sacrifice he was about to make.

She was worth it. Bachelorhood had been great, but saving Winnie from Buck Landen was far more important.

At least now his great-great-grandfather realized how much Paul and Winnie had sacrificed—without their consent—to help Sam take his killer to justice. Now if only Paul could keep his mind off Winnie's backside pressed so enticingly against the most vulnerable part of his anatomy . . .

"You better try harder," Sam quietly warned, guiding Lucifer through a ravine and up an incline.

Gravity pressed Winnie against his body, making Paul realize that he and Sam—damn, he hated sharing this—were already responding to her soft, feminine bottom. Paul's memory only fueled his desire.

"I ain't gonna be able to stand this, Paul," Sam mentally relayed, reaching up to mop perspiration from his forehead. "Especially not with you flashing them kinda pictures through my mind."

Then let me take over, Sam. He held his breath as the silence in his head mounted and Winnie's soft form became increasingly difficult—impossible—to ignore. He wanted to take her in his arms, to kiss her and touch her . . . to make love to her again. That marvelous release he'd found in her arms was the only thing he could think of right now. Would his great-great-grandfather deny him even this?

"No, I don't reckon I can," Sam's silent communication continued, as he shifted uncomfortably in the saddle. "But what in hell makes you think she's gonna believe it's you even if I leave?"

Good question. All Paul knew for certain was that he needed some time with Winnie, to explain this mess to her. And to be with her again . . . if she'd have him. This woman, who'd started out as nothing more than a spontaneous night of sexual abandonment, had become important to him. Hell, she was everything to him. Maybe it was their desperate situation fueling his emotions right now, but he knew what he felt for Winnie was worth pursuing. It might even be something lasting. After all, no matter what century they remained in, Sam couldn't possess his body forever.

Could he?

Sam sighed before conveying his speechless reassurance. "Nope. I told you once we take Landen to trial, I'll let you be."

Paul felt Winnie's tension. She looked left and right, then straight ahead, as if searching for something. For him? The way she'd brightened when Sam told her he was taking her to see Paul made him feel warm inside. She cared. He didn't know yet how much, but he knew she cared for him, as he did for her. More than he'd realized, hoped . . . or feared.

"I'll leave you for a while," Sam mutely promised, shifting

again in the saddle. "I sure as hell can't stand bein' this close without—ah, damn."

An irritating thought barged into Paul's mind. If Sam left his body in the obvious sense of the word, did that mean Paul would really be alone with Winnie? Or would Sam share everything in some spiritual way?

"What d'you think I am?" Sam's thoughts raged through Paul's head. "I may be a bit rough around the edges sometimes, but Ma raised me right."

Paul thanked God, and for the first time in weeks he felt there might be hope. *Thanks, Sam. I mean, Grandpa.* If Sam was willing to leave him some privacy tonight, then one day soon he'd give Paul back to himself permanently. Paul was sure of it now.

Guilt weighed heavily on his conscience as his ancestor's situation forced itself home. His great-great-grandfather was dead, and had only asked—well, maybe not asked—to borrow Paul's body long enough to avenge Sam's own death. That was all. And Sam was granting Paul this night of privacy. For a price. Winnie's safety plus this night with her in exchange for "doing right by Winnie."

He had to ask himself again. Was it worth it? Was *she* worth it? Unfortunately, yes. Winnie Sinclair was worth any sacrifice Paul had to make. If marriage was what Sam had in mind, then so be it. Paul was as good as married. Assuming of course, that Winnie'd be willing. She might very well take Sam's gun and blow Paul away once and for all. Hell, she had every right to do that and more. Look at the mess he'd dragged her into.

What was wrong with him? He was getting soft in his old age. Thinking about doing the honorable thing and such. This was nuts . . . but it was right. A word Paul hadn't thought much about in years sprang to his thoughts.

Honor.

For the first time since this ordeal had begun, Paul realized he *wanted* to help Sam take Buck to justice. There was a need running deep through his soul that knew helping Sam was the right thing to do. It was a family obligation—duty.

Damn.

"It's about time," Sam muttered quietly, then smiled.

"What did you say?" Winnie asked, half-turning to look over her shoulder.

"Nothin'." Sam clenched his fist and pounded his right thigh, clutching the reins in one hand. "We'll settle for the night in a cave I know just up ahead."

Paul couldn't wait to hold Winnie in his arms. Even though she was leaning against his body at this very moment, it just wasn't the same.

Sam guided Lucifer up onto a bluff and through a thick stand of scrub oak. The dark outline of a cave was evident in the limestone cliff just ahead. "Here we are," he announced, bringing the horse to a halt and swinging himself to the ground.

Sam lifted Winnie down from the saddle and pointed to the cave. "I'm gonna start a fire in there, but first I wanna make sure it ain't already occupied."

"Occupied?" Winnie repeated in a very small voice. "By . . . by what?"

"Well, let's just have a look." Sam slid the saddle off Lucifer and rubbed the animal down with the wool saddle blanket. Then he set it free to graze through the night.

"I'll be back in a few minutes." He pulled the revolver out of his holster. "You know how to use this?"

"N—no." Winnie took a step back. "And I don't want to, either."

You'n me both, Paul thought, counting the moments until he could actually speak to her as himself.

Sam shrugged and shoved the gun back into his holster. "Suit yourself."

"Wait." Winnie touched his sleeve. "I'll hold it, but I won't shoot it."

Chuckling, Sam handed her the weapon, butt first. "Sit down there on that boulder, then . . . and just hold it."

Sam walked slowly up the incline to the cave, removing his other gun from its holster in the process. His movements slowed as he neared the opening, making Paul wonder what the lawman was so worried about. What were a few bats, after all? He wanted this over with so he could have his body back.

What are you waiting for? Let's get that fire started, Paul urged.

"Hush up," Sam whispered, then he stooped to pick up a rock and tossed it into the opening, backing against the wall of the cliff in one smooth motion. "Some of these caves along here are dens for bears and cougar. Ain't much bear around anymore, though, and that's a real shame. This'n seems to be safe, though."

Safe? Paul would've rolled his eyes, but consoled himself with the knowledge that he'd be able to very soon. And that wasn't the only thing he'd finally have the opportunity to do again.

Would Winnie let him hold her? Right now he could be content with only holding her, if that was all she wanted, though he hoped her memory of their night together was as vivid as his. Letting her know he was here with her and that he intended to do everything possible to ensure their return to the twentieth century, was of paramount importance. But even more crucial was the knowledge that neither one of them was alone in this involuntary adventure.

Paul was surprised by the flicker of a flame near the cave opening. His thoughts had been so distracting that Sam had gathered firewood and started a small blaze without Paul's awareness. The time was coming. Sam was going to leave him . . . at least for a while.

"Yeah, for a spell, I reckon I am." Sam straightened from his crouch beside the thriving fire. "You know how to keep this goin'?"

I was an Eagle Scout.

Sam chuckled. "Well, I wouldn't know what that is, but just remember to keep feedin' the fire. It'll keep animals away during the night." He scratched his head, then glanced out at the night sky. "I'm gonna scout around for some sign of Landen while you . . . uh . . ."

Paul felt like laughing, and soon he'd be able to. He couldn't wait to have control of his own body again.

"When I git back, we'll decide where to go for the hitchin'."

Paul resigned himself. *All right.*

"Good."

Paul waited. How would this happen? He had a vague recollection of the day Sam had first possessed him. There'd been some pain, but not much. Mostly, he'd been frightened, but not anymore.

"I'll be back in two days." Sam brushed off his jeans and fell silent for a moment.

What's wrong? Paul was terrified that Sam would change his mind at the last minute.

"I was just wonderin' . . ." Sam laid a larger log across the fire. "What if . . . I ain't able to come back? Suppose I'm taken, you know, to wherever it is I'm supposed to spend eternity?"

Paul didn't need this burden of guilt or responsibility. Damn, but he had enough problems of his own without dealing with his great-great-grandfather's as well. But he knew fate had brought him here. Sam's problems were Paul's problems. Paul had a duty to perform and would do it. Somehow.

If that happens, then I'll . . . I'll do everything in my power to take Buck Landen to trial. There. He'd said it—thought it, rather.

Sam nodded and grinned. "Good." He took a deep breath, then let it out very slowly. "That's gonna have to last me a while, I reckon. See you in two days. I hope."

Thanks.

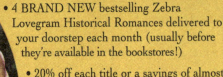

"No problem."

Paul was vaguely aware of a pressure in his middle as Sam stepped from his body. Then a brief but searing pain shot through his head as his mind suddenly took full control of his body.

He blinked, then focused on Sam's iridescent shape just in front of him—the bloodied hole appeared again in Sam's shirtfront. Paul's heart raced. This was his great-great-grandfather's spirit. Sam Weathers was dead. For the past few weeks, it had been almost possible to forget that.

Sam looked at Paul—his eyes filled with sadness. The seasoned lawman looked lost, an emotion Paul felt certain was as alien to Sam as this time and lifestyle were to Paul. A lump formed in Paul's throat and his eyes burned.

"Thanks," Paul repeated, feeling selfish and cruel for asking this huge favor of his ancestor. But Winnie needed to know he was here, that she wasn't alone in this mess . . . in this time.

Besides, Sam *was* already dead. That was a fact Paul couldn't change, no matter what concessions he made.

"I'll be back." Sam smiled sadly, then floated away from the cave, in the opposite direction from where they'd left Winnie.

Paul watched until the faint glow completely vanished. Sam was out scouting for Buck Landen . . . and the nearest preacher.

And Paul was alone with Winnie.

Filled with purpose, he half-slid down the embankment to the boulder where they'd left Lucifer and Winnie. Paul froze when he caught sight of her, sitting there in the darkness and actually carrying on a conversation with the horse. What an amazing woman.

"See, Lucifer," she said. "I don't belong here." Her laughter was cynical. "I'm from the future. Really, I am." She sighed and reached out to stroke the animal's neck. "I guess you're not quite as terrifying as I thought you were. I wish you'd believe me, though."

"*I* believe you." Paul's heart swelled in his chest as he took a few more steps toward her. Moonlight broke through the few scattered clouds and bathed her in silver. "You're beautiful, Winnie."

A tiny gasp preceded Winnie's lurch to her feet. Sam's pistol fell from her skirt to the ground. She stood staring at him for several minutes, then took a tentative step toward him. "Say something else."

He knew she wanted to hear his voice—his *real* voice, so he searched his mind for something only he could know. "We'd better go up to the cave for the night. It isn't the Holiday Inn, but it'll do in a pinch."

"Holiday—" Winnie covered her mouth with her hand, then took another step toward him. She stopped suddenly and stooped to retrieve the discarded gun.

When she straightened with the weapon aimed at his abdomen, Paul stared at her in shock. He couldn't blame her for being pissed. She'd been dragged back in time after a night of fantastic sex, believing she was totally alone, only to find that he was here, too . . . and had been all along. He had to find a way to make her understand that he was as much a victim in this as she.

"Winnie—"

"What the hell kind of game are you playing with me, Paul Weathers?"

Eleven

Winnie gripped the gun so tightly her fingers started to feel numb. "You'd better start talking," she warned, her mind whirling in confusion, her heart constricting with a sense of betrayal.

"Winnie, it's really me—it's *been* me all along. Sort of." He reached out to her. "Come up to the cave and let me explain."

"Explain? *Explain?*" Tears stung her eyes and her hands wavered beneath the gun's weight. Even if she managed to pull the trigger, she wouldn't be able to see what she was shooting at. How could he do this to her? *What* was he doing to her? Even Paul Weathers couldn't have the kind of power it would take to perform the class of miracles—rather, disasters—she'd encountered.

"It hasn't been you all along," she spat, clutching at anything concrete, though nothing made sense anymore. "Dammit, Sam doesn't even have blue eyes. How the hell are you going to explain that?"

Paul dropped his arm to his side. "It's a long story, Winnie. A very long story." He sounded exhausted—defeated. "This is the first time in weeks I've been . . . myself."

Winnie blinked back her tears. Had she been right about Paul having a mental illness? Could it be true? "What about the gray eyes? How can you explain that? I already ruled out contacts." She leaned slightly toward him, wishing she had more light to discern the exact shade his eyes were now.

"Yeah it was weird. When I first saw those gray eyes staring back from my face . . ." Paul chuckled and shook his head. "That old fart. Well, he isn't really old . . . and never will be. It was a long time before I finally saw my face in a mirror. Sam didn't even use one to shave, not that he bothered shaving on a regular basis. Or bathing, for that matter." He rubbed his cheek with the palm of his hand. "I'm probably permanently scarred. Battle scars."

"He? Who and what the hell are you talking about?" Winnie's heart thundered along at a dangerous pace. This was all so terrifying—outrageous. "What old fart? Do you mean Sam?"

Paul's ragged sigh was the only sound in the darkness except the frantic beating of her heart. "Sam is—was—my great-great-grandfather." He held his hands out, palms up. "Come up to the cave and hear all of this. Please. The mosquitoes'll eat us alive out here."

She lowered the gun with both hands as tears rolled unheeded down her cheeks. "What difference does it make anymore?" She shook her head and let him take the gun from her limp fingers. She was lost. It didn't matter whether this was reality or fantasy, she was defeated. Sanity couldn't possibly save this situation.

"We're in this together, Winnie," he said quietly, slipping the gun back into its holster at his hip. He reached for her again. "C'mon."

She didn't resist when he gripped her elbow and led her slowly up the hill. This was Paul—*really* Paul. She could sense it somehow, the difference in him from when he'd been Sam just a little while ago. *God, Winnie—do you know how crazy that sounds?*

He guided her to a blanket that had been spread on the ground just beyond the fire, then bent down to place a huge log on the blaze, even though it wasn't cold. As she sat down on the blanket, Winnie stared into the fire, watched the orange and yellow flames dance in the darkness. There *really was* only one explanation, and it was past time she faced it. She'd gone insane and none of this was actually happening— none of it had *ever* happened. All these weeks she'd been rotting away in a mental hospital somewhere. She should've known right away. Time travel. The mere notion was ridiculous.

"This isn't happening," she said in a voice she didn't recognize as her own. "None of this is real. You're not real. Maybe even that night . . ."

He walked over and reached for her hand, then pulled her up to stand in front of him. Winnie dragged her eyes up to meet his gaze. Firelight danced in his blue eyes. *Blue eyes.* "Damn you," she whispered, mesmerized by the tenderness and naked desire she saw clearly reflected there. Her insides coiled into a tight spring of hunger so intense she thought she might die from it. And she hated herself for feeling it.

"Winnie, I'm real," he whispered, wrapping his strong arms around her shoulders to pull her closer. "We're real. *This* is real. All of it."

She shook her head and her knees trembled. Why did he have to make her want him? How *could* she want him after all this? "You promised me answers. Someone did." She blinked back her tears and took a shaky breath. "I want those answers and I want them now."

Paul sighed and rubbed her upper arms with his open palms, sending whispers of conflicting emotions skittering down her spine. *Oh, it's not fair. Why does he have to affect me this way?* "Answers, Paul."

"Winnie, do you remember . . . us? That night?" He inched his way closer, tightening his grip on her shoulders. Rhythmically, he massaged the tight muscles at the base of her neck where her shoulders flared. "It was the best. The very best."

He moved his highly effective massage technique to the back of her neck and Winnie thought she'd pass out right on the spot from the torrent of blatant desire that surged through her. Heat engulfed her body, made her tremble as his gentle movements continued. "The best," she repeated, permitting her head to loll to one side as her demand for answers was overpowered by a stronger need.

Physical desire mingled with a desperate need to deny all this. She was vulnerable right now. A voice deep in her subconscious told her to put a halt to these proceedings, but she didn't want to. It was that simple—she wanted and needed Paul. He could make her forget, for a little while, the topsy-turvy world she'd fallen into.

Correction—*they'd* fallen into.

Was it true? She wasn't alone in this bizarre nightmare? She wasn't insane? Paul had accompanied her, followed her, into the storm that swept them both back in time. She had no explanations for their situation, nor did she care at the moment. All that mattered were his strong hands kneading her flesh.

And, more importantly, his presence.

"Winnie." His whisper was a caress against her cheek as he lowered his lips to hers.

Winnie whimpered as her insides came to life with such force she thought she might scream out loud in pure ecstasy. This was maddening, bewildering. How could she respond so easily to his touch after all that had happened?

Yet how could she not?

His mouth was sweet and soft, yet hard and invasive with its intensity. He wrapped his arms completely around her and pulled her against his full length, flaunting his engorged sex against her lower abdomen, as his tongue met and melded with hers in a primitive and unmistakable dance.

Winnie's insides turned to jelly. She was on fire, losing complete control of her ability to form a conscious thought as he pressed himself more fully against her. She craved this—wanted *him*. Denial was futile. All these weeks, when she'd thought Paul was still in the next century, Winnie'd remembered their night together, dreamed of it, prayed for a repeat performance. Now that impossibly wondrous experience was becoming reality.

She sagged in his embrace, unable to support her own weight any longer as he dragged his mouth from hers. He didn't say a word—he didn't have to. Winnie knew what he wanted, what they both needed.

Their gazes fused together and her heart sprinted away in synch with her libido. Winnie saw candid hunger and desire in his crystal blue eyes, and something more she was afraid to define. He wanted her as desperately as she wanted him. What possible reason could there be to refuse? Considering . . .

The silence between them was charged, tinged with regret and desperation, yet vanquished by pure, carnal yearning. There was something distinct, something far more powerful than their first time, which commanded Winnie's immediate surrender. Need—raw, basic human need. It wouldn't be simply sex this time, though their first encounter had been anything but simple. There was genuine human emotion fueling her desire, driving her on, weakening her resistance, making her seek more of what Paul Weathers had to offer.

And Lord knew he had more than his fair share to give. . . .

"I want you," he whispered, his fervor reflected in his hooded eyes. "But I won't—can't—persuade you to do something you don't want to. If you don't—"

Winnie very gently pressed her fingertip to his lips. "Shh." She moistened her lips with the tip of her tongue and smiled slowly.

"Oh, Lord." His gaze was fixed on her mouth. "Winnie . . ."

She needed this night of abandonment. The explanations, the answers she'd been promised, could wait. They'd have to. The need coursing through her veins was so sweet and fierce, there was no way she could deny it.

Nor did she want to.

"Paul." She laid her cheek against his shoulder, savoring

the rough feel of his shirt against her skin. "Make love to me. Again and again . . . like before."

She felt him tense in her embrace. Would he deny their mutual gratification? She knew he wanted this as much, or more, than she did. What price would this single night of pleasure in the midst of all the turmoil and uncertainty exact from her? It didn't matter. Whatever the price, she'd already paid it—with interest.

Pulling slightly away, she searched his eyes for a solution. She saw his doubt, his reserve, which made her want him all the more. Somehow, knowing he cared enough about her to deny himself warmed her heart. Filled with purpose, her fingers made short business of unbuttoning his chambray shirt and slipping it from his broad shoulders.

The crisp dark hair on his chest felt wondrous beneath her open palms. "It really is you, Paul." She smiled up at him, feeling a joy sweep through her that left her breathless for a few glorious moments. What power did this man have over her? She really didn't know him, though Winnie felt connected to him in more ways than one. They were soul mates, fellow time travelers on an uncertain adventure.

This was *right*. Inevitable.

With a low growl, Paul quickly released the buttons at the front of her dress, then slipped it from her shoulders. As she fumbled with his belt buckle and the buttons at his fly, Paul unlaced her archaic shift, permitting it to join her dress, then kicked off his scarred leather boots.

Winnie felt, savored, his gaze on her hardening nipples. They puckered and grew hard beneath his inspection. She was eager to feel his hands and lips on their sensitive peaks. Her insides turned to liquid fire as his gaze possessed her. God, how she wanted him—needed him. As she eased his jeans lower on his slim hips, she realized he wasn't wearing briefs. Of course, Jockeys hadn't been invented yet.

Good.

His flesh felt warmer as her fingertips inched closer and

closer to that part of him she wanted so desperately. When his jeans fell to his knees, she closed both her hands around his shaft to savor the rigid flesh that would bring them both so much pleasure.

"Oh, Lord," he whispered, gripping her shoulders and pulling her full against him.

Nothing separated them now except her Victorian pantalettes. Winnie giggled, despite the fiery passion which leapt between them. Here she stood, in a cave with a naked man, wearing nothing but a pair of cotton pantalettes even Scarlett O'Hara would've found too modest.

"What's so funny?" Paul's voice was hoarse with longing as his rough hands stroked her back and cupped her buttocks. When she wrapped her arms around his waist, he suddenly lifted her up and against his erection. He gasped and held his breath for a second, then released it very slowly. "I'm not laughing."

Winnie's laughter abruptly ceased and her breath froze in her throat. "Oh, Lord." She swallowed with difficulty, remembering in detail their night together on the boat. He was a lot of man for any woman, but at least for tonight he was all hers.

He lifted his gaze and stared down at her upturned face through half-closed eyes. With one open palm, he caressed her cheek. "I want you, Winnie Sinclair. There's never been a woman who makes my blood boil the way you do. How do you do it? What's your secret?"

Stunned, Winnie relished his words. She'd had no idea such power was hers for the taking. Did Paul mean he believed their physical bond was something special and unique—as she did? And dare she hope it could be something more?

"Do you want me, Winnie?"

She nodded and tears stung her eyes. There was so much more to this than physical gratification, but she was too terrified and aroused to define the emotions just now. There were far more pressing matters demanding her undivided attention.

Winnie pressed her hips more fully against him, savoring the way he throbbed against her. He was so hot and engorged, making her acutely aware of the differences between man and woman. Soft met hard. Positive countered negative. Abundance filled emptiness. . . .

Groaning, Paul kissed her again, but the gentleness she'd noticed earlier was now marvelously absent. His tongue probed deep into her mouth as Winnie returned his kiss with a fury born of desperation. He lifted her completely off the floor to press her against him, their lips never parting.

Winnie tasted fervent desire mingled with desperation on his lips, and she enhanced the flavor with her own parallel emotions. When he lowered her feet to the floor, she moaned, but his searing lips blazing a trail down the side of her neck quickly negated her protests.

He kicked his jeans away, then kissed his way across the curve of her shoulder, pausing to trace warm wet circles on her tender flesh. Winnie's legs weakened as he dropped to his knees in front of her, kissing her just beneath her swollen breasts, impatient for his touch.

"Sweet," he murmured kissing his way lower and releasing the drawstring at her waist. Slowly, he eased her pantalettes downward, kissing her flesh as he bared it.

When he fused his lips to the reddish brown triangle of hair which shielded the part of her that ached for him, Winnie's knees buckled beneath her weight. He eased her down to the blanket, hovering over her for a few intensely sensual moments.

Winnie arched upward when at long last his warm lips found the cusp of her breast. She gasped in joy when he drew her nipple deep into his mouth, suckling her flesh until she thought she'd die from the exquisiteness of the moment. He cupped her breasts in his large hands, alternating his delicious mouth between them, never allowing her the opportunity to come back down from the high plateau of ecstasy he'd brought her to.

She entangled her fingers in the soft dark hair at his nape, longer now than when she'd last touched it. The immaculately groomed, suave, metropolitan divorce attorney was nowhere to be found. This Paul Weathers was far more open, eager and honest than the man she'd known before. Though, at this moment, Winnie wouldn't have objected to either version. As long as he was really Paul, and she knew without a hint of reservation that he was.

He flicked his tongue across her sensitive flesh, looking up at her as he slowly swirled circles around her tender nipple. The passion blazing in his blue eyes made Winnie melt. She wanted him to fill her so full she'd never want again, though this forbidden fruit wielded a lure surely no woman could resist. Winnie yearned to touch him . . . taste him.

Very gently but firmly, she pressed his shoulder until he rolled to the side, releasing her nipple from his potent lips. "What . . . ?"

Her wicked smile was nearly Paul's undoing. "Oh, Lord," he whispered raggedly as she pressed him flat, then eased herself atop him. This woman was as devastating now as that first night. He wanted and needed her more than anything or anyone he'd encountered in his entire life. The thought gave him pause, made him wonder about the significance of these feelings.

Until her lips toyed with his, then moved lower to tarry over his flat brown nipple. Winnie eased her leg over his body, straddling him as she kissed her way lower, then sliding her legs down between his as the velvet tips of her breasts tickled and tantalized his skin.

Paul groaned in anticipation mingled with fear. He wasn't sure if he was afraid she would or afraid she wouldn't. All he knew was that he was helpless to prevent her from doing anything she wanted. Anything at all.

And she did.

She kissed the tender flesh on his upper thighs, laved her

tongue along the edges of the crisp dark hair at the base of his pulsating erection. Her fiery mane mingled provocatively with the crisp dark hair surrounding his sex. He was sure there'd never been a more erotic sight than what his captivated gaze feasted upon at this very moment.

Then Winnie's lips found the part of him that screamed for release. She planted tiny, torturous kisses along his taut flesh, up and down the length of him, pausing just short of his burgeoning tip. He couldn't take much more. She was driving him insane.

She was coming dangerously close to detonating a ticking bomb. The big one. "Winnie."

He wound his fingers through her cinnamon curls, gently urging her to abandon her quest in favor of something mutually satisfying, but Winnie persisted with her delicious torture. Her talented tongue glided along his turgid flesh, higher and higher until he thought he'd die right on the spot. Then boldly—marvelously—she found his aching tip.

He gasped and bit the inside of his cheek, hoping to prevent his immediate release. Wincing, he prevented it barely in the nick of time. It would definitely be short-lived if she continued on her present course of the finest persecution he could've imagined.

Winnie lifted her face a few inches and looked up at him with sultry green eyes. That slow sexy smile of hers gave him little warning of her intentions as she parted her glistening lips. Ever so slowly, inch by devastating inch, she bent closer until she encircled him with her warm, silken lips.

Paul's self-control wavered, nearly drawing him over the edge, into that pit of consummation he wanted so desperately. He should make her stop before it was too late, but he couldn't bear for her to stop *too* soon. Holding his breath, he permitted her intimate torture to continue, as he traveled along a path of sexual arousal unlike anything he'd ever experienced. Soon, he would surge beyond the point of no return. But just for a moment . . .

He couldn't drag his gaze from the sight of her lovely face against his engorged body. Her mouth formed a perfect circle to accommodate him in his inspired state. Her brownish gold lashes rested against peach-tinged cheeks with just a sprinkling of freckles. Her bare breasts tickled his thighs, augmenting the entire experience. Dangerously so. He moaned again and closed his eyes, until her seduction grew even more dauntless, jarring him from the land of self-indulgence. Another moment and it would be too late. He'd relished her seduction as long as he possibly dared.

Winnie whispered in mild protest when he gripped her shoulders and lifted her away from him. Gasping, he struggled for control. "No more. Can't take it."

She smiled again and ran her tongue along her bottom lip, then bit down on it with straight white teeth. He moaned helplessly as she slithered slowly back up his body, pressing herself against him in all the right, and most devastating, places. "You're a cruel woman—a gifted one, for sure—but this torture is about to cease."

Winnie moaned softly as he gripped her hips and guided her astride his dangerously stimulated body. As she hovered over him, just beyond reach, he felt like a gun about to discharge, hammer pulled back and prepared to fire. The anticipation was killing him. Just when he thought he couldn't bear another moment, her silken folds enveloped him in sheer heaven as she slid down his length until he was fully sheathed within her receptive body.

Paul bit his lower lip, trying to bring himself under control while he throbbed within her, right on the verge of losing complete control. It was too soon. Again, he was reminded of that other night, when he'd first discovered that Winnie Sinclair was the sexiest woman alive. There was no doubt about it—he hadn't dreamed it, after all.

Thank God.

She closed around him, drew him within her warm circumference. His sense of urgency ebbed very slightly as she moved against him. He savored the way she fit and held him, as if she'd been made just for him.

Paul's state of sexual exigency prevented him from dwelling on the perplexing thought—that she was meant for him—but he filed it away for future reference. Right now there was no room left for logic or consequences. His ability to concentrate was limited to the heady sensations leaping between he and Winnie. The intensity of their union would not permit intrusion.

She tightened around him, angling her hips to more fully meet him as she sat upright with her knees bent and feet slightly behind her. No other woman had ever brought him such utter fulfillment, in any century. Somehow, he knew none ever would.

Or could . . . ?

He wanted to watch her, to see her pleasure etched across her delicate face. Pleasure he was responsible for. As he opened his eyes, his heart soared with a sense of purpose. He drove upward to meet her thrusting pelvis, intent on bringing her unparalleled fulfillment.

Her head was tilted slightly back and her hair loose and sexy around her face, grazing her shoulders with graceful curls. Her breasts . . . Winnie had the world's most tempting breasts. He reached up to hold them in his hands and was rewarded by her tiny gasp of pleasure and a glimpse of those gorgeous green eyes.

She leaned slightly forward to accommodate him, as he craned his neck to tease the puckered brown nipples with his tongue. Her immediate response was nearly his undoing as she convulsed and pulsated around him. His head fell back weakly as he neared his climax. He rolled her responsive nipples between his thumbs and forefingers, watching the mounting pleasure he was giving her combine with the explosive sensations coursing through his own body.

Her soft murmur, followed by a sudden gasp, alerted him to her completion. He watched her lovely face in the firelight as she bit her lower lip and the veins distended on her neck. Her breasts swelled in his hands as he felt her contracting body possessing and swallowing his in a sexual vise which left no room for self-restraint. He lifted himself up and into her as she pressed against him in primal urgency.

She drew the essence from him, demanding all he could give as she arched and writhed against him. Paul strained as his strength culminated and exploded within her, filled her with the product of their union, the results of their mutual desires.

Spent and panting, she slumped against him, planting tiny kisses along the side of his neck as their heartbeats thudded together. Words popped into his mind, things he wasn't ready to accept or say, as he gathered her into his arms and rolled her to his side.

"God, woman," he whispered into her hair. "What you do to me should be illegal. Hell, it probably is in at least three states."

Sexy, intelligent, charming, witty and beautiful.

He was in big trouble.

Her giggle broke the tension between them. "Including this one?"

"This isn't even a state yet, love."

Paul immediately regretted his words, but he couldn't take them back. For a few glorious minutes, they'd both been able to forget their predicament. Now, with his thoughtless remark, reality was thrust to the forefront again.

Damn.

He felt her tense in his arms, though she made no effort to move away. Nevertheless, it was painfully evident the exquisite moment was lost.

Forever? *No, please not forever.*

"I'll . . . have my answers, now," she stated very simply. Quietly.

Paul squeezed his eyes shut, wishing the mood didn't have to change so soon. But it was too late. He swallowed hard, then dragged his eyes open again. Her head was nestled on his shoulder in a place that seemed to have been made just for her. It was almost frightening—too many things about this woman felt so damned right. He played with her hair while searching his frazzled mind for the right words.

Winnie, I'm possessed.

Maybe something that sounded slightly less insane would be easier for her to accept. "I'm not sure where to begin," he said honestly, then drew a deep breath. "During the storm, when I found you gone . . ."

Winnie nodded against his shoulder. "That was really dumb. I should've known better."

"I noticed the missing life vest. Thank God you put it on." He remembered that morning, the terror he'd felt while searching for her on the boat.

"I'm sure it saved my life."

"Me, too." *And mine.*

"Go on."

Paul watched her long, creamy leg shift to drape across his darker one. The relaxed intimacy of the simple act pulled him from his train of thought with a jolt. What was it about this woman?

"Paul?" She lifted her head to look into his eyes. "I need some answers."

He nodded and she laid her head against him again. *She feels so right—so good.* "I was searching for you on deck when a wave washed me into the lake. Damned thing almost seemed to have fingers. It sort of reached up and grabbed me."

She nodded again. "Same thing happened to me." There was a pregnant pause. "Coincidence?"

"No way."

"Then . . . what?"

He shrugged and wrapped his arm completely around her shoulders. "I don't know. Something more powerful than either of us. God, maybe?"

Her head shot up and she stared at him as if he was out of his mind. There was probably a better than fifty-fifty shot that he was. *Not of sound mind and body.*

"God? The God I was raised to respect wouldn't do something like this." She laughed bitterly and shook her head, then rested her cheek against his shoulder. "Go on. I want to know how we got back in time." He felt her holding her breath, then she let it out in a rush. "And I also want to know who the hell Sam is."

Here comes the tricky part. Paul chuckled and kissed the top of her head. "Are you sure you're ready for this?"

"I wasn't ready for any of this, Paul," she said tiredly. "I don't think you were either."

"No, that's for sure." Paul searched his mind for the details of that fateful day. "After I was washed ashore and realized the lake didn't exist, two men suddenly appeared on the riverbank. They were fighting."

Winnie took a deep breath. When she released it, he knew what she was thinking. "Sam was one of them?"

Paul nodded. "Yeah—Sam Weathers. My great-great-grandfather."

Winnie laid her palm on his chest. "I knew he had to be your ancestor the minute I saw him."

"But you thought he was me."

"At first." She shrugged. "Until I realized his eyes were gray."

"His gray eyes." Paul hugged her close when he felt her tremble. "Cold?"

"No, just finish the story."

Tension was mounting. He'd have to tell her everything. She had a right to know, having been dragged back in time with him. This mess certainly wasn't her fault. He owed her the truth. All of it.

"Winnie, Sam was . . . killed in that fight."

Her head shot up again. "Killed?" Her brow furrowed and her green eyes narrowed. "But he's been up walking and talking for weeks since then." Her voice rose a bit higher with each word. "Paul Weathers, so help me—"

"It's true, Winnie." He watched the stunned expression in her eyes. "It was a knife wound. After the killer rode away, I tried CPR, but he'd already lost too much blood."

A tremor racked her body and he rubbed her upper arm. "Paul, what are you saying? This is scary. How . . . ?"

Paul drew a deep breath. "Sam Weathers—my great-great-grandfather—has been sort of borrowing my body since the day we came back in time."

"Whoa. Hold on a minute, buster." She pulled away from him and sat up at his side, wrapping her arms around her knees. "I don't buy this—not for one minute."

"It's true." Paul sat up and faced her, gritting his teeth for a moment while he searched his mind for the right words. "Sam borrowed my body, so he could take his killer to justice."

Winnie looked at him as if he was absolutely insane. Hell, he probably was. How else could he have accepted this mess so easily? Now what was he supposed to do? Continue to deny the obvious?

"True, Winnie. All true." He reached for her hand, but she jerked it away. "Sam wanted to take his killer to hang, but he couldn't very well do that in his condition." Paul winced as he recalled Sam's body that day. Dead—very dead. "When he saw how much I looked like him . . ."

Winnie grunted in disbelief. "So, he just crawled right inside and made himself at home? Tell me, Paul. Isn't it just a little crowded in there?"

Paul chuckled, amazed at how accurate her words really were. "Something like that. Yeah."

"Oooookay." Winnie looked at him through one eye. "So you're . . . possessed?"

Paul grinned. "Not right at the moment. He left."

Winnie shook her head. "Without calling an exorcist? No

head turning three hundred and sixty degrees? He just up and left? For good?"

Paul cleared his throat, trying desperately not to burst out laughing. As horrible as this mess was, hearing it put into words was too ludicrous. "No, he'll be back in a couple of days."

Winnie giggled in disbelief. "Oh, this is good. I'm sure you'll have no trouble selling this story to a movie producer when—if—we get back."

"We will get back, Winnie." Paul reached out to her again and took her hand in his. She didn't withdraw this time, but her fingers were icy. "And if we don't . . ."

Winnie's eyes widened and moisture glistened in their emerald depths. Her lower lip trembled and her chin quivered. "If we don't . . . ?"

Paul squeezed her hand and drew a deep breath, knowing what he must do. Even if Sam hadn't insisted. "Then I'll take care of you in this century."

"Paul Weathers," she said very quietly, her tone devoid of emotion. "Winnie Sinclair does not need a man to take care of her anywhere, in any century."

He smiled in approval. "I know you don't. God save anyone who doesn't realize that." He traced circles in her palm with his thumb, lowering his gaze, then lifting it to meet hers again. "Winnie, I care about you. I feel like we belong together. *Especially* if we're stranded here."

She was silent for several moments. He watched her fluctuating expression, felt her hand warm within his grasp. Color crept back into her cheeks and when she looked up at him again, his breath caught in his throat. An almost ethereal beauty possessed her. It was almost as if she'd accepted this and was at peace with all of it. Amazing.

"You're right, Paul." She smiled sweetly. "If we're stuck here, then we're the only people who could possibly understand each other."

Somehow, that wasn't what he'd hoped to hear, though he

wasn't prepared to admit what words he had wished for. "Good." He cupped her chin in his hands. "We're both consenting adults. I can think of a . . . very pleasant way to spend the next couple of days."

Winnie giggled nervously and a tear trickled down her cheek. She quickly wiped the glistening droplet away as if she didn't want him to see it. But he had seen it, and for some reason he knew he'd always treasure the memory.

"Oh, Lord," she murmured, then giggled again.

He smiled in remembrance. "Is this where I'm supposed to say I don't have—"

"Oh, damn." Winnie covered her mouth with her hand. "Oh, no—we didn't."

Paul's heart sank as he followed her thoughts. "We did." They'd engaged in unprotected sex. Very *enthusiastic,* unprotected sex. If performance was any indication of successful conception, they were as good as parents. He searched her gaze. "You know I really don't have anything with me."

She rolled her eyes and shrugged. "It's a little late to worry about that now. Maybe later than you think." She moistened her lips, then rose onto her knees. "Besides, I don't intend to waste any of the time we have left until . . . Sam comes back."

There was a flicker of sadness in her eyes when she mentioned Sam's name. Didn't she believe him? At this point, he had to assume she did. "And once Sam does return, he's under strict orders not to lay a hand on you."

Paul held his breath and raised himself onto his knees. She inched toward him and he was struck dumb for a moment by the contact of her cool flesh against his warm body. "Of course, you do realize the possible consequences of our . . . intentions?" He had to ask. It was the least he could do, though the thought of having a baby with Winnie wasn't the least bit disturbing. In fact, the possibility made him feel kind of nice.

Winnie blushed prettily. He hadn't seen her blush since that first night. It was a pleasing sight.

"Yes, I know. My mother taught me all about it when I was ten. Well, maybe not all." She lifted her gaze to meet his. Something poignant passed between them in that hand's breadth of time. "My biological clock is ticking away. If . . . it happens, and we're able to return, then it'll be the longest pregnancy on record."

"Oh, Lord."

Twelve

"What am I gonna do?" Winnie whispered, as she poked a long stick at the glowing embers of the dying fire. She was alone for the first time since she'd confirmed her suspicions about Paul's insanity.

He was nuts. Certifiable in a court of law—an appropriate way for an attorney to go insane.

She raked her fingers through her hair, wishing for a hot shower and a gallon of her favorite conditioner. Paul would be back at any moment, so she had to get her thoughts together before then.

"Okay, Winnie. Think." She laid a small log on the red-hot coals, watching it ignite immediately. The yellow-orange flames licked up the sides of the log until it was completely engulfed.

She chewed a ragged fingernail, forcing herself to think about the changes Paul had undergone just before and after his transformation into Sam. This was all so strange.

Could Paul summon Sam at will? The thought made her blink in surprise. Was this alter ego capable of doing the primitive things he'd been doing all these weeks? It was far from likely that the Paul she knew would be able to handle a gun with the expertise Sam had displayed. Riding a horse was even questionable, and she'd certainly seen him do that.

Mental illness was a powerful force, but could it give a person the knowledge and skill necessary to perform acts he'd never done before? The fact that Paul went to all the trouble to insert blue contacts when he was himself—

"Uh-oh." Winnie's heart raced and she felt cold all over, despite the warm day and the hot fire. She had no way of knowing who the real Paul Weathers was. Which persona was the real Paul? Rolling her eyes, she rubbed the back of her neck. That was a stupid question to ask. She'd seen the real Paul Weathers in action during her divorce hearing.

Or was he really a combination of the two personalities? Sam and Paul? Or maybe Paul number one, the barracuda lawyer, and Paul number two, the lover. For some reason, this thought warmed Winnie. She drew a deep breath, then held it a few moments before releasing it. She sure had a knack for picking the wrong man.

Wrong man? Guilt welled within her, crowding her confusion for supremacy. She tried to ignore the burning sensation in the pit of her empty stomach.

How could he be the wrong man, when no other had ever taken the time to show her the tenderness and passion he'd shared so openly? She trembled as the memory of the past twenty-four hours assailed her. No, she couldn't call Paul the wrong man. Far too many things about him were so very right.

So perfect.

"Damn." She kicked at a loose stone on the cave floor, watching it skitter along and roll into the fire. How had she gotten into this predicament? Not only was she sexually involved with a man who needed intensive psychiatric care, but she'd traveled back in time with him to complicate matters even more. This had to be one for the record books. She could already see the headlines in the *Tulsa World*.

Local Woman Finds Time Love Tunnel.

Knowing he was crazy, why had she fallen into his arms again with only the slightest impetus? She closed her eyes as the longing for Paul renewed itself in all its fury and glory.

None of this was fair. She'd been married to a jerk who cheated on her, then fell in lo—

No. Winnie felt her heart swell in her chest as the thought took root and grew. Was she in love with Paul? The thought, despite his certain insanity, didn't bring an immediate denial. Surprised by the realization, she smiled a secret woman's smile, then poked at the fire again with the stick.

She could do worse.

Shaking her head, Winnie chuckled. She couldn't very well tell herself to take things slowly with Paul, because she'd already been *very* intimate with him on more than one memorable occasion. And there was the matter of her missing period. Lord knew they'd done everything right, or wrong, to create a child. Heat flooded her face as her breasts swelled within the confines of the old-fashioned, cotton dress.

Paul was the kind of lover women's magazines said every woman wanted—caring, patient, gentle yet passionate, physically incomparable, and eager to please. Yes. *Oh, my.* Fanning herself with her open hand, Winnie dropped the stick and moved outside for some badly needed air. The heat in the cave, with the fire blazing suddenly became oppressive. It seemed an appropriate symbol for the slow burn taking place inside her.

It was already hot outside, though the sun hadn't yet reached its zenith. Right. She was a real pro at telling time by the sun and navigating by the stars. Laughing, she shook her head, then leaned against the limestone wall behind her. At least it felt cool.

Paul should be back soon. Squinting, she looked down the side of the hill at the dense oak forest. A feeling of déjà vu washed over her, prompting Winnie to look into the distance at the surrounding countryside. There was something intensely familiar about the hills and forests.

With a rush of childhood memories, Winnie realized where she was. This was the Osage Hill country in what would one day be called Washington County. Her father had rented a cabin up in the hills north of Tulsa every year during Christmas. It had been a luxury they could ill afford, but it was something he'd wanted for his family. Those had been the best times of her life, her most cherished memories.

She racked her brain, trying to remember the history of the region in 1896. She wasn't sure. Was the Phillips family here, yet? Had Bartlesville been settled? Had oil been discovered?

If only there were some way for her to prevent the discovery of oil. Wouldn't that be a boon to the ecological implications of the next century? That was unrealistic and she knew it. If oil wasn't discovered here, it would be in the Arab nations eventually anyway. How would that alter history? The thought brought a shudder from deep inside her.

"Imagine Saddam Hussein, dictator of a superpower." No, that wouldn't happen. Winnie knew there was nothing she could or should do to prevent the discovery of fossil fuels. She was no history whiz and had no idea exactly when it was first discovered, anyway. Though she had a hunch it had been—would be—near the turn of the century.

"Stop it, Winnie," she commanded, placing both hands against her temples. If only she could blot out her knowledge of Paul's insanity. But what good would that do her, even if she could? Knowing what she was dealing with seemed far preferable when she considered the possible alternatives.

Paul was obviously suffering from a multiple personality disorder—schizophrenia? Winnie sighed and pushed away from the natural stone wall. She should've paid closer attention during psychology class. Maybe there was something she could do to help Paul—to help them both. She needed him.

Placing her hand low on her abdomen, Winnie drew a deep breath. She'd give anything for an in-home pregnancy test. Would the stick turn pink or blue?

And more importantly . . . which color did she *want* it to turn?

Winnie squeezed her eyes tightly shut. She knew the answer to her question hovered on the fringes of her subconscious, but she wasn't ready to acknowledge it yet. The feelings she had for Paul were terrifying. She needed him more with each passing day.

With a sigh she looked down to where her hand rested against her abdomen. It was beginning to look as if she might not be the only one who'd be needing Paul.

Paul looked up at Winnie from his vantage point at the bottom of the hill. Standing up there with her hair and skirt blowing in the steady breeze, she looked like a character from an epic motion picture. *Pioneer woman blazing trail,* he thought with a surge of pride. She was a pioneer all right—of time travel.

Considering all she'd been dealt since that damned storm, Winnie Sinclair was displaying amazing fortitude. She was, quite simply, one hell of a woman. One he was growing more fond of by the minute.

It was more than mere fondness that made his heart swell in his throat. It wasn't even her incredible sex appeal that really got to him, though it was certainly a contributing factor. It was *her*—whatever it was that made her Winnie Sinclair. Not genetically, but spiritually. That was it. He loved her spirit.

Loved?

Paul held his breath for a moment of serious contemplation. Yes, he loved her spirit and courage, but did he love *her?* He hooked his thumb in his belt loop. The timing was all wrong. What an understatement. It just wasn't the right time or place for him to think of anything long-lasting with Winnie or any other woman.

Winnie'd ruined him for life. Now, every time Paul had sex with a woman—though at the moment he couldn't even conjure a picture of himself with anyone else—he'd compare her with Winnie Sinclair. Somehow, he knew everyone else would come up short when equated to Winnie. No contest.

She took a few steps away from the side of the cliff, reaching up to loosen the top buttons of her dress. She folded back the fabric to expose her moist flesh to the fresh air.

Paul's heart skipped a beat, then thudded loud and strong as his blood supply redirected itself to another, very enthusiastic, part of his anatomy. It was a miracle he didn't pass out from lack of circulation to his brain.

But his brain was just fine—at least his memory was sharp and clear. In his mind's eye, Winnie bared herself before him, offering what they both wanted and needed.

His throat went dry as he started up the hill toward her. An eerie sensation—a very familiar one—washed over him. Paul froze, then turned slowly to his left. There, in the trees, stood Sam. A myriad of emotions pummeled Paul for control. Such a large part of him—at this moment, very demanding—wanted to prevent Sam from regaining control. As Sam, Paul couldn't be with Winnie, and there was nothing Paul wanted more at this moment than to *be* with Winnie in a very literal sense of the word.

Then there was his sense of duty. Where had that irritating emotion come from anyway? He'd never had to deal with it before. Why the hell'd it have to choose now to screw up his life?

He met Sam's glowing gaze. This was the reason he'd been brought here. Sam. Destiny. Honor. *Duty.* It was Paul's duty to follow through with Sam's mission. He had to take Buck Landen to Fort Smith. Only then would Paul feel he'd achieved whatever prophecy he'd been brought back in time to fulfill.

Pretty grandiose, Paul.

Less than a dozen steps separated him from Sam. Maybe Paul could convince his ancestor to grant him a few more hours with Winnie. Even one would be welcome. Paul closed the distance between himself and the specter, holding his hand out when Sam started to move toward him. The two days were gone already.

"Wait. Please." Paul sighed in relief when Sam ceased his forward movement. "I need just a little longer. More time. Please?"

Sam grinned and nodded his head. "I understand." He looked up the hill toward Winnie. "I was always partial to redheads myself. Must run in the family."

Paul swallowed hard. Why did Sam have to go and remind him of his familial connection right now? "Just a little longer, then we'll . . . get back to work."

Sam studied Paul with something resembling regret flickering in his lifeless eyes. "I'm sorry you got dragged into this, Paul." He looked upward, then met Paul's gaze again meaningfully. "It weren't my idea, but I reckon somebody thought they knew what they was doin'."

"Yeah. Somebody." Guilt weighed heavily in Paul's conscience as he tried to meet Sam's gaze and failed. Forcing himself, he lifted his gaze again to meet his great-great-grandfather's solemn expression. "You understand what I'm . . . feeling. Don't you?"

Sam chuckled and rolled his eyes. "Yeah, I been sharin' your thoughts for weeks now. Whew. It ain't been exactly easy to keep my distance from that filly, lemme tell you."

Paul felt the stirrings of jealousy deep in his gut. And he didn't like it—not one bit. "You wouldn't—"

"Nope." Sam shook his head. "I couldn't. It'd be wrong, and I'm a man who spent my life doin' what I thought was right." He chuckled again. "Seems kinda foolish to change now. I'm an honorable man, Paul. I reckon that must be a family trait, too. I weren't sure at first, but now I'm right proud to know you're my kin."

Relief flooded Paul and he released a breath he hadn't realized he was holding. "Thanks." Sam wouldn't touch Winnie. Then why had that lump formed in Paul's throat?

Guilt? Remorse? Sam was "proud" of Paul, the way a grand-parent should be of a descendant.

But was Paul deserving of such pride?

Sam shook his head and clicked his tongue. "Seems sorta strange for you to thank me." His gaze was worth a million words. "I thank you, though."

Something hot pricked Paul's eyes and he silently cursed himself. At least Sam couldn't read Paul's thoughts while outside his body—he hoped. The last thing he wanted or needed was for his great-great-grandfather, Rooster Cogburn tough guy, to realize Paul was on the verge of shedding real tears. *Damn.*

" 'Course," Sam continued, glancing up the hill at Winnie again. "It's time to do right by Winnie. I kept my end of the bargain."

Paul's eyes widened and he nearly gagged on the lump in his throat. His time of reckoning had arrived. He'd given his word—in exchange for Sam's help in getting Winnie away from Landen, Paul would . . . would . . . what? They'd never actually spelled out what Sam meant by "do right" by her. Of course, Paul had a very clear idea of what his great-great-grandfather probably meant. "My intentions?" Paul laughed quietly and shook his head. "That's a good one. My intentions."

Sam loomed nearer. "I ain't laughin'. You gave your word. Don't that mean nothin' in your time?" He folded his arms across his translucent chest. "She's a nice woman and you're gonna do right by her."

Paul quelled his laughter and inclined his head. "I prob-ably *should,* according to your ideals, but I'm not sure she'd want me to," he said thoughtfully, as much to himself as to Sam. "She's politely informed me that she doesn't need a man to take care of her in any century." Paul smiled in open pride. "She's one helluva woman."

"Feisty, that's for sure." Sam looked at Paul in open disbelief. "Will women really change *that* much between now and your time?"

Paul whistled low and rolled his eyes. "That's just the tip of the iceberg. Believe it or not, a woman ran—will run—for vice president in the 1988 presidential election. And there's a woman on the Supreme Court, too."

Sam squinted in amazement. "You must be joshin' me." He shook his head and rolled his glowing eyes again, then leaned closer with a conspiratorial air. "This woman . . . she didn't win, did she?"

Paul laughed quietly. This was great, though his thoughts were persistently drawn to the woman who waited for him. It was almost as if there existed a connection between them— a bond that distance couldn't sever. Was there some significance in the fact that he and Winnie'd been dragged back in time *together?*

"Well, did she win or not?" Sam repeated with obvious concern.

"Worried that women'll take over the world?" Paul teased, then realized his great-great-grandfather was genuinely concerned. "No, she didn't win, but it's only a matter of time before some woman does." *Damn.* There was that word again. Time.

Sam seemed to sense the shift in Paul's mood and backed away. "I think I might've found Buck's hide-out, so I'll just mosey over and have a peek while you . . ."

Paul nodded and cleared his throat. "Thanks . . Grandpa."

"Grandpa. Huh." Sam chuckled as he raised himself about two feet off the ground. "I gotta be the world's youngest great-great-grandfather."

"No doubt." Paul watched Sam float through the trees until he was out of sight. A sense of urgency swept through Paul. He only had a couple of hours at the most alone with Winnie . . . as himself. Turning to scramble up the hill, the need to hold her in his arms spurring him on, Paul knew he'd have to face his growing feelings for Winnie soon.

There was much more to this than sex, even though the fact that she was the best lover he'd ever been with sure as hell didn't help him think straight. Pausing when he reached the flat area in front of the cave, his breath caught in his throat when he met her gaze.

He saw desire and compassion in those gorgeous green eyes. And something more—undefinable. He took a step closer. Was this love? Was it love he saw glowing in her eyes right now? Was it love that made his heart seem to somersault in his chest when he saw her from a distance?

Was it love that made him realize he'd rather die than face a future without her?

There's your answer, Einstein. He was awestruck. Love? Who would've thought that the barracuda divorce attorney, as Winnie had so affectionately called him, could fall in love? Real, true, genuine love. He wanted to tell her so badly he could almost hear the words leave his lips, but he suppressed them. It wouldn't be fair to profess his love to her now, here . . . in this time. At least, not until his mission was finished.

Now I'm starting to think like a spy.

"Paul," Winnie said, taking a step toward him, then hesitating. "Are you . . . okay?"

She looked very intently into his eyes, and he realized with a sinking sensation that she was checking their color. No, he couldn't tell her his feelings yet. Not with this possession thing hanging over their heads. *This possession thing? You're not exactly Linda Blair.*

The bottom line was he had only a couple of hours before Sam would again take control of Paul's body. His gaze lingered over the outline of Winnie's nipples. Her soft intake of breath told him she knew the direction of his thoughts.

Part of Paul felt guilty for even thinking about making love to Winnie right now. He felt deceitful, though he'd been totally honest with her. It was evident she didn't believe him, though. That knowledge didn't offend him, because he doubted the feasibility of anyone believing such an outlandish story.

As his gaze traveled upward to her lips and he saw her tongue sweep across the surface, leaving a glowing pink sheen in its wake, he knew she wanted him, too. When he detected the glitter in her green eyes, he understood for the first time in his life what it really meant to love a woman. He'd do anything, go anywhere, conquer any foe to be with Winnie Sinclair. He wanted to spend the rest of his life with her, to build a home and a family with her. Only her. There'd always be only Winnie for him.

The thought struck him hard, nearly making him blurt out his feelings. But he didn't. Biting the inside of his cheek, he reached out to her, took her hand in his and held it tight. For a few glorious moments, he saw something in her eyes that gave him hope for the future. The future in any time—their time or this time. It didn't matter. All that mattered was being with Winnie, sharing the joys and sorrows of life with her at his side.

He drew a deep breath, knowing he'd have to wait to reveal his true feelings. It wouldn't be fair to tell her now, then change back into Sam later in the day. He was sure she wouldn't appreciate that. Hell, *he* wasn't exactly crazy about the idea.

Winnie reached up to touch his face with her open palm. It felt cool against his sun-warmed skin. Unable to restrain himself, he turned to kiss her palm, then found her in his arms, his lips covering hers with a sweet desperation which nearly unhinged him.

Winnie battled with the nagging voice in the back of her mind that shouted warnings against being intimate with Paul again. He was mentally ill, yet she was powerless to halt the onslaught of desire which exploded within her at his touch. She felt so giddy and foolish at times when he was near, but that was ridiculous, considering her disposition and her attitude toward women's rights.

That hadn't changed. She was still independent and liberated, but she was also in love. There was no point in denying it to herself any longer, though she wasn't ready to reveal this discovery to Paul just yet. She had to get him back to the twentieth century where modern medicine could try to help him through this nightmare.

Then they could be together—forever.

Wordlessly, he lifted her in his strong arms and carried her into the cave, where he laid her on the blanket near the dwindling fire. He dropped to his knees at her side and very slowly undressed her, making love to her with his eyes, looking at each inch of skin as if he'd never seen it before.

Winnie's gaze riveted to his as she was bared to his gentle hands and enigmatic expression. There was something almost pristine between them. For her, she knew it was the knowledge that she loved Paul that made being with him so special. But for him, she couldn't be sure. Perhaps he was sensing and responding unconsciously to her emotions. Whatever it was, it was spectacular.

He was naked beside her a moment later, caressing her breast with the palm of his hand. He brushed the eager peak with his thumb, then his mouth—his wonderful, talented mouth. Winnie moaned as he drew the peak inward, taking her beyond the realm of reality and into that surreal world of total bliss only Paul had shown her. She knew that place had always been there, waiting for her to discover its existence. But it had taken Paul to show her the way, to unlock the door and remove all barriers.

And now that she'd found it, there was no going back. Paul had to get well, so they could have a future together. Anything else was unthinkable.

Each stroke of his tongue against her nipple sent Winnie higher, closer to that state of semi-consciousness his touch always promised . . . and delivered. And as she'd recently learned, Paul Weathers wasn't a man to break his promises. Thank goodness.

He stroked her abdomen with the flat of his palm, then moved lower. He found her woman's flesh with his finger and parted her. She was swollen and empty, throbbing with longing for him. Waiting. Ready.

Winnie moaned and arched against his hand as he filled her, then withdrew, driving her nearly mad with the fierce hunger he always created within her, the longing ache which would not be denied. No part of his body was benign, nor was any part of her safe from his potency. And now, at least, she knew the reason.

"Winnie," he whispered, moving his lips down her abdomen, kissing her tingling flesh until she thought she'd shout her need for him to touch her with his lips. She wanted him to taste her, possess her, make her forget everything else for as long as possible.

Or forever.

She dragged her eyes open to watch his descent as he stroked her inner thighs with his tongue, while his fingers continued to tease and tantalize her to her core. But it wasn't enough. She had to have all of him. Everything. All he had to give . . .

Then he lifted his face and gave her a look that made her breath catch in her throat. The expression in his blue eyes made her heart surge with love, even as her body cried out with need for him.

No words passed between them, but she was sure she heard them seconds before he lowered his head to taste her. She was so aroused by the time he covered her tender nub with his mouth that she thought she might explode into a million pieces. The sensation of having his mouth and fingers loving her simultaneously was devastating. Wonderful.

Winnie whimpered and angled herself against him, wrapped her fingers in his hair as she was carried into another dimension. She saw pinpoints of light against blackness as she surpassed a pinnacle of pleasure again and again beneath his talented touch.

Then he moved and shifted himself above her, thrusting himself deep within her before she ever had the chance to float back to earth. Her body was still climaxing as it closed around him like a vise, swallowing his erection with a hunger born of love and desire. She wanted to feel him take her beyond the limits of sanity, into a realm of pleasure so intense only love could pull her from its clutches. And she knew, somehow, that he could. And would.

Wrapping her legs around him, Winnie welcomed his ardent thrusts with equal vigor. This was a desperate coupling, a union erupting from mutual enthusiasm. There was no longer anything gentle about Paul's possession, but that was as it should be. She was ready to receive him in all his primal, male fury.

Her finale neared; she knew it was mere seconds away as she tilted her hips to welcome him even deeper into her body. Winnie felt them join, like two streams swirling together as one river, merging and blending into a single entity.

The only sound in the cave was their breathing as it slowed and returned to normal. Winnie blinked back the tears that stung her eyes as he laid his head against her shoulder. She'd heard of women who cried after great sex. Now she knew why. Her emotions were raw and vulnerable, yet she had to suppress them somehow. At least for a while.

Paul raised up and sighed heavily as he met her gaze. At least his eyes were still blue. "I'm sorry."

"Sorry?" she repeated, frowning as she wondered why he regretted such fabulous sex. "Why?"

He chuckled and kissed the tip of her nose, then pulled back to smile down at her. "Not about . . . this." He looked at her naked breasts, then met her gaze again. His message was clear. "I could never regret making love with you, Winnie. Do you know that?"

Those wretched tears. They stung and pooled in her eyes

until a steady trickle of the liquid traitors managed to find their way down her cheeks. She drew a ragged breath and smiled through her tears. "Yes, I know," she whispered, not trusting herself to speak in a normal voice. At any moment, she feared she'd break down and sob out loud, then do something really foolish, like tell him she loved him.

He nodded, then rolled onto his side, raised up on one elbow with his face resting in his palm. "Good. I'm glad you realize that." He cleared his throat. "What I was sorry for was lunch."

"Lunch?" Winnie suddenly remembered that Paul had left the cave earlier to find them something to eat. "Oh."

"I managed to pick some berries." He sat up and reached for the cloth pouch he'd worn over his shoulder when he left the cave this morning. "Blackberries, I think."

"Blackberries?" Winnie sat up quickly, forgetting her thoughts of unrequited love. "You have blackberries and didn't tell me? Don't you know that blackberries are my favorite food in the whole world?"

Paul chuckled and held the bag out to her. "You mean I could exact some . . . payment for these?" His eyes smoldered with desire as he stared at her.

Winnie grinned, feeling very wicked and hungry for much more than blackberries. "Anything you want . . . cowboy, but first, the berries."

She noticed the way his eyes lit up at her words, and despite her best efforts, she couldn't prevent her gaze from drifting downward. *Oh, Lord.* He was already engorged again, ready to please them both. She looked away to gather her wits. Her heart thudded loud in her chest, echoing in her ears as she forced herself to meet his intense gaze.

"The berries?" He extended the bag toward her. "I'm feeling sort of . . . magnanimous, so I'll let you have them on credit."

Winnie moistened her lower lip, then took the bag from his grasp, reaching inside to remove a plump berry. Her mouth watered at the sight, then she put it between her lips and chewed very slowly. The juice filled her mouth and made her wonder why something as benign as blackberries should make her think about sex. For some inane reason, each time she popped a succulent berry between her lips, she became more aroused.

Of course, she knew the answer. The reason the berries made her think of sex was the promise of payment she'd already extended. "Credit, huh?" she asked quietly, popping another berry into her mouth. She really should've kept her mouth shut, but the banter was addictive. The prospect of ending it precluded the realm of plausibility. "My . . . credit's good. I really do have an, uh . . . excellent rating."

Paul gasped, and she saw his Adam's apple bob up and down in his throat. "Yeah," he said in a hoarse voice, reaching into the bag for a berry himself. "Damn good. Excellent."

Winnie shivered in anticipation as she ate another blackberry. She laid back on the blanket, unashamed of her nakedness as Paul sat watching her and slowly chewed blackberries. He ran his fingertips along the curve of her calf, just below her knee.

"You're beautiful," he said quietly, continuing to torture her with his gentle touch. Then his expression darkened and she saw the muscles in his jaw twitch. "I wish we had more time before . . ."

Winnie's hopes plummeted. For a while, she'd thought perhaps his alter ego was gone forever, but it was clearly evident that Paul was thinking about it. If he could think about Sam, he could become Sam.

She sat up abruptly, hugging her knees to her chest. "What?" she asked, wishing she hadn't, but unable to retract her question. Besides, not facing this thing wouldn't make it go away.

Paul sighed and met her gaze. "I wish like hell I could change this mess." He narrowed his sensuous lips into a thin line. "I'm sorry. I shouldn't have brought that up again right now."

"You . . . need to talk about it." Winnie rested her chin on her knees, praying she could suspend its quivering. "It's all right. Go ahead. Tell me about . . . Sam."

Paul nodded as his hand fell away from her leg. "I've already told you about how he was killed, and what he wants from me." He chuckled cynically and rolled his eyes. "I'm his . . . host, I guess."

"Uh, yeah." Winnie avoided Paul's gaze. This was worse than she'd thought. He'd never be able to handle a child along with time travel and insanity. *Please, God, don't let me be pregnant.* "And?"

"He won't rest until he's taken his killer to hang in Fort Smith." Paul shrugged. "All I know is, having met Sam Weathers, I sure as hell wouldn't want to be Buck Landen when Sam catches up with him."

Buck Landen? All the air rushed from Winnie's lungs as if she'd taken a direct hit between the shoulder blades. She jerked her head around to stare in horror and disbelief at the man she loved . . . and shouldn't. Surely she hadn't heard him correctly. "Who—what did you say?"

"I said, I sure as hell wouldn't want to be Buck Landen when Sam catches up with him." Paul chuckled, obviously unaware of Winnie's reaction to that name.

The roaring in her ears drowned out the rest of Paul's words. Winnie sat staring beyond him, at the dying embers of the fire. Her heart felt like that fire—consuming itself, then dying a slow death, never to burn again.

The man she loved was determined to see *her* great-grandfather hang for murder. He'd just as well put a bullet in her brain now, because Winnie's grandmother couldn't have been conceived yet.

And if her grandmother was never born, then Winnie couldn't possibly exist.

Thirteen

This can't be happening.

Winnie tried to draw a deep breath, but found it eluding her. Paul had somehow convinced himself that his mission in life was to see to it Winnie would never be born. The man she loved . . .

"What's wrong, Winnie?" Paul reached out to her, but Winnie shied away. "Did I say something wrong? Too many blackberries, huh?"

Winnie shook her head wordlessly before reaching for her discarded clothing. Shrugging into the dress, she searched her mind for some means of preventing this nightmare. She couldn't let Paul take Buck Landen to trial. Her heart swelled into her throat as she pulled on the narrow shoes she'd hoped, somehow, she'd never have to wear again.

Unshed tears filled her eyes, threatening to spill over and trickle down her face, betraying the depth of her pain. She mustn't let him see. Knowledge was power. The last thing in the world she needed was for Paul to realize he possessed the ability to hurt her. As long as he didn't realize how she felt about him, perhaps there was still hope for her.

Get your act together, Winnie. You don't love him—he was Dirk's divorce lawyer, for God's sake.

"Where are you going?" Paul asked, reaching out to touch her shoulder as she shoved her foot into the other shoe and tugged at the laces.

"I don't have that blasted hook thingie with me." Winnie

struggled with the laces, then finally stood up and hobbled out of the cave without closing the shoes. "Stupid, stupid, stupid."

"Winnie."

She paused, turning to glance over her shoulder as Paul leapt to his feet and reached for his jeans in one smooth motion.

"Winnie, wait."

No, she wouldn't wait for Paul Weathers, or any man. She'd struggled most of her adult life, first with an impossible marriage, then a financially devastating divorce. Now she was living a nightmare of immense proportions. Was there no end to her agony?

Fury slowly overtook heartbreak as Winnie stepped outside the cave opening and stared down at the countryside. She knew this area—sort of. If she could find the river, there was a good chance she could find her way back.

Back to where?

"Damn." She bit her trembling lower lip, commanding her tears to cease. Winnie Sinclair in love with Paul Weathers? Ridiculous. Her libido'd taken over her sense of reason for a while. That was all. Love was out of the question. Impossible.

Insane.

Like him.

"Winnie."

Paul came to stand behind her. She felt him—smelled him. Every nerve in her body came to life whenever he was near, and she hated herself for it. He was like a deadly narcotic—insidious in its subtlety. He'd wormed his way into her life and into her heart.

"What's wrong?" he repeated, reaching out to touch her hair. "Is it something I said or did?"

Winnie shook her head. For some reason she didn't want to confront him with her newfound knowledge yet. There'd be time later, once she'd determined a way of protecting her great-grandfather from Paul's insane plan.

"The blackberries," she lied, finding their aftertaste bittersweet. "My stomach."

"Ah." He placed his hands on her shoulders, then nuzzled the back of her neck. "I'm sorry you're not feeling well. I was kind of hoping . . ."

Winnie closed her eyes against the stinging sensation. Yes, she'd been hoping, too. Now it was ruined. Over. There was only one chance of a relationship with Paul. He had to recover and realize that taking Buck Landen to stand trial wasn't his responsibility. He mustn't change history. Winnie's very existence depended on that.

Still, Winnie knew she shouldn't *want* a relationship with him ever again. Surely she'd learned her lesson by now. Not only had he made her pay dearly during her divorce, now he'd turned her entire world upside down. She'd be much better off without either Paul or Sam Weathers in her life. Past, present and future.

Much better.

Her throat went dry and tightened; her lower lip trembled again. If she was better off without Paul, then why didn't she feel better?

Winnie's heart raced. She was cornered. Her instincts zeroed in on the need to escape in a big way. She had to get away from here. Away from Paul and his illness.

She stole a quick glance at him over her shoulder, then faced forward again. Would he be all right without her? *Sure. Sam'll take care of him.*

This was so crazy it was almost believable. Winnie knew practically nothing about psychology. At this moment, she wished she'd majored in it in college. How could Paul do things he couldn't possibly know how to do when he was Sam? She closed her eyes again and sighed. Well, he obviously could and that was all that really mattered. The how wasn't important.

He'd be all right without her. She had to look out for herself and her future. Winnie's throat constricted again as realization forced itself to the forefront of her thoughts. She couldn't leave Paul. If she left him, his other personality would see to it her grandmother was never conceived. What would happen to Winnie if that happened?

Would she simply disappear? Was there another dimension she'd be whisked into? A place for people who didn't really exist?

Oh, Lord. Winnie, this is really nuts.

Still, she had to consider the consequences of Paul's—Sam's—possible success. What *would* happen to Winnie if her grandmother was never born?

"Winnie?" Paul gently massaged both her shoulders and rested his cheek against the top of her head. He drew a deep breath, then kissed her gently before releasing her.

Winnie swallowed hard as he turned her slowly around to face him. The expression in his eyes was nearly her undoing. Deep concern mingled with naked desire as he smiled down at her. *Oh, Lord.*

"Winnie, are you okay now?" His gaze searched hers as his hands remained on her shoulders. His crooked grin suddenly broke the intensity of the moment. "I dunno about you, but I'd kill for an order of Hunan Beef from Egg Roll Express."

Despite herself, Winnie laughed. She couldn't leave Paul, at least not completely. He was her link to her world—the future. He'd even mentioned her favorite fast food restaurant. Those little details which had once been so trivial, now seemed paramount in importance.

Her subdued laughter trailed to silence after a moment. "I'm . . . feeling better now," Winnie said, then drew a deep breath for reassurance. "I'll be all right." But what would she do if he tried to make love to her again now? Her heart gave a small lurch of anxiety blended with anticipation. No, she mustn't let that happen again. Not yet. Not until she was certain he'd fully recovered from his illness.

Not until Sam was gone for good.

"Good." He pulled her against him and stroked her back with his fingertips. "I want you healthy and strong for what we have to face together. And we are together, Winnie. I hated it when I couldn't get out to tell you I was here with you."

Winnie's mind reeled. This was his insanity talking—not Paul. "You couldn't . . . get out?" Maybe if she understood his illness better, its particular manifestations, she'd be able to help him.

He sighed, then led her to a flat boulder near the cave entrance. Even after she was seated, Paul continued to stare into the distance. "He'll be back soon."

Winnie closed her eyes for a few moments, then stared at Paul's profile as he stood silently gazing into the distance. *He really believes this possession thing.* Mental illness was powerful. Consuming.

In a way it was true. This illness possessed Paul. Sam wasn't exactly what Paul thought he was, of course. Sam was . . . the illness. Wasn't he? Had Paul given his illness a name?

Sam Schizophrenic Weathers.

Winnie frantically searched her mind for words of wisdom. She had to help Paul. He was all she had here . . . in this time. Her feelings stemmed from far more than their bizarre situation, though that should surely be an adequate catalyst for any level of emotional response. Her feelings for Paul were far too powerful for that.

Did she love him?

Was she carrying his child?

"Oh, God."

Paul dropped to his knees at her side, searching for her hand with his in the folds of her skirt. When his warm hand closed around her icy one, Winnie's tears broke free. She was in his arms a moment later as he cradled her against his strong chest. Enfolded in a cocoon of warmth, Winnie's tears flowed as he gently rocked her to an ancient rhythm of soothing comfort.

"There, what's all this about?" he asked in a gentle voice as he shifted himself onto the boulder and her into his lap. "Tears aren't going to take us back to 1996, Winnie. Is that why you're crying?"

That was but a small portion of what precipitated her tears. Winnie sniffled, then dabbed at her eyes with the back of her hand. Paul's arms felt so right—so strong. She made no effort to leave the comfort of his embrace. For a while, at least, she needed to feel his strength surround her in this unblemished manner.

Dare she tell him about her possible pregnancy?

Their child?

Lifting her head to meet his solemn gaze, Winnie felt the words on her lips, heard them form in her mind. But for some reason she couldn't speak them. Until she felt more confident about Paul's mental health, her potential condition must remain her secret.

Her tribulation.

"Better?" he asked, staring at her as if he thought she might break.

Winnie felt fragile, but she'd always been a strong person in every sense of the word. It was past time for her to summon every iota of strength—both physical and mental—she could scrounge from the depths of her soul. She nodded, then forced a shaky smile to her lips. "Yes, I'm feeling better." *As much as possible, that is.*

"Good. I was worried about you." Paul rested his cheek against the top of her head. "I'm sorry about all this."

Winnie leaned her head back to study his expression. He seemed so sincere. She reminded herself that he believed every insane word he'd said about Sam possessing him. A shudder was born in her belly and spread throughout her body before she quelled it.

"Cold?"

"No." Winnie drew a deep breath and looked out across the valley again. "What are we going to do now?" She had to learn his plans in order to develop her own strategy. Somehow, some way, she must prevent Paul from taking Buck Landen to jail.

She needed more information about the real Sam Weathers and his demise. For a fleeting moment, she considered the possibility that Sam Weathers had never really existed. But the Hopsadors knew him—had obviously known him for quite some time. There must've been, or still was, a Marshal Sam Weathers.

Was Sam Weathers still alive?

Winnie jerked her head around to stare at Paul's face. If she could find the real Sam Weathers, would that snap Paul out of his fantasy?

She tried to ignore the lump in her throat. Her skin felt clammy and her pulse was doing the minute waltz. Was she as insane as Paul for thinking such nonsense? No, she wasn't insane. This was all too painfully real. Perhaps finding Sam Weathers really would put an end to this nonsense.

She had to at least try.

"It's getting late." Paul sighed, then eased Winnie from his lap. Sam would return soon. It was nuts, but there was a big part of him that almost feared Sam wouldn't come back. That was really crazy.

Still, he felt a connection to his ancestor in more ways than one. Paul had made a commitment to Sam; there was a job to finish. Lord knew Sam couldn't do it alone.

But Winnie needed him. Her vulnerability shook him. She'd been so strong and self-assured before all this. Even back at the Lazy H, before she'd learned that Paul was here with her, she'd seemed fairly confident. The only difference now was him—his presence as himself.

Not good, Paul.

It wasn't a sexual problem—that was for sure. Her response to him these past two days had been utterly incredible. Fan-damn-tastic.

Something had changed suddenly and drastically. Maybe he was being paranoid. It probably was just her stomach reacting to the quantity of blackberries she'd consumed.

"Paul?"

"Hmm?" He nuzzled her hair, inhaling deeply of its clean fragrance.

"I need to, uh, visit the ladies' room."

Her giggle warmed him, gave him reason to feel confident again. "Sure." He stood and helped her to her feet, then kissed her on the forehead. "The latest in modern conveniences are at your fingertips, Ms. Sinclair."

She smiled again, but lowered her gaze. Such demureness wasn't like Winnie. His Winnie was outspoken and confident. He missed that Winnie. Hell, he *needed* that Winnie.

Damn.

"Let's just hope it isn't a pay toilet. I'm fresh out of quarters." Winnie slipped from his embrace, winked, then turned to walk down the hill.

Paul stared after her for several minutes, pondering her shifting mood. Maybe it was that time of the month. He'd known enough women in his life to recognize the possible symptoms of PMS. Could that explain her moodiness? Her lack of confidence and the uncharacteristic tears?

Somehow, he knew it was more than simple hormones affecting Winnie's disposition. It was him and his big confession. When Sam came back . . .

"Guess you two didn't miss me very much. Huh?" The hollow, echoing sound of Sam's voice intruded on Paul's concentration.

"Sam." Paul looked around him until his gaze rested on

the glowing figure near the ledge. He was hovering just above the surface. "Uh, no. We didn't miss you . . . much."

Sam grinned, then moved closer. "I feel kinda funny about . . . doing this again." He continued to stare, but moved no nearer.

"Funny?" He was sure Sam couldn't feel nearly as funny as he did at this moment. The woman he loved thought he was nuts. Well, maybe he was. Why else would he be standing here waiting—expecting—his ancestor to take possession and control of his body again?

Winnie needed him—the real him. Paul's gaze darted from Sam's hovering figure to the trees at the bottom of the slope. There was no sign of Winnie, but she'd be back soon. She'd take one look at him and see those gray eyes. Those dead, gray eyes.

Not Paul's eyes.

He raked his fingers through his hair. "This is weird." He looked at Sam again. "Winnie doesn't understand any of this."

Sam chuckled. "You surprised?" He made a whistling sound. "Would *you* believe you?"

Paul smiled and shook his head. "Not a word."

"Well, then?"

"I guess I shouldn't have told her." Paul glanced again toward the trees. "She'll be back soon. You'd better . . ."

Sam looked at Paul for several moments before advancing on him. He paused directly in front of Paul. "You, uh, ready?" Sam asked.

Paul swallowed again, then nodded. He had no choice. Sam's murderer must be taken to justice. That was the purpose of this involuntary pilgrimage. Who the hell was he to disregard fate? How could he simply turn his back on such responsibility? He couldn't.

Then how could he turn his back on Winnie?

He couldn't.

"Just what the hell am I supposed to do?" Paul struggled

against the impulse to run away. He cast a furtive glance in Sam's direction. The specter's expression was filled with something resembling remorse. Paul realized with a start that his ancestor shared his uncertainty. The cocky lawman who'd originally taken over Paul's body without a qualm was curiously different.

Sam shook his head. "Like I said, I don't feel right about this no more. When I didn't know you, it weren't a problem."

Paul chuckled. "Tell me about it. I know the feeling well." This was really bizarre. "When I didn't know you, I could hate you for taking over my body. Now I feel sort of obligated to let you borrow it."

Sam nodded. "I'm much obliged, Paul." He shrugged, then moved closer. "I know where Landen's holed up. He's so close I can almost smell the son of a bitch."

A sudden chill gripped Paul. "How close?" He looked anxiously down the hill for some sign of Winnie in the trees. There was nothing. No sound or movement. The air was heavy and oppressive as storm clouds gathered overhead. "Sam, how close is he?"

Sam seemed to sense the impetus for Paul's anxiety. "He weren't no more'n a mile downriver about an hour back." Sam turned to look down the hill, too. "How long has Winnie been gone?"

Paul held his breath. "Longer than she should've." He turned to make his way down the slope again, then froze. Slowly, he turned to face his great-great-grandfather. "Dammit, Sam. I can't shoot, ride a horse, or take a man to hang by myself. I don't know how."

"But I do."

Paul nodded, then held his hands out to his sides and waited. He closed his eyes as Sam's spirit loomed nearer, then encompassed him with its penetrating coldness. The pressure in his head didn't seem as pronounced this time, though the wrenching sensation in his gut nearly made him double over in pain.

After a moment, he knew the process was complete. He was no longer in command. Without hesitation, Sam straightened, then ran into the cave and retrieved his holster and gun. As he strapped it on, he asked, "Which way'd Winnie go?"

Down the hill about a hundred yards, then into that stand of oak. Paul followed Sam's gaze until it rested on the right area. *There. That's it.*

"I reckon we make a pretty good team, after all." Sam checked his weapon, then placed it in the holster. "I don't think Landen'd come this close, but you never know."

I'm not taking any chances with Winnie.

Sam smiled. Paul felt the tugging sensation at his lips and couldn't help wondering if his ancestor had set him up for this. Was this Sam's way of making Paul "do right" by Winnie? Not that it would take much coercion at this point. He'd do anything to keep Winnie safe—to keep from losing her forever.

Anything at all.

Including marriage.

"Let's go, Sam."

Winnie stared in horror at the man's face.

"Well, well," he said in a slow drawl, circling her as if she were an animal caught in a trap.

He held a gun in his hand as if it was nothing more than a toy, twirling it from time to time as he watched her through hooded eyes. Green eyes.

Like hers.

His fiery red hair was shaggy and unkempt, curling against his collar and sticking out around the bottom of his hat. Winnie knew who the man was without hearing his name. There was no mistake. This was the infamous outlaw, Buck Landen.

Her great-grandfather.

"Oh, Lord," she whispered, glancing anxiously up the hill. She knew Paul would come searching for her after a few more minutes. She'd been gone too long already, delaying her return in order to gather her thoughts. An impossible task.

"I've been called lotsa things, but Lord's a new one." He threw his head back and bellowed with laughter.

Obviously, maintaining silence to avoid capture wasn't uppermost on his list of priorities. It was almost as if he *wanted* to attract attention to his whereabouts.

To lure someone into a trap.

Winnie's heart swelled in her throat as she continued to study her great-grandfather. Did she dare tell him her identity? Would he believe her?

If she hadn't been so terrified, she would've laughed at her ludicrous thoughts. Believe her, indeed.

Hello, Mr. Outlaw—you don't want to hurt me, because I'm your great-granddaughter, dropping in from the future for a little visit.

Yeah, right.

Did he intend to harm her? Winnie's gaze rested on the shiny weapon in his hand. The memory of Paul's story about Sam's murder returned to haunt her. Was Buck Landen capable of murder?

Her gaze drifted back up to meet his. Her breath caught in her throat as she studied his fluctuating expression. Through shuttered eyes, he studied her. Confusion flashed across his face, then quickly vanished as careful contemplation replaced it. Yes, she believed maybe her great-grandfather was capable of murder.

Had part of Paul's story been true? Perhaps Sam Weathers really was dead and Paul had conveniently assumed his identity. It was entirely possible that Paul had actually witnessed the crime, then used Sam as a convenient persona, behind which to hide his mental illness.

A vehicle for insanity.

"God, this is nuts."

Landen tilted his head to one side and grinned. It was an almost boyish smile, though tiny lines crinkled at the corners of his eyes. "Who are you?" he asked suddenly, his expression growing solemn.

Winnie took a step backward. How much longer before Paul would come searching for her? She didn't want him to walk into a trap. The bottom line was, she didn't want Paul to get hurt. She cared too much about him. Loved him. He was an attorney—not a lawman as he'd been pretending. Paul Weathers was no match for Buck Landen.

"I asked you a question."

"I—I'm Winnie Sinclair." She took another step backward as he took two toward her. "I'm Amanda Hopsador's new governess."

Buck grinned again, but it was a wicked expression. His chuckle revealed open disbelief. "Amanda don't need no governess. 'Twouldn't do her no good anyway." He shook his head and clicked his tongue. Devilment danced in his eyes. "I already seen to that."

Winnie's ears filled with a roaring sound as her heart rate escalated to an alarming pace. Amanda. Why did the sound of that name make her gut twist and her heart palpitate? It hadn't bothered her before. For some reason, when Buck Landen said it . . .

"Oh, my God." Winnie brought her hand to her mouth to smother her gasp. She couldn't breathe; her vision blurred as comprehension dawned. Why hadn't she made the connection before? "Oh, no."

"What's matter?" Buck twirled the gun in his fingers, then gripped it firmly in his fist as a snapping sound shot through the trees.

He moved toward her with lightning speed. Gripping her

elbow, he led her behind a large oak near the river's edge. "Don't you make a sound, woman."

The lump in Winnie's throat enlarged as he tightened his bruising hold on her arm and pulled her down beside him. She wouldn't dream of making a sound. Not for a few moments, at least.

Tears stung her eyes, threatening her ability to see as Paul emerged from the trees. Stealthily, he crept a few steps into the clearing, then paused. A speculative expression crossed his features as he perused the small clearing beside the river.

The urge to shout a warning to her lover surged through Winnie. She bit her lower lip to quell it, knowing that to make a sound at this point would endanger both her and Paul.

"Damned lawman's gonna meet his Maker for sure this time," Buck vowed, quickly clamping one hand over Winnie's mouth, while cocking his pistol with the other. Raising his gun hand, Buck slowed his breathing, though his heart thudded dangerously where his chest pressed against Winnie's shoulder.

Winnie couldn't let him shoot Paul. Her gaze darted frantically around the clearing as Buck's gun followed Paul's movements. What could she do? How could she stop this senselessness?

"Winnie," the other man called, cupping his hand to the side of his mouth to shout again. "Winnie."

Winnie's gasp was smothered by Landen's sweaty hand. That voice didn't belong to Paul. It was the low, growling drawl of Sam Weathers.

Tears stung her eyes as the lawman ducked into the trees again. She saw him skirting the clearing, weapon drawn. In and out, he wove his way around the circle, ever closer; danger spiraled closer with every step.

She couldn't let him be harmed, even if he wasn't Paul anymore. At least, she didn't think he was Paul. Desperate, she opened her mouth as far as Buck's grip would permit, then brought her sharp teeth down on Buck's palm.

"Yeeoow." Buck instinctively released Winnie and jerked his injured hand away.

Leaping to her feet, Winnie ran into the clearing and toward Paul. This was her only hope. She could only guarantee that neither man would come to any harm. Again, she was faced with her own mortality. Her existence.

If it came down to a choice between Paul and Buck . . .

Winnie's heart hammered at a dangerous pace as she darted into the trees near where she'd last seen Paul. She knew Buck would've recovered enough by now to renew his aim.

"Winnie," a whisper rasped from behind.

Jerking her head around to look over her shoulder, Winnie was relieved to see her lover making his way toward her. He seemed alert and capable as his gaze scanned the trees across the clearing.

A shot rang out from across the clearing, ricocheting off the tree in front of them. Terrified and confused, Winnie gasped as Paul crouched even lower, pulling her down at his side. Their opponent made not a sound as they waited for what seemed like forever.

"Landen, this ain't gonna do you no good. Give it up."

"I want the woman, Weathers."

The figure beside Winnie tensed. What was his answer? She held her breath.

Paul cupped his hand around his mouth. "No, she's my woman."

Heat suffused Winnie's face. She had no idea whether she was angry or embarrassed. A combination of the two made more sense. Paul was sick. This sick side of him had no idea how sexist he sounded.

Nor did it matter, considering how much danger they were in at the moment. Getting out of this predicament must take priority, then Winnie could sort through this jumbled mess.

Paul thought he was a nineteenth-century lawman. At the moment, she couldn't think of a better identity for him to assume.

At least he didn't think he was Marilyn Monroe.

Paul returned the shot. Winnie winced and covered her ears at the explosive sound, followed by ricocheting rings around the clearing.

"Give yourself up, Landen," Paul called in his perfect law-man's voice.

"No way." A shuffling noise from the area where Winnie'd left Buck drew her attention. She felt Paul turn his head in the same direction in which she jerked hers. A flash of red hair was the only glimpse they saw through the dense trees. A moment later, they heard a horse galloping away.

They remained cloistered in silence for several moments while Winnie considered the enormity of all that had transpired in the last few minutes. She'd seen for herself how powerful this illness of Paul's was.

And she'd remembered her great-grandmother's first name.

Her stomach lurched and burned as she considered this revelation. It was ludicrous, but she knew without a doubt that Amanda Hopsador was . . . is . . . would be—if all went as it should—Winnie's great-grandmother.

The girl was but a child. There was time for her to mature, and hopefully improve with age.

Enough to marry a known outlaw?

"He's gone." His voice was rough and rich.

Winnie stared at the man in horror mingled with amazement as he straightened, pulling her up with him. He wasn't Paul anymore. This was Sam. Paul's illness was far more powerful than Winnie'd realized. It was all-encompassing. Overpowering. Her lover actually *became* his alter ego, making him capable of performing all sorts of feats.

Her breath froze in her throat as she stared at the man who stood directly behind her right shoulder. The face was the same, as were the clothes. The voice was different. It was Sam's voice.

And the eyes . . .

They were gray.

Fourteen

"I wanna know what the hell's going on," Winnie demanded, as Sam, or Paul, guided his horse alongside the Verdigris River, en route to the Lazy H. "And who said I wanted to go back to that archaic ranch, of all places?"

She'd had enough. No man was worth all this. She'd been shot at, dragged around on a wild horse, and exposed to insanity at its worst. And best.

No, Winnie. Don't think about that.

She drew a deep breath, then forced herself to concentrate on the very real and necessary. "And I want to know what Buck Landen meant back there? Why'd he want me?" Her own great-grandfather'd held her at gunpoint. She swallowed the burning sensation creeping into her throat as her stomach contorted in fear and hunger.

Paul or Sam didn't bother to respond, though she felt the muscles in his back tense at her words. "C'mon. Enough of this," she argued, desperate to goad him into true confessions, or out of his bizarre mental state.

She needed the real Paul back now, so they could try to sort through this mess together. If that was possible. What, exactly, was she supposed to say to Paul when—if—he became himself again?

And when had he either removed or replaced his tinted contacts? They'd been so intimate the last few days—surely she would've known if he'd removed them for cleaning. No, it wasn't possible. That had to mean he was wearing contacts now. Gray ones.

Didn't it?

"I reckon Amanda might have somethin' to tell us," he said quietly. Ominously.

Winnie stiffened. Amanda. She'd pushed that revelation to the back of her mind, unable to deal with the knowledge that Amanda Hopsador—the teenager from hell—was Winnie's own great-grandmother. Compared to this, Marty McFly'd had an easy time of it with his ancestors. At least they hadn't tried to kill him.

Groaning, she laid her cheek against the strong, male back in front of her, savoring the smooth chambray shirt stretched over warm, rippling muscles. Paul's back—she'd recognize it anywhere.

Not Sam's.

There is no Sam. He doesn't exist.

She was back to square one. When she'd first arrived here in the nineteenth century, she could've sworn Sam had really been Paul in disguise. Now she had proof. He was Paul in disguise. Sort of.

Worse and worse.

"Damn."

"You got to be the cussingest woman I ever did see." He shook his head and clucked his tongue in open disapproval. "My ma would've washed your mouth out at least ten times with lye soap by now."

Winnie sighed, wondering how long she was going to have to play this stupid game with Paul's alter ego. The sad part about all this was that Sam—or Paul acting like Sam—was a congenial character. "Well, your *ma* would've had one helluva fight on her hands, then."

"There you go again." He reached up to push his cowboy hat back from his face and scratched his head, then guided his horse down an embankment, toward the river. "Paul don't seem to mind your cussin', though."

Stunned, Winnie lifted her cheek from its soothing resting place. "Paul?"

"What about him?"

"You said Paul as if . . ." Winnie rubbed her cheek for a moment, where it still tingled from resting against his back. This was really starting to get complicated now. "As if he's another person."

He chuckled. She felt his laughter through his back. It rumbled into her, filled her with something so pleasant it was downright dangerous.

Terrifyingly so.

"Paul *is* another person, Winnie." He brought the horse to a stop near a rocky outcropping where the river had formed a small pool along the bank. "Don't you got that figgered out by now? We gotta stop for a spell. Lucifer needs a drink and so do I."

"I . . . I don't know what to think anymore." Winnie's face warmed with humiliation and confusion as he swung his leg over the saddle horn, then dropped to the ground. When he pulled her from the saddle to stand in front of him, Winnie stared intently into those gray eyes. They returned her stare with a hint of amusement dancing in their depths.

"I don't understand any of this," she whispered.

He sighed and shook his head, gently rubbing her upper arms with his strong hands. "Winnie, Paul's in here." He moved his hand away from her left arm and patted his chest, then he touched her cheek ever so gently with the back of his fingers. "Don't you know he's in here? In your heart, don't you feel it?"

In her heart? Feeling immediately defensive, Winnie furrowed her brow and tilted her head back in order to see his face more clearly. He'd found his mark, and was far too close to the bull's eye for her comfort. "Of course Paul's in there. He's been there all along." She swallowed hard, searching for the right words. It was past time someone just said it outright. Perhaps Paul could be shocked back to reality.

"Paul's in there because you *are* Paul." She sighed and shook her head when he parted his lips as if to speak. "Shh. Let me finish." He nodded slowly. "Good. Paul, you're ill. You have something called schizophrenia. This Sam person doesn't really exist. He's someone you made up, so you could pretend to be him. Maybe your parents didn't let you play cowboys and Indians enough when you were a kid. Who knows? Or maybe you've always had a Roy Rogers fixation, or the Lone Ranger. That's it. It'd explain the badge, t—"

"Oh, good Lord. I dunno who all these people are, but they ain't me." He started to laugh, but Winnie didn't see anything funny about this. "Is that what you really wanna believe? 'Cuz I gotta tell you . . . this ain't no game."

Winnie drew a deep breath and laid her hand on his chest. "You *are* Paul, dammit. Why won't you just admit it, instead of standing there lying to yourself and me?" Her voice rose a little with each word until she jerked her hands away from him and covered her face. Sobs tore at her throat as tears slid unheeded down her cheeks. She didn't want him to see her cry. Feeling vulnerable wasn't exactly her idea of pleasant.

"Don't cry, Winnie." He patted her shoulder in an uncharacteristic, almost fatherly, manner. "I ain't gonna lie to you. I ain't Paul. I just borrowed his body for a spell. Who do you think you . . . been with the past two days? Me? Or Paul?"

"Paul, of course. You don't think I'd have sex with just anyone, do—" Her hand flew to her mouth. Isn't that exactly what she'd done in the first place? What had led to this entire stupid episode in the soap opera she called life? "Oh, my God." Feeling as if she'd been struck, Winnie tucked her chin and refused to meet his gaze, hating herself for breaking down in front of him.

Barracuda Lawyer was still in there. This was just the sort of tactic he would've used in the courtroom. Why not here, to her, when she was most vulnerable? "I was with Paul.

With you. Just like . . . just like on the houseboat. The first time. The first mistake . . ." Her voice was barely above a whisper as she waited for his response.

Silence stretched between them, pregnant with possibilities as Winnie waited for him to attack again. *Could* Paul be shocked out of his split personality? There was one possibility. Something so surprising, that it might do the trick. Did she dare?

What did she have to lose at this point?

Winnie dried her tears with her grimy sleeve, then slowly turned to face him. She looked up into his eyes, so filled with concern and helplessness. Perhaps she'd been mistaken about him deliberately trying to hurt her. At least, she hoped that was the case.

She had to try something.

Would this work? She didn't know what else to attempt. Besides, if it didn't work, she'd have to accept his illness and determine what to do with herself and her situation. Survival, if she existed at all after all this, must take precedence over all else.

"Paul—"

"Sam."

Winnie bit her lower lip and briefly closed her eyes as she struggled with her temper. Adrenaline pumped through her veins, threatening to override her precarious thread of control at any moment. It was nothing less than a miracle that she'd maintained her own sanity for this long.

"Sam, Paul. Whatever." She shrugged and sighed, then reached out to hold his rough hand in hers. Not a lawyer's hands now. A cowboy's—a lawman's—rough and blistered, tanned to a leathery brown from the summer sun. A lump lodged in her throat. She had to do this, not only for him, but for her. It was time she faced this very real possibility—probability. She cleared her throat, then met his gaze again. "I think I'm . . ."

He tilted his head to one side. A muscle twitched in his

jaw. "What is it, Winnie?" His brow furrowed in obvious concern. "Tell me."

Tell who? Sam or Paul? She hated this, but the circumstances necessitated it. "I think, that first night we were together—"

"Whoa. Hold on there, missy." Reddening, Sam held his hand out in front of him and backed away. "I don't reckon Paul wants me hearin' none of this. Matter of fact, I don't *wanna* hear it. No, sirree. Not this lawman."

"Ah, dammit, Paul." Winnie stomped her foot and doubled up her fist. "Why don't you just shut up and listen for a change? Always the lawyer—you have to argue every single thing that comes along. Well, argue *this,* Mr. Barracuda Lawyer."

Biting her lower lip, Winnie drove her clenched fist into his firm abdomen. "Ow." Her wrist wrenched and she felt the vibrations clear to her shoulder. It was like hitting a brick wall, but he grabbed his gut while she tucked her wounded fist beneath her armpit as if to protect it after the fact.

"Why'd you do that?"

"Because I *wanted to."* Tears stung her eyes, but she refused to heed them again. This was classic. He was the crazy one, yet a passerby would've suspected her as the mental hospital escapee.

He stood in front of her with his hand across his abdomen, no injury evident to Winnie's shuttered gaze. That figured. She'd done something impetuous and it hadn't even fazed him. "Argue . . ."

She froze, unable to form the words. Struggling against the closing sensation in her throat, she lifted her gaze to more fully meet his. He stared at her in total confusion and indisputable shock at her outrage.

"Argue what?" he asked calmly, after a few moments when she made no effort to complete her unfinished statement. "I'm listenin', Winnie." His expression softened and he nodded. "So's he."

Groaning, Winnie examined her wounded hand, gingerly flexing her fingers. Just a little bruised, nothing compared to the rest of her. She lifted the hair off the back of her neck to permit the warm breeze to dry the perspiration there as she gathered her thoughts. This was going to be tricky.

"Okay, have it your way," she said quietly, dropping her hands to her sides, then staring at him through one eye. This was really nuts, but she'd play along if there existed any possibility of snapping Paul out of this. "Listen up, Sam and Paul. Is everybody in there, now? I don't want to have to repeat this later."

Sam shot her a crooked grin that would've made her melt at another time and place. The Marlboro Man had nothing on this cowboy.

Except sanity, of course.

"Go ahead. Tell us."

Us. Winnie covered her face with her hands for a moment, then dragged her fingertips down her cheeks and neck. *Just get it over with, Winnie. Do it.*

"I think I'm . . . pregnant."

Winnie watched as his stunned expression fluctuated between scandalized and concerned. She anchored her gaze on his, waiting for any sign of Paul inside that handsome face. The lawman's facade had to give. If this was going to work, Paul should show himself right away.

But he didn't.

Still, as she stared intently into his eyes, a spark of light and color appeared in the gray, near the pupils. Color. Blue lights. Wishful thinking? Squinting, she continued to stare.

And wait.

"Well?" she asked, when he seemed unable, or unwilling, to speak. "So, tell me how you feel about the possibility of becoming a . . . a father?" Winnie'd never expected to say those words to a man. She'd abandoned all thoughts of a home and family following her divorce, resigned to living out her life as a single career woman.

But that had been another time and place. This was now.

His eyes widened and he shook his head as his increased blood flow stained his face from red to purple. *"Me? Now, wait just a minute here, Winnie. You and me both know it weren't me who . . . who—"*

"Paul. I want Paul." Tears stung her eyes again, but she lifted her chin stubbornly and folded her arms across her middle. "This . . . is his baby. I'd think the least he could do is come out and face me like a man. It's not as if I did this all by myself, you know. He wanted it—enjoyed it—as much as I did." *A baby? Really? Have I accepted this as true already?*

"Dang it, woman." Sam covered his face and shook his head. "Paul, just what in tarnation am I supposed to do about this mess?"

Winnie waited. Paul had been summoned. Surely, any moment now . . .

Dammit, Sam. Let me out. Did you hear what she said? Paul raged from inside his prison of flesh and bone. How could this be? They'd been so careful. Except for the last two days, of course. She couldn't possibly know already that she'd conceived during their cave rendezvous. *Ask her . . . how it happened, Sam.*

"I ain't gonna ask her no such thing. I reckon you both know the *how* of it anyways." Sam clenched his teeth and stared over Winnie's head, into the trees. "It ain't my place to ask a lady such questions, and you know it."

It's my place. My baby. God, a baby? A melée of emotions swept through him as he considered what a child created between he and Winnie might look like. *A baby.* Red hair or dark brown? Blue eyes or green? Or maybe they'd be gray like Sam's. Wouldn't *that* be appropriate?

Here I am accepting this like . . . it's really true. Paul wished Sam would look down at her face again. All he could see was the top of her head and the trees behind her. *Sam, I need to make sure.* He searched his memory for details of their first night together. A vivid and delicious memory of Winnie's cool fingers rolling a condom down the length of his heated—

"Stop that right this minute, Paul," Sam warned, his voice dropping to a menacing whisper. "This ain't none of my business, and I don't wanna know about it."

"Stop what?" Winnie demanded, taking a step nearer. "Let Paul out. I want the real Paul."

You heard the lady. Paul waited, sensing Sam's indecision as the seconds slipped by. *If you won't let me out, then you're going to have to ask her some questions for me. I need to know.* Of course, Winnie wouldn't lie to him. Paul was certain of that above all else. He ached to gather her in his arms, to comfort her, to tell her he loved her.

He really loved her.

"Well, it's about time." Sam chuckled and shook his head. "Reckon you're ready to do right by her now."

"Excuse me?" Winnie's voice was a combination of outrage and disbelief. "What did you just say?"

I tried to warn you about liberated women, Sam. It served the lawman right. He was hogging Paul's moment, so he could just take the heat, too.

"Well, I just said . . . I thought . . ." Sam jerked his hat from his head and slapped his thigh with it, then shoved it back onto his head. "All right. I give up. To hell with everything. Landen can just—"

A bullet zinged overhead, making Paul thankful that Sam was still in control. The seasoned lawman had Winnie in the water behind the rocks in less than a second. Sam drew his weapon and waited with Winnie, her body sheltered between his and the rocks.

"C'mon out, Weathers," a voice called from the trees. "I told you earlier, I just want the woman."

Paul was aware of Winnie tensing against his body. If only he could touch her of his own volition. But no. She was in danger and, Lord forgive him, Sam was more qualified to

protect her than he. Winnie's, and their baby's, safety must
take precedence.

There I go, sounding like a lawyer again.

As Sam scanned the wooded bank with his keen vision,
Paul's gaze followed. There was no sign of anyone, though
Paul was sure they both knew who was out there. It was
Buck Landen. Maybe this time, Sam could put an end to this
nightmare, once and for all.

"That's the plan," Sam whispered, shifting himself to
search the bank on the other side of the rocks. "There. See
him? That durned red hair'll do him in yet."

Yeah. Why the hell's Landen want Winnie?

"Amanda."

"Who are you talking to?" Winnie slowly shook her head,
then half-turned to look behind her through the corner of
one eye. After a moment, she closed her eyes. "Never mind.
Don't answer that. I don't want to know."

You have to keep her safe, Sam. Paul knew what he was
really asking Sam was to do what Paul wasn't capable of
doing himself. Sam had been on the verge of abandoning
his quest, of returning control of Paul's body to its rightful
owner. Now, that just wasn't possible. Winnie's safety came
first. *You know I can't do it by myself. Not in . . . this time.*

"Yep. I know."

Winnie muttered quietly to herself. Paul recognized a word
here and there, with "insane" and "crazy" most prevalent.
Would he ever convince her he wasn't crazy? That could
wait. Her safety came first. Why the devil did Landen want
to harm her anyway? None of this made sense.

Of course, it never had.

"It's . . . Landen, isn't it?" she asked after several long
moments of silence. Then another shot rang out and she
pressed her face against the rock. "Answer me."

"It's Landen, all right. I seen his red hair in the trees a
minute ago." Sam squinted and levelled his weapon in the

direction of a slight movement. "Redder even than yours.
He's gonna meet his Maker real soon, though."

"No. Stop. You can't do that." With sudden violence, Winnie pushed herself back against him, making Sam lose his
aim as Landen darted into the open.

"Dang it, woman. You made me miss my shot."

Wondering why Winnie had interfered, Paul watched as
Landen ducked into the trees less than fifty yards away. Landen was getting closer and closer.

And he wanted Winnie.

Why does he want Winnie? Sam must know something.
There was no possible motive for Landen to harm Winnie
Sinclair. She was from another century, for Christ's sake. He
didn't know her at all. *Why, Sam?*

"I reckon it's gotta be Amanda's doin'." Sam closed one
eye and waited. "Why'd you mess up my shot, Winnie?" he
asked the now quiet woman.

"I . . . I had to." She released a long sigh. "I'm a pacifist.
I hate violence."

Sam chuckled. "Coulda fooled me, the way you slugged
me in the gut."

"I . . . I'm sorry."

Paul felt a tremor sweep through her slender frame. *She's
cold, Sam. The baby.*

"Oh, yeah." Sam watched in the trees for several moments
more.

"I just want the woman, Weathers," the voice called again.
"Send her out into the open then I'll let you get on your
horse and ride away."

"Like you did the last time, Landen?"

A long pause made Paul aware of the thundering of Winnie's heart through her back. She was frightened. Hell, he
was terrified. Why wouldn't she be scared? And why did
that maniac want Winnie?

"Yeah. How'd you do that, Weathers?" the man asked. The

question was punctuated by a menacing chuckle, carrying on the summer breeze. "I was sure you was dead."

"Your aim was true, Buck." Sam swallowed hard. "I was dead. Heck, I *am* dead."

Bravo. Paul couldn't have done better himself. Sam'd have Landen running scared in no time with this line of conversation. All he needed were the Ghostbusters to show up with Slimer. They'd have that murderer running in the opposite direction just as fast as his boot-clad feet could carry him. Landen'd be looking for the nearest priest to perform an exorcism.

Which was precisely what Paul needed at the moment.

"Then what the hell you doin' up ridin' around the countryside?" Landen's voice sounded less confident now. "I left you for dead, but it was your own danged fault. Then you go and show up at the Lazy H to spark my woman."

"See?" Sam whispered. "I know'd Amanda had something to do with this."

I still don't get it, Sam. Paul would give anything to have Winnie in his own time, to treat her like a queen and pamper her until their child was born. To protect her . . .

But he wasn't her best protector right now. *Why would Amanda want—*

"Me." Sam sighed. "You know how Amanda's been after me. How could you miss it? That day out by the corral . . . ?"

Yeah. I remember.

"What are you talking about? And who are you talking to?" Winnie squirmed, pressing her soft bottom against the region below Paul's—Sam's—belt.

Despite their precarious situation, Paul's body had a mind of its own. Actually, that made a total of three minds—two too many. Blood pooled in his groin, making him harden and thrust against his button fly . . . and Winnie's softness.

"Dammit, Paul." Sam sighed in exasperation. "This ain't the time for such foolishness."

Foolishness? Yeah, I suppose. Winnie was strangely quiet.

It wasn't like her to stand by in silence while someone tried to kill her. Not that Paul thought she'd been in similar situations before, but he knew her well enough to recognize her subdued behavior as uncharacteristic. This wasn't his Winnie at all.

My Winnie?

"I reckon."

"Will you stop talking to yourself for a few minutes and help me figure out how to get us out of this mess?" Winnie pushed her soft bottom back against him again. "And stop sticking your erection at my butt. I hardly think this is the time or the place. Have you no shame?"

Sam's face flushed hot and he sputtered incoherently. He drew a ragged breath, then released it very slowly. "Shame is right. I reckon this was all nothin' but a big mistake."

Sam? An uneasy feeling swept through Paul. Were they driving Sam away? He couldn't let that happen. Sam had to take his killer to justice, and Paul was his only chance. His only hope. Winnie had to stay out of it. Yet how could she, when the man he and Sam were trying to capture was after Winnie?

He had to redirect Sam's thoughts back to capturing Landen. *So, why do you think Amanda asked Landen to take Winnie?*

Sam sighed, then swallowed hard. "This is pure hell, Paul," he whispered as Winnie's pressing shifted to a side to side motion. "I don't like this one bit."

You didn't answer my question, Sam.

"I reckon she was jealous, 'cuz she's sweet on me."

I see. By the way, I think you like being this close to Winnie a whole lot more than you ought to, judging from your— our—reaction. Here he was, forced to share Winnie with Sam, at least in theory. Thank God he'd avoided making it fact.

So far.

"You know how I feel about that, Paul." Sam clenched

his teeth. "She's your woman, by God. She's gonna be your wife, if it's the last thing I ever do."

Winnie tensed, but made no comment. Strange. Paul would've expected a response—a very vehement one.

Yeah, Sam. This might very well be the last thing Sam Weathers ever did. Paul struggled with his warring libido and common sense. Of course, common sense didn't enter into any of this. *I told you I'll marry her.*

"Darn right you're gonna marry—"

"What did you say?" Winnie demanded, looking over her shoulder with an expression that could melt uranium. "Marry who? *You?* Pray tell, who'll officiate? Sigmund Freud? Some other mind doctors like Jung? Or how about Sybil, the woman with split personalities?"

"Never heard of them." Sam chuckled, then another shot whistled overhead and he jerked her hard against him. "Hush, woman. Your jabberin' is distractin' me," he whispered fiercely.

She gasped and Paul felt her tense even more. A tremor swept through her and into him. Her bravado was being sorely tested by flying bullets.

Winnie sputtered incoherently for a few moments while Sam's gaze swept the clearing along the bank. Paul knew this wasn't the time to discuss their future as a married couple. Triple? *Oh, God.* And parents. Staying alive took precedence.

A flash of red hair in the trees preceded a horse's shrill whinny and galloping hooves. "He's gettin' away again," Sam said sadly and his shoulders slumped. "I dunno . . ."

Paul sensed what his ancestor wasn't saying. Was there some sort of time limit on Sam's continued presence? Would the powers that be sweep Sam away to whatever plane would be his eternity?

Damn.

"Yep." Sam shook his head and eased himself away from

Winnie. "I think it's about time I gave this up, Paul. I reckon Landen's gonna get away with killin' me."

Winnie turned very slowly to face Sam. She shivered and hugged herself against the cold, thigh-deep water. Her green eyes flashed in anger, then something resembling amusement. "There's one problem with that, *Paul*," she said carefully, ominously. "You aren't dead. Yet."

Fifteen

"I think he's gone," Sam said quietly, then grabbed Winnie's hand and led her from the water. "I missed him again. I reckon I won't get another chance."

Winnie shook her head and jerked her hand from his grasp. "Another chance to what?" She rubbed her arms to warm herself. Standing waist deep in a river wasn't exactly her idea of an afternoon of fun and games. "Play the Lone Ranger? Well, I'm not in the mood to be Tonto, so you'll have to go it alone, cowboy."

Sam sighed and shook his head. "Winnie, you gotta be the most confusing woman I ever know'd. Unless she was powerful riled, even my wife was quiet and respectful." He arched a brow. "The way a woman was meant to be."

Winnie drew a deep breath and squeezed her eyes shut. When she released her breath, she wondered what force would be powerful enough to prevent her cold-blooded murder of Paul Weathers. Right now, at this moment, she could very easily—

No, she couldn't.

Wimp. She shook her head and commanded herself not to cry, but traitorous tears stung her eyes despite her insistence. "And, as you obviously realize, I'm anything but quiet and . . . respectful," she said steadily, pinning him with her gaze. "It's time for the real Paul to come out and play. Sam can go away. We need to play grown-up stuff now."

Avoiding her gaze, Sam chuckled as he gathered Lucifer's

reins in hand and led the animal to the river. The black stallion lowered his muzzle to the water and drank.

"I ain't Paul," he said finally, then returned her steady stare. "You know I ain't Paul, but you keep insistin' I am. I'm Sam. Paul said he told you about me. Who I am and . . . what happened to me."

Winnie bit the inside of her cheek and took a few more steps onto dry ground before slumping down next to an oak tree. She'd tried everything. What possible way could there be for her to bring Paul out of this? She'd even confessed her possible pregnancy. Surely there was some way of making him acknowledge that.

She'd played her trump card—now it was time to raise the ante and call his bluff. Clearing her throat, she smoothed her skirt and turned as demure an expression as she could muster in his direction. "Why . . . Sam," she said, batting her lashes a mile a minute. Lure? "You tellin' me you're a married man?" Bait. Lure. Time to play dirty.

He swallowed hard. A surge of satisfaction swelled within Winnie as she watched his Adam's apple bob nervously in his throat.

"Was. Was married. My wife, God rest her soul, died a couple years back." He pulled his kerchief from around his neck and mopped his brow. "Warm today."

His imagination was certainly fertile. Unfortunately, that wasn't the only part of him that could claim such distinction. Involuntarily, she laid her hand across her lower abdomen. Surely this child—their child—would bring him out of this. If not . . .

If not, then she had to find a means of supporting herself and Paul's child alone. Here and now. She'd wasted enough time trying to help Paul with his problem. She had problems of her own to contend with.

Problems he'd helped create.

Heat flooded her cheeks, but she turned to face him anyway. Let her blushing work to her advantage. If he truly believed himself a nineteenth-century gentleman, chivalrous to the end, then so be it. She'd play along with that angle until a better one presented itself. Maybe she could still shock him back to reality.

I'm talking reality in the middle of a quantum leap? Winnie suppressed the groan which threatened to betray her true feelings. She needed to appear demure and vulnerable—a helpless female in a . . . family way. "Okay."

"Pardon?" He led Lucifer back up the embankment. "I didn't rightly hear what you said."

He had the cowboy vernacular down pat. For a while, she'd been convinced Sam Weathers was a different person. But not after these last few days.

A wild thrill swept through Winnie as she recalled, against her will, the way Paul had touched her, possessed her . . . loved her in his special way. Her lower lip trembled as a sense of loss so intense it threatened her sanity descended over her. Her throat constricted, felt as if it would close completely in another moment.

Leave it to me, Winnie Sinclair, to fall in love with my ex-husband's divorce attorney. Correction—my ex-husband's insane divorce attorney.

Her plan to play the injured female had backfired. She wasn't supposed to succumb to her own devices. If she didn't feel so sad, she would've laughed at the irony. Covering her face in her hands, Winnie cried. Exhaustion combined with desperation and held her in a tenacious grip—a prison bent on preventing her escape.

"Aw, don't you start bawlin' on me, woman."

She heard him take a few steps toward her, then he slapped what she assumed was his thigh in obvious frustration. He took a few more steps, then touched her shoulder.

The feel of his rough, warm hand through her cotton dress snapped Winnie back into control. For a moment, she'd almost lost sight of her goal. Drawing a shaky breath, she grabbed his hand with both of hers, then brought it to her lips. Tears could help her cause.

"Oh, Paul," she sobbed, laying her cheek in his palm, struggling with her own rising emotions as she tried to play this game. Melodrama in action. Continuing to hold his hand against her face, she stood before him, staring intently into his eyes. "What am I going to do?"

His expression wavered and she gave herself another point when his Adam's apple bobbed again. Was it working? Would her ploy drive Sam away once and for all? Could Paul's sanity be saved?

Could he care as much for her as she did for him?

Stop, Winnie. He's crazy.

Paul needed her help, not her love. At least, not right now. If they were to survive in this time, with their child, she had to bring him out of this. There was no modern medicine to help. She was on her own.

"Do about what?" he asked in a strained voice.

"About . . . our baby?" Renewed sobs burst forth, and for a few moments they were very real. Gut-wrenching. Dragging another deep breath, she renewed her efforts at self-control. This was a ploy, an acting technique. It wasn't real. At least, not entirely. "What am I going to do, Paul?"

"I ain't—" He bit his lower lip, then put his arms around her shoulders and pulled her into his embrace. Very gently, he stroked her back and held her against his firm shoulder. "I can't do this anymore." His sigh was filled with desolation. Failure. "It's time I let go of this foolishness. What's done is done. Meant to be."

Yes, it is. Winnie's hopes soared as she struggled against the persistent feeling that something was very wrong with all this. Why didn't she feel victorious? Success loomed within her grasp, yet no torrent of satisfaction appeased her need for triumph.

Why?

This Sam persona was surrendering his control of Paul.

Hadn't he just said as much? Winnie felt almost guilty about it. Ridiculous. This was what she wanted. What she needed. Wasn't it?

Stop it, Winnie. She drew a deep breath. Paul needed her to maintain her facade a while longer. Sam wasn't gone yet. More importantly, Paul wasn't back yet.

"What . . . what do you mean?" she asked in a shaky voice, lifting her face to stare into his eyes. "What can't you do anymore?"

He clenched his teeth and a muscle twitched between his ear and jaw. "This." He cupped her chin in his hand and lifted her face until she met his gaze. "I can't keep you two apart anymore. It's wrong. I feel lower than a sidewinder." He drew a sharp breath, almost as if he'd been wounded.

"Oh, shut up, Paul."

This is scary. Winnie winced beneath his self-directed verbal assault. Was Sam capable of violence? She swallowed hard, then pressed ahead. She'd gone this far . . .

"Wrong?" Winnie tilted her head back even farther, raising herself up on tiptoes to bring her mouth dangerously close to his. "Is it wrong to want a man the way I do you, Paul?" Though her words were true, Winnie hated herself for saying them. She could pretend they weren't valid, that she didn't really care for Paul, but *she* knew the truth. This was all for a purpose, she reminded herself. She needed Paul, because he was the only person in this world she could be herself with. Only Paul would—*could*—understand when she developed a sudden urge for pizza, her position on politically correct language, or why she couldn't bear the thought of wearing furs.

"Watch it, woman. You're gettin' way too close." The warning in his husky voice was unmistakable. "He ain't gonna like this one bit."

He tried to back away, but Winnie slipped her arms around his neck and held him fast. "Kiss me, Paul."

"I . . . *ain't* . . . Paul." He grabbed her wrists and yanked her hands from behind his neck. "You gotta let go, Winnie. You're Paul's woman, and I ain't of a mind to trespass on another man's territory."

"Trespass on another man's territory?" When he released her hands, Winnie let them fall to her sides as she stared at him in mute indignation. Trembling in rage mingled with defeat, she stepped away. "I'm no man's *territory,* buster. And you'd better never forget it."

She turned her back, overcome with the sagging acknowledgment of defeat. Paul was lost. She'd have to get on with her life in the nineteenth century alone.

Correction—with her baby.

"I guess . . . you don't want the baby. Don't care . . ." She couldn't prevent her words, even though she knew she'd hate herself later for them. She sounded like a helpless woman trying to trap a man into marriage. That was the farthest thing from her mind at the moment. Right now, it didn't matter to her whether Paul ever married her. All she wanted was his company and his devotion to the child they'd created together. "We don't need you anyway. I'll take care of my baby all b—"

"That's it. We're goin' to town."

He grabbed her upper arm and wheeled her around and toward the waiting horse. "Hey, what do you think you're doing?" Winnie tried to jerk herself free from his bruising hold, but his superior strength allowed none of that.

"We're goin' to town," he repeated, his jaw set in a hard line. "It's past time I made Paul hold up his end of the bargain."

"Bargain?" Winnie stared in outrage as she pulled against his grasp. "Let me go, you sexist pig. I'm part of no man's bargain." Had Paul's two personalities gambled for her? Was she the booty in a high stakes game of some sort? A sinking feeling swept through her as he held the reins and shoved her into the saddle with one hand.

Which one of them had won the prize?

* * *

What the hell are you doing, Sam? Paul couldn't believe how domineering Sam was being with Winnie. *Be careful. You're going to hurt her.* And make her really angry, too.

"Shut up, Paul and let me do what I gotta do." Sam swung himself into the saddle behind a still struggling Winnie. "Be still, woman."

"Let me go, you bully. Who the hell do you think you are?" Winnie tried to jerk the reins from Sam's grasp, but he quickly foiled her efforts with a flick of his wrist. "Why are you doing this to me?"

"This is for your own good." Sam nudged Lucifer with his knees, then pulled the reins to the side until the animal turned away from the river. "Don't know why Landen's after you for sure, but we can't set around here all day waitin' for him to come back. Can we?"

"No. I suppose that wouldn't be very smart." Winnie's voice fell to a low whisper, in stark contrast to her anger only moments ago.

Sam, what's wrong with her? Did you hurt her?

"No, I didn't hurt her," Sam said in what Paul thought was a perfect Archie Bunker voice. The only thing missing was "Meathead."

"What are you going to do to me?"

Winnie's voice trembled, making Paul realize she was genuinely afraid of him. Winnie thought he was crazy. She'd made that perfectly clear. *Sam, what are you going to do with her?*

"Exactly what I said I was gonna do when I first agreed to take her away from the ranch." Sam urged Lucifer up a slight hill and into heavy woodlands. "Make you do right by her, like you promised."

Fine. Whatever. Let's just do it and catch Landen so we can get this over with.

Silence.

Right?

Nothing.

Sam?

"Make who do right by whom?" Winnie asked in a voice dripping with sarcasm. "Exactly what sort of maneuver is this?"

She'd regained her cocky demeanor, but a telltale tremor revealed her true feelings. Was she afraid of him? Of them? The thought gave Paul reason to pause—made him sick to his stomach, as a matter of fact.

"There you go upsettin' my gut again."

"What?" Winnie sat very stiffly in front of him, her back rigid and her chin held high. "Upsetting what?"

"My gut." Sam clenched his teeth and looked off to his left. "I been powerful distracted. Sure hope Landen didn't follow us."

Winnie stiffened even more. "Follow?" She looked over her shoulder. "You wouldn't . . . shoot him. Would you?"

Sam was silent for a few moments. Then he sighed long and slow. "Winnie, why don't you want me to shoot him? He's killed more'n one man in his life."

Strangely silent, she turned to face forward again. After several moments, she sighed. "I just don't want you to shoot anyone. Okay?"

There's more to it than this, Sam. She's not telling you everything. Paul didn't know exactly why, but he was positive Winnie was hiding something. *She's up to something, Sam. I can feel it in my bones.*

"And in your gut." He shook his head and chuckled quietly. "We're goin' to town, Winnie."

"You already said that." She remained stiffly erect, facing forward as she spoke. "Why?"

Sam sighed. "You'n Paul is gettin' hitched."

Winnie's head shot around—her mouth formed a perfect circle. After a moment, her face turned fiery red. "By God, I'm not marrying you until you come out of hiding and act

like yourself. The only way I'll give you the time of day is
if you're Paul and stay Paul."

With a gasp, Winnie brought her hand to her mouth and
turned her back to him again. A tiny sob broke through,
despite her fingers clutched over her mouth. Her shoulders
shuddered and heaved as she wept right in front of him. Each
tear that fell unheeded to Lucifer's mane could just as easily
have been a nail in his coffin.

And Paul could do nothing to prevent it. Nothing to comfort her or ease her suffering.

This was all his fault. Every bit of it.

"Nope. It's my fault," Sam said simply, then sighed as if
a great weight had been lifted from his shoulders. "It's past
time this come to an end. But right now, we got us a wedding
to go to."

"I told you . . ." Winnie drew a shaky breath, but didn't
turn around as she obviously struggled with her words. "I'm
not marrying you. Not like this."

"You said you'd marry Paul." Sam clicked his tongue and
turned onto a rough road. "Bartlesville's over the next rise.
We'll find a preacher there, I reckon."

"Preacher?"

Preacher?

"Yep. Preacher."

Yeah, I remember. Okay. Paul was getting married. That's
all there was to it. If there was one thing he'd learned to
recognize by now, it was Sam's obstinance. His great-great-
grandfather'd made up his mind and there was no changing
it.

And Paul wasn't at all certain he'd try, even if he could.
This might very well be the only way he could tie Winnie
to him. He loved her and their unborn child. It still seemed
impossible that there could be a baby on the way—they'd
been so careful on the boat . . .

Of course, if Winnie hadn't conceived on his houseboat,
it was entirely possible that she had in the last few days.

More than possible—probable. Lord knew they'd done everything right to bring about such an occurrence.

And then some.

"Stop fillin' my head with them pictures, Paul," Sam said in a low growl. "Dammit, do you think you can control yourself for just a little longer? Then I'll be outta your way once and for—"

No. This was precisely what Paul had feared and wanted most. *You have to finish the job, Sam.*

"Well, that's a switch, ain't it?" Sam chuckled low in his throat and clicked his tongue to urge Lucifer over a narrow stream. "Who'd have thought you'd want me to stick around?"

I know, but I do. I want you to catch Landen and take him to jail.

"To hang."

"Hang?" Winnie looked over her shoulder again. Tear tracks marred her face with salty streaks down her cheeks; her eyes were red and puffy. "You can't take Buck Landen to hang. I won't let you."

Sam sighed in exasperation. "Why in tarnation don't you wanna see justice done, Winnie? The man's been tryin' to get his hands on you for days, in case you didn't notice."

"I . . ."

She turned to face forward again, but not before the expression in her green eyes revealed something Paul couldn't define. *Keep after her, Sam. She's keeping secrets.* Paul couldn't imagine why Winnie would want to interfere with the wheels of justice. If anyone ever deserved hanging, it was Buck Landen.

"Sometimes hangin's the only way." Sam leaned to his left and spit on the ground. A clap of thunder filled the sky, making Lucifer tense and shy to the side. "Whoa, boy." Sam leaned forward to stroke the beast's neck. "Blowin' up a storm."

Keep after her, Sam. Find out why Winnie doesn't want you to catch Landen.

Lightning split the sky, followed by a sudden boom and a long rumble. "It's buildin' up to a biggun." Sam glanced up at the darkening sky. Dark clouds roiled overhead, obliterating the sun and sky. A sickly greenish gray had replaced the crystalline blue.

You're avoiding the issue. Paul was beginning to wish he had the mental equivalent of a cattle prod for Sam. Why was he circumventing the topic of conversation here? *Sam?*

Winnie sighed. "Does this thing go any faster? I really don't feel like getting wet right now." She shivered as if to punctuate her request. "Standing in the river was enough for one day. Unless it's hot water with bubbles, I'm not interested."

"Suits me." Sam squeezed in gently with his knees, urging Lucifer into a slow trot.

Within a few moments, they left the dense oak forest behind and rode into a clearing. Glancing up, Sam sighed. "Looks like we might beat the storm to town."

Winnie nodded, but made no comment. Paul couldn't help but wonder what she was up to. Winnie was becoming secretive and conniving. Was she capable of outright deceit?

I want to know why she doesn't want you to catch Landen, Sam? Ask her again. Please.

"All right." Sam sighed and looked down a long sloping hill. "Winnie, Paul wants to know why you don't want me to catch Landen."

Gee, that was subtle.

"Shut up, Paul."

Winnie shook her head very slowly. The red curls swayed against her shoulders, making Paul want to run his fingers through them, to bring each shining strand to his nostrils and inhale its clean fragrance. Catching himself before he filled his mind with vivid images, Paul waited for Winnie's answer. He must have it. For some reason, he knew it was important.

"I wish you'd stop talking to Paul as if he's a different person." Her voice was small and subdued. She sighed, then glanced over her shoulder. Her expression broadcasted distrust in a big way. "I . . . I don't believe in violence. I'm a pacifist."

"Did you hear that, Paul?" Sam asked in an exasperated tone. "Now will you shut up and let us get this wedding on the road?"

"I told you—"

"I know what you told me, Winnie," Sam interrupted, then he clenched his teeth and sighed. "I'm sorry. I ain't got no right to talk to a lady like that."

Winnie shook her head again. It was obvious she still believed Paul suffered from schizophrenia. *Tell her I'm not crazy, Sam.* It wouldn't do any good, though. Paul knew that. As long as Sam possessed his body, Winnie Sinclair would continue to believe Paul was insane.

That was the way it had to be, then. Paul had a job to do—a duty to perform. His mission—the reason he'd been swept back in time—must be accomplished. It was crazy. Taking Buck Landen to stand trial and avenging Sam Weathers's untimely death, was something Paul *must* do. There was no other way.

"How much farther is it to town?" Winnie shifted uncomfortably in the saddle, inadvertently rubbing her backside against his groin.

Oh, no. Don't do that, Winnie. Paul tried not to respond to the direct physical stimulus, but he and Sam combined couldn't prevent his body's immediate reaction. It would always be that way with Winnie. Paul knew that. Sam must surely be learning that by now. *Sorry, Sam.*

"Yep." Sam's voice was thick and low, more like a growl than human speech. "It ain't much farther."

"You said Bartlesville. Right?" Winnie glanced over her shoulder, then turned quickly toward the front again. "Forty miles from Tulsa. Home."

"Tulsa?" Sam shook his head. "Only visited Tulsa once. Only thing I saw besides mud was that hole down by Chelsea, full of oil. Some say it'll be worth as much as gold someday." He chuckled. "I dunno. I think I'd a lot rather have the gold myself."

"The world'd be a lot better off if more people had felt that way." Winnie covered her face and sighed. "I'm starting to sound like I believe your crazy stories. Paul, stop doing this to me."

"I ain't Paul." Sam chewed the inside of his cheek and guided the horse onto another rough road. "There's Bartlesville yonder."

Paul followed his ancestor's gaze, shaking the guilt which continued to torment him. Winnie had to accept facts—Paul and Sam were two different people. Then Paul saw a crude collection of buildings in the distance. The trees had given way to open, rolling prairie around the town. *Whoa. That's Bartlesville?*

"That's Bartlesville?" Winnie echoed, then laughed nervously. "Oh, God. I really don't believe this."

"Believe it, Winnie." Sam urged Lucifer into a trot. "By sundown, you'll be a married woman."

She jerked her head around and glowered. "I told you I'm not marrying you unless you become yourself, Paul." Her lips turned white as she pursed them together.

"So be it." Sam stared over her head, into the distance at the bustling town. "I always liked Bartlesville. Some folks think it'll be bigger'n Guthrie someday."

Guthrie doesn't amount to much in my time, Sam. Paul could hardly believe the dirty little town would one day be a rich oil-producing community. The Bartlesville, Oklahoma, of 1996 would be clean and prosperous, with good schools paid for by taxes from oil revenue. *I'd sure like to have a chat with—*

"Hush."

"Excuse me?" Winnie glanced over her shoulder again

with a withering glare. "Who do you think you're telling to hush, buster?"

"Not you, Winnie," Sam said with a chuckle. "I reckon that'd be a waste of breath. Not that I got any of my own to speak of."

Her eyes grew round and her lips parted, though no sound escaped them. After a few moments, she turned around and looked straight ahead.

She's speechless, Sam. How'd you do that? Paul was incredulous. True, Winnie's behavior had fluctuated from one extreme to the other the last few days, but to be genuinely speechless, when she had no ulterior motive, was a first.

"I wish I knew the answer to that." Sam shook his head. "It's gonna be your cross to bear, I reckon."

I reckon. Christ, he was developing Sam's diction. A lawyer with cowboyese? Actually, now that he considered it, the concept had possibilities. Right now, he needed to get his attention back on Winnie, and figuring out exactly what Sam was up to. *So we're going to get married. Then what?*

Paul felt Sam's face flood with heat. "Well, what do folks usually do . . . after?" Sam swallowed hard, then brought the horse to a stop in front of a white church with a pair of double doors in front. A steeple reached to the sky and crowned the structure.

A bolt of lightning split the sky just above the steeple. *That's probably an omen of things to come.*

Sam shook his head and swung his leg over the rump of the horse, then grabbed Winnie around the waist and lifted her to the ground. She swayed and leaned full against him. "Yep, I reckon it could be."

"What could be?" Winnie whispered, staring into his face. "I'll tell you one thing, Sam—Paul, or whoever you think you are—if you want me to say 'I do,' you'd better have the real Paul front and center in about five seconds, less the guns, the star and the cowboy slang. Got it?"

That's my Winnie.

"Yep, it sure is."

"Well?" Winnie placed her hand on her hip and continued to stare.

And wait.

Her resolve was obvious, unerring. There was no way she'd back down on her ultimatum and Paul knew it. Sam must've realized it, too.

"I'll let him out when the time's right," Sam promised, then gripped her elbow and led her and Lucifer across the street, away from the church. "Lucifer's earned himself a dry stall and some grain."

"Of course. By all means." Winnie remained stiff but co-operative while Sam paid the livery man to care for his horse.

She still made no protest, even when Sam led her back across the street toward the church. Paul didn't like this. She was up to something. *Sam, watch her. I'm worried.*

"Um," Winnie hesitated at the steps in front of the white building. "Is there an . . . uh, outhouse around?" She cast a furtive glance toward the back of the building. "Back there, maybe?"

Sam's face flushed hot and fast, but he nodded without looking at her and escorted her to the back of the church. "Best hurry. It's gonna start rainin' buckets any minute now."

"Some things really never change," Winnie muttered, then stepped inside the small structure, letting the door slam shut behind her.

What do you think she's doing in there? Paul asked, then could've kicked himself for his stupidity. *I mean besides that, Sam?*

Sam cleared his throat. "I don't know. How we gonna do this, Paul? She ain't gonna agree to the weddin' unless you stand up for yourself." Sam leaned against the trunk of a tree a few yards from the outhouse door. "I can't say I blame her none."

Paul followed his ancestor's gaze skyward. The dark clouds intensified, gathering strength. This was going to be one hell of a storm. *It's up to you, Sam. However you want to handle it.* He couldn't believe he was letting go that easily. Paul sensed that he could press Sam to leave, but he was afraid to. He knew, somehow, that Sam was ready to abandon his quest, to let Buck Landen get away with murder.

Literally.

The outhouse door opened and a white-faced Winnie stepped out. Her eyes were wide, startled.

"What is it?" Sam rushed forward and grabbed her arm. She swayed against him, then laid her head on his shoulder and cried.

What's wrong with her? Winnie, what is it? Panic struck from all sides. He had to help her, touch her. *Sam?*

Winnie pulled back just enough to see his face. "I'm sorry. For a minute I thought . . . maybe I'd been mistaken about the baby," she whispered, then laughed nervously. Cynically. "I'm sure that would've been a big relief to you. Me too, of course. See, I . . . I felt sort of funny and thought maybe it was a false alarm. I thought I'd started my—"

"I don't need to hear this." Sam looked upward and shook his head. "If there's a baby, there's a baby. It don't make no difference to this wedding. Besides, even if the seed didn't grow, it was sowed, just the same. Paul promised me he'd do right by you, and by God he's gonna."

There's still a baby? Funny, but Paul had actually feared the possibility that the baby didn't exist. He should've felt relief. Strange.

The color returned to Winnie's face in a rush, flushing her cheeks pink behind her freckles. Her green eyes snapped with anger. "Fine. You want a wedding? We'll have one just as soon as the real Paul Weathers comes out to say his vows." She threw her arms up in surrender. "Do you understand that? I'll marry Paul—not Sam. Just Paul. Right now. Right here. Today."

Sam nodded, then led Winnie inside the church just as the

skies opened and dumped sheets of rain. "Anybody here?" he called into the cool, dim church.

Pews of solid oak lined both halves of the church. A cross hung behind the pulpit, simple and serene. After a moment, a tall man stepped through a door near the back of the building. He walked slowly down the aisle and paused before Sam and Winnie.

"May I help you with something?" the man asked, glancing from one to the other. His gaze rested on the star pinned to Sam's chest. "Marshal?"

"Yep, I reckon you're just the man we been lookin' for." Sam's grip on Winnie's elbow tightened as if in warning. "We wanna get hitched, Reverend."

The man smiled, then nodded. "Very well. I'll get my wife to witness the ceremony." He hesitated. "Will there be another witness?"

"Oh, yeah." Sam nodded and smacked his lips, then eased the hat from his head to rake his fingernails through his hair. "Trust me, Reverend. I'm more'n qualified to be my own witness."

"Well, Territorial law only requires one, so suit yourself. I'll be right back. This'll only take a moment." The minister shook his head, then left them.

Once the door closed behind the man, Winnie turned to face Sam. "Well? Where's the groom?"

It's show time.

"Yep."

There was only one way Paul could think of to prevent Sam from leaving for good. He didn't need the kind of guilt that would follow such an occurrence. *If you leave, I won't go through with the wedding.* There, that would take care of it.

"I already thought of that," Sam whispered, baring his teeth in something that might have been a smile. "I can let you out part ways, I think."

You think?

Sixteen

"Well?" Winnie tapped her foot impatiently on the smooth oak floor. Her charade of cool self-assurance was wearing thin in a big hurry. For those few agonizing moments when she'd thought her pregnancy was nothing but a false alarm, the relief she should've felt had been overshadowed by grief.

Gut-wrenching angst.

Why?

She drew a deep breath to steady her nerves and, with any luck, prevent her tears from emerging. Now was not the time to cry. That vow she'd made about not letting her feelings show was making a liar out of her in every way. Besides, she still couldn't be positive about the baby. Her PMS was alive and well. Either that, or the symptoms of early pregnancy were very similar.

No tears, Winnie. She wouldn't allow herself the luxury of succumbing to her true feelings. Not yet. Maybe not ever. Determined, Winnie straightened and met his gaze. She held her hands out to her sides, palms up, silently questioning. "Where's Paul? No Paul—no wedding. I think I made my position clear."

"I reckon so." Sam's gaze shifted, then he rolled his eyes upward and shook his head. "How do I know you'll go through with the wedding if I let Paul take over?"

"Take over?" Winnie laid the back of her hand against her warm cheek. Lightning flashed outside, followed immediately by a ground-shaking explosion. This storm was almost as violent as—*No, I won't think about that night.* "So, let Paul take over, or whatever you want to call it. In the words of Saint Nike, just do it."

"You didn't answer my question." Sam folded his arms just above his belt buckle and shifted most of his weight to one foot. "Well?"

It was a stand-off. Winnie should cry, but instead she felt like laughing. Even if this Sam character was Paul's sick side, he was likeable. In fact, a large part of her hoped certain aspects of Sam's personality were really Paul's. Barracuda Lawyer could use more than a little mellowing around the edges.

"I told you I'll go through with it and I will." Her eyes pricked and her vision blurred as the liquid turncoats threatened her resolve yet again. "Damn." She blinked and rubbed her eyes. "Will you just—"

"Here we are," the minister called, stepping through the door at the back of the church. "This is my wife, Naomi. She'll be your witness. Come on up here and sign my register, then we'll get on with the ceremony."

Winnie swallowed hard and held her breath. She didn't resist when the groom gripped her elbow, none too gently, and led her up the aisle. He took the pen the minister handed to him and dipped it in the inkwell, situated in a hole in the upper right hand corner of the table.

With rapt attention, Winnie watched him scrawl his signature across the page. A lump formed in her throat when she read the name.

Paul J. Weathers, Esquire.

He looked up at her and smiled as he held the pen out for her to use. Winnie gasped when her gaze met his. "Blue." Incredulous, she brought her hand to her mouth and stared. "Your eyes are blue."

"He got you to the altar without you knowing what color his eyes are?" Naomi shook her head. "I don't know what this world's comin' to."

"It isn't for us to pass judgment, Naomi," the minister gently reminded his wife, though his own expression mimicked her disapproval. "Are you ready to begin?"

Winnie nodded very slowly, then dipped the pen in the ink and signed her own name beneath Paul's. *Paul's.* Her hand trembled, but somehow she managed to complete the task and return the instrument to the minister without incident.

There'd been no opportunity for Paul to remove or insert contacts this time. None at all. This was insane. Humans couldn't change their eye color at will. Perhaps she'd been mistaken. Stealing another glance, her heart leapt into her throat at the smile that greeted her.

It was Paul—the real Paul.

Her Paul, with chameleon eyes.

His grin was reminiscent of the lone wolf expression he'd given her on the boat in another time and another storm. His beautiful blue eyes . . .

"Oh, Lord."

"Oh, He's here," the minister said with a nod of his head. "The Lord's always here in His House."

"Y—yes." Winnie held her breath as Paul took her hand in his and faced the minister.

"Dearly Beloved . . ."

It's really Paul. Winnie only heard a phrase here and there as she stared in wonder at the man beside her. Was he insane or not? Symptoms of mental illness didn't include fluctuations in eye color. This was nuts. Maybe that was the problem. *She* was insane—not Paul.

"You may kiss the bride."

"What?" Winnie jerked her attention back to the man who stared at them so solemnly.

"I said he can kiss you now, Mrs. Weathers."

Mrs. Weathers? With a small gasp, Winnie turned to face her groom. Her husband. Was this real? She felt so strange, so lost. In a moment, she'd know if this was the real Paul.

If his other personality still held him in its grasp, she'd know when their lips met.

Wouldn't she?

As he pulled her toward him, Winnie remembered another night, when he'd held her in his arms and made passionate love with her, again and again. This time was different though. She was his wife. *His wife.*

Paul's mouth was warm as he kissed her, very softly staking his until-death-do-us-part claim. Winnie banished thoughts of marriage and divorce from her mind as that magic which always erupted within her from his touch made its presence known. Her knees felt weak and watery as his arm slipped lower around her waist and pulled her firmly against his solid body.

Definitely Paul. No doubt about it.

He deepened his kiss, reminding her of their other encounters, their physical and emotional bond that even the constraints of time itself were unable to sever. Her feminine instincts answered him with a hunger which unfolded from a shadowy, private place, buried all her life beneath the veneer of competent determination she'd permitted society to see.

Was Paul as moved as she? Did this marriage mean anything to him, other than an inconvenience? Startled by the intensity of her feelings, Winnie realized she wanted this moment to touch Paul, to bond him to her so certainly that nothing could ever tear them apart. She shouldn't want this, but she did. An invisible silken thread connected them—she felt it, knew it existed, even though their circumstances threatened to negate something so fragile.

Naomi cleared her throat and the minister sighed.

Paul lifted his mouth away from Winnie's, but his eyes—so beautifully blue—bored into hers with an intensity that took her breath away. An unspoken message, a vow, relayed from his piercing gaze into her heart and mind, her very soul. The message was unmistakable.

She belonged to him.

"I reckon that's enough to seal God's work." The minister shook his head and closed the Bible on the pulpit.

"Uh, right." Paul reached into his pocket as he stepped away from Winnie, then retrieved some coins and handed them to the man.

"Thank you. The church will put this to good use."

Paul thanked the minister and his wife, then led Winnie outside. The sun had broken through the clouds, making Winnie wince against the bright intrusion. A gentle breeze stirred the rain-washed town and brought its clean scent wafting to her nostrils.

"Look." Paul stepped behind her and pointed over her shoulder to the east. "A rainbow."

Winnie stared reverently as the colors materialized. The sun was low in the west, filling the eastern sky with color and magic. Her heart leapt, then raced as she grappled with a myriad of emotions, so poignant she scarcely believed this was real.

Tears trickled down her face as Paul slipped both arms around her waist and rested his cheek against hers. His warmth radiated into her. She had his name, and she knew she could have his body whenever she wanted—a definite benefit of matrimony if one had ever existed—but would she ever have his love?

The colors lasted mere seconds as the clouds dissipated and the sun sank lower behind them. "Beautiful," she whispered, closing her eyes for a precious moment, hoping she could preserve this memory for all time. She performed a mental filesave, then backed it up on a floppy. "I wish . . ."

"What do you wish, Winnie?" Paul nuzzled her cheek with his lips, then traced her jaw with his tongue. "Hmm?"

She trembled as naked desire surged through her. He planted kisses down the side of her neck, filling her with warmth. She tilted her head to the side. "Paul," she whispered, moaning as he brought his hand dangerously near her breast.

Clearing his throat, he brought his hands to her arms, then lifted his head away from her. "We're in public, and what I want to do to you is very . . . private."

"Oh, Lord." She half-turned in his embrace. Lifting her gaze so she could see his face, she reached out to touch his cheek. The rough whiskers grazed her palm, sending shivers of excitement skittering down her spine. "Private. Yes."

"We'll find a hotel." Paul tucked her hand in the crook of his elbow, then they stepped off the porch and into the muddy street.

Winnie remained silent, feeling downright giddy as Paul led her through the door of what appeared to be the only hotel in town. He removed his hat and walked to the front counter with her at his side.

The ceiling was high, going up two stories. A rail wrapped around both sides and the back of the floors above, giving the impression the establishment was larger than it seemed. Dark paneling covered the walls where gas lamps burned, casting a yellow glow against the polished wood. It was like something out of a John Wayne movie. Winnie was no Maureen O'Hara, but at least her hair was the right shade.

As if in a dream, Winnie watched Paul ring the bell on the long counter. His profile, and everything else about him, was absolutely inspiring. In a few moments, they'd be upstairs together. As a married couple.

On their wedding night.

Oh, Lord.

A small Native American man wearing a visor came to the counter and turned the register around for Paul to sign. "Right here, please," he indicated a blank line on the page. The man glanced up, then smiled in obvious recognition. "Marshal Weathers. It's good to see you again. Been a while since we seen you through these parts."

Marshal Weathers? Winnie winced. How many people in

this time knew Paul as Sam Weathers? Doubts flooded her, but she held them at bay. *Maybe Sam's gone for good now. Maybe.*

She could hope, couldn't she?

Paul hesitated, then greeted the clerk as he signed the register: *Marshal and Mrs. Sam Weathers.* He really hadn't wanted to do that, but the clerk wouldn't understand him using the name Paul.

"Got yourself hitched, I see." The clerk smiled at Winnie. "Welcome, Mrs. Weathers. I have a bottle of real French wine tucked back for a special occasion. Looks to me like a woman catchin' this mean old cuss might be worth celebrating. I'll send it up to your room."

"Thank you," Winnie murmured as her gaze darted from the clerk to Paul. "And could we have hot water for a bath, please?"

The clerk beamed with pride. "Got runnin' water upstairs in the hall water closet, and one suite with its own. I'm puttin' you in that one." He leaned across the counter. "It's the least I can do. Your husband run some rowdies outta here one night for me. Don't know what might've happened if Sam Weathers hadn't come along when he did."

Paul searched Winnie's face for clues to her reaction. If hers was anything like his, every time she heard him addressed as "Sam" should make her wince in agony.

And where the hell was Sam? Paul hadn't heard his great-great-grandfather utter a single syllable since he'd let Paul take command. But one thing was certain, the spirit hadn't left Paul's body. He felt him—sensed him. Sam was still possessing Paul.

The clerk made a passing comment about their lack of luggage, then led them upstairs to an elegant suite in the back corner of the hotel. Paul slipped the man a coin, uncertain of its actual value, then turned to face his bride.

"I'll be right back with a light supper and the wine." Fol-

lowing the promise of food and wine, the door closed behind
the proprietor with a faint click.

Paul stared at her for several moments, acutely aware of
her emotional turmoil. It flickered in her eyes as she looked
from him, to the bed, then beyond him at something only
she could see.

"Winnie," he whispered, then slowly approached her. "I'm
sorry."

She jerked her head around to meet his gaze. The hurt and
confusion vanished as anger flashed in her eyes. Good,
healthy, reassuring anger. Winnie wasn't in shock. She'd be
all right.

"He called you Marshal Weathers." She shook her head
and met his gaze without faltering. "I thought I had this all
figured out, Paul. Who are you? What are you? How can
you be two men at the same time?" She laughed, but it wasn't
a pleasant sound. "There must've been a real Sam Weathers
before we came here."

Paul nodded, still wondering why Sam hadn't made his
omnipotent presence known. It wasn't like the old fart to
stay gone this long. Surely Sam wouldn't give up the quest.
Not yet. They still had a killer to catch.

"I told you about Sam, Winnie," he said, laying his hands
on her shoulders. "In the cave, remember?"

"Oh, boy." Winnie shook her head and a suspicious glitter
appeared in her eyes. After blinking a few times, she pursed
her lips and tilted her head at an angle to stare at him. "We're
back to that, eh?"

Paul nodded. What the hell was he supposed to say now?
Party's over, Winnie? He sighed and gently caressed her upper arms, wishing the clerk hadn't recognized him as Sam,
and that he could take his bride into his arms and make
passionate love to her. A fierce need coursed through his
veins, shocking him with its potency.

Paul Weathers wanted—needed—to consummate his marriage.

Was it insecurity that made him need that bit of insurance? Yes, that and much more. He cupped her chin in his hand and lifted her gaze to meet his again. "Winnie."

She squeezed her eyes shut and a telltale tear trickled down her cheek. He reached out with his fingertip and gently brushed it away. "Look at me, Winnie."

She shook her head, but he placed one hand on each side of her face, gently but firmly holding her fast until she opened her eyes. It was there, the love he thought he'd seen. Joy swept through him, startling Paul and making the ache in his heart compound the throbbing in his loins. This was natural and right.

Inevitable.

"Winnie, I love you."

Her eyes widened and he heard her breath catch as she stared unerringly at his face. Was she waiting for him to retract the declaration? If so, infinity would fall short, for he would never withdraw the words. Instead, he planned to say them again and again.

"I love you, Winnie."

She shook her head. "No, don't say it, Paul. Don't lie to me." There was a pleading tone in her voice. "I can't . . . stand it."

He lowered his mouth to hers, very gently caressing her lips while tasting the salt of her tears. After a moment, he lifted his face to gaze into her eyes. "I love you," he repeated. "In the future, the past, and now. Always. Forever."

"I can't . . . do this."

Her voice quivered, then she threw her arms around his neck and clung to him. His strong, independent Winnie conferred something more precious than anything he could've imagined in any century. Her self-constructed barriers, which he knew had shielded her feelings, crumbled while she stood here in his arms. Had he finally won her trust?

Did he deserve such faith?

She clung to him in silence while he held her. Nothing

would please him more than to make her his wife in every sense of the word. Here. Now.

But he couldn't.

Group sex still wasn't for him, and it sure as hell wasn't for Winnie. *God, I sound like a jealous husband already.*

Jealous of sharing his wife with a dead man?

Paul winced, torn apart by the abominable sense of duty he'd discovered, thanks to his time share vacation with a twist, and his desire to consummate their marriage. How was he going to get through this night without suffering permanent damage to his reproductive organs? Surely this sort of unfulfilled arousal—both physical and emotional—wasn't healthy.

"Paul, I—"

A knock at the door interrupted her words. With a sigh, Paul released her and turned to open the door. Their overzealous host walked in with a smile and placed a food-filled tray, complete with the promised wine, on a table near the hearth. Uncertain as to current practice, Paul passed the man another coin of unknown value. He didn't care what it cost him to get rid of the intruder.

"Thanks, Marshal."

The man must've had the good sense to realize he'd intruded on a private moment, for he quickly left them alone again. God, he was actually nervous—as a bridegroom? Paul found himself unable to meet Winnie's gaze. He uncorked the wine and poured them each a glass.

"I, uh, probably shouldn't drink," Winnie said without looking at him.

"Why n—" Paul could've kicked himself. He'd almost forgotten about the baby. He held his breath for a moment while taking inventory on his wits. *All right, use your brain for a change.* How could he have forgotten something so important? No, he hadn't forgotten—he'd just been sidetracked for a few moments. "Right, you probably shouldn't."

"I'd really like to take a bath right now." Winnie looked

lost, standing there in her torn dress, with dirt smudged across her forehead and the bridge of her nose. She smiled tiredly, then held out her skirt. "I'm afraid there wasn't time to pack."

Paul chuckled, amazed by Winnie's resilience. "I guess we didn't give you much of a chance."

"We?" Winnie shook her head and rolled her eyes. "Paul, when are you going to stop with that nonsense? There is no *we*. No Sam Weathers."

Paul drew a deep breath and clenched his teeth. How did he answer this one? At the moment, he didn't know where Sam had gone.

Or if he'd ever return.

Instead of arguing or reasoning with her, Paul nodded. "I'm sure a hot bath will make you feel better." *And some time alone might help me get my hormones under control and my brain back in function mode.*

She met his gaze for a few precious moments. Paul couldn't believe how far they'd come since that night on board the *Sooner Sunset*. Literally. Not only had they traveled through time, but their emotional journey had proved even more phenomenal.

She turned and took a few hesitant steps, then reached for the bathroom doorknob. When she paused, Paul waited for her to speak. Would she? Could she say the words he needed to hear? The words he'd shared with her from his own heart?

Silence.

"I remember . . . another doorknob," she said just above a whisper, then laughed wearily. "Another bathroom. Another night . . ."

Paul's stomach did the limbo as he recalled that night, a night he'd never forget as long as he lived, in any century. A smile tugged at the corners of his mouth and he took a step closer.

"Winnie," he said gently, laying his hand on her trembling

shoulder. "I just want you to know . . . I meant what I said. All of it. I *do* love you."

Winnie shook her head, then looked down at where his hand rested on her shoulder. "Paul, right now I'm so tired and confused I don't know what to believe." She laughed—it was a derisive sound. "So, tell me." Her tortured gaze met his. "Which one of you loves me? Paul . . . or Sam?"

Bull's eye. Paul stared in silence as she dragged her gaze from his and turned away. What more could he say? His arm fell limp at his side as she stepped into the bathroom and closed the door.

Resting his forehead against the cool wood for several moments, he drew deep breaths to quell the panic that urged him to break down the door and demand that Winnie admit she loved him. *Fool.* It wasn't possible to force Winnie to love him.

Either she did . . . or she didn't.

Consumed with doubt, he turned away and trudged wearily to the tray bearing their dinner. Their wedding supper. That was a laugh. He picked up the bottle of wine and stared at its ruby contents, where light danced in a broad array of colors. His grip tightened little by little as the injustice of their situation overwhelmed him. His eyes stung and his stomach burned.

He envisioned the bottle striking the plastered wall, splintering into millions of shards of glittering glass, each one dripping with wine as it soaked into the brocaded carpet. Holding it out in front of him, he gritted his teeth, then brought it back over his shoulder, prepared to launch the missile. Anything to relieve the life-threatening tension building within him. He was a bomb about to explode.

Winnie's life was in chaos and it was all his fault.

No, it ain't your fault. It's mine.

"Shit." Paul dropped the bottle and watched it land without incident on the settee beside the table—far less gratifying than seeing it shatter. He stepped back, struggling with his initial shock and confusion as he came to terms with the thought's origins. "Sam."

Who the hell else'd be yackin' away inside your head?

"This is a switch." Paul raked his fingers through his hair and slumped down on the settee beside the bottle of wine. Not only hadn't it broken, but the cork was still securely lodged in place. He placed the bottle back on the table and released a ragged sigh. "What took you so long?"

I was thinkin'.

Paul nodded. "Well, that makes two of us." He chuckled and laced his fingers together and cradled his pounding forehead in them. "What are we going to do now?"

I think it's time I give up on takin' Landen in.

"No." Paul straightened and dropped his hands into his lap. He couldn't let Sam do this. It was too important. "You think I made this trip into the *Twilight Zone* for nothing? I won't let you do this, Sam. You have to finish the job."

No, I don't reckon I do.

Several moments of silence compounded the tension, made Paul's heart thud so loudly in his chest he heard it in his ears. All this for nothing? "No, you have to finish the job, Sam. Why else would I be here? And Winnie? If you give up, then all this has been nothing but a travel agency discount tour gone sour."

That's the reason I gotta give it up, Paul. Don't you see how I'm messin' things up with you and your wife?

"My wife," Paul repeated, rubbing his sweaty palms on his jeans. "My wife." He glanced up at the closed door again. "She doesn't want me, Sam."

Yep, she does. She just ain't figgered it out yet. That's why I gotta let it go so you'n Winnie can get on with livin'. I had my chance—lived a pretty good life for a while. But it's done.

Paul swallowed the lump in his throat and pounded on his knee with his fist. "This isn't fair, Sam."

Life ain't fair.

"I won't let it go." Paul stood and retrieved the bottle of

wine. Rather than throwing it, he opened it and filled a glass. "What'll it take to make you pursue Landen? Finish this job?"

He brought the glass to his lips and tilted his head back, draining its contents within a matter of seconds. The sweet wine hit his empty stomach and created a roiling sensation, then threatened to exit via the same route it had entered. "Whoa."

Paul placed his hand across his abdomen, then reached for the bottle again. Maybe another glass would settle his stomach. Or kill him.

"Well? I'm waiting for an answer," he said before tasting the wine. The second glass went down easier, then warmth spread through his veins and his stomach grew accustomed to the wine's presence. "What'll it take, Sam? Name it. I don't plan on wasting this trip through time. I'm here for a purpose, dammit."

Anything? Remember last time?

"Yeah, I remember," Paul growled, then gulped a mouthful of wine. "What'll it take?"

Make Winnie your wife in every way.

Paul coughed and choked on a mouthful of wine, grabbing a napkin from the tray to mop the mess from his shirtfront. "What did you say?"

I said I want you to make Winnie your wife in—

"I heard you." Paul clenched his teeth and returned his empty wineglass to the tray. "You know how I feel about . . . sharing that."

Hold on there. I ain't got no hankerin' to be here when . . . when . . . well, you know.

Oh, yes. He knew all right. Involuntarily, Paul's gaze found the closed door again. "What are you saying, then?" He knew damned well what Sam was saying. It was simple and clear—no possibility of a misunderstanding. His heart hammered against the walls of his chest, his blood thickened and pooled in his groin. The damned wine wasn't helping the situation any either.

I'll leave for a spell, but only if you gimme your word that you'll . . . you'll . . . Ah, hell—you know what I mean.

Paul laughed and shook his head. It wasn't as if he needed any encouragement in that direction. Making love to Winnie was at the top of his list of favorite pastimes. "I don't understand this."

Paul, you're my kin. Winnie's part of the family, too. I can feel it.

Paul nodded. Crazy as all this was, Sam's words made sense. "All right, that's true." He rubbed his chin with his thumb, waiting for Sam to explain this bizarre request. "I still don't understand all this. Why is it so important to you that Winnie and I—"

I want it legal—sealed. Understand, Paul? I wanna go to meet my Maker knowin' my great-great-grandson's married and is gonna stay that way.

Stunned, Paul digested Sam's words. He understood all right. What his great-great-grandfather didn't understand was that marriages weren't always permanent. At least, not in the twentieth century. "What if Winnie doesn't want to stay married to me, Sam? Have you thought about that?"

She will. I told you I know it—feel it in my bones. Get it through that thick skull of yours.

"Not thick enough to keep you out," Paul muttered, shaking his head. He glanced at the door again. Nothing would please him more than to consummate his marriage. To bind Winnie to him, for better or worse, at least in a spiritual way.

But, by God, he'd damned well make it for the better.

I'm gonna see how far this flyin' stuff'll take me. I gotta hankerin' to see George one more time.

"Yeah." Paul blinked back the burning sensation in his eyes. Clearing his throat, he nodded. His great-great-grandfather was going to see his son—Paul's great-grandfather—

one more time. "I understand. When will you be back? Should we wait here?"

You can find your way back to Hopsador's, can't you?

Paul nodded. "Sure."

Don't forget what I said now.

"No." Paul took a deep breath. "I won't forget. Be careful, Sam. Grandpa."

What could happen to me, Paul? It done happened already.

"Yeah, I suppose."

Sam stepped from Paul's body, then stood for a few moments in the center of the room. The glow around him had faded from the last time Paul had seen Sam in this form. "Sam?" Alarm shot through Paul as he took a step toward him. "You're . . . fading."

"I feel different, that's true enough," Sam said in his hollow spectral voice, then shifted toward the window. "I'll meet you at the Lazy H in a few days. Don't try nothin' with Landen."

Paul watched Sam fly through the window, past the glass and all, then vanish. A gut-wrenching sense of loss filled Paul. He had a nagging suspicion that Sam wouldn't be able to return. Whatever power had enabled Sam to remain on earth for this long was fading.

"Dammit."

Splashing. Water sloshing over bare skin. The sound drifted through the bathroom door, jarring Paul from his musings about the unexplainable. His thoughts gathered and focused on the woman—undoubtedly naked—behind the door.

His wife.

Seventeen

"God, I don't believe this." Winnie stared at her reflection in the full-length mirror. What she wouldn't give for her own bed, her own tub, her own *life*. Enough of this adventure through wonderland. She'd surpassed her lifetime quota of adventure quite some time ago.

The warm water perked her up somewhat. At least she didn't feel like a zombie stand-in for a horror film anymore. *Progress—how nice.*

What was she going to do about Paul? Sam? Buck Landen and Amanda Hopsador? Groaning, she dunked her head under water, then came up sputtering for air and pushed her hair out of her face. What a paradox. If she let Paul do what his Sam persona wanted him to, then Winnie's great-grandfather might be hanged for murder before her grandmother was conceived.

By the same token, for some insane reason, Buck Landen seemed determined to kidnap her. Why? She lathered her hair with the perfumed soap while contemplating this dilemma. She was damned if she did and damned if she didn't. The way things were going, she was damned anyway. Why else would she be living this hell?

She was receiving ample punishment for every possible transgression she may have committed during her entire lifetime—and beyond. Her feelings for Paul were interfering in all this. Winnie Sinclair should be tough enough after her divorce to know better.

Especially with her ex-husband's divorce attorney.

Scrubbing her scalp as if that might purge her mind of uncertainty, Winnie blinked back the tears that threatened to escape again. *Enough already with all this boo-hooing.*

The worst part of all this was that she was crazy about Paul. She even liked Sam, though it was Paul she—

"No."

She wouldn't permit the word to form in her mind. Not right now. There were far more important things to contend with at the moment. Her love life, such as it was, could wait—had better wait.

Did Buck Landen want her dead? Winnie shuddered, lowering herself to her chin in the warm water. Her own ancestor, though he didn't realize that, of course. She knew now where her red hair had come from. A smile tugged at her lips, but quickly vanished.

My great-grandpa is a murderer.

If Paul's alter-ego's claims proved true . . .

"Great," she whispered to her reflection. "I'm the descendant of an outlaw and a spoiled brat."

Wrinkling her upper lip, she scowled at her sunburnt face while questioning the wisdom of the person who'd elected to place the mirror so near the bathtub. Humans tended to have a natural urge to stare at themselves when mirrors were handy, and if Winnie Sinclair was anything, she was human. Unfortunately.

Wishing she'd noticed the freestanding mirror before climbing into the tub, Winnie wadded up her washcloth and hurled it at the silver. The oak frame teetered to one side, then crashed to the floor, sending shards of silver splintering across the room.

Winnie sat upright and stared in horror. She'd had no intention of breaking the mirror. It seemed the cost of venting her anger escalated with each occurrence.

Status quo.

Shrugging, Winnie sat upright and poured a pitcher of

lukewarm water over her soapy hair. She'd just as well finish and get out so she could clean up the mess.

"Winnie, I heard a crash. Are you all right?" A knock followed the query. *"Winnie?"*

Sputtering at the water running down her face, she called, "Just a mi—"

The door opened and Paul poked his head around the corner. "Are you—"

"I said, I'm fine," Winnie said through clenched teeth, wishing she still had the washcloth with which to cover at least a small part of herself. Not that it made any difference, of course. Paul had seen, touched, kissed, every inch of her. *Oh, Lord. Don't think about that now, Winnie.* "Will you just get out?"

"Sure, I'll . . ."

Winnie wiped her hands over her face to clear her vision, then turned her gaze on the ogling man who'd invaded her bath . . . and her life. "Did you ever hear of privacy? You're staring at me, Paul."

"Yeah, I sure am." His Adam's apple bobbed up and down, he moistened his lips, then raked his fingers through his hair. "You're all . . . wet."

Winnie strangled the laughter that threatened to spring forth. "People generally do get wet when they bathe. Or hadn't you noticed?"

"Yeah." He grinned suddenly and his gaze dipped lower. His pulse visibly quickened at the base of his throat and his temples. Those eyes seemed to caress her bare flesh, her breasts.

His eyes were still blue—very blue.

Winnie felt her heart do a little flip, then race along at a startling tempo. It didn't matter how much she tried to convince herself that Paul wasn't the right man for her, that he was insane and maybe even dangerous. None of that mattered when he looked at her . . . like that.

Hot—*blue* hot.

He'd said he loved her. The expression in his eyes said that and much more as he took a tentative step toward the tub—closer to her. She shouldn't want him, but she did. *Damn.* She felt her breasts swell right before his eyes. The cooling water didn't help matters any. She felt wet and wild beneath his heated gaze.

"Winnie." His voice was hoarse, thick with emotion and desire as he took a few more steps, then knelt beside the tub. There was no sign of his alter ego as he reached out and lifted a damp red curl from her shoulder and wrapped it around his index finger. "Winnie," he repeated.

"Paul, don't." She closed her eyes as he trailed his fingertips along her cheek, then lower to her chin and the side of her neck. "We can't."

"Can."

She opened her eyes and found him closer, mere inches from her face. His breath cooled her damp flesh and enticed her blood to a fevered pitch. She wanted him so much she ached inside. It wasn't just sex anymore—not with Paul. There was an emotional link between them now that eternity couldn't sever. She knew it, felt it, dreaded it all in one pithy moment.

This man—this mixed up, sexy lawyer—had turned her world to misery and joy with very little effort. She bit her lower lip as his caressing fingers moved lower, inch by devastating inch, touching the curve of her shoulder and turning her insides to jelly. She should resist and deny her arousal and his. She should . . .

"I love you, Winnie," he whispered, leaning closer to claim her lips in a kiss so soft, if it hadn't been for the explosion in her core, she might have questioned whether it had actually happened.

The significance of the moment rippled between them.

As his lips very gently possessed hers, Winnie was cognizant of his fingers gliding along her wet skin, finding the side of her aching breast to impart additional torture. He cupped her breast in his hand, lifting her and flicking his thumb across her puckered nipple.

"Oh, God," she whispered as he kissed his way across her jawline to the lobe of her ear. "Paul." Winnie entwined her fingers in his hair as he trailed kisses across her shoulder to the upper curve of her breast.

She was lost.

Her nipple throbbed and pouted, waiting for him to sample it, but instead he lifted his head and stared long and hard into her eyes. An unspoken challenge leapt between them. Winnie sucked in her lower lip in anticipation of his words— words she both dreaded and craved.

"I want you, Mrs. Weathers," he said quietly, his voice low and rough, slithering deep inside her to perform an erotic cotillion with her already rampant libido.

She nodded, mesmerized by the intensity in his voice, his eyes, his open invitation. There was no point in denying it. She couldn't even if she tried. By this time, he knew her well, her needs, her responses. She'd be lying to herself to think otherwise.

"I know," she managed, holding her breath as his hand again found her breast and he circled her impatient nipple with his thumb. She released her breath very slowly as he moved steadily closer, then kissed her again, more firmly this time.

Winnie moaned as he parted her lips and filled her mouth with his tongue, painfully reminding her of all the other ways a man filled a woman. She needed him, wanted him . . . loved him. Yes, she loved him. No more denials—no more sidestepping around the issue. She was in love with Paul and he claimed to love her, too. His illness was something they'd work through together.

The water had grown cool even as her body warmed beneath an onslaught of hormones she was certain would've stymied modern medicine. This felt so right, so wanted, so inevitable.

When he dragged his mouth from hers, they both gasped for air. He continued to hold her breast in his hand as his gaze probed hers. "I want you, Winnie," he repeated raggedly, his nostrils flaring as he obviously struggled with his desire. "Do you . . . ?"

It was her call. Winnie struggled with the differing voices inside her mind. The voice of her conscience said, *No, this is wrong.* Her liberated woman persona shouted, *Are you going to let this man have his way with you again?* The inner woman's voice quietly reasoned, *You love him—he loves you. We're married. What could be more right?*

What, indeed?

"Yes, Paul," she whispered, choosing her answer from among the various choices. "I want you. God help me, but I do want you."

He lifted her wet body from the bathtub and carried her from the room. She shivered from a combination of damp skin and anticipation as he lowered her to the bed.

"Are you cold?" He hesitated, standing beside the bed.

"No." Winnie reached out to him, took his callused hand in hers. "All I want right now is you."

Desire darkened his eyes to cobalt as he slowly unbuttoned his shirt and eased it from his shoulders. The lamp burned brightly, casting dancing yellow fire across his magnificent body.

Winnie felt downright decadent, sprawled atop the quilt, waiting for her husband to join her. It was marvelous. There was something painfully right, above reproach, about sharing this time with Paul in the traditional way of wedding nights since the advent of civilization.

Were they legally married? Was it possible, since neither of them had actually been born? Yet here they were, flesh and blood man and woman, beyond ready to consummate their marriage. Yes, this was real. They were married, at least in every way that mattered.

He dropped her hand for a moment to loosen his belt and

the buttons at his fly. Winnie's heart soared when he suddenly shot her a devilish grin, then slid his jeans down past lean hips to expose that part of him she remembered so well.

Accurately, too.

Heat flowed like honey through her veins as he rested one knee on the edge of the bed and paused, his gaze raking the length of her. Winnie's body anticipated his touch, his kiss, and craved his expert way of loving her.

She wanted him to blot the unpleasantness from her mind, to obliterate the pain and uncertainty with ecstasy. With these thoughts fueling her desire, Winnie rolled onto her knees to face him, marveling at what a beautiful man she'd married.

"Winnie." His whisper was a caress against her cheek and a key to her soul. He reached up to outline her lips with his fingertip, then inched his way closer until the crisp, dark hairs on his chest brushed against her susceptible nipples.

"Oh, Lord," she whispered, remembering against her will their first time together. She should've known then that Paul was in her blood. This desire he'd created and now commanded with his merest touch, wasn't something she could willfully suppress. It was a powerful force, a potent drug, addictive in the best and worst possible ways.

She reached between them and grasped his engorged sex with both hands, savoring the velvet hot feel of him, intense and pulsating with lifeblood. Hers—he was hers. Overcome with a feeling of power, Winnie rubbed herself against his impressive erection, felt their hairs mingle and tease, tantalizing the other to greater expectations.

"God." His voice was thick with passion as he reached behind her to cup her bottom in his large, callused hands, then lifted her slightly up and against him.

Winnie gasped. She wanted more—she wanted *him* deep inside her, filling, giving and taking. This was far more than mere need or desire. It was necessity. Paul's love, his possession, her possession of him, were a part of her now. This

was who and what she was, would always be. What she
wanted to be.

"I want this, Paul," she invited, tilting her head slightly
to watch his fluctuating expression as she continued to hold
him. There was no doubt he was as hot as she. "Inside me."

He flinched at her words, gritting his teeth as she slid her
hands to the tip of his erection to tease in slow, erotic circles.
His breathing became erratic as her manipulations increased
with her own escalating passion.

Growling, he gripped her waist and wrenched her away
from him, throwing her none too gently onto her back. He
hovered between her thighs, panting and staring at her. Winnie reached between them again, but he grabbed her wrists
and foiled her attempt.

"No more of that," he said harshly, then gently pinned her
adventurous hands on either side of her. "Now it's my turn."

"Promises, promises." Wickedness flowed through her as
he claimed her lips in a searing kiss, plunging his tongue
into her mouth to suggest more intimate endeavors.

The curling hairs on his chest rasped against her breasts,
making her nipples hard and eager for his touch. Easing his
grip on her wrists, he dragged his mouth from hers and kissed
his way down her neck to her breast.

With his tongue, he traced teasing swirls around her nipples, then released her wrists to cup her breasts, molding
them into greater prominence as he enticed and promised.
Winnie pressed herself against his mouth when he at long
last found one nipple and further tested her endurance by
barely grazing the tender cusp with his tongue.

"Paul." She moaned impatiently, then gasped outright
when he fastened his mouth to her breast. Hot and wet, he
drew on her with his mouth until she thought she'd go mad
from the want of more.

Paul wanted her even more than he'd realized. Never in
his entire life had he suspected that the desire for a woman
could become such a powerful, driving force. Winnie was in

his blood, his life, his heart. She was a part of him, the very best part. Life without her wasn't worth a restraining order against a dead man.

Without Winnie, that's what he'd be inside—dead.

Like Sam.

She laced her slender fingers through his hair and held him against her, banishing conscious thoughts as he tasted her, relished the miraculous realization that she was his. At least for now.

"Now Paul," she whispered urgently, wrapping her legs around his waist to pull him against her in open invitation. "Now."

How could he resist such an invitation? Paul reluctantly released her breast, then lowered his engorged body to meet her tempting folds. She was ready for him—warm and wet, softly opening to take him inside.

Lord, he was going to die right here on the spot. Biting his lower lip in an effort to control his nearly explosive level of arousal, Paul entered her slowly, savoring each devastating millimeter. She encompassed his sex in a vise that nearly unhinged him, drove him beyond sanity to a new plane reserved just for men who'd surpassed turned on and moved ahead to ballistic with no effort whatsoever.

Dangerous territory.

Uncharted waters.

Winnie arched against him, taking him more fully into her. Paul squeezed his eyes closed, battling with the urge to release himself here and now. This was a job for Superman, but Paul vowed to rise to the challenge. The possible rewards were worth any level of temporary self-denial.

Moving rhythmically against her, Paul nearly lost the gossamer thread of self-control remaining to him when she tightened fiercely around him. Winnie pulled him into her, locked her ankles behind his back and met him thrust for thrust.

Wild abandon swept through him. This was like that first night all over again, except they were sober . . . and married.

Even marriage, that he'd denied and forbidden himself for so many years, couldn't dampen the passion he felt for Winnie. As he drove into her, he felt her gathering climax. She tightened around his shaft with a tenacity that pulled him beyond any semblance of sanity.

He was lost and glad of it.

Hot and fast, he exploded inside her as she clenched him in a stronghold of sexual bliss, clutching him tight with her legs and woman's flesh. Together, they strained against one another until the throbbing between them eased slightly and enabled Paul to lift his head to study her face.

"I love you, Winnie," he whispered, marveling that he'd finally found a woman he could say those words to.

And mean them.

A slow smile spread across her face and she moistened her lips. She nodded very slightly, then her smile broadened. "I know." Sliding her legs down the length of his, her expression grew solemn. "I love you, too, Paul. More than anything or anyone in the whole world. I never thought it was possible, but it's true. And it's frightening."

His throat filled with something—tears?—as he stared at her lovely, freckled face. At this moment, he was the happiest of men, in his honeymoon suite with his bride. Such a simple yet complex situation. People fell in love and were married every day, all over the world. But they didn't travel through time to accomplish it.

He smiled and kissed the tip of her nose, rolling onto his side to stroke her cheek and brush her tangled hair from her face. "You're beautiful."

She laughed. It was music, floating around him and filling his heart and soul with its beauty. "Yeah, right. Sunburnt with freckles, and a mane of hair Phyllis Diller would envy."

He had to chuckle along with her. It was true. The well-dressed, manicured, coiffed woman he'd first seen in the courtroom would bear little resemblance to this nymph. "Hmm. I think I like this Winnie better."

Her expression grew solemn and he saw her pulse quicken at the base of her throat. She nodded. "It's funny, but I like me better, too." She giggled, and pushed his hair back from his eyes. "I like the you who's here with me better, too. You know that?"

Paul stiffened. What did she mean? Did she like Sam better than Paul? No, of course not. She hadn't permitted Sam to make love to her. But what if Sam had tried to seduce her? Would she have . . . ?

Stop it, Paul, he cautioned himself, realizing his jealousy of a dead man was foolish, unfair and unwarranted. Winnie loved him—not Sam. And nothing could change the fact that Sam Weathers was very dead.

Maybe even his ghost was gone for good.

A cold sweat popped out on his forehead and he wiped it away.

"Are you okay?" Winnie furrowed her brow and reached out to feel his cheek. "You don't have a fever."

"I was just . . . thinking about something." Paul covered her hand with his, then turned his mouth into her palm and kissed it. If only she'd believe him. For some reason, it was important to him that she understand why he had to capture his great-great-grandfather's killer and take him to stand trial.

That was like asking Rush Limbaugh to endorse national health care, gun control, and the gay rights movement.

Hell, he didn't understand any of this. All he knew was that Sam Weathers had taught Paul something he'd never known he could feel—a sense of duty, obligation and honor. Paul was honor bound to see Sam's killer stand trial. Even if Sam didn't—couldn't—return.

The yuppie divorce attorney had found something more important than making a buck. Love and honor.

Winnie and destiny.

Nothing else mattered.

How the hell had this happened?

Paul gave an amazed chuckle and kissed Winnie on the

forehead. He was one of the good guys now and it felt damned good. Pride nudged its way into his heart, mind and soul, something Paul hadn't felt since his early college days. He felt ten years younger.

He pulled Winnie against him and kissed her beautiful mouth, hoping she felt his happiness. This was a moment he'd never forget. He'd found the woman he could spend the rest of his life with and himself all in one day.

Their wedding day.

Winnie moaned and leaned into the kiss, trailing her fingers along his rib cage and making him harden in anticipation. He'd never have his fill of her. She touched something so deep inside him it was terrifying yet priceless—definitely a risk worth taking.

He cupped the back of her head in his hand, tasting and exploring as her caresses grew bolder. Her cool palm came flat against his lower abdomen, mere inches from the part of him that screamed for her touch.

Filled with purpose, he gathered her close and rolled onto his back, taking her with him to pursue what only she could make him want—a hunger so profound it could never be slaked.

Breaking the kiss, she lifted her face to stare into his eyes. "I do love you, Paul." She bit her lower lip and he saw tears pool in her eyes. "I hope we both know what we're doing— that we won't be sorry for this . . . later."

Paul understood her meaning—that there was so much more involved here than either of them could possibly put into words. "I'll never be sorry for marrying you, Winnie," he said quietly, pushing a stray curl behind her left ear. "I love you more than I ever thought possible. Yeah, it makes me feel vulnerable, but that doesn't lessen it any. I love you, no matter what, where . . . or when we are."

A tear rolled down her cheek and dripped onto his forehead. It felt warm and wonderful, because it was part of

Winnie, and because it had been caused by the love they shared.

"I love you, too, Paul," she whispered, obviously trying to repress more tears. She shook her head, then kissed his cheek. "You're right about it being scary, too."

She looked away, but not before Paul saw a moment of doubt flicker in her gaze. He clenched his teeth, realizing in that second that she still questioned his sanity, and perhaps even his motives. If she couldn't trust him, then how could she truly love him?

"Winnie?" His tone was serious, carefully controlled. "Look at me." Reminding himself that she had every reason in the world, and then some, to doubt him and their situation, he cupped her chin in his hand and turned her to face him. "Winnie?"

She met his gaze. Guilt and doubt mingled to form an expression that tore at his heart, strangled his throat and tied his gut into an agonizing knot. She doubted him and felt guilty as a result. It was painfully obvious in her tear-filled green eyes.

"I'm not crazy, Winnie."

"What?" She looked away again. "I didn't say that."

"Not now, but you did earlier, and you're still thinking it." He stroked her cheek with the backs of his fingers. "Winnie."

She turned slowly to face him again, blinking several times in an obvious attempt to dam her tears. "Then how do you explain . . . ?"

Paul grinned, knowing he shouldn't, yet unable to prevent it. This was so absurd it defied explanation, making laughter a last ditch offense. Or perhaps defense.

"Sam?" He quirked an eyebrow. "I told you back in the cave about Sam."

"I remember."

She tensed, then rolled to his side, severing—temporarily, he vowed—their physical and spiritual link. Determined that they maintain some physical contact during his conversation, he turned halfway to face her, propping himself on his side.

"I saw Sam, my great-great-grandfather, stabbed to death with my own two eyes." Paul placed his hand on her upper arm, massaging very gently as he spoke. His chest tightened and burned as he recalled the vivid image of Landen's knife finding its mark. "It was on the banks of the Verdigris, right after the storm. Sam was stabbed—murdered by Buck Landen."

Winnie's soft intake of breath was undeniable and confusing. He slid his hand up her arm and touched the side of her face. "What's wrong, Winnie?"

Her face paled beneath her sunburn and she moistened her lips, then met his gaze. "I'm listening."

Frowning, Paul nodded. "All right." He knew she was keeping secrets—what he didn't understand was why. "Sam sort of . . . borrowed my body. Remember, I already told you all this."

She nodded and her expression issued a silent challenge. "Oh, I remember all right," she said tightly, her tension radiating into him. "I also remember your eyes changing color and you walking around thinking you were Sam Rooster Cogburn Weathers, U.S. Marshal. That doesn't qualify as mentally ill? Give me a break, Paul."

"Winnie, I—"

A knock at the door made her pull away. Gritting his teeth in frustration, Paul leapt from the bed and pulled on his jeans. "Just a minute." Before he could say a word to Winnie, she left the bed and ran into the bathroom. He stared forlornly at the actual and emotional door as it closed between them.

Again.

"Damn."

"Marshal?" The knocking resumed.

"I'm coming." Paul clenched his fists, prepared to do battle, then crossed the room shirtless and barefoot to jerk open the heavy door. "What is it?"

The proprietor took a step back. "I'm s—sorry to interrupt, Marshal, but they got trouble across the street in the saloon."

Great, now I get to come to the rescue. "What kind of trouble?" This was Sam's forte, not Paul's. *Sam, where the hell are you when I need you?* Then he remembered where Sam had gone—to see his little boy one last time.

"Remember that redheaded fella who gave us so much trouble summer before last?"

Paul's stomach lurched and an adrenaline rush flew to his toes, then back to his brain. "Redheaded?" His mouth went dry and every nerve in his body advanced to alert mode. It was fight or flight time. "You mean . . . Landen?"

"Yeah, that's the one." The man shook his head and whistled low. "He's downstairs lookin' for you. Says he's gonna tear the place apart unless he finds you real fast. Claims he saw your horse at the livery."

Paul winced. Lucifer was indeed at the livery, and was probably as singular in 1896 as a DeLorean would've been in 1996. Hiding was pointless.

So Buck Landen was downstairs looking for Sam Weathers, undoubtedly planning to finish what he started back on the banks of the Verdigris. The outlaw might have a little trouble killing a dead man, but he sure could do some damage to the still living—like Paul.

"Better get your guns, Marshal," the man said, his face flushing and perspiring. "That guy's in an ornery mood."

Guns? "Great, just what I needed right now." Paul glanced back over his shoulder at Sam's holster and pistols. Just what he needed . . . Landen would eventually find his way to the hotel in search of Sam. It was the most logical place to search after the saloon.

"Better hurry, Marshal." The proprietor shifted nervously and chewed his bottom lip. "He's . . ."

"He's what?" Paul narrowed his gaze and shot the man

what he hoped was an ominous, Clint Eastwood, look. "Spit it out, man. What's he doing?"

"He's . . . got one of the girls, and says if you don't come over there right now, he's takin' her with him." He shook his head and gave a helpless shrug. "No tellin' what'd happen to her . . ."

Paul understood more than the man was saying. "She your girl?"

The man's Adam's apple bobbed up and down in his throat. "Yeah. We're fixin' to get married next month."

Paul released a long sigh, knowing his options had all vanished. He couldn't let the girl be harmed in order to protect himself. Where the hell had all this honor come from anyway? It was all he could do to keep from laughing out loud at the ridiculous situation.

Without a word, Paul rushed into the room and pulled on his boots and shirt, then picked up the holster and buckled it around his hips, low the way Sam had worn it. He swallowed the lump of apprehension that formed in his throat. When Sam had controlled Paul's body, wearing the guns hadn't been an option. There was an incredible difference this time—one Paul didn't like in the least.

He paused outside the bathroom door and knocked softly. "Winnie?" he called, then pressed his ear against the wood. Her muffled sobs tore at his gut—twisted it into a hard core of self-loathing. "Winnie, I have to step out for a few minutes. I'll be back as soon as I can. Will you be all right here by yourself?"

Silence.

"Winnie?"

Something solid hit the door, making Paul jerk his ear away, startled.

"Oh, just go away . . . *Sam*," she shouted, then another object hit the door.

Her anger was a good sign. Wasn't it? Right now, it was

better to have her angry than crying. He couldn't bear to hear her cry. "I'll be back in a little while." *I hope.*

"You comin', Marshal?"

"Yeah, I'm coming." Paul dragged himself away from the door, but allowed himself one more glance before leaving the hotel room. Surely whatever power had brought him back to this time wouldn't let anything happen to him. Winnie needed him. They were together in this nightmare. The thought of being alone here in the nineteenth century settled in him with an ominous sense of dread. Not that—not for either of them.

"Marshal, c'mon." The man walked ahead of Paul, but glanced back several times.

"Afraid I'll chicken out?" Paul cursed the shudder that shot through him. Chicken out was exactly what he'd like to do most right now.

The man cast Paul an expression of total bafflement. "Everybody knows Sam Weathers is anything but yellow. You're a legend in these parts, Marshal. Now let's get."

Dammit, Sam. What the hell am I supposed to do now?

Eighteen

Paul hesitated just outside the saloon entrance. *This is nuts.* He knew better than to just walk in through the front door with a crazed outlaw waiting for him.

"What you plannin', Marshal?" The small man wrung his hands while Paul stood silently in the dark, deserted street.

"Beats the bloody hell outta me." He shoved his hat back and ran his fingers through his hair. "I don't think walking in and saying how the hell are you is a good idea. Do you?"

The clerk chuckled, then nodded in agreement. "Nope. That's a fact."

"Can you go back inside without . . . triggering anything?" *Great word choice, Paul.* "I mean—"

"I know what you meant." He sighed and stepped onto the boardwalk in front of the saloon. "I can go back inside, but you'd best use the rear entrance."

Paul couldn't argue with that logic. A back entrance was just what he had in mind. "All right, but don't let on that I'm coming." *As if I know exactly what I'm doing.* Who was he fooling anyway?

As the man moved toward the swinging doors, Paul shifted into the shadows near the edge of the building. A shout sounded from inside, followed by a long string of curses. Landen wasn't happy that the man had returned without Sam Weathers.

Paul laid his hand on one pistol at his hip, then the other. They were both there and loaded. He knew that from the last time Sam had used them when Landen had them pinned down by the river. "God, I wish Sam was here."

"I am."

Stunned, Paul whirled around to face the glowing image at the side of the building. "Where'd you come from?"

Sam shook his head. "I couldn't leave once I heard Landen shouting and carryin' on in there," he said, his voice weak and shaky. "Besides, I don't got enough strength left in me to get clear to Fort Smith."

Paul held his breath for a few moments while he struggled with a surge of emotions. "I . . . I'm sorry. I know how much you wanted to see George again."

Sam moved closer. "Seein' me woulda scared him, so it's probably better this way."

Paul nodded, knowing his great-great-grandfather was right. A small child would either be terrified, or accept without question, the appearance of a ghost. Sam had obviously decided it was a risk not worth taking. "I understand."

"Yep, I reckon you do."

They stared at each other for several minutes. "You done the right thing, marryin' Winnie," Sam said finally, then turned toward the saloon when Landen shouted again and a woman screamed. "We gotta put a stop to that."

"I know." Paul sensed something different about Sam—a resignation to his fate, perhaps. "I'm . . . glad you're here. You know I don't know how to use these at all." He patted the holster. "But you do."

"In my sleep—er, dead or alive." Sam shot Paul a spectral grin. "Sorry."

Paul managed a wry smile. "It's all right." Silence again. Not a soul stirred on the dark streets of Bartlesville. "We'd better just do this."

"Ready?"

Paul nodded, preparing himself to be possessed again. The first time Sam had taken over his body, Paul never would've guessed that he'd ever willingly invite the spirit to possess him. Here he stood, in the dark streets of a town in Indian Territory, welcoming a ghost into his body.

Weird.

It took less than a moment, then a slight pressure in his abdomen, followed by a brief shooting pain in his head, told Paul the deed was done. Sam controlled Paul's body again.

"Y'all set?" Sam asked, shrugging his shoulders as if checking Paul's body for fit.

Yeah, all set. Paul felt like an airline passenger, placing all his trust in the pilot. In this case, the man at the controls was far more qualified than Paul. *Let's get that girl away from Landen before somebody gets hurt. Uh, and make sure it isn't me. Okay?*

"I know. You've sure as hell told me enough times." Sam chuckled. He sounded stronger from inside a living body. "This is your body and I'd best treat it right."

Damn straight.

"Just tell me one thing, Paul, before we go in there," Sam said quietly.

What?

"Did you—is Winnie . . ." He sighed, then drew a deep breath. "Did you make Winnie your wife in every way, Paul?"

Paul hesitated, then realized how important this was to Sam. *Yes. And thanks for letting us have a wedding night.* At this moment, Paul figured it was more than likely that this would be the last time Winnie ever let him touch her. Everything was fine—much better than fine—until she'd heard the hotel manager call him "Marshal."

Sam moved to the rear entrance of the saloon, then paused in a square of light coming through an open window. He quickly checked both guns for ammunition, then replaced them. After glancing in the window to ensure the room was vacant, Sam swung one leg over the sill and slipped silently into what appeared to be a kitchen.

You're pretty good at this, Sam.

"Shh." Sam crouched low behind a long counter, then slowly straightened, drawing his weapon at the same time. "Now hush so I can think."

Of course, no one else could hear Paul, but his thoughts would probably distract Sam, so the request made perfect sense. Paul didn't want anything to interfere with Sam's ability to reason right now. This was a matter of life and death.

Paul's.

Sam took several quick strides in total silence, then stopped near a partially open door to listen. Through the narrow crack, Paul saw Landen. He sat at the bar with one arm draped over a young woman's shoulders. The hotel proprietor stood less than ten feet from the pair, his eyes wide and frightened.

"Just let her go," the man pleaded. "She can't help you."

Landen snickered, then tilted his head back to look at the woman at his side. "I dunno," he said sarcastically. "Weathers'd probably come after her. 'Course, it would've worked better if that redhead would've come after me."

Was that why Landen had wanted Winnie? To use her as a lure for Sam? *Sam? What does he mean?*

No answer. Of course, Sam couldn't speak right now without risking being overheard.

Sam straightened from his crouch, then locked the hammer of his pistol in place and stepped through the door, leveling his weapon at Buck Landen. "Let the girl go, Buck," Sam said in a deep snarl. "I'm the one you want, so turn around and face me like a man."

Landen stiffened, then turned very slowly to face him. This was the first time Paul had been close enough to the outlaw to actually see his features. He was obviously well into his thirties, with a ruddy, sun-weathered complexion. A mass of red curls stuck out around the brim of his cowboy hat, probably like Harpo Marx would've looked as a redhead.

"Tell me, Marshal," Landen said in a quiet voice, com-

pletely opposite of his usual manner. "How is it you got up
and just walked away after my blade found its mark?"

Sam clenched his teeth and stiffened slightly, but to anyone else, Paul knew his great-great-grandfather appeared
poised and ready to do battle. God, Sam Weathers was one
hell of a man. Pride swelled within Paul—not only in his
ancestor, but in himself as well.

"Reckon that's for me to know." Sam waved his weapon
toward the door. "Just step away from there and I'll let you
walk out that door."

Landen chuckled and pushed himself away from the bar.
His left hand was less than six inches from his own gun,
fingers poised and curled, obviously prepared to draw the
weapon with the slightest impetus.

But Sam already had his drawn, clutching it tightly with
his index finger poised to squeeze the trigger. Paul felt a
huge relief sweep through him. There was no way Landen
would get the better of Sam. The odds were in Sam's favor.
And Paul's.

Footsteps sounded on the boardwalk just beyond the
swinging saloon doors, then they swung open suddenly, re-
vealing a man in a black hat and long coat. Obviously drunk,
the man swayed as he squinted to focus on the group. "What
the devil's goin' on in—"

The shot seemed to come from nowhere. If it hadn't been
for the searing pain in his right arm, and Sam's sudden lurch
as he clutched the injury, Paul would've questioned whether
it had actually happened. But this was real—his arm was on
fire.

But Sam didn't drop his gun as he staggered after a re-
treating Landen. The outlaw bounded past the newcomer,
then vanished in the dark street as Sam followed.

A shout of victory erupted from the darkness, followed
by hoofbeats echoing through the deserted town. "Damn,"
Sam whispered, and Paul realized they couldn't pursue Lan-

den in the dark, especially not with an injured arm. "He got away again."

But you saved the girl. Paul felt compelled to comfort Sam, sensing his ancestor's frustration. The hoofbeats grew distant until no longer audible. *We'd better find a doctor.*

"Yep." Sam turned back to the saloon and stepped inside.

"Thank you, Marshal." The woman rushed over to Sam and looked at his arm. "Thank you for helping me."

"Yes, thank you." The woman's fiancé came forward and offered Sam his hand. "I think we'd better have that arm looked at."

A real doctor, Sam. Not a horse doctor or the local barber. Sam gritted his teeth, then nodded. "Get the doc."

"Right here." The drunk who'd inadvertently assisted Landen's escape stepped forward. "Lay him out on this table and I'll have a look." The man looked at the hotel manager. "On second thought, we'd best get him to my office in case I need my bone saw."

"Sure, Doc."

Bone saw?

"They don't call him a sawbones for nothin'." He chuckled, then turned to follow the physician into the darkness.

I'd better come out of this with both arms intact, Sam, Paul insisted, wishing Winnie'd come out of the hotel to find him. Right now, he felt the need for an advocate, and it wouldn't hurt if she held his hand through all this either.

The doctor unlocked the door to his office and lit a lamp. "Sit down over here, Marshal." At least he seemed sober now.

"Doc, no saws," Sam said quietly.

When the doctor turned as if to protest, Paul knew it was only Sam's warning glance that stayed him. "Whatever you say, but if you get gangrene you'll be beggin' somebody to lop it off."

"I doubt it."

Me, too.

* * *

A shot echoed through the darkness, making Winnie pause at the door to the livery stable and hold her breath. A figure dashed across the street, no more than twenty feet in front of her, leapt onto a horse tied in front of the livery, then galloped away.

She brought her hand to her throat. Where had Paul gone? Had he been involved in the shooting? Was he hurt?

"Stop it, Winnie."

Wiping angrily at her tears, she opened the door and slipped inside. Except for the horses and a cat perched in a moonlit window, the stable was vacant. She breathed a sigh of relief.

Now, if only she could summon the courage to ride Lucifer.

Alone.

Why would anyone name a horse Lucifer? Suppressing a shudder and deciding she didn't want to know the answer to that question, Winnie approached the beast, recognizing him immediately, even in darkness. He was taller, stronger and far more terrifying than any of the other horses in the livery.

Taking Lucifer wasn't stealing, exactly. Winnie was no horse thief.

"Horse thief, indeed," she muttered, reaching out to touch Lucifer's velvety muzzle with trembling fingers. "There, there. Winnie's going to take you for a midnight ride. Won't that be fun?" *Oh, yeah—a real blast.*

Assured that the horse recognized her, Winnie searched around for the saddle. It was slung over the wall separating the stall from the next one. Grabbing the saddle horn and the back of it, she heaved.

It didn't budge.

"Damn." Gritting her teeth, Winnie tried again, but the heavy saddle wasn't about to succumb to her meager strength. The effort brought an unwelcome thought rushing back with a vengeance. At least she didn't have to worry about lifting heavy objects, or going horseback riding now.

Not now that she was certain . . . no baby was on the way.

Trembling, she turned back to face the horse, feeling his muzzle for the halter. The nasty bridle with the hard bit was gone. Well, that was fine with her.

Why am I sad? Her period should be welcome assurance. Instead, when she'd discovered her pregnancy was nothing but a false alarm, Winnie'd felt devastated. Dizziness washed over her, threatening her ability to reason and survive in this ridiculous situation.

Well, she'd had enough of that. It was time for Winnie to take control of her destiny again. She wasn't pregnant, and as far as she was concerned she wasn't married either. How could her marriage to Paul be legal when neither of them had been born yet?

It couldn't be. Simple answer.

Her mission must be to ensure that she would be born one day. She drew a shaky breath and decided she could ride Lucifer bareback. She really had no choice in the matter, she decided, laying the wool saddle blanket across the horse's back.

Would the horse allow her to ride him? She gently stroked his muzzle for several minutes, hearing the thunder of her heart and the voices echoing through her mind. She had to get out of here, back to the Lazy H and Amanda—her great-grandmother. Perhaps the girl could tell Winnie where to find Buck, so she could reason with the outlaw.

Reason? *Hey, Mr. Landen, you don't want to hurt me. I'm your great-granddaughter.*

She'd deal with that when she found him. First things first. Climbing onto Lucifer's back and finding her way to the Lazy H were all that mattered right now. Nothing else could be accomplished until those simple—*ha!*—tasks were completed.

A lead rope hung over the stable door. Winnie looped it through Lucifer's harness, then stepped onto an overturned bucket and swung her leg over the animal. He bobbed his head up and down, then snorted once, almost in approval.

"A saddle would be so much better." Winnie looked down at the dark back and head, wondering how she could make him go. Cars were so much simpler. Accelerate or brake—elementary. "Go?" Nothing.

She chewed her lower lip, trying to remember how Paul, when he thought he was Sam, had made the horse move. Maybe he'd used his legs somehow, but she couldn't be sure. Besides, she might accidentally make the horse move too fast and make her fall. That was a very distinct possibility. Talking to the beast seemed her only alternative. "Giddyup, Lucifer."

To her utter astonishment, the horse walked slowly from the stall. Winnie clung to his mane and the lead rope, wishing the flesh on his back wouldn't roll from side to side with her. She felt as if the slightest shift would deposit her on the ground.

It would.

Chuckling, she realized the livery stable door was only partially open. Lucifer stopped in front of it, then nudged it open with his muzzle.

This is spooky. It was almost as if he understood what she wanted from him. Who was she to question a miracle? Lord knew she could use a few about now.

"Okay, Lucifer," she whispered, as they emerged from the livery and into the street. "Let's go to the Lazy H."

C'mon, Winnie. He isn't a cab driver. "Um, to see Rufus?" she asked, and the horse turned to the east and continued his slow pace.

"This must be what they mean by horse sense." At this moment, she knew Lucifer had a lot more common sense than she did. The events of the last few days had all but killed her. Learning of her true feelings for Paul and the magnitude of his mental illness had been devastating, to say the least.

And the realization that her great-grandfather was the same man Paul thought he was duty bound to take to justice . . .

"What a mess."

Lucifer nickered in response.

"Now I'm talking to horses and they're talking back." She shook her head, relaxing somewhat. Lucifer seemed to like her for some reason, and she had no choice but to trust him and his instincts.

She looked around her, allowing Lucifer to continue in whatever direction he chose, not that she had any choice in the matter. She could either look at what she could see of the passing scenery, or linger on the traumatic events which had disrupted her life.

Easy choice.

It was a beautiful night. Like a black shroud, darkness enveloped the land as the horse plodded slowly along the road, through thick wooded areas, then emerged onto high plains where the stars seemed so close she felt certain she could reach out and pluck one from the sky. The night was warm and quiet, mocking the apprehension which filled her heart.

She hurt. Deep inside where the most damage could be inflicted, Winnie ached. All her life, without realizing it, she'd wanted a man she could truly love with all her heart and soul. For a little while, she'd convinced herself that the youthful attraction she once felt for Dirk had been something lasting, but now she knew better. Now she'd experienced the real thing—true love.

And it hurt like hell.

Exhaustion settled over her as Winnie slumped forward against the horse's neck. Emotionally and physically drained, she wrapped the rope around her wrist and laced her fingers in Lucifer's mane. With any luck at all, she'd maintain her seat until they reached the Lazy H.

And Amanda-the-Hun-Hopsador.

Sunlight blasted Winnie in the face, jarring her awake to cuss the morning with a vengeance. She must've forgotten to close the shade last night.

Then the shifting animal beneath her reminded her where she was.

And when.

"Damn." She pushed her hair back from her perspiring face and straightened, groaning as her stiff muscles protested the movement. "Where are we?"

She blinked several times until her eyes adjusted to the bright light, then stared in disbelief. "Good God, Lucifer," she said in awe. "You did it."

He whinnied and bobbed his head as Winnie slid from his back, flexing the hand which had been wrapped in Lucifer's mane. Hitting the ground with bone-jarring impact, she kept one hand on the horse's back until she was certain of her ability to remain upright.

The Lazy H sprawled out before her. A smile tugged at her lips as she turned toward the stable with Lucifer's lead rope in hand. He more than deserved whatever it was horses received after hard work.

"Well, if it ain't the fancy governess, come back to beg for her job." He chuckled. "You're too late, though. The real one done showed up."

Winnie squinted and stared at the man standing near the barn door. Immediately recognizing one of her rescuers from the quantum boating accident, she forced a smile to her lips and walked into the barn when he opened the door. Was it Stinky or Oscar?

Stinky Lemuel—that was it.

Real one?

"What do you mean the real one showed up?" She bit her lip. Now what the devil was she supposed to do? "The real governess—that Kathleen MacGregor person?"

"That's the one." Lemuel spit in the corner and tilted his head at a cocky angle. "Says a family fished her outta the river, then took her in a spell. Helped her figger out the Indians around here ain't nothin' to be scared of."

"I see." She took a deep breath. This could complicate things considerably.

"In fact, she ain't a bit scared of them anymore." Lemuel chuckled and shook his head. "She up and married Rufus the other day."

"Married?"

"Is that Sam's horse?" Lemuel stared in obvious awe at the docile beast, seeming to completely forget the news he'd just delivered. "How the hell'd you git him to let you ride? And bareback, no less."

Forcing thoughts of Kathleen MacGregor's arrival and subsequent marriage to Rufus aside, Winnie suppressed the urge to gloat about the horse. "I asked him to let me and he did," she stated simply, then smiled again when the man stared in astonishment. "Amazing what being nice to people and horses can accomplish. You should give it a try sometime."

"Well, I'll be." He moved around and opened a stall for Lucifer, then stepped aside when the animal bared his teeth as he passed.

Winnie laughed softly. "I guess he must like me for some reason."

"Yep, that's for sure." Lemuel turned his attention to his chores, though he continued to chatter as he worked. "This horse lettin' you ride him is just 'bout as crazy as the boss gettin' hisself hitched like he done."

"That does seem strange." Winnie frowned.

"Yep."

"I'll bet he was mad at you for bringing a substitute like you did." Winnie shrugged.

Lemuel cast Winnie a sidelong glance as he rubbed down the horse. "I reckon it was downright mean, the way we made you pretend to be the woman who was s'posed to come be Miss Amanda's governess."

"Yes, I remember." How could she ever forget that fateful day?

"Boss took a likin' to the real one when she showed up here, then they up and got hitched, the same day she showed up. I ain't never seen the boss so taken. Went to Wichita for a weddin' trip." Lemuel paused in Lucifer's grooming to stare curiously at Winnie. "Where'd you run off to?"

"It doesn't matter now." It shouldn't matter to Winnie that the real Kathleen MacGregor had finally arrived. Her trunk had been here all along, waiting for her.

And being used.

"Uh, thank you for taking care of Lucifer." She needed to get away from here, before her great-great-grandfather and his bride returned.

Lemuel grinned and nodded. "No trouble. I don't mind tendin' the horse." He shot the beast a wary look. "If he'll let me."

"He will." Winnie gave Lucifer a stern look. "Won't you, Lucifer?"

The animal bobbed its head.

"Well, I'll be damned," Lemuel said quietly, scratching his head as he stared at Winnie. "How'd you do that?"

"I told you—he likes me."

Sighing, Lemuel turned his attention to feeding and watering Lucifer.

Winnie turned to leave the barn just as a shadow appeared in the doorway. She looked up to meet Amanda's angry gaze.

"Well, how'd you get aw—I mean, why'd you come back?" the girl asked, her expression filled with confusion and distrust. "I didn't expect you. What . . . changed your mind?"

Amanda Hopsador is my great-grandmother, Winnie reminded herself, drawing a deep breath to steady her nerves. She wanted desperately to love and respect this girl, though at the moment all she could do was remind herself of all the mistakes Amanda would make in her early years. If not for those mistakes, however, Winnie wouldn't exist. Buck Landen and Amanda Hopsador were responsible for Winnie's very life—her existence.

Moistening her parched lips, she took a step toward her. "I was convinced I had to leave for my safety," she explained, wondering how she'd ever manage to make Amanda and Rufus understand the truth.

"Your safety?" Amanda's brow furrowed in open disbelief. "What do you mean?"

She glanced over at Lemuel and frowned again. "That's Lucifer, Sam's horse. Is he here?" She met her gaze. "Did *he* bring you back?"

Now just how was she supposed to explain this? She'd abandoned Paul and taken the horse without permission. "I . . ."

"Well?" Amanda folded her arms across her middle. "I'm waiting, *Miss* Sinclair."

"I just borrowed his horse." Winnie laughed nervously and shrugged. She was too tired to think straight right now. Her serious talk with Amanda would have to wait. "I really need some sleep, Amanda. If you'll excuse me?"

"Not so fast." Amanda grabbed Winnie's arm when she tried to leave the barn. "I asked you about Sam. Were you . . . *with* him?"

Unsettled by the vehemence in Amanda's tone, Winnie met her great-grandmother's youthful gaze. "We need to talk," Winnie said after a few moments. "Alone, but not right now—a little later."

Amanda's expression shifted from anger to suspicion, then after a moment she nodded. "In my room."

Winnie sighed. "Give me an hour to clean up, then I'll meet you there."

Amanda seemed reluctant to release her hold on Winnie. "You better, 'cuz if you don't, I'll come lookin' for you."

Winnie waited in silence for Amanda to release her. Her great-grandmother was a hard woman even at seventeen. What would she be like by the time Winnie's grandmother would be conceived? It was a heinous crime for a girl, in any century, to grow up so fast. Amanda had skipped sweet and innocent and moved on to hard-core in a big hurry.

"I'll be there."

Amanda released her arm and stepped away, though the girl's gaze held Winnie's for several seconds.

"Miss Amanda?" Lemuel asked, stepping across the barn, apparently oblivious to the heated exchange between the women. "I need to shoe that mare of yours. You wanna have a talk with her so's she'll let me?" He chuckled, displaying a near toothless grin. "Seemed to work on the Marshal's mean old horse."

Winnie couldn't suppress the smile that tugged at her lips as she stepped from the barn amid Amanda's tirade. The girl was obviously unimpressed with the possibility of communicating with animals.

"Talk to her?" Amanda asked in a curt tone. "I don't talk to animals, Lemuel. Do you?"

Winnie drew a deep breath, then rushed across the lawn to the house. With any luck, by this time tomorrow she'd know Buck's whereabouts and could warn him of the impending danger. Her stomach lurched in response.

Her life depended on it.

Nineteen

Winnie hesitated at Amanda's bedroom door. She lifted her hand to knock, but froze as a sense of dread settled over her. What was she going to say to the girl? This was so crazy, no one could possibly believe it.

She closed her eyes for a moment. She had to at least try. Drawing a deep breath, Winnie opened her eyes and knocked, vowing to do anything necessary to win Amanda's aid.

The door was jerked open mere seconds after Winnie's knock. "Well, it's about time," the girl said with a toss of her head, then she crossed the room and sat on her bed. "Now tell me."

Winnie watched as Amanda flung her dark hair over one shoulder and glared, obviously prepared not to believe anything Winnie said. *Not a good beginning.* She searched her mind for words, then decided simply to start and see where it led her.

"Amanda, I'm . . . not who or what you think." She cast the girl a slight smile, but quickly squelched it when she saw Amanda's raised brows and pursed lips. "I guess that's obvious."

"Yep, I'd say so." Amanda folded her arms across her middle and tilted her head to the side. "Just tell me what you want with Sam."

"I'm . . . I'm . . ." *From the future?* No, not that—not yet. "I can predict—see into the future."

The girl's eyes grew round and she straightened, dropping

her hands to her lap. "You *can?*" Then her brow furrowed in obvious doubt. "Prove it. Wish you coulda predicted my pa runnin' off and getting himself married to that uppity stranger."

"I'm sorry." Winnie's stomach lurched, then started to burn. She'd kill for a couple of antacids about now. Laying her hand across her forehead, she closed her eyes and called upon what she hoped was a mystical expression. She pretended to concentrate very hard, then opened her eyes as if she'd seen something miraculous.

"Oh, I saw *your* future."

Amanda's eyes grew even wider. "You did?"

"Yes, I did." Winnie rushed over and sat on the bed beside the girl. "I saw the man you'll marry."

Amanda's cheeks flushed and she looked quickly away, then back again. "Who'd you see?"

Winnie chewed the inside of her cheek, hoping beyond hope that this would work. It had to. "I don't know the man's name," she lied. "But I can tell you what he looks like."

Disappointment filled Amanda's eyes as she looked anxiously at Winnie. "Not Sam Weathers?" she asked in a small, almost age-appropriate voice.

Winnie shook her head, maintaining her steady gaze, though it was difficult not to break down in the midst of this charade. "Not Sam."

"Then what'd he look like?" Amanda moistened her lips and waited, eyes wide and curious.

"He's older than you—quite a bit, I'd say." Winnie chewed her lower lip and hoped she appeared serious and thoughtful. "The man's tall and slender, with lots of curly hair."

Amanda frowned. "Curly hair?" She narrowed her gaze. "What color?"

"Why, it's red, like mine." Winnie laughed and picked up a strand of her own hair, hoping the fear in her own heart wouldn't betray her. She looked down at the curl wrapping itself around her index finger. "Imagine that."

Amanda's face reddened even more. "Buck," she whispered, looking down at her lap, then back at Winnie. "But Sam's the man I want, so I reckon I can change the future you see."

Oh, God, please don't let her change the future. I want *to be born.* Panic threatened Winnie's resolve, but she drew a deep, fortifying breath, then forged ahead.

"Sam Weathers—I don't see him living long." As she spoke, Paul's words returned to haunt her. She hadn't taken time yet to sort through what had happened to the real Sam Weathers. Buck Landen had questioned how Sam could possibly be up walking around. That her great-grandfather had killed Paul's great-great-grandfather had to be true.

Perhaps seeing his ancestor brutally murdered had triggered Paul's illness. Paul *thought* he was possessed, though it couldn't possibly be true.

Could it?

Then how could Paul know so many things only this Sam person should've known? Riding a horse and shooting a gun, for example? The Paul Weathers who'd represented Dirk Sinclair in court couldn't possibly know how to behave in such a manner. The mere notion was ludicrous.

Asinine.

"I don't believe you." Amanda eyes glazed over and she narrowed her lips. "Ain't nobody could hurt Sam. He's too strong, and fast with a gun."

Winnie fought against the tears pricking the backs of her eyes. Oh, how she wanted to give in and confess everything to this girl, but she knew that wouldn't do her any good. "I'm only sure of one thing," she continued, bracing herself against escalating anxiety. "Someday, you'll marry this redheaded man. You know such a man. I could tell from your reaction. You even said a name. What was it, Amanda?"

Amanda's gaze shifted, then fell to her lap. When she looked up to meet Winnie's gaze again, indisputable guilt made the girl's eyes glitter. "A man I used to know." She gave a nervous—guilty—laugh, then shrugged. "He worked here on the ranch."

Winnie mentally counted to ten, then summoned an innocent mien. "Oh? What was his name?" *Come on, Granny. Don't make me drag it out of you.*

"A man named Buck Landen." She tossed her head as if the name and the man meant nothing to her. "He worked here until Pa fired him about a year ago."

"Fired him? Why?"

Amanda looked away again and her cheeks reddened beneath her tan. She was definitely hiding something. Winnie's pulse pounded in her temples as she watched her great-grandmother's face flood with color, then grow pale as if someone had turned off the color controls on a television set.

The answer exploded in her mind as she stared open-mouthed at the woman-child who controlled Winnie's very existence. Amanda's reaction to Buck's name was blatantly obvious. The girl looked like a dog who'd just been caught marking the living room carpet.

Buck and Amanda were already intimate.

"Amanda." Winnie reached out and took the girl's hand in hers. "Have you . . ." Her breath caught on the words and nearly choked her.

Pulling her hand from Winnie's grasp, Amanda looked up as a tear trickled down the girl's cheek. Her lower lip trembled and she suddenly covered her face in her hands and cried, huge racking sobs that tore at Winnie's heart.

Stunned, Winnie put her arm around Amanda's shoulders and pulled her against her shoulder, where the girl wept for several minutes. It gave Winnie time to gather her thoughts and to plan her strategy.

She needed a bit more time to gain Amanda's trust, then perhaps the girl would reveal the location of Buck's hideout. Winnie remembered few details from her family history, but the infamous Buck Landen had been a favorite legend of her ancestors. Though Amanda Hopsador had never been mentioned, her notorious husband's name had crept into conversation at nearly every family gathering Winnie could remember.

The Osage Hills. Her grandmother had told her about a place in the Osage Hills where Buck had allegedly hidden from the law during the years before his marriage. Winnie's stomach rumbled and burned again.

She couldn't bombard Amanda with questions yet. The girl needed a little time. Winnie patted Amanda's shoulder and coaxed her to look up.

"Amanda, I think a little rest would do you a lot of good." At the girl's nod, Winnie stood and waited until Amanda placed her head on the pillow. "Good. I'll come in and check on you a little later, then we can finish our little talk."

"Maybe . . . maybe I was wrong about you." Amanda sniffled, then turned her face toward the window, silently dismissing Winnie.

Holding her breath, Winnie turned and left the room, pulling the door closed behind her. She'd made considerable progress with Amanda this afternoon. Maybe by tomorrow she'd have the information she needed.

And could ensure her own birth in about seventy years.

Paul's arm burned like the fires of hell.

And Winnie was gone. She'd abandoned him on their wedding night. Where the hell was she?

God, she had to be here at the Lazy H. If she was out wandering around the countryside, lost and alone . . . *I hope Winnie's here.*

"Where else would she go?" Sam asked in an even tone. "But I hope she's here, too. I can't imagine her takin' Lucifer, but better Winnie than some lowdown horse thief. 'Course, I can't rightly believe he'd let himself get stole in the first place."

No, I can't see that myself. The thought of Winnie actually riding that beast from hell terrified Paul. He'd known she was upset when the hotel manager called him Marshal, but they'd been so close. Intimate.

Loving.

She'd said she loved him.

Then how could she just leave the minute the opportunity arose? *Oh, my God.* Cold fear flooded his mind as a possibility he hadn't considered crept into his thoughts. *Landen. Sam, could Landen have Winnie?*

Sam brought the rented horse to a stop just inside the gate at the Lazy H, then swung his leg over the back of the animal and dropped to the ground. "The thought crossed my mind. And I don't much like it neither."

What are we going to do now? How can we find Landen? Sam? We have to find her. We have to.

Leading the horse toward the barn, Sam scratched his head beneath the rim of his hat. "Yep. I reckon we do." He looped the reins over the top fence rail, then stepped into the stable's dim interior. "Don't appear like we gotta look no more."

Lucifer. Paul had never imagined himself being happy to see that monster, but right now the sight of the huge black stallion munching hay brought sweet relief. If Lucifer was here, that meant Winnie was here. *Thank God.*

"Yep." Sam walked over to the horse and stroked its muzzle for several moments. "So, you let a woman mount you?" He exhaled in disgust. "Never thought I'd live to—"

Sam's unfinished sentence hung in the air, an ominous reality check. *I'm sorry, Sam.* Sorry was an incredible understatement of Paul's true feelings. George would grow up without his father, and Indian Territory would lose a great lawman.

"Don't matter none. It's high time I accepted it. Past time, I reckon." Sam cleared his throat, then gave Lucifer one last pat before turning toward the open stable doors. "Reckon

I'd best see to this nag out here, then we'll go check on Winnie."

I don't know how I get into these messes, but I'm sure glad you came back when you did.

"Never thought I'd hear you say you was glad to have me around."

Neither did I. Paul had sure changed his point of view where being possessed was concerned. Of course, being possessed was better than being dead.

Like Sam.

"Let's go find your wife." Sam almost collided with Winnie in the doorway, then grabbed her arm to prevent her fall. "Pardon—"

"Let's?" Winnie glowered up at him while regaining her footing. Balling one hand into a fist, she perched it stubbornly on the curve of her hip. "Still playing that stupid game, Paul?"

"Winnie, it's Sam—not Paul." He slipped his hat from his head, then sighed. "I know you didn't believe Paul when he tried—"

"Believe what? That he's insane? Oh, God. Now I'm doing it, too. That *you're* insane?" She laughed and shook her head. "Oh, trust me, Paul. I believe it. You're certifiable. But heck, you're an attorney. If we ever get back to the real world, you can file your own papers."

God, Winnie. I'm not crazy. This is real. Paul wanted desperately to talk to her, to hold her, to make her understand. He'd already told her everything *and* held her in his arms, but she still didn't—couldn't—believe him. *Winnie.*

Paul sensed Sam's growing unease, the hard set to his jaw, the slow, purposeful breathing. Sam was up to something. *Remind her we're going to catch Landen, then maybe she'll start to understand this a little better.* As if any reasonable human being could understand this.

"Winnie, I dunno what to say, but I'm Sam . . . borrowin' Paul's body. He's told you that."

Winnie's eyes glittered, then tears spilled over the rims and trickled down her cheeks. She shook her head and looked heavenward as if seeking answers. "Sure, Paul," she whispered, then turned away. "So, ask this Sam person when he's going to leave you alone so we can . . ."

Sam reached out to touch her shoulder. "So you can what?" He just stood there with his hand resting on her shoulder, struggling with a multitude of readable thoughts that stunned and worried Paul. "I reckon you must be worried 'bout the youngun."

Winnie's laugh was cynical and short. "Oh, I'm sure you'll be happy to hear that's no longer a problem," she said flippantly, though the tremor in her tone betrayed her true feelings. "Turns out it was a false alarm. Quantum-induced cycle screw-up. No biggie. Don't sweat it. You're off the hook, Romeo."

No baby? Amazed by the intensity of his reaction to her news, Paul felt as if she'd reached inside him and grabbed his heart, twisted it, then wrenched it from his body. *Damn.* Until this moment, he hadn't realized how much the child meant to him. There was no child—no physical link with Winnie. Could he hold onto her without it?

Sam bit the inside of his cheek. "What'll it take, Winnie?" he asked quietly, coaxing her with the slightest pressure on her shoulder to turn around and face him.

Sam, what are you doing? There's a killer out there to catch.

"Nope, it's done, Paul."

Sam.

Winnie watched his fluctuating expression with growing disquiet. Paul looked so lost, so confused. A part of her ached to help him, to take him in her arms and offer soothing words and reassurance.

But she couldn't. The tightening in her chest foreshadowed a resurgence of tears and she blinked rapidly to prevent their onslaught. She had to be strong. Drawing a deep breath, she renewed her determination.

"What'll it take, Winnie?" Sam repeated.

"What'll it take?" she echoed, her gaze focusing along with her resolve as she looked directly into his alluring face. "The truth, Paul. The complete truth, unadorned with insane ideas or the barest hint of any creative right-brained thinking. Simple facts, like in the courtroom. Spill it now . . . or never."

Her voice fell with that last word—that horrible, final ultimatum. *Never?* She had no choice. Psychiatric help was unavailable and even though she'd tried shocking him into reality before without success, there seemed no readily available alternative.

"Well, I reckon that settles it." He dropped his hands to his sides, then slumped his shoulders in defeat. "Paul showin' up here like he did seemed like the answer to a prayer. I shoulda known better."

Winnie shook her head. "You're really far gone, aren't you?"

"Not yet, but I will be shortly."

Winnie sighed and pressed her palm against her forehead, hoping to force the growing sense of helplessness from her mind. Nothing seemed to work.

"I gotta go."

"You have to leave? Please, don't let me keep you." She rolled her eyes dramatically, then snapped her fingers. "Go ahead, then. Leave, or whatever it is you're going to do. Trust me, Sam. Paul doesn't need you. All you're doing is interfering in our lives right now. Buzz off—I've had enough." *Good Lord, I'm talking to this guy like he's real.*

"Hush, Paul."

"Oh, God." Winnie groaned and closed her eyes for a moment. She wasn't at all certain how much more of this she could take.

"I will go." Sam bowed his head for a few moments, the

faced her. Unshed tears glittered in his gray eyes when she met his gaze. "This is real hard, Winnie. Between Paul tellin' me one thing and you another . . ." He drew a ragged breath, then chuckled quietly. "But it's time now. Past time."

Winnie stared in amazement. This "possession" was so real to Paul. The finest actors on Broadway would kill for control—botch a mental illness. They'd probably consider it a gift—to her it was a curse.

"I gotta ask you to do somethin' for me before I go." He cleared his throat and sniffled, then slipped the kerchief from around his neck and dabbed his eyes. "Guess I'm gettin' soft in my old age."

The hardness in her heart softened as compassion crept in to replace most of her cynicism. She swallowed the lump in her throat and nodded, deciding it best to hear him out. Maybe then he really would leave them forever. "Go ahead . . . Sam. I'm listening." Her voice was steady and quiet, rebutting her true feelings.

"Paul was sure right about somethin'. You're one helluva woman." Sam sighed and shoved his hat back on his head, then audibly gritted his teeth before speaking again. "I want you to promise me you'll make Paul happy—that you and him'll stay together and have lots of babies and grandbabies together."

Winnie's breath entangled in her throat. Now what? "I . . . can't promise that." She looked at the ground, then back at his face and gave a little shrug. She was so tired. "This whole thing has been like a nightmare, and I'm not making any promises until the real Paul comes out and asks me for himself." That was a lie—it hadn't *all* been a nightmare. Some of it had been an exquisite dream.

His eyes shifted as if a thought—or voice—had just burst into his mind. She felt certain he was talking to that voice again—Paul's voice. Reminding herself that the man she loved was in there, trapped inside his own body, Winnie bit her lower lip to cease its tremor.

"Gotta do it, Paul. Now hush." Sam cleared his throat again. "I wanna make sure you'n Paul's gonna be all right before I . . . go. This is all my fault. I can't rest in peace thinkin' you'll never forgive him for what I done."

This was cruel. How could his delusions seem so real even to her? His alter ego had a conscience. "Let me make sure I understand. You'll go for good if I promise to make Paul happy. Is that right?" Her pulse throbbed at her temples, roared in her ears and pounded in her head. "If I agree, you promise never to return to bother Paul again?"

He nodded. "That's right." After rolling his eyes, he chuckled to himself. "That's a damned good question."

"Question?"

"Paul wants to know why the hell he was brought back here if I was gonna give up on catchin' Landen. I reckon he—both of you—needed to do some learnin' about livin'. That and get together like you was meant to."

"Enough of this." Winnie closed her eyes for a moment of pained realization—Sam was Paul's more human side. It seemed a shame to completely banish him, but the alternative was continued insanity. Sighing, she opened her eyes to face him. "All right, I promise to try. I do care about Paul—about you, I mean. I'm so confused." She covered her face with her hands and groaned. "That's the best I can do."

"Then I reckon that'll have to be good enough." He lifted the corners of his mouth in a sad smile. "That's right, Paul. I'm givin' up. Now, hush.

"I want one more thing," Sam said, earning Winnie's scornful gaze.

"Figures."

"I want you to watch."

Winnie narrowed her gaze and took a step back. "Watch what? This is weird. Kinky."

"Maybe if you see me and Paul apart, you'll believe what he's been tellin' you all along."

"Paul, give me a bre—"

"Promise me."

Winnie stared in silence as the moments ticked by. Pink and gold bathed the western horizon as the sun vanished from sight. Darkness battled with twilight for supremacy, as logic struggled futilely against an inner voice which insisted Winnie play along.

"Sure, I'll watch. What are you going to do?" Winnie took another step back. With her back to the little remaining light, she saw Paul clearly. "Let's get on with it. It's time you let Paul have his life back, even if you are just a figment of his sick imagination."

"I reckon we'll see what you really think in just a spell." Sam drew a deep breath. "Reckon I won't smell any more of this sweet air after this."

Guilt crept into Winnie's thoughts. No, she shouldn't feel guilty. She was helping Paul, not hurting Sam. The lawman didn't exist, even though all the evidence proved he had at one time. The Hopsadors' easy acceptance of him in their home, the hotel proprietor's obvious recognition . . .

Buck Landen's murder attempts.

Oh, God.

"I gotta gather my strength. Been dependin' on Paul's and I ain't got much left of my own." He shot her a crooked grin. "Now, you watch like you promised, but don't be scared. This ain't gonna hurt Paul and I reckon I'm ready to go. I got me a wife up in heaven waitin'."

Winnie's eyes stung and she took another step away, giving him room to do whatever he was going to. If she truly thought this was insanity talking, then why this sense of expectancy that swept through her?

"This ain't her doin', Paul," Sam said quietly. "You been a godsend to me, an' I wanna thank you for bein' here for me. Just remember, it ain't Winnie's fault I'm goin'. It's my time. You oughta know that better than anybody."

I can't stand this anymore. Chewing the inside of her cheek, Winnie listened to her heart hammer in her chest, her gaze riveted to Paul's shifting expression. What was he doing? The next moments were critical—she sensed that, though she couldn't explain it.

"Funny that you want me to stay now." He chuckled, then shook his head. "One more thing, Paul."

"How long is this . . . going to take?" Winnie asked, hoping to find a way to halt the bizarre conversation between Paul's personalities.

"Not long." He turned himself inward again—she saw it in his eyes. "You promise? Anything?" A look of satisfaction crept over his face. "Good. Just in case you'n Winnie don't get to go back to where you come from, I'd like it if you'd get to know George." Sam blinked rapidly and sighed. "It'd help me rest in peace a powerful lot."

"Who's George?" Winnie asked, sensing something powerful and imminent. She was terrified yet hopeful at the same time.

"George is my son, over to Fort Smith." He sighed, a long ragged sound. "My wife died a few years back, so he's been livin' with my sister and her family. I wanted to see him once more . . ."

Winnie brought her knuckles to her mouth and bit down hard, hoping the pain would ease the guilt and pain surging to the surface. This was ludicrous. She shouldn't feel guilty for helping Paul through his illness. If, in fact, she was helping at all.

"Nope, Paul. I'm done." Sam took Winnie's hand in his and met her gaze. "You're gonna see now that I been tellin' the truth all along. Sam Weathers—that's me—is dead. Buck Landen killed me."

"Buck Landen's . . ." Winnie swallowed hard. "He's my . . ."

Frowning, he shook his head. "Just watch, Winnie. It'll be over in a minute."

Over in a minute? Such a rapid cure for schizophrenia.

Winnie drew a deep breath and focused her gaze on Paul's shadowy figure in the twilight.

His head lolled to the side and a strange glow surrounded him, clearly visible in the semi-darkness. "Oh, my God," Winnie whispered, covering her mouth with trembling fingers. A strange sensation swept through her, almost like an electrical current tingling along every nerve ending.

Could this be real?

The glow intensified and expanded, then seemed to separate from Paul's body, moving to the side as Paul staggered and grabbed his head. A second figure now stood beside Paul, translucent and iridescent, a bloodied hole in the front of his shirt.

Sam.

"You're . . ." Winnie looked from one to the other, noting that Paul seemed to have regained his strength and stood glowering at her in the twilight. "You're Sam Weathers. Aren't you?"

The figure nodded. "Was." His hollow voice echoed around her. Lucifer snorted in the background, obviously protesting the proceedings. "You take good care of my horse, Paul."

Paul nodded and took a step toward his ancestor. Reality surrounded Winnie as she watched this profound interchange between Paul and Sam. Why shouldn't she believe this? She'd accepted time travel, so why not a spiritual possession?

"Paul? What does this mean?" Winnie asked, taking a step toward him, but his look of fury tinged with hatred stayed her.

"Winnie, this is all my fault," Sam insisted, moving closer. "See this?" He indicated a large bloodstain and tear on his shirtfront. "This is where Landen's blade found me. Paul saw."

"I did."

His voice—his real voice—surrounded Winnie with hope

and dread all in one pithy batch of sound waves. He was here, real and hers, yet his anger was unmistakable.

Paul met Winnie's gaze. "I want Sam to stay and finish his mission."

"To . . . take Buck Landen to stand trial," Winnie supplied. Her great-grandfather had murdered Paul's ancestor. She pushed her hair out of her eyes and stared at him. "I don't understand any of this, Paul. I'm sorry I didn't believe you." She turned her gaze to the other figure, which seemed to be diminishing in shape and substance—fading. "Sam? I'm sorry."

A sob tore at her throat as another light filled the stable. Glowing steps leading upward to infinity appeared beside Sam. What was this? Her stomach lurched and tightened as a squeezing sensation began in her chest. This was a miracle in action, right before her eyes.

"Sam, don't go." Paul's voice cracked as he turned to reach for the specter. "Don't . . ."

Sam shook his head and smiled, then pointed up the ghostly staircase. "It ain't my decision no more. Probably never was." Sam reached out and touched Paul's hand, then he turned away and started up the steps. After a few steps, he turned around and waved. "Remember, both of you— your promises."

Winnie nodded, then stole a glance at Paul. The ethereal glow from the staircase bathed him in an unnatural light.

"I promise, Sam," he whispered. "And I promise to finish what you couldn't."

"Let it go, Paul."

Winnie gasped as the staircase and Sam vanished simultaneously. Lucifer voiced a shrill neigh, as if he understood the permanence of what had just occurred.

The horse's distress seemed to snap Paul back to reality as his head shot around to face Winnie. Darkness had settled over the land, so his eyes weren't visible, though she knew without seeing that they were blue. Now they'd always be blue.

His anger was a palpable thing, crackling and surging through the air around them. He reached out and gripped her shoulder with one hand, making her suddenly aware of the sling on his other arm.

"Paul, your arm. What happened?"

"I got shot," he said venomously, still clutching her shoulder. "By Buck Landen, last night while you were sneaking away like a thief."

Winnie shook her head. "No, Paul. I was frightened of your . . ." She bit her lower lip. "I thought you were crazy. Don't you understand? Even though I lo—"

"Don't say it." He released her and looked away. "You drove Sam away before he'd finished his mission." Paul released a long sigh, then looked up at her again. "It's my duty to see it through. Landen will go to jail—maybe even hang."

"No." Winnie reached for his hand, but he jerked it away before she found it. "Please, you can't hurt Buck Landen."

"Why, Winnie?" He chuckled low and held his good hand out in front of him, palm up. "Why in God's name shouldn't I hurt him? He hurt me and murdered my great-great-grandfather."

"Oh, God." Winnie's stomach lurched and twisted into a knot. "Paul, he's . . ."

"Well?"

"Buck Landen is *my* great-grandfather," she said barely above a whisper.

Paul stared at her for several minutes in the darkness. Winnie sensed it, though she couldn't actually see the direction of his gaze.

"Are you sure?" he finally asked in a low voice, no trace of disbelief evident in his tone. "Very sure?"

Winnie nodded, then realized he probably couldn't see her gesture in the darkness. "Yes, I'm sure." Tears slid unheeded down her cheeks, falling in plops at her feet. "Don't you see? If he dies before my grandmother is conceived . . ."

Paul chuckled. "What's wrong? Are you afraid you'll disappear or something?" His laughter was downright evil. "I don't buy into that crap and neither should you. Human beings don't just disappear. You've been born, even though you're back in the past now. You wouldn't be standing here in front of me right now if you hadn't been born."

Winnie lifted her chin and squared her shoulders. "I won't let you interfere with history, Paul." She suppressed the tremor which began in the depths of her very soul, threatening to reduce her to nothing more than a worthless blob of blubbering DNA. "I won't let you kill my ancestor."

He came toward her so fast Winnie winced, even though she knew he'd never lift a hand to strike her. Paul wasn't that type.

"Winnie, listen well, because I won't repeat this." His breath scorched her cheek as he spoke. "Buck Landen *murdered* Sam Weathers, and some force swept me back in time to witness it. Gee, color me stupid, but I happen to believe that miracle occurred for a reason. It's my duty to take Buck to stand trial. It's a matter of honor."

Winnie stared at him, wishing for enough light to enable her to see the expression in his eyes. "No, Paul," she whispered. "There's nothing honorable about any of this. It's a horrible mess—nothing more. This is all so ironic. You want to see my ancestor hang, even if that means I'll never be born. Tell me how can I stand here . . ." She shook her head . . . "And still love you?"

Silence. Only Lucifer's nervous whinnying marred the menacing silence.

"You drove Sam away, Winnie," he whispered, turning away as he spoke. "I'll never forgive you for that."

His words hung in the air between them as he walked away, then emerged from the stable a moment later leading

Lucifer. In silence, he saddled the horse and put a booted foot in the stirrup.

"I sure as hell hope I can remember how to do this without Sam." He swung his leg over the back of the stallion, then patted the animal's neck. "Lucifer, let's find Landen's hideout and finish what Sam couldn't."

The horse bobbed its head as if understanding and sharing Paul's mission. Winnie stared mutely, wishing she could think of something—anything—to say which might stop him, but the words didn't come.

As Paul rode away into the night, Winnie's throat threatened to close. She clutched at her collar and drew a ragged breath. "Please, God. Keep him safe, but don't let him find Buck."

Guilt and her own hunger for survival bombarded Winnie from every direction. The image of Sam's pained expression when he'd spoken of his son, tore at her. It didn't matter whether Paul forgave her or not, she realized, turning to run toward the house.

She'd never forgive herself.

Twenty

I have to stop him—help him. Thankful Rufus was still away honeymooning in Wichita—an oxymoron if she'd ever heard one—Winnie hurried to Amanda's room, then hesitated in the hall for a moment.

What did she want to accomplish—to rescue Paul from Buck or Buck from Paul? A lump threatened her ability to breathe as she pondered this.

The answer stunned her. She wanted both, but if forced to choose, she'd rather see Paul live than Buck.

Even if it meant she'd never be born.

God, not that. She must try to prevent them from harming each other, and hope that in doing so, she might save herself as well.

"Amanda," Winnie whispered as she opened the girl's bedroom door. "It's me, Winnie."

"Miss Sinclair?" the girl's sleepy voice answered. No trace of her earlier nastiness remained in her tone. "What are you doing here?"

"I need to talk to you right away about something." Winnie closed the door and tiptoed over and sat on the edge of the bed. "I have to know where Buck Landen's hideout is. Can you tell me?"

The seconds of silence which followed seemed like an eternity to Winnie. "Please?"

"I don't know exactly," Amanda said, scooting back and sitting upright in the bed. "He told me it was in the Osage

Hills, just north of here a piece. Why do you wanna know? You ain't . . . gonna sic the law on him, are you?"

The girl obviously cared for the outlaw. For some reason, even though a physical relationship between Buck and Amanda was manifest to her plan, Winnie felt guilty. She hated being even indirectly responsible for seventeen-year-old Amanda's involvement with any man. But things were different now. Girls grew up and assumed adult responsibilities at a much younger age in this time. It was a way of life, one over which Winnie had no right to pass judgment.

Nor was it in her own best interest to do so.

"Can you lead me there? Pa—Sam's life may be in danger." She gripped the girl's hand in hers, hating the lies, and knowing Sam Weathers was far beyond mortal help. "Please, tell me." She had to remain calm. If she frightened Amanda, the girl might not be willing to tell. "I'm sorry. I didn't mean to—"

"Yes, I'll take you there. I think I can find it." Amanda swung her legs to the floor and stood. "I got somethin' to tell Buck anyway, especially if . . ."

"If what, Amanda?" Winnie stood beside the girl. "What is it?"

Winnie stepped to the table and turned up the lamp. Light bathed the girl's guilty, frightened expression. The full impact of this truth struck Winnie full force.

"You've been with Buck already. I sensed it earlier." Her heart hammered against her ribs as she waited for an answer. Had Winnie inadvertently changed history already simply by her presence? It was too soon for her grandmother to have been conceived. Too early. Winnie was almost positive that her grandmother'd been an only child, though she couldn't be certain.

"I shouldn't have sent for him when I did." Amanda shook her head, then looked directly at Winnie. "I thought you was after Sam, so I . . . asked Buck to take you away. I'm sorry."

Amanda bit her lower lip as silent tears trickled down her cheeks.

Sam had said as much the other day, that he suspected Amanda of playing some role in Buck's determination to capture Winnie. It was outrageous—her own great-grandmother'd had her kidnapped. Almost.

Standing here in a long white gown buttoned to her throat, with her glossy black hair hanging over one shoulder in a thick braid, Amanda fit the image of a demure young lady in every sense of the word. Winnie's heart swelled with pride in her heritage, though she knew Amanda'd made some very foolish mistakes. She was young and proud—mistakes were an unavoidable part of the growing up process.

"Tell me something, Amanda," she probed, hoping she was mistaken. "When you sent for Buck, did he—did something happen between you?"

Looking at the floor, Amanda nodded very slowly. "Yep. It happened a lot, but it wasn't the first time." Her face flushed bright red beneath her tawny complexion. "Buck makes me want him in a bad way. I know it's wrong, but I can't help myself when he . . . touches me. He makes me feel important, even if he don't love me."

Now what, Winnie? "Maybe he does love you, Amanda." *He has to.* She touched the girl's shoulder, then smiled when Amanda looked up at her with eagerness and hope shining in her eyes. "I'm sure of it."

"I sure hope so." Amanda's voice was very faint, almost inaudible. "For our baby's sake."

Oh, not that. Was she doomed now? It wasn't as if she could find a means of traveling back a couple of months to change things back to the way they were. Winnie sighed, forcing herself to accept the facts as they unfolded. So be it. Maybe there'd be this child, then another one in a few years who would be her grandmother.

"Take me to Buck, Amanda," she said quietly. "Then we'll try to make everything right again for both of us." *I hope.*

Amanda nodded. "I'll get dressed, then we'll go right away." She rushed to the bureau in the corner. "I wonder how Buck'll feel about bein' a pa."

Winnie wondered about that herself. The Buck Landen she'd seen and heard was a hardened criminal. She found it impossible to believe he could be a gentle or loving man under any circumstances.

Watching her great-grandmother prepare to ride into the night at her side, Winnie realized a truth. She wanted—no, needed—to share everything with this girl. Winnie wanted Amanda to realize that she was in the company of her own descendant.

Whether or not Amanda chose to believe her was an entirely separate issue.

"On the way, I'll tell you a story, Amanda." Winnie prayed her mission would prove successful. "A true and very bizarre story."

Brilliant move, Einstein.

Paul's gaze swept the area as he watched his captors mill around the fire, occasionally refilling their coffee cups from the metal pot hanging over the blaze. Many of them laced the beverage heavily with liquor from an earthenware jug being passed between them.

He tugged at the rope which held his hands tied around the base of a small oak, wondering how he could be so stupid. Riding in here like he owned the place wasn't exactly the most intelligent thing he'd ever done.

It sure as hell wasn't what Sam would've done.

"Shit."

At least he'd been smart enough to stop in town and send an anonymous telegram to Fort Smith. With any luck, help would soon be on the way.

Here he sat, tied to a tree in a notorious outlaw's camp, while his wife thought he hated her guts and never wanted to lay eyes on her again. Well, it was beginning to look as if that was precisely what would happen.

The ground was hard and cold, slightly damp from the dew. "What I wouldn't give for my nice warm bed, a snifter of brandy and a good book." *And a warm Winnie at my side.* But of course, then he wouldn't need the book or the brandy.

Now that he was away from the Lazy H, and in big trouble, Paul realized how foolish he'd been to get angry at Winnie. None of this was her fault. Sam had realized that, even if Paul didn't.

Looking down at his legs stretched out in front of him, Paul wondered how Winnie could possibly be related to Buck Landen. His beautiful Winnie, the descendant of a notorious outlaw—the very man who'd murdered Sam.

Whoever said life wasn't fair had summed up all of mankind's little idiosyncrasies in one phrase—the understatement of all time.

A shadow passed between him and the fire, jarring Paul from his thoughts and forcing him to lift his gaze. Landen. Even in the dark night, firelight danced off the criminal's red hair.

Red like Winnie's.

Paul knew in that moment that her story was true. He should've noticed the resemblance earlier. In fact, he remembered thinking the outlaw's green eyes were similar to Winnie's. Great—validation, just what he needed.

"Who the hell *are* you?" Buck asked from a few feet in front of Paul as he stooped low to the ground. "You look like Sam Weathers, but you sure as hell don't act much like him."

"Why do you say that?" Paul narrowed his gaze, watching for any sign from the outlaw which might indicate Paul's emancipation. If Buck's genes were part of Winnie, then there must be some good in the man. But good luck and Paul seemed destined to remain strangers.

"First of all, me and the boys took you too easy. The Sam

Weathers who's been doggin' me for nigh onto three years wouldn't have let that happen." Buck laughed and shook his head. "Either that, or he'd find a way to talk his way out of this by now. You ain't said much, and what you have has been pretty strange."

"Strange?" Paul grinned, deciding to let it all hang out. What the hell did he have to lose at this point? "Yeah, I'm strange, and you're right. I'm not Sam Weathers. I'm Paul Weathers."

"Paul?" The firelight outlined Buck's silhouette enough to make Paul aware that Buck had tilted his head to one side to study his prisoner. "I didn't know Sam had a brother. But I felt sure you wasn't Sam when we first grabbed you."

Paul laughed and he knew it was an insane sound. Good, the crazier the better. "I'm not his brother." He leaned his head against the tree's rough bark. "I'm his great-great-grandson."

Silence.

Good, he had the outlaw's attention now.

"Sure, and I'm Robert E. Lee." Buck laughed nervously and inched his way closer. "Tell me the truth now, and maybe I'll let you go. I wanna know what really happened to Sam."

Paul winced. The man wanted to know if Sam was really dead. It was too late for lies. "He's dead, but I think you knew that."

The man sighed. "I was kinda afraid of that."

"What do you mean, afraid of that? That's what you wanted, isn't it?" Paul lifted his head away from the tree. "Why you stabbed him that day at the river . . ."

"How'd you—"

"Riders comin'."

Buck shot to his feet and rushed away from Paul, jerking a rifle from his bedroll before throwing himself to the ground with his companions. Paul strained his eyes in the darkness, trying to discern the identity of the visitors. Maybe it was the cavalry, riding in to rescue him from the bad guys.

Yeah, right.

"Buck. It's me, Amanda."

Amanda Hopsador? Paul couldn't see the girl through the darkness, but there were definitely two horses standing on the far side of the fire.

"You alone?" Buck asked from his position on the ground. "I heard two horses."

"I brought . . . Winnie with me."

Buck's laughter split the night. "Anybody else?"

"No. Just us."

Buck straightened from the ground, followed by his cohorts. The outlaw walked purposefully toward the pair of horses. "Why the hell'd you bring her here? Do you want rid of her that bad?"

Rid of her? Paul's gut twisted into a knot of cold fear. He couldn't let them hurt Winnie.

"No, not anymore." Amanda's voice was low, but clearly audible in the night air. "She's with me. We're together in this."

"In what?"

"Mr. Landen?"

Winnie. She was really here. Paul strained his eyes in the darkness for a glimpse of her, and was rewarded when she dismounted and walked closer to the fire. She and her great-grandfather stood on opposite sides of the campfire, their red hair identical bookends flanking the dancing flames.

"Mr. Landen? Yeah, that's me." Buck took a step closer to the fire. "Why'd you come here? Amanda, you recollect I told you how I don't want nobody to know about this place?"

"Yes, Buck. I remember, but Winnie has somethin' to tell you." Amanda stepped over and stood beside Winnie. "So do I."

Buck nodded. "Fair enough." The outlaw turned toward Paul. "I got me a feelin' we oughta just head over there to have our say with . . . whoever that fella is."

Paul watched Winnie and Amanda follow Buck over to his tree away from home. His gaze remained on Winnie's face when they stopped and sat on the ground in a semicircle around him.

Pow wow time.

"Paul," she whispered, reaching toward him.

Buck's hand snaked out and grabbed her wrist. "No."

Winnie returned her hands to her lap, though Paul felt her gaze on him. He'd said terrible things to her, made her think he didn't love her, couldn't want her. Sam's death wasn't her fault. He knew that now, just as he knew that his great-great-grandfather had never blamed Winnie for any of this.

Paul returned his gaze to Buck, reminding himself who was responsible for Sam's death. "Why'd you murder my great-great-grandfather?" he asked very slowly, and waited for an answer.

Winnie and Amanda looked on in silence while Buck laughed—alone. "Amanda, did you ever hear such foolishness?"

"What? That you killed a good man like Sam?" She pointed at Paul. "Or that he's from the future?"

Winnie must've told the girl the truth. But why? Paul glanced from face to face in the darkness, wishing for enough light to read their expressions. There was much more going on here than he'd realized.

"Winnie?" He knew she'd understand his unspoken question, but would she answer?

"Mr. Landen—Buck," Winnie said, turning to face the outlaw as she spoke. Paul was sure only he could've recognized the slight tremor in her voice. "We might just as well get this out in the open right now. I'm from the future and so is Paul." She gestured toward him with a slight but purposeful nod of her head.

"What is this?" Buck sounded angry now, not merely skeptical. "You been out in the sun too long, woman."

"Buck, it's true." Amanda reached over and touched the

outlaw on his forearm. "Listen to them. This man's Sam's great-great-grandson, and Winnie's . . ."

"What?" Buck's voice sounded worried now. "Amanda, how'd this woman get you to believe this foolishness? Weren't too long ago you wanted me to take her away and get rid of her for you. Remember?"

Amanda nodded. "I was wrong. Buck, you have to listen to me. Winnie's your . . . your great-granddaughter. She's *our* great-grandchild."

Talk about a double blow. Christ. Poor Winnie.

Buck's laugh began as a low chuckle, then slowly built to a loud guffaw. The outlaw stood and strode over to his circle of thieves. "Hey, fellas. This woman here claims to be my great-granddaughter. What do you think of that?"

A round of raucous laughter gave way before Buck ambled back to the small circle beneath the tree. "I dunno what kind of game you two is playin', but I ain't believin' none of it."

"Buck, you gotta listen to her." Amanda stood beside him and held his hand. "She knows things about the future that can help you. Help both of us."

"You mean she's a gypsy?" He shook his head and chuckled again. "I don't recall ever seein' a gypsy with hair that co—"

Buck's head shot around and he stared at Winnie. "Well, I'll be damned." He reached down and jerked her to her feet. "Woman, you better tell me everything." He picked up a strand of her red hair between his fingers, then let it slip through very slowly. "It's almost exactly the same. I reckon I got cousins runnin' around the country that could have the same color hair, but I'm tellin' you right now I don't believe this from the future nonsense."

"I can . . . can tell you when and where you'll die," Winnie said quietly. "I don't know about you, *Grandpa*, but I'd sorta like to have that information in advance." She laughed in that same cynical tone she'd used with Sam. "Just imagine the possibilities."

Buck stood silently for several moments. "I've heard about, even seen, some Indian magic before, but nothin' like this." He whistled low. "I ain't a man to risk passin' on the chance to postpone my own judgment day, whether this be true or not."

"Good, Buck. I'm glad." Amanda moved closer and laid her cheek against his upper arm. "I want you around for a long time."

"You do?"

The outlaw actually sounded surprised. Paul couldn't believe this turn of events. Not only was Buck Winnie's ancestor and Sam's murderer, Amanda was now Paul's great-grandmother-in-law. Talk about skeletons in the closet.

Winnie's courage astounded Paul. Pride permeated him as he watched her in action. She'd risen to the occasion in a big way. Like Sam had said, Winnie Sinclair . . . Weathers was one hell of a woman.

God, but he adored her.

Silently, Paul waited for the last shoe to drop. Somehow, he knew there was more to come. The stage had been set very effectively. Now it was time for a well-orchestrated, hopefully successful, finale.

Then what?

One step at a time here, Paul. Let's just get us both out of this mess alive first.

"I thought you had plans to marry somebody else," Buck said slyly, obviously realizing everyone knew by now that Sam was really dead.

"That was before," Amanda said quietly.

"Before I killed Sam?" Buck sighed and shook his head. "Y'know, I didn't wanna kill him, but he dogged me until I couldn't even get a good night's sleep. There just didn't seem no other way. Except for him, I know'd I could live out my days here in the Territory a free man. I been ready to hang up my guns for a couple years now."

"You really did kill Sam?" Amanda pulled away and stared up at his face. "I kinda hoped it was a mistake. Oh, Buck."

To Paul's amazement, Buck looked down at the ground as if actually ashamed of his dastardly deed. *God, here I am almost understanding why this man murdered my ancestor.* Somehow, Paul knew Sam would forgive him. The lawman was dead, and though Buck's knife had inflicted the fatal wound, Paul sensed that Sam would consider the outlaw's motives reasonable.

Sick, Paul. But true.

Sam Weathers had possessed a gift for seeing the positive in the very negative. Maybe Paul could keep that part of Sam inside himself. It might come in handy, especially if Winnie didn't forgive him.

Then I'll just file an appeal—Winnie has to forgive me.

"So you killed Sam because you thought you'd never have a moment's peace otherwise?" Winnie asked, then sighed. "Well, it can't be undone, though I don't understand how anyone would kill another human being for any reason."

"No, I don't reckon you would." Buck put a protective arm around Amanda's shoulders. "So, you think you're my . . . great-granddaughter?"

"More than just think."

"Time to prove it."

Winnie glanced at Paul for the first time. He held his breath, wondering if she'd speak directly to him, if she'd ever forgive him for turning her away back at the ranch.

Without a word to Paul, she turned to face Buck again. "You marry Amanda and go straight, then in 1916, you'll be shot during a bank robbery in Tulsa. After years of leading a crime-free life, you'll make one more mistake and die for your bad judgment."

Buck chuckled, but quickly fell silent. "The hell you say." He looked over at Paul, then back to Winnie. "Tell me why I oughta believe you."

Winnie shook her head and folded her arms across her

middle. A pinkening sky framed her silhouette, reminding Paul of more pleasant times with Winnie. "It's your choice. I don't think I'd ever rob any banks in Tulsa if I were you, though."

Buck nodded. "I don't reckon I will. Thanks for the warnin'." The outlaw turned to face Paul again, then stooped beside him. "I'm cuttin' you loose. I dunno who you two are, or where you're really from, but you sure as hell ain't Sam Weathers."

"No, I'm not." Paul found Winnie's gaze on him as the sun bathed the landscape in pastels. "I'm Paul Weathers, his great-great-grandson."

Buck gave a derisive snort, though the rising sun revealed a modicum of doubt in his green eyes. He reached behind Paul and quickly sliced through the ropes with his knife. Was it the same blade that had snuffed out Sam's life?

"Tell me, Buck." Paul met the outlaw's gaze, though he ached to look at only Winnie. "How can you look at Winnie in the daylight and deny she's your blood relative?"

Buck straightened and looked at Winnie. "Don't reckon I can, but that don't mean she's my great-grandkid."

"Whatever. It doesn't really matter anyway." Here Paul stood beside Buck Landen, so close he could've reached out and strangled the outlaw with his bare hands, but he didn't. Violence wasn't his way, never had been. For a while he could've done it, but no more.

"You two get on outta here before I change my mind." Buck turned to face Amanda, summarily dismissing Winnie and Paul. "You goin' or stayin'?"

Amanda placed her hand on his arm and looked directly into his face. "It depends. You marryin' me before the baby, or after?"

Buck stared openmouthed at Amanda. "Baby?"

" 'Course, I could just go on home and tell Pa all about it, if you'd rather."

Buck straightened and a huge grin split his freckled face.

"A baby, for real?" He picked her up and swung her in a circle. "We'll find us a preacher and I'll beg your pa for my old job back."

Amanda stared at him in silence for several moments after he'd lowered her feet to the ground in front of him again. "Only if you swear to mend your ways, Buck Landen. I know I did somethin' awful wrong when I asked you to take Miss Sinclair—I mean Winnie—away."

"I wouldn't have hurt her anyway, Amanda. That ain't my way." He sighed long and slow. "Honey, I told you I been wantin' to hang up these pistols for a couple years. You're forgettin' I'm older than you—ready to settle down and raise some younguns."

Me, too. Paul caught and held Winnie's gaze with his own. "Let's go."

She watched him warily, he knew for any sign that he might turn on Buck. "I'm not going to try anything," he promised, hoping to reassure her. "Sam's gone and I'm letting it go. That's what he wanted in the end."

Winnie nodded, then turned to her ancestors. "Amanda, will you do something for me after I'm gone?"

"Gone?" Amanda stared at Winnie. "Aren't you coming back to the ranch with us?"

Winnie shook her head. "We can't." She shrugged, then cast Paul a glance filled with uncertainty.

"No, we need to at least try and find our way home," Paul said, not realizing he felt that way until the words left his mouth.

"We do?" Winnie turned to stare at him again. "How?"

Paul chuckled. "Beats me. The devil made me say it." He touched her then, very gently at first. "Wherever we go, we're going together."

Her green eyes filled with tears as she blinked, then nodded. "Together."

Winnie embraced both her great-grandparents as Paul stood by watching. After a few moments, he reached out and took Amanda's hand in his. "Sam was fond of your Pa, Amanda," he said slowly. "I think he'd want Rufus to have Lucifer. Will you and . . . Buck take him back to the Lazy H for me?"

Amanda nodded. "Pa'll like that."

"Let's go."

Winnie knew that Paul giving Lucifer away was symbolic of releasing all the demons that had been chasing him. Was there hope for them? Could they find their way home and be together in any century?

The gaze he held her with touched her heart, where her love for him had been stored all this time. As they turned and walked away from the outlaws' camp, Winnie felt a surge of freedom sweep through her. They were starting a new life together somewhere.

Some *when*.

Less than a hundred feet from the camp, Paul turned and gave her a smile that melted her heart. God, how she loved him, despite everything that had happened. He pulled her into his arms and kissed her, long and hard and deep.

Winnie melded against him, opening her mouth to receive his kiss, savoring the sweetness of surrender—of sharing and belonging.

When he lifted his face to stare into her eyes, Winnie knew this was real and right. Wherever their lives steered them, she knew they'd be together.

"I love you," he whispered, then kissed her again, sealing an unspoken vow that left her trembling.

He shifted his lips to her cheek, resting them against her face. Winnie's heart swelled and her eyes stung. This was real and forever. "And I love you," she whispered, holding him against her for several moments.

Thunder rumbled in the distance, then lightning streaked across the morning sky. "One of those morning popcorn thunderstorms," Paul said, glancing up at the darkening sky.

Then he looked at her and Winnie realized they were thinking the same thing. *Could* they find their way back to the twentieth century the same way they'd left it? It would be a miracle, for sure, but it was worth a try.

"Let's find that damned river," Paul said urgently, then grabbed her hand and started to run.

The wind howled around them and rain pelted them, but they kept running, never looking back or considering the consequences of their actions. They must try.

She had no idea how, but when they crested a small rise, nearly blinded by the pummeling rain, they found the river. The Verdigris wound its way through a small valley below. Paul lifted his arm and pointed to his right, upstream from where they now stood.

"Over there," he shouted above the wind. "I think that's where I came ashore."

Winnie nodded, though she had no idea where she'd come ashore. Placing her life and her love in his care, she ran down the hill, still clutching his hand. The rain poured down the embankment in rivulets of red, making their footing precarious at best.

Near the bottom of the hill Winnie slipped, taking Paul with her on a giant slide of red Oklahoma clay. She shrieked, then laughed hysterically when she landed face down across his lap.

As she lifted her gaze to stare at him through the driving rain, Winnie blinked and her laughter froze in her throat. He was remembering that night . . . and others. His body and his eyes told her.

Oh, Lord.

"Come on," he growled, lifting her from his lap and leaping to his feet, pulling her up beside him. "Let's go."

The worsening storm surrounded them, giving Winnie a wild thrill of expectancy as they neared the water. This was insane, but they had to do it. It just might work, crazy or not.

Paul stooped down near the water and pulled something

bright orange from the river. He held the objects out in front of him—muddy and barely identifiable, were two orange life vests.

Theirs.

"Oh, my God," Winnie whispered as he handed one of the coveted objects to her. This was a link to the future.

A sign?

Paul started to put on his vest, but Winnie hesitated, quickly unbuttoning her dress. She wasn't about to let the long skirt pull her under.

He nodded in understanding, then kicked off his boots and jeans. Within moments, dressed only in the pantalettes and chemise, Winnie donned the life vest as Paul tied his, then they waded into the water.

When he paused to face her, waist deep in the cold river, Winnie nodded, knowing his unasked question.

As long as they were together, she was ready to face destiny.

They held hands and floated out toward the middle of the river, allowing the buoyant life vests to keep them afloat. The storm crashed and churned overhead, making the river angry and dangerous.

And familiar.

Something tugged at her toes, pulling and sucking at them as she began to spin. Then Winnie remembered the last time, the strange whirlpool that must've drawn her back in time. Had Paul's experience been similar? They'd never discussed it, so she couldn't be certain. It must've been, but right now it didn't really matter. They were well beyond the point of no return.

The sucking and whirling grew stronger, tearing her hand from Paul's grasp. She struggled in the angry water, the whirling, sucking *thing,* knowing it was the same as before. They'd rediscovered the time portal . . . or it had redis-covered them. She could only hope they'd both survive and come through this together.

And in the right century.

"Paul," she cried out against the wind and the roaring river. She lost sight of him in the torrent and found herself alone in the powerful current.

Again.

Winnie dragged her eyes open to survey her surroundings, spitting fishy-tasting water out of her mouth as realization dawned. It was night. Moonlight glittered across the calm water as she clung to the life vest and kicked until she'd turned a complete circle.

No sign of Paul.

Panic threatened to overpower her, but she bit back her sobs and started to paddle and kick. He could be here in the water with her, very near.

And dead?

"No, not that." Winnie blinked back her tears and continued to paddle, afraid to remain too long in one place in case the whirlpool returned to grip her in its aquatic clutches again.

And take her to another time—alone.

No.

A dark shadow on the water drew her weary gaze. Lifting her face to stare at the ominous form, Winnie's breath seized in her throat as comprehension unfolded.

"A boat." Could it be the *Sooner Sunset*?

Tears stung her eyes as she paddled furiously until she touched the side of the boat with her hands. It drifted in the darkness, no running lights or motor sounds. Winnie felt her way around the side of the boat until she found what felt like a ladder. Holding it with one hand, she pulled herself up to the first rung.

Yes, it was a ladder.

She was much heavier out of the water, but Winnie pulled and strained until she had her entire body halfway up the boat's side. As she heaved herself over the rail and landed on the deck, Winnie sighed, then struggled to a sitting position.

"Is anybody here?" she called, almost afraid to hear an answer.

After a few minutes, when no one responded to two more calls, Winnie breathed a sigh of relief. Maybe this was the *Sooner Sunset*. Still afraid to remove the life vest, she crawled along the deck until she found an open hatch.

Half falling, half climbing down the ladder, she went below deck and felt her way around in the dark. The boat was about the same size as the *Sooner Sunset*. She swallowed a lump in her throat. Surely, if she'd found her way here, Paul would, too.

Fighting back a sob, Winnie fumbled around in the dark until she discovered a bunk. Exhaustion prevented any further exploration. In the morning when the sun rose, she'd learn for certain where she was.

And with any luck, she'd find Paul. Alive.

A strange sound woke Winnie with a start. She blinked and tried to move, but found her efforts hampered by the soggy life vest. Sunlight burst through the porthole, hitting her full in the face.

Groaning as her muscles protested any movement whatsoever, Winnie sat up and unhooked the vest. Her lips were parched and rough as she drew her tongue across them and looked around the room.

"Oh, my God." She brought her hand to her mouth and surveyed the familiar surroundings. On the far wall, the door with the missing doorknob seemed to mock her. The floor was littered with empty condom packages and two discarded brandy snifters. Her overnight bag lay forgotten on its side, its contents haphazardly scattered about.

"It really is the *Sooner Sunset*."

The sound that had awakened her came again. It was outside, sort of a scraping and banging noise. Slipping the open life vest from her shoulders, Winnie stood and walked stiff-legged to the ladder and climbed up to the deck.

She blinked against the intrusive sunlight, thankful the storm had passed. Once her eyes adjusted to the brightness, Winnie shaded them with her hand and looked out across a broad expanse of water.

A lake—not a river.

"Lake Oologah," she said with wonder, then turned toward the scraping sound again. She moved slowly along the deck, wondering who or what it was, then realized just before his dark head popped above the rail, who it must be. "Paul."

She ran to him and grabbed his hand, remembering his injured arm as he hoisted himself over the rail and landed near her feet. "Winnie," he whispered, then grinned sheepishly.

Crying and laughing at the same time, she helped him to his feet, then pulled the life vest off and his shirt away from his wound. "At least it isn't bleeding," she said, struggling with a bombardment of emotions unlike anything she'd experienced in her entire life.

So this was love. It hurt like hell at times, but it was the most wondrous experience she could've imagined.

Right now it was perfect.

He pulled her into his arms and held her close, stroking her hair with his hand as she marveled over the miracle which had safely delivered them back in their own time. "I'm okay," he whispered against the top of her head. "Are you all right?"

She nodded, not wanting to pull away from him far enough to talk right now. Just feeling his solid warmth was all she wanted or needed at this moment. Some hot food and ice water wouldn't hurt, but this would do.

"We made it," he said, still holding her against his chest. "I can't hardly believe it, but we're here. We're home."

"Home," Winnie murmured, savoring the moment. "Together."

He nodded and sighed, then pulled slightly away. "What's this? I don't remember this."

She winced as he plucked a hair from her head and held it out in the bright sunlight to examine it more closely. "See?"

Winnie frowned and took the wiry silver strand from his hand to see for herself. "Oh, no." She looked up at him, then laid her hand on her head as if to will the truth away. "I'm older. That baby *was* my grandmother."

"Looks that way to me." He grinned and pulled her into his arms again. "It's okay. I like foxy older women."

"Hey, who said I'm older than you?"

"Nobody." Paul sighed. "I love you, Winnie Sinclair Weathers, and I think we'd better make this marriage legal for this century, too. And, if it's okay with you, when we have a little boy someday, I'd like to name him Sam. What do you say?"

"Sam or Samantha for a girl. I think that's appropriate." Winnie leaned away from him to study his face. Those marvelous blue eyes twinkled back at her from a face with several days' growth of beard. She smiled, then put her head back on his shoulder in that place that seemed to have been made just for her.

"Well, you answered half my question. Will you marry me again?"

"We'd better hurry. I'm sure not getting any younger."

Dear Readers:

A Willing Spirit is an outrageous story—no doubt about
it. I had more fun with this book than anything I've ever
written, and I hope it shows.

This story is about finding love in the most unlikely
places, but it's also about discovering the good with the bad.
Winnie and Paul's greatest fears become life's most precious
rewards.

My husband was a primary source of inspiration for *A
Willing Spirit*. He's one of those people who bounces through
life with a smile on his face, and he's always willing to share

I hope you have as much fun reading *A Willing Spirit* as
I did writing it. I'd love to hear from you. Write to me at
P.O. Box 1196, Monument, CO, 80132-1196
e-mail: debstover@market1.com
http://members.aol.com/debstover2/debhome/

Deb

DANGEROUS GAMES   (0-7860-0270-0, $4.99)
by Amanda Scott

When Nicholas Barrington, eldest son of the Earl of Ul-
combe, first met Melissa Seacort, the desperation he
sensed beneath her well-bred beauty haunted him. He
didn't realize how desperate Melissa really was . . . until
he found her again at a Newmarket gambling club—being auctioned off by her father to the highest bidder. So,
Nick bought himself a wife. With a villain hot on their
heels, and a fortune and their lives at stake, they would
gamble everything on the most dangerous game of all:
love.

A TOUCH OF PARADISE   (0-7860-0271-9, $4.99)
by Alexa Smart

As a confidence man and scam runner in 1880s America,
Malcolm Northrup has amassed a fortune. Now, posing
as the eminent Sir John Abbot—scholar, and possible
discoverer of the lost continent of Atlantis—he's taking
his act on the road with a lecture tour, seeking funds for
a scientific experiment he has no intention of making.
But scholar Halia Davenport is determined to accompany
Malcolm on his "expedition" . . . even if she must kidnap
him!